SOMETIMES ANGELS WEEP

One Soul's Journey Through This Valley

By

C. S. Hanson

ISBN: 0-75962-386-4

This book is printed on acid free paper.

1stBooks - rev. 02/19/01

PROLOGUE

The golden cloud swelled to fill the whole temple of God. Eelima avoided looking at the high Serif. He sat in the middle of the crowd, so as not to be too noticeable. It was a vain hope... even now he could feel the piercing eyes focused on him. He peeked up, and was riveted to those eyes that told him he had put it off long enough. It was time for his trial, the test that would establish his rating in the realms and orders of Yahweh's universe. Around him hundreds of other golden beings, the Sons of God, the Elohim sat in solemn assembly before the throne of Yahweh. Each waited to receive his assignment for the journey through the dimension of time. The Father, Yahweh, would give each one a body of flesh and blood, and set him in place on the Earth.

Now as the High Serif read the list of placement possibilities, one by one the members of the Elohim chose their earthly roles.

Eelima's mind drifted, wondering what it might be like to be constrained by time. How could I exist in a universe where I could only experience a small piece of Yahweh's vast creation, bound in and unable to move about propelled by thought? And how could I be expected to overcome the extreme difficulties humans face with their fleshly needs and desires? I am Eelima and I don't want any other identity! I don't want to leave this glorious home — to be away from the throne room!

He looked down again, avoiding those compelling eyes. But Jesus the Lamb went through that valley. He laid down His life there for us to show us the way...and I know I have to go sometime...I suppose it might as well be now.

Reluctantly he raised his head. The golden cloud seemed to pull him up. "This placement will be a great challenge," the Serif was saying, his eyes still fastened on Eelima. There didn't seem to be any way around it. This was his time. Most of his colleagues had already gone through the great test, and were now waiting in Paradise for their placement in eternity at the judgment seat of Christ.

"This life will be born to a young woman rejected by her family. The soul will be a girl who will go through much torment and trouble in the earthly body. If you can come successfully through the time element and serve our Lord Jesus even through such trials, there will be great reward at the judgment." Those eyes seemed to look into Eelima's soul. "Great reward," he repeated.

Eelima squirmed in his seat, but then he felt the Spirit come over him and he rose. "I can do it!" he heard himself saying. "I can overcome all the obstacles and come back bringing many souls with me...I know I can!"

The Serif nodded. "Then go, and God grant you His help and grace. The assignment is yours!"

Eelima held out his hand to receive the pattern. Instantly he was gone from the assembly in the heavenly realm, and found himself in a small dark space, where he floated in warm fluid and soon lost all memory of where and what he had been.

CHAPTER ONE

1915

Mary Louise frowned as she tried to rub the spot off her white glove. It was no use. She'd have to arrive and stand inspection with the obvious defect. It was the last straw...almost more than she could bear! Her chin trembled, but then she shook herself, straightened her back and raised the chin defiantly, refusing to give in to tears.

She felt strong once more by the time the carriage swept up the familiar drive under moss-draped oaks. They pulled to a stop at the stately house with its white-columned porch, and the driver waited while she gathered her things, and then helped her down.

"Thank you, George." She gave the old man a tight little smile as she paid him.

He nodded back at her, sympathetically. "Good luck, Missus." He turned the team and headed back toward Savannah.

She left her suitcases beside the driveway, and gathering her skirt in one hand, her handbag in the other, she climbed the steps feeling like a condemned prisoner making her way up to the gallows. The huge brass knocker reverberated under her resolute hand. She took some deep breaths to calm herself while she waited. The door opened suddenly and eager hands pulled her into the entrance hall, upsetting her dignified stance.

"Mamie, you'ah heah! Motheh...Mamie's heah!" Lucy Ann hollered as she gave her sister an enthusiastic hug. "My," she stepped back, "y'all are a sight, Mamie!"

"Lucy Ann!" The voice stiffened Lucy's back and she braced, like a solider ready for inspection. "Go upstairs and help Millie with the linens." Lucy Ann gave her older sister a wry look, but turned and started up the broad winding stairway without argument, though she dragged her feet and turned to look back as much as she could. Mrs. Wilson surveyed Mary Louise critically, seeing in a moment everything about her eldest daughter, from the blue straw hat with its small white feather perched on dark blonde curls, to the neat brown ankle-high shoes that showed under the long blue skirt of her best dress. She didn't notice the pleading of the bright blue eyes or the embarrassed red of the cheeks, but she did see the spot on the white glove and raised a critical eyebrow. She remained focused finally, on the obvious bulge of Mary Louise's belly.

"So he left you, did he...and you in this condition! Papa and I warned you this would happen, but would you listen? No! Not you, Miss high and mighty...Miss know it all!" Her voice was tight and high-pitched, to match her outlook. "Now see the mess you're in! And here you come crawling home, expecting us to take you back in and care for you and your pitiful child! Well let me tell you Missy, we're a respectable family, and I won't have you influencing your sisters with your willful, sinful ways!"

The words kept coming, but Mary Louise couldn't hear them any more. As in a dream, she watched her Mother's mouth moving, saw the frowning face, the judgment in those cold gray eyes. With her dark hair severely parted in the middle and caught up into a knot in the back, and the dark dress relieved with only a bit of lace that seemed out of place at the neck, Mable Wilson seemed all dark, all judgment...no warmth...no hope.

"Oh Ma!" Mary Louise choked, as she turned and fled out the imposing door and down the steps. She grabbed up her bags and ran awkwardly, seeing her way as well as she could through tears that now flooded her eyes and flowed down her hot cheeks. She stumbled to a grassy spot in the shade of a familiar welcoming oak a little way off the road, where she sank down on her knees with her head resting on her valise and wept for the first time since John had left her standing alone in the train station. Deep sobs racked her frail body and left her finally exhausted, empty, drained.

Nobody came after her. The big door remained closed. Slowly she rose and stripped off the gloves, throwing them on the grass under the tree. She would never wear white gloves again. They were her mother's way of judging a lady. Still gasping with left-over sobs, she straightened her dress, picked up her things, and started down the dusty road away from the only real home she'd ever known. Whatever shall I do now? How can I take care of myself, much less a baby? Dear God, what will become of me?

The sun was hot on her back and the bags were heavy and she was so tired she could hardly keep going. She stumbled. Why didn't I ask George to wait?

But her stubborn will, much like her mother's, caused her to keep putting one foot in front of the other, determined to maintain her independence.

Far ahead at the crossroads, she could see the white wooden steeple of the family church waiting for her, welcoming her. She reached the building gratefully, pushed the tall green door open, and dropped her bags just inside it. The slightly musty smell of the old sanctuary made her stomach uneasy as she tiptoed into the almost cool gloom. She genuflected before the altar and sidled into the back pew, wishing she'd remembered to pack her rosary. Light strained to penetrate the towering stained-glass windows, each with its plaque at the bottom in dedication to someone long dead. Two or three almost expired candles flickered before the statue of the Blessed Virgin. She could see better, now that her eyes had become used to the half-light. It was peaceful here in the church, and gradually her mind began to function again. The pain of Ma's rejection was almost more than she could bear, but she shoved it aside for now. She had the baby to think about.

She rubbed her belly gently. Maybe I'll take a little rest before I start again.

She stretched out on the hard wooden pew, pulling her shawl over her like a blanket. Almost immediately she was in a strange sleep, where she tried to save her baby from some terrible danger...she couldn't make out what the danger was exactly, except it was dark and evil. She knew she had to get away and she tried to run, but couldn't move her legs.

She woke abruptly nearly falling off the pew, and sat up, rubbing her eyes. She had to go...bad! She hurried out of the church and around to the back, where there were two outhouses. They were big ones with plenty of space for two or three people. She went into the one for ladies, avoiding the long sticky spiral of fly-paper covered with dead and dying flies that hung near the door, and sat there half breathing against the familiar smell. She listened to the frantic buzzing of the trapped insects and fancied she knew how they felt!

After she had managed to work the pump nearby, she washed her face and hands and took a long cool drink from the tin dipper that hung by a thin rope from the spout. Then feeling somewhat better, she gathered her things again. Mrs. Mary Louise Wilson Shane had just made a decision. She didn't really like the decision, but she couldn't see much choice.

A hot and weary hour later, she reached Savannah and found the boarding house she had noticed earlier as the wagon passed. The sign said rooms were reasonable and they gave meals. Mrs. Barrett, the landlady, took one look at Mamie and beckoned her in, "Y'all come on in here. Let me take that bag for ya, Love." She took the biggest one out of Mamie's hand. "My land, child! Have you been carryin' that very far?" She eyed the forlorn looking girl, who was obviously in some kind of trouble. "You must be hungry?"

Mamie nodded gratefully, and Mrs. Barrett ushered her into the kitchen. Mrs. Barrett's solution to the problems of the world was to feed them, and soon she placed a big plate of chicken stew and homemade biscuits in front of the famished girl. It smelled heavenly and tasted even better, and Mary Louise could feel her strength returning even while she ate.

"Thank you so very much, Mrs. Barrett...guess I didn't realize how hungry I was! I do feel so much better now. You are such a blessin'!" She hesitated, then went ahead and asked, "Do y'all have an ink-pen I could borrow?" The older woman nodded and went to the big carved wood living room desk, where she rummaged in the little compartments for the required instruments. She brought them to the kitchen and handed them to Mamie, who was just finishing her cup of tea.

Mamie thanked her again, then taking the pen and the bottle of ink, she excused herself before Mrs. Barrett could begin the questions she was obviously dying to ask, and went to her room.

She put her purse on the dresser, sighing deeply. I guess I have to do it, so I might as well just go ahead and get it over with!

She found the small box of stationery in the bottom of her bag. Then she sat on a straight chair at a wobbly little table by her bed and slowly wrote out the whole sad story of her situation, stopping often to think. She read it over, then finished, "If you're still interested in me, let me know and I will go with you after all...and I'll try to make you happy." She folded the letter, sealed the envelope and addressed it to 'Mr. Frank Gibbs, c/o the Sheffler Bros. Circus, Sarasota, Florida.' Then she carried it downstairs and walked directly to the post box before she changed her mind. With some trepidation, she dropped the letter into the slot. Then she leaned against the box wishing she could retrieve it somehow. What have I gone and done? ... Oh what have I done? She went back to her room, crawled into the bed and wept again with regret and sorrow.

A few days later the landlady called her. "Mrs. Shane...there's a telegram for you!" Mary Louise hurried downstairs and took the yellow envelope. "I hope it's not bad news?" Mrs. Barrett hovered expectantly in the doorway.

"I hope not too," she answered, as with some misgiving she opened it. "I guess it's *good* news," she told the curious landlady, and left her still wondering as she climbed slowly back up the stairs. In her room she read the wire again. I'LL MAKE A HOME FOR YOU AND THE BABY. COME RIGHT AWAY. LOVE, FRANK.

She sank down on the bed. *Oh, Lord, I hope this is the right thing!*

She there a long time staring into space, then she sighed a deep sigh as she got up and packed her few things. She dragged the bags downstairs again, where she said good-bye to Mrs. Barrett, and set off for the train station. The now familiar nausea rose up in her throat, nearly choking her as she stood on the platform with her ticket in hand, waiting for the train to Florida.

She thought about her family. The Wilsons were a genteel family, well respected in their community and their church. They supported many good causes, entertained fairly often, and served as a model for many a young couple just starting married life. The outward appearance, however, was far from the reality. Mrs. Mable Wilson ran her husband and daughters' lives by her own set of standards, allowing no independent ideas to upset her regime. Mr. Wilson was a weakling who found it easier to give his wife her way in everything having to do with the home and family than to stand up for his rights...or those of his three daughters, whom he really loved very much.

Lucy Ann and Millie chafed under the rules and restrictions, but they hadn't the grit that Mary Louise had. Anyway, just look at what rebellion had gotten for her! She'd known their handsome young neighbor John Shane all her life, and loved him wildly. So she was in heaven when he asked her to marry him. Her mother wouldn't hear of it, as she planned for her oldest daughter to marry into money...notably Judge Howard Runyan, a widower more than twice Mamie's age. The Judge was ugly and smoked big black cigars. Mamie detested him, and anyway he had a son older than Mamie! She ran off with John Shane and they found a Justice of the Peace in a small town south of Savannah. They stood before him holding hands as they said the words that made them man and wife. It wasn't the kind of wedding Mamie had always dreamed of, but she was happy anyway.

The first few months went pretty well, until the United States got into the war in Europe and John joined the Army. He was assigned to a base in Florida. They met some other young couples there and made a few friends, but money was tight, so Mamie found a job in town at the millinery shop.

She remembered when she'd met Frank. She'd been rearranging the window display one afternoon when she noticed a dark-haired man outside watching her. She smiled at him and went on with her work, but he stood there staring until he made her nervous and she retreated back to the counter. The man was there again the next day and came into the store pretending to look at the hats. Mamie waited on him and sold him a hat 'for his mother.' He came back again a couple of days later and started a conversation with her. He told her his name was Frank Gibbs, he worked with the circus and he thought she was the prettiest thing he'd ever seen.

Mamie was flattered by the attention, but a little intimidated too by his intense manner. She told Frank that she was married. Then they talked about John and the war and just chatted for a while. Frank wanted to know everything about her, and kept asking questions until she finally told him that either he had to buy something or leave, so she wouldn't lose her job. He left, but came back a few days later and hung around again. This time he bought another hat, after spending as long a time as he could manage. "You really belong with me, you know," he told her several times. "Let's run away together!" At first he sounded like he was teasing, but then she was afraid he was serious. She laughed at him, but she couldn't help being flattered by his attention, especially since John was acting so strange lately.

John had begun staying on the base rather than coming to the apartment on weekends. He was restless, and chafed at being 'tied down,' resenting Mamie's wanting him to spend his time with her, rather than drinking with the other guys in the evening. The last straw was when she told him she was pregnant. He panicked at that news...he wasn't ready to be a father! He wasn't ready to be a husband either...he was sorry, but maybe she'd better just go home to her folks and forget about him!

The last time she saw John was at the train station when his company shipped out to France. "Forget me, Mamie! I'm sorry about everything. Your mother was right about me...I'm no good." He turned his straight young back on her and climbed onto the already moving train. The band was playing "Over There." It seemed she heard that song everywhere she went these days. She hated it. Steam chuffed back from the big black engine, as the cars filled with soldiers clattered past her, picking up speed. She stood there as though frozen to the spot, watching John leave her, wondering what to do now, wishing she were dead!

That's when she had reluctantly decided to go home and face her mother and dad...with such disastrous results.

Now she set her purse down on top of her bag. Wish I could have talked to Daddy though. I bet he would have hugged me and said how sorry he was...

She shook herself and fought against the tears and the nausea. The train bound for Florida steamed into the station like a black dragon ready to swallow and digest her, and she submitted herself to that fate as she stepped up into the coach. She found a space on the thinly padded seat across from a dour-faced couple, who argued when they spoke at all.

Mary Louise was about to give up to despair, when she felt the baby kick and remembered why she was doing such a completely unbelievable thing...going to live with a man she hardly knew! She was scared, yet hopeful...maybe things would work out really fine! She prayed it would be so, as the train clack, clack, clacked down the tracks carrying her relentlessly toward her destiny.

CHAPTER TWO

1921

Screams of rage and anger filled the drab little room and echoed into the cluttered hallway of the cheap apartment building. Mary Louise stood with tears streaming down her face, hardly able to believe what she was seeing.

Frank Gibbs brandished his scissors, ignoring the pitiful screams of the small child who knelt on a kitchen chair before him. On the floor lay a golden heap of baby curls that only moments before had crowned the now desecrated little girl.

Five-year-old Jenny sobbed, her skinny shoulders shaking. She couldn't understand it... Why did he do it? Why did he take my hair? Why does he hate me? What did I do wrong?

"Momma!" She jumped down and ran to her mother to hide the poor shorn head in her skirt, and the two of them wept together. Jenny's heart was sore, and her head felt light and strange. She rubbed it with the hand that wasn't busy holding Mamie's skirt.

Mamie took a deep shaky breath and straightened up. Her hands curled into tight fists at her sides. She raised her white face and looked him in the eyes, "I don't know why you have to be so mean to her! I thought you said you'd take care of us both! I guess I'd better go back to Georgia and find my father. He'll make some kind of a place for us where we'll be safe! I can't believe you did this to Jenny!" She turned her back on him.

"Don't go turnin' your back on me, woman! The kid looks a lot better! Ya won't have ta spend so much time fussing with combin' and curlin'. Now she won't get food in it all the time. And besides, it'll be cooler too!" Frank put the scissors down and turned to Jenny. "Get the comb and bring it here!"

Jenny obeyed against her will. She knew what would happen if she didn't. Her sobs subsided to long shuddering breaths. She handed the comb to him tentatively, looking up at him, her large blue-green eyes now red and swollen, the long lashes wet with tears.

"Stop that blubbering!" He grabbed the comb and dragged it through her ragged hair, then glanced at Mamie. "Well, I'll take her to the barber shop and they'll make it look better. It'll be fine, you'll see. Now, stop bawling, the two of you or there'll be more trouble than ya can handle!" He started for the door, "Come on, kid, let's go!" He looked back at Mamie, "An' I don't want to hear any more about you going back to your father...not ever again, you hear me?"

Jenny needed to go potty, but she didn't dare say so. She followed him down the smelly hall and out into the fresh air of the street, her small heart aching. She didn't understand why he treated her so mean. She tried hard to make him like her. After Mom taught her to print, Jenny even left little notes on his pillow every night, until he complained to her mother "She just says the same thing every time." She was scared of him. He was gruff and mean and never smiled at her.

He didn't take her hand now, just went striding down the street, making her run to keep up. They turned in at Floyd's Barber Shop and waited their turn, sitting in straight chairs in front of the big window. Frank smoked a cigarette and read the newspaper while they waited, but Jenny watched in fascination as the barber wrapped a man's head in a hot towel, and then put soapsuds all over his face. Jenny caught her breath when he picked up a long sharp knife. But he didn't cut the man, he just scraped the soap off again. When he was sure he had all the soap off, he rubbed some nice-smelling stuff on his hands and slapped the man's face! The man got out of the chair and gave the barber some money and left. The barber swept up a little pile of hair, leaned the broom against the wall, and then looked at her and said "next!"

She really 'had to go' now, but she looked at her Dad and didn't dare tell him so. He'd be mad at her again, she knew. She tried to hold it. The barber put a board across the arms of the big black leather chair and lifted her up to sit on it, with her feet in the chair cushion. Then he took out some sharp black-handled shears and began to comb and snip. Jenny watched in the big mirror, fascinated. It didn't look like her in the mirror, and she really had to go. She began to cry softly. The men thought it was because of the haircut, but it was really from the pain of the full bladder. Suddenly she couldn't hold it any more, and to her horror, she felt the warm liquid pour out from her body, soaking her clothes, running down into the seat of the chair and dripping off onto the floor to make a yellow puddle.

Dad looked really mad! The barber lifted Jenny down from the chair, swearing, and started wiping it out with a towel. Dad gave him some money, grabbed Jenny by the arm, jerked her out the door and dragged her down the street toward the apartment. She ran to keep up, but half the time he had her feet off the ground. Her arm hurt and she was cold from the wet clothes. Her dad was so angry that Jenny was really scared now. She didn't know what he'd do to her this time!

He banged the door open and flung her at her mother. His face was red and his dark eyes fairly bulged. The veins on his neck stood out as he screamed at her. Jenny couldn't stand it any more. She ran and hid under the bed, way back in the dusty black corner, where she knew the monsters were. She'd rather be with them than with him right now! Her thumb went into her mouth and she tried to find the lock of hair she usually held and twisted, but it wasn't there any more. Her hand felt the satin ribbon bow that trimmed the neck of her underwear and she wound that around her fingers instead, pulling her knees up in the fetal position and listening to the adult voices arguing.

Above her, a bright angelic being watched, unseen.

Mary Louise wrote to her sister Lucy Ann the next day, carrying the letter to the post box herself to make sure it got mailed. She didn't hear back for a couple of weeks, and then a long letter arrived. Lucy Ann was so glad to finally hear from her, but sorry to tell her their father was dead. He died of a heart attack not long after their ma made Millie marry Judge Runyan. Mamie put the letter down, buried her head in her arms and wept. She wept for her father, and she wept for poor Millie, and she wept for herself and Jenny. They were trapped! There was nowhere else to go for help.

CHAPTER THREE

1924

The circus headed back to Florida for the winter, but Jenny and her mom and dad boarded a train to Chicago, where Frank would work at a factory until spring. Jenny could hardly wait to get back to school."I hope I'll be in the third grade this year!" she confided to Mamie. But she knew that would be up to Sister Francine; and Sister Francine was not happy with Jenny...not after the episode with the rope and Libby Spaulding. Jenny was sorry about that.

It seemed like yesterday. Jenny hadn't meant to get Libby's hair tangled in the swing rope...it was an accident. But Libby had long blonde hair that blew in the wind, and somehow it got tangled around the swing next to her and when Jenny gave Molly Benten a big push, a whole handful of hair came out, along with part of Libby's scalp. Libby screamed and ran for the school, crying and holding on to her head, while blood oozed out between her fingers. Jenny grabbed the swing, jerking Molly to a halt, and they stared at each other, not knowing whether to run hide, or go in and face the wrath of the nuns.

Jenny remembered, as the train rattled along the tracks. She stared unseeing out the window, watching the whole thing again in her mind.

The little girls didn't have to make a decision after all, because Sister Martha appeared at the door, beckoning them to come immediately. They did, and stood trembling as Sister Martha scolded them severely, "There are many sins involved here, I can see that! There is envy, and coveting, and there is willfully doing harm to another person." Sister Martha's expression changed from anger to sorrow. "You will both have to be punished severely. Libby is hurt very badly, and will probably take a long time to heal! Go and sit in the cloakroom until I send for you."

"But Sister Mar..." Jenny started to try to explain.

"Not another word!" Sister Martha cut her off. The two culprits sat in the cloakroom whispering and listening to Libby's sobs, which finally died down to quiet weeping, after Sister Francine finished bandaging her head and sent for her mother to come get her. Jenny ran her fingers through her own short hair...dark blond and cut in a Buster Brown style, as she looked over at Molly's fuzzy black mop, and slowly she understood what Sister Martha thought.

"She thinks we did it on purpose 'cause we're jealous of her beautiful hair," she whispered to Molly, "and how can we prove we didn't?"

Molly looked scared. "Whadda you think they'll do to us? My mother'll kill me!"

Jenny sympathized...she knew what her dad would say! They hadn't been able to mention the subject of long hair since he cut hers off when she was five. He'd be really mad now!

Sister Francine came into the room and stood looking down at the two unfortunate little waifs. She frowned as she saw them cringe in fear. She beckoned them into the empty schoolroom and sat in the teacher's chair facing them as they stood trembling before her. "Now," she said, firmly, "let's hear what happened."

"It was an accident, Sister...honest it was. I didn't know Libby's hair was caught in Molly's rope!" Jenny spoke earnestly, looking into Sister Francine's eyes with her clear blue-green ones.

"And then when Jenny pushed me, and Libby's swing went the other way, it just happened! We didn't mean it, Sister! We feel so bad about it...honest we do!" Molly rubbed her head. "Jenny says Sister Martha thinks we did it on purpose because we don't have pretty hair like Libby's, but we didn't, Sister!"

"Honest, we didn't, Sister Francine!"

Jenny still remembered the relief that flooded her when Sister Francine believed them. But her dad made a big fuss over the affair when he found out about it, and he kept Jenny out of school the rest of the year. "Girls don't need schooling anyway... just makes 'em more trouble! Ya can stay home an' learn how ta work!" Mom had taught her at home, though, and she was a good reader. She really hoped she could be in the third grade this year.

"Smarty, smarty, smarty! You thought you had a party! Don't forget what the teacher taught, you'll be sorry if you get caught! I'm going to tell your mother, just see if you don't care... you're nothing but a smarty pants so there, there, there!" The song pounded through her head over and over, in time to the clicking of the wheels.

The train bumped and swayed along, passing through cities and towns that all looked alike to Jenny. She waved through the windows at children when she saw them watching along the tracks. They had to stand back far enough to avoid the black smoke that occasionally belched out from the big engine, but lots of times they waved back to her. It made her feel good, just as performing with the clowns did. She didn't have any friends her own age, so she pretended the children she waved at, and the ones she performed for were all her good pals. She made up stories about some of them in her mind.

Jenny liked circus life, and she enjoyed being a clown, wearing the silly ruffled polka-dot dress and the straw hat with its tall bobbing red flower, and acting ridiculous with the other clowns. It was great when everybody laughed at them. What she really wanted though was to be an acrobat or an aerialist... one of the big stars! She constantly practiced doing back-flips, and was getting good at it. She pretended she was Lillian Russell, whom she'd seen one time, dressed in beautiful pink satin tights, the spotlight shining on her supple body, back-flipping the whole length of the big tent. She had decided then to try to do the same thing herself. She could do some tumbling acts just for fun, but she wanted to be one of the headliners.

Now she watched out the window as the train steamed along through countryside and small towns, not really seeing them. I'm gonna practice my back-flips all winter until I can do them all the way around the tent! I just hope we have someplace I can practice... I wonder why Dad won't let me play with the other circus kids. He never lets me have any friends my own age! Well, at least I have lots of grown-up friends. And the circus folks are like a big family. I love them all ... and they love me too... they do!

She was lost in thought as the miles clicked by. Jenny's dad had a pretty good job with the circus. He worked in the front office, helping keep things organized and running smoothly. He made sure the circus traveled efficiently and on time, and he helped keep order in the ranks, soothing the feelings of Murphy, the elephant man and keeping Mr. Clyde, the lion tamer happy, as well as making sure the ring artists were being taken care of. There was a lot of work to do with a circus the size of the Sheffler Brothers Big Show. The sideshow attractions each had their own tents, as did all the performers. When they camped, they treated the tents like their homes, making such family routine as they could manage.

Jenny was special friends with John Gandella, one of the Great Gandellas, a tumbling act. He was teaching her a trapeze act. (John was drawn to the strange little girl...happy-go- lucky and full of ambition, ready to try almost anything, but sometimes so desperate for approval and love that she'd do things that weren't sensible or safe. John wondered why Frank Gibbs was always so stern with his daughter. He never seemed to smile at her, only found fault. John tried to make it up to her. His own sisters were being trained for the trapeze, and he arranged for Jenny to practice with them.)

I really love John, she thought...I wish he was my real big brother! He's always nice and smiling, and ready to help. I wish we didn't have to leave him and the girls when the circus left for winter quarters!

The train whistle interrupted her thoughts, and the porter came through calling, "Next stop Chicago." Mom and Dad started gathering their things. Soon the engine rolled to a stop at the station, and they got off, but they had to wait awhile to get out through the crowds, all pushing and milling around, looking for luggage, or meeting and greeting people. There were lots of soldiers too, coming and going. Dust, stirred by hundreds of feet, rose from the platform and mixed with the steam from the locomotive. Jenny coughed, and tried to keep her hand over her nose and mouth. The confusion was almost overwhelming, but she held on to her Mom's hand through it all, and finally they found a cab to take them to Morton's Boarding House.

"Did you get all our stuff, Frank? You remembered the extra boxes, didn't you?" Mom always asked that, and Dad always got disgusted. He dropped his cigarette butt and ground it into the gravel with his heel and helped her into the Model T. They settled in as well as they could for the ride across town.

"It'll all be coming along as soon as possible. They had ta wait for the dray to get back. Why do ya always hafta ask? Ya'd think I don't know anything about moving goods and people...whadda ya think I been doing all summer?" He frowned and rubbed his stomach. "Sure hope we're in time for dinner...I'm real hungry!"

When Jenny enrolled in classes at St. Francis, the other kids had already been in school for three weeks. She stood outside the door a moment, then swallowed hard, and went into the office where Sister Francine sat behind her big black desk. "Hi Sister Francine. My mother wants me to be in third grade this year," she lied, keeping her fingers crossed behind her back.

"Well then, get your books from Sister Susanna and go on down to the third grade room. I'll tell Sister Agnes you're coming." Sister Francine surveyed the skinny little girl, "You'll need to buy a uniform, of course. Please have it on tomorrow." She smiled, "I'm glad you're back, Jenny. I hope things go better for you this year."

Jenny returned the smile, happy and scared at the same time, "Thanks, Sister Francine. I hope so too!" She went to get her books, and settled into a desk near the window, ignoring the stares of the other kids.

As it happened though, she only got to spend a couple of months at St. Francis, then her dad decided to move on to Atlantic City, New Jersey, where he worked at a small shop. She hardly got settled into class at St. Steven's there, when they moved on again, this time to Birmingham, Alabama. "I sure hope I get to finish third grade here!" she told her mom.

But only a few weeks later her mom was sick, and Dad said, "I want you here at home to help in case your ma needs something while I'm gone. You've had enough school anyhow...girls don't need school!" So she stayed at home again, in the one little rented room, and Mom taught her from the schoolbooks. It was like that a lot. They moved so often Jenny never got to finish a grade in the same school she started it in, and as often as not, she was home schooled. She skipped some grades, and caught up with her age group as well as she could. Fortunately she was smart and caught on to things quickly.

The rest of that winter seemed very long to Jenny, cooped up with her mom in their smoky room. She dreamed about going to school and making real friends, and she dreamed about performing on the trapeze in the circus, while she studied history, geography, arithmetic and spelling under Mamie's patient tutelage.

Sometimes she talked to God in her mind. She somehow felt a drawing to him that she couldn't explain. But she never felt the presence of the angel assigned to be her guardian, who was always with her.

Frank joined up with the circus again in the spring and Jenny was beside herself with excitement, finding all her old friends again, and catching up with the news from the winter. She inhaled deeply of the ripe circus smells. Hammers rang against metal stakes, as the tents went up all around. She ran from one tent to another, greeting all the performers, checking that everyone was back again this year.

"Hey, Jerry!" she yelled, catching sight of her friend the sad clown. "I'm so glad to see you again...isn't it great to be back?"

Jerry grinned and hugged her. "Sure is, Jenny! There's a lotta work to be done now though. Be sure you come to practice this afternoon...we've got a new act all planned."

Happily, Jenny agreed, "I'll be there, Jerry...see ya later!" Then she ran to check on the elephants and the big cats, and stood in front of the gorilla's cage talking to him. But she was especially anxious to see John Gandella and his family.

When she found them in the practice tent, John was teaching one of the older girls to dangle from the high wire and spin on a rope by holding on to it with her teeth! It took a lot of work and time to learn that trick, and you had to be older so your teeth were well enough set in your head so they wouldn't just get loose and fall out. "Hi, Jenny," John called when he spotted her, "Hope you're ready to learn some real flying this year?"

Jenny grinned from ear to ear. "Boy, am I ever, John!" She hugged him enthusiastically. "It's sure good to be back!" She settled down on an upturned bucket to watch Andrea work.

"How are the back-flips coming?"

"Well, I didn't have as much chance to practice as I wanted, but I can still do quite a few. I'm gonna get really good this year." And to prove herself, she stood, poised carefully, and did a series of ten flips in a row, her skirts flying over her head in a most unladylike manner.

"Not bad, kid, but you'd better get yourself some tights if you plan to do that a lot." John turned to hide his grin.

She borrowed some old tights his sisters had outgrown, and practiced her flips religiously to get her arms in shape, in between practice sessions on the one arm trapeze. She was getting pretty good on the trapeze, but as the weeks passed she became really expert at the back-flip, and could finally flip her way the whole length of the big tent and back. She dreamed of being a star with her own act...being in the spotlight, with the band playing music for her. The dream kept her practicing every day.

Her big chance came quite 'by accident' one day when Mr. Sheffler himself just happened to come into the tent while she was practicing.

"Say, you're quite an acrobat, aren't you?" He grinned at her.

"I can flip all the way from this end of the Hippodrome to the other end!" Jenny bragged. (They all called the big tent the Hippodrome.) "I've been practicing ever since I saw Lillian Russell."

"No kidding? Well, let's see what you can do, OK?" He beckoned Hiram the ringmaster to join him. "The kid says she can back-flip like Lillian Russell!"

"Oh?...Yeah, I heard somebody was practicin' a lot lately." Hiram raised his eyebrows, "she gonna show us?"

Jenny poised herself, took a deep breath and began flipping. Over and over and over she went, never missing a beat. All the way to the end of the tent and back again she flipped, her short blonde hair whipping back and forth at each turn, until she ended up in front of the men where she'd started. She stood before them dusty and panting, and grinning triumphantly.

"Say, that's pretty darn good!" Hiram sounded really impressed. He turned to Mr. Sheffler, "You think we could use her for black-out?"

"Exactly what I was thinking." He turned to Jenny. "What do you think, young lady, do you want to do this every day for the crowd?" Jenny grinned wider than ever and nodded emphatically. "Well, I'll talk to your dad about it then. You're Frank Gibbs' kid, aren't you?" Jenny nodded again, losing some of her enthusiasm. Would Dad let her do this, or would he have some rule against it, like so many other things she'd wanted to do?

But they would pay her for the act, of course, so Frank agreed to let Jenny perform, and Mamie bought her a beautiful costume with white spangled tights and top, and fixed her short hair attractively. They realized how dangerous it could be if Jenny got too near the row of tent stakes along the edge of the bleachers, so they had a clown stand by the stakes, every few feet, where Jenny could see them even though the tent was darkened. That way she could stay far enough away from the edge.

The night of her first performance, Jenny stood waiting at the north entrance. Her heart was beating fast as the lights went out. She heard Hiram announce "The Remarkable Miss Jenny Gibbs." The band stopped, the drums began to roll, and the spotlight swung toward her. Jenny stepped into the light, bowed to the crowd and began flipping her way down the 200-foot length of the tent, the drum accenting every time her feet touched the ground. Time seemed to stand still, as she spun around and around and around, endlessly and forever.

When finally she ended back where she'd started and stood for a bow, applause surged up around her, wrapping her as if in a blanket. To a child so starved for approval, it felt like love! When she ran out of the tent to meet her parents, it even seemed to Jenny for a second, as though Frank smiled at her. And her angel guardian touched her, ever so gently.

CHAPTER FOUR

Jenny worked as a regular part of the circus each season, while she continued to practice on the trapeze. She was getting to be a pretty good 'flyer', too, so when they moved to Washington D.C. the next year, her dad actually built her a small trapeze in their campground. She practiced long and hard, while Frank worked at the Kroger store there. She went to school sporadically, when he would let her, and practiced on the trapeze whenever the weather would allow. Her mother smiled, hearing Jenny sing as she practiced, "Ohhhh, she flies through the air with the greatest of ease... the daring young girl on the flying trapeze!"

When they went back to the circus the following season, Jenny was given her own trapeze act. She worked without a net, 30 feet up. Frank kept all the money from that too, although he gave her a little spending money now. But Jenny was happy. She was a star! She still wasn't allowed to make friends with other kids, though. She was watched wherever she went and whatever she did, and someone always reported back to Frank Gibbs.

One evening after the show, Jenny was tired and hungry. She trudged toward the Gibbs tent, then stopped and turned. "Guess I'll stop at the mess tent and get a sandwich." She went in, took a chair and ordered a burger.

A couple of sailors sitting in the mess tent drinking coffee looked at her curiously, and as Jenny started to eat her hamburger, one of them asked, "Hey, you one of the acts?"

Jenny brightened, like a flower responding to the sun, and told them about the circus and how great it was to be a star in it, and then, feeling really good, went 'home' to bed. The next day, someone kidded Frank Gibbs, "Hey, Frank, your daughter was getting cozy with a couple of 'flatties' last night! Better watch it, or she'll be running off with somebody."

Frank came home in a towering rage and confronted 11-year-old Jenny. "What's the matter with you? Are you turning into a whore or something?" He shook his finger under her nose." You keep your @#$@# mouth closed around strangers. Do I have to be with you every single minute, or lock you up somewhere?" He ranted and raved, using words Jenny had never heard before. She was devastated, and confused. All she had done was to respond proudly to someone's interest in the circus. Wounded in her spirit, she curled up on her cot with her hurt, wondering once more why her dad hated her so much. Why was it that no matter what she did, he was angry at her? She remembered what the Sisters at school had said about praying when you were in trouble, so she fingered her rosary and recited the Hail Marys in her mind. She fell asleep in mid-prayer.

At the end of that summer, they went to New Jersey again. New Brunswick. It was where Frank had grown up. His mother was there, and his brothers and sister. He hadn't seen them for years, and now he took his family home to meet them. Jenny was surprised to discover she had a Grandma and Aunts, Uncles and cousins. Dad never talked about them at all, and she hadn't thought to ask him whether she had grandparents, she just figured she didn't.

The funny thing was that Dad looked different in New Brunswick. He wore dark glasses all the time, and he grew his mustache and combed his hair different, and wore a hat most of the time. And Grandma and the Uncles were really surprised to see her and her Mom. "My, Frank, you must have gotten married right after you left here!" was Grandma's comment. How come you never told us about your family?"

Frank made some sort of explanation and changed the subject.

"Grandma isn't like I thought a grandma would be," Jenny confided to Mamie later as they settled things into the nice little apartment they rented in town.

"Oh? How did you think she'd be?"

"You know, nice and comfortable, with gray hair and an apron and cookies and smiles and hugs...you know..." Jenny wrinkled her nose. "But Grandma smells funny, and she doesn't really hug..." she trailed off. "It's kind of nice to have cousins, though. I like Alice, but I wish she was my age. The boys are kind of fun. I'd like to get to know them all better. Do you think we'll stay here now?"

Mamie had a strange expression. She was thinking of her own mother, and wondering suddenly what she was like as a grandma. She shook her head, "I don't know, but probably not, Jenny. Your dad likes to move around. Just enjoy it while we're here, Honey."

Jenny did enjoy it for a while. She started 5th grade in the public school. She was the star of the gym class when the teacher asked them to climb a rope. A couple of the boys tried, and one of them managed to get most of the way up the rope. Then Mr. Burns turned to Jenny, and indicated it was her turn. Jenny grabbed the rope and nonchalantly went up it hand over hand, as easily as breathing. Of course, that's how she had gone up to her trapeze all season.

Mr. Burns' mouth dropped. "That's it! That's the way. Show them again!" He was so pleased with Jenny he had her teach the other kids how to climb. Later on she told them she was in the circus, bragging about her experience, and most of them were jealous of her, so she didn't find any friends there right away. She was beginning to get to know Shirley Peters, though, and hoping maybe Shirley would like her.

Frank got a job at the steel mill where his brothers worked, and things went along pretty well, until one day right before Christmas. He came home early looking different...it took Jenny a few minutes to decide what it was... he actually looked scared! That scared Jenny too, because something had to be really bad to scare Frank! He called Mamie, "Come on, pack up quick, we're leaving!" and began throwing things out of the closet.

"What? Whatever for now? I thought you liked it here." Her mother protested, even as she began taking their suitcases down.

"Come on, move...move! Detectives were at the factory today looking for me! I think that stupid Flora turned me in! Don't know why Elmer married such a rotten egg!" He threw things into boxes wildly, as he ranted. "The boys hid me in the big shovel till the 'dicks' left, but they'll be hangin' around now looking for me."

Jenny listened, wide-eyed, as she packed her own things. What in the world was Dad talking about? Why should detectives be looking for him? She didn't say anything, but she wondered a whole lot as they finished gathering their belongings together. "Where are we going?" she asked.

"We'll stay with Uncle Pete until after Christmas, then we'll go back to Chicago I guess." He looked at Mamie, "I really want to spend Christmas with Ma and my family first, but it's a lot easier to hide in Chicago."

So they arrived with all their bags at Uncle Pete's house, where they crowded into one bedroom, as usual. There was a lot of confusion, and that night Jenny lay still, straining her ears to hear what the adults talked about around the dining table after the children were supposed to be asleep. They mentioned something about a manslaughter charge, and Uncle Pete said, "It wasn't easy breaking you out of the county jail and getting you safely out of the area. Why in the world did you decide to come back, anyway? You know they're still looking for you!"

"Wanted to see Ma again, and the rest of you. Thought maybe they'd have forgotten about me by now! That good-for-nothing Flora of Elmer's… I'd like to fix her wagon good!"

"Give me one of those cigarettes Frank," Jenny heard her Mom say, "I guess if all the rest of you are going to smoke all the time, I might as well smoke too!"

Jenny didn't hear any more. She woke up in the morning wondering where she was, and then remembered what had happened. She dressed slowly and went downstairs looking for cousin Alice. "Alice, what is manslaughter?" she asked, after she'd finished her oatmeal and before Alice left for school. They were alone in the big kitchen for a moment.

"Why, I think it's like murder only not quite as bad." She glanced over at her cousin, "Why do you want to know that, anyway?"

"Oh, I just heard the grownups talking about it, that's all." Jenny changed the subject and they discussed whether she would have to change schools now, but inside she felt strange. Her thoughts churned inside her, and slowly she began to understand why they moved so much, from one little room to another, in one city after another. Like murder...that's killing somebody! And they broke him out of jail! I'll bet that's why he works at the circus! We travel all the time...I wonder who he killed? I wonder why he did it?

She never mentioned what she'd heard to her mother, but she thought about it a lot and she was even more afraid of Frank.

CHAPTER FIVE

1929

Frank must have been really worried, because he signed up with a carnival that summer instead of the circus. It wasn't the same, but it was fun.

On a fine June morning, Jenny moved down the line of booths listening to the cacophony of voices and music. Shills tried to entice the suckers into spending their cash on the various games and shows. Each of the many rides added its own voice to the symphony of sound, their engines revving up and then easing back alternately, as the whirligigs whirled and the Ferris wheel spun. The calliope on the merry-go-round played loudest of all. Jenny loved every speech, every tune, every sound, every smell...they were all part of her life. She loved the sickening sweet smell of cotton candy and caramel corn, as well as the smell of the spicy hot dogs Max sold at the big white vendor's wagon. She loved the smell of grease and gasoline at the rides. She knew everyone in the Carnival, and they all knew Jenny. Frank's daughter was the favorite with everyone at the Jimmy Johnson Shows.

She arrived at Frank's assigned show and swung up into the ticket booth. Her dad grunted..."Bout time ya showed up! Here now, you take over selling tickets while I drum up some business. Remember how I showed you to make 'em forget the change! You better come up with more extra than yesterday, Missy!" He frowned at her.

She grinned back "OK Dad." She leaned over the edge of the booth, "That's 10 cents" she answered a small boy standing there. She dropped the coin into the box and handed him a ticket. Frank grunted and stepped down from the booth. He reached back for his straw hat, which he perched jauntily on the side of his head and mounted the small stage in front of the show's entrance.

"Girrulls, girrulls, girrulls" he sing-songed. "Beeyooteefull girrulls! Blondes, brunettes. red-heads...and real princesses, every one of 'em! See them dance the fantastic dance of the veils. You've never seen *anything* until you've seen Fatima and her sisters dance, wearing only the flimsiest of silken garments. Ya won't believe yer own eyes!" He chanted on and on while Jenny took in the money and gave out tickets, being careful to put the change on top of the box the way her dad showed her, so that some customers forgot to pick it up. He always got mad if she didn't get at least $5 a day that way. She was very good at it now.

In late afternoon Jimmy Lee took over the booth and Jenny gratefully jumped down and headed for the trailer. She was hungry...boy was she hungry! The smell of onions browning came out to meet her as she opened the trailer door. "Hi, Mom! What're we havin' for supper?"

"Hamburger and peas." Mamie turned from the stove, "How did things go today?" She lit a cigarette and took a long drag, exhaling the smoke through her nose.

"Good, I guess. I got an extra $5.60. I gave it to Dad." Jenny pulled a chair up to the table and waited while her mom poured the juice off a can of peas and added them to the onion and hamburger in the frying pan. As soon as it was warm enough, Mamie put some on a plate and set it in front of her daughter. Jenny spread some oleo on a slice of bread and began to eat hungrily. "It's good, Mom. I wish sometime we could have real butter though."

"When our ship comes in we'll have real butter, and not until then. Maybe we'll have milk then too," she added, as she poured Jenny a cup of coffee.

"Yeah, I know," Jenny nodded. "When do you think that'll be, Mom?" Mamie just sighed a deep sigh, and Jenny changed the subject. "Oh, Mr. Baker wants me to work for him tomorrow if it's OK?"

"That's nice Honey, I'm glad they all like you so much! Of course, you'll have to ask your dad."

"Yeah. Oh, and he wants me to wear my red shirt if I can. Is it clean?"

"Yes, I managed to wash out a few things today. I'll have to iron it though." Mamie got the iron and plugged it in. Then she got the sprinkling bottle and shook water on the shirt and rolled it up into a tight ball to dampen. She proceeded to dampen the rest of the cotton things too. It was such a blessing to her to finally have electricity...so much easier than when she'd had to heat heavy sad-irons on the stove. She picked up the iron and nearly scorched the handkerchief she started with. She unplugged the iron for a couple of minutes, then plugged it back in and tried again. "There, that's better." She took a closer look at Jenny. "Why don't you go on over to the bath house and take a shower?" she suggested.

"Oh, Mo-om," Jenny protested, but she got her towel and soap and went over to the bathhouse anyway. She stood under the warm water a minute, turned it off while she soaped herself, then turned the water on again and rinsed off. After rubbing herself good with the rather stiff towel, she had to admit she did feel better.

In the morning she ran to the Bakers' booth. They owned the ring-toss, and Jenny really liked that concession. She stood outside and played shill, getting the customers to stop and spend their money to take a chance on winning a big teddy bear. There were a lot of cheap smaller prizes, and it wasn't easy to win the big bear. "Come on Mister, try your hand and take home the prize for your kids!" she'd sing out at one prospect. "Just toss the rings over the pegs, and your girl can walk away with the bear. Come on, be a sport...be a hero" to another.

Jenny was very good at getting money out of people. At only 12 years old, she was an expert shill, in demand down the main street of the carnival. Her dad kept all the money she earned, though, so lately in her spare time Jenny often disappeared for a while. Her dad was busy most of the time and couldn't get away to look for her.

Jenny had discovered the Charleston contests. She was so limber, and such a 'ham' that she nearly always won, until they finally caught her. One of the kids watching recognized Jenny, and when she won the prize again, the kid reported her to the manager. When the people running the contest realized she was with the show she couldn't compete any more, though they just laughed about it and sent her away. Of course then someone told Frank about it, laughing about his crazy daughter. Dad was really mad though, because she hadn't given him her money from winning.

"OK, Missy, if you're so anxious to dance in front of everybody, and you're so all-fired good, you can just jolly well dance to ballyhoo the girlie show! Now get yourself decked out in a proper outfit and get on down to the stage!"

"Oh Dad..." she began.

"Oh, Jenny!" he mocked..."just do as I say. Your mother'll help you get inta some kinda costume. Then you get yerself on down there, and fast!" He nodded at Mamie, meaningfully.

Mamie knew better than to stand up for her daughter. Obediently, she got out the boxes of clothes and dug through them. Finally she came up with a short-fringed red and black dress, which she put on Jenny, pinning up the shoulder straps and taking a tuck in the middle of the skirt to shorten it. It was a typical flapper outfit, and when they added a headband around her forehead, with a black feather, she looked pretty good. Mamie finished the outfit with Jenny's good black silk socks and black patent shoes.

Jenny looked in the mirror. She was surprised to see how good she looked...almost like the grown-up girls! She smoothed the fringe on her skirt. Well, OK, I guess I might as well do it...anyway Dad'll really be mad if I don't. Maybe it'll be fun.

She stopped at the Charleston contest and borrowed a danceable record for the machine, then reported to her dad. He was pleased at her appearance, and more pleased when he watched her dance. She threw her whole body into the rhythm, crossing her hands on her knees, and kicking her feet out stylishly. He sold tickets at a great rate, people eagerly handing in their dimes, anxious to see the show inside, if the show outside was a good representation. Jenny enjoyed the dancing, and the rhythm of the Charleston music. She always loved being the center of attention, and applause was food for her soul. For the rest of the tour she danced ballyhoo for 20 shows a day, from 9 AM to 11 PM and earned $11 a week. She danced through a pair of black silk socks every day. Her dad took the money...every cent. She got fed, and he figured that was enough for a kid!

"Mom, why doesn't Dad like me?" she asked Mamie for the hundredth time. "No matter what I do, he's not happy." She looked up at her mother with those big clear eyes, "And I really do try to please him, Mom."

Mamie hugged her, "Of course he likes you, Honey. It's just his way."

"But he's nice to some of the other kids, Mom, and he even smiles at Tilly Richards sometimes!"

Mamie turned her back to hide her expression. There was nothing she could say to explain Frank's behavior. She had tried everything to get Frank to love Jenny. He provided a home for her, and that was all he had promised to do. "I know what let's do," she suggested, forcing her voice to sound bright, "let's go over to Max's wagon and get a hot dog instead of cooking!"

The angel went with them.

CHAPTER SIX

1930

When the season was over, they went back to Chicago, where they found lodgings in a rambling rooming house on the West Side. It was a friendly kind of house, with big windows and a wide front porch with a swinging wooden 'couch' that creaked rhythmically when they used it. There was a Victrola in the parlor, with great records. They played everything from opera to cowboy songs to popular love songs, depending on who had control of the machine at the time. Whenever Jenny opened the front door, music and the smells of baking bread or other wonderful foods welcomed her in.

A disparate lot of interesting people lived there. Mr. Jones, a balding book-salesman who always wore the same ratty brown suit and derby hat. Mr. and Mrs. Smathers, a middle aged couple who argued all the time. Miss Mattie Pearson, a refined maiden lady who, judging from her clothes and demeanor, must have had money once. The one Jenny liked best was Mrs. Rabb, a fat, happy woman with several chins, who lived in the back room upstairs. Mrs. Rabb made lampshades for some of the stores downtown. They were lovely creations of crimped georgette. She hired Jenny to thread needles for her.

Jenny spent every minute she could manage, when she wasn't in school, with Mrs. Rabb. She threaded needles and knotted the threads, as she chattered happily about anything and everything that came to her mind, without a thought to family privacy, telling her the most intimate details of their lives. Mrs. Rabb became the 'best friend' that most 13-year-old girls have in school, since Jenny still wasn't allowed to play with other kids.

One afternoon when she bounced into the cluttered room to start threading and knotting, Mrs. Rabb stopped her. "Look here, Jenny. I got something for you that I think you'll like." She held out a book. "The Secret of the Old Clock" Jenny read. "Oh thanks, Mrs. Rabb! I've never had a book of my own...I love it!" She leafed through the pages. "I just love it!" She sat down and started to read then and there, quickly becoming completely involved with the adventures of Nancy Drew and her friends.

Mrs. Rabb bought her another book whenever she could manage it, and from then on, any time she wanted to, Jenny lived in a borrowed world of wealth and leisure, with a family who had servants and undreamed-of luxury. She read everything she could get her hands on after that, getting a lot of her education that way.

But Mrs. Rabb reported back to Mamie and Frank the things Jenny told her about the family, and they punished Jenny time and again. There couldn't be any family secrets, since they lived in one room, and Jenny faithfully repeated everything her folks said to Mrs. Rabb, in spite of the punishment. Jenny honestly didn't think she did anything wrong...she didn't know what else to talk to Mrs. Rabb about. Mrs. Rabb wasn't a kid, and Jenny wanted to talk to her like an adult. Since Jenny wasn't allowed to play with other kids, and she was a naturally outgoing personality, the "adult-type" talk continued no matter what the consequences later.

"Listen, you two," Mamie said. Jenny was at school, and Frank and Mamie were talking together with Mrs. Rabb. "I have an idea... let's make up some outlandish story and see if Jenny can keep it quiet. I think she's learned her lesson, but ... "

Frank grinned wickedly. "Great idea, Mamie! We'll check the kid out."

Mrs. Rabb looked doubtful, but she nodded. "What'll we tell her?"

"Oh, let's invent something fun. She'd really love to live in one place like 'real people' as she puts it. Let's tell her ... oh... if we can just save another hundred dollars somehow, we can start a new business! Then we can make a fortune, and buy our own big house to live in." Mamie rocked back in her chair, remembering better times.

Frank slapped his knee, "That'll really get 'er! She's always yammerin' about havin' our own place so she can have friends!" He challenged the two of them with his look. "As though she doesn't have any now!"

That evening they carried out the plan. They closed their door tight and Frank began to tell Mamie about the new business they could start, "If we could just manage to save another hundred dollars!

Jenny was breathless with the thought of it. "I can help! I know I can earn that much this season!"

Frank and Mamie went on and on, finally cautioning Jenny not to tell anyone else about their plans. "It would ruin everything if this gets out before we're ready!" Mamie cautioned her.

"OK, Mom." Jenny agreed. She really meant not to say anything about it, but she hadn't been at Mrs. Rabb's room more than 10 minutes before she'd blurted out the whole thing.

Mrs. Rabb reported back to Frank and Mamie, and Jenny was trapped! "Lean over the table!" Frank told her, as he removed his belt. She took the stinging blows that hurt her soul as well as her body, then retreated to her cot, covered herself completely with her blanket and wept.

But for the most part, it was a happy winter for Jenny. She got to finish seventh grade in Chicago, and even though they moved on again in the spring, they remained friends with Mrs. Rabb. They even called her once the next summer and took her along on a camping vacation at Fox Lake. That was a memorable event in Jenny's life, since it was one of the only real vacations they ever had together. Jenny had a wonderful time swimming and playing in the water. Frank even bought her some rubber water shoes. It was one of the happiest times of her childhood.

They spent the whole next year with the circus. Jenny had her own little trapeze act, and also did her back-flip act for the blackout. She worked hard every day, earning the respect of the circus folks, who watched over her like a group of concerned aunts, uncles and grandparents, reporting to Frank everything she did. For her part, Jenny tried to avoid her dad as much as possible. Since they all worked hard, including Mamie, who sold cotton candy at every performance, they didn't get in each other's way much.

"You're getting really strong, Jenny. Maybe we should teach you a new act for next year." John Gandella said, as he tested a guy rope carefully, making sure things were set for The Flying Gandellas' next act.

"Really, John?" Jenny stopped beside him, looking up at his muscular frame. John, at 20, was a handsome fellow, who attracted a lot of attention from the younger women in the circus. Jenny idolized him, feeling jealous of Andrea, Joya and Rhonda, his sisters, who worked together with him and their parents every day.

"Really! I saw you trying some wire walking the other day. You're not bad, Jenny, but with some practice, I'll bet we could have you doing some really interesting tricks on the wire." He walked over to check the net, talking back over his shoulder, "You think your dad would let you spend some practice time learning something new?"

"Sure...at least I can't see why not! He likes to have me earn money any way I can." She said the last with a mixture of sarcasm and sadness that John missed.

"Well, OK, let's get in some time early in the morning, before our regular practice sessions. I'll meet you here right after breakfast."

"Gee, thanks, John. I'll be here!" Jenny's shoulders straightened with pride, as she walked over to the 'hotel' to get some lunch. She was careful to eat only a light meal, so she would be able to perform without problems at the 2:00 o'clock show. She passed the sideshow tent, waving and grinning at the fat lady and the midget, who stood outside enjoying the sun. The pungent smell from the elephant area faded a little as she reached the cookhouse.

She stopped by a hose to wash her hands, and surveyed what she could see of herself. Boy, I'm really dirty. I'd better get cleaned up before I get into my costume!

It wasn't easy to keep clean in the circus surroundings. Most of the time, the performers looked in need of baths, their hair dusty, their feet dirty. But when they went into the ring dressed in their gorgeous costumes, and the spotlight shone on them, they were people out of a fairy tale, glamorous and immaculate. Jenny was no exception. Most of the time, she looked like a neglected waif, but when the spotlight caught her at the foot of the rope, ready to climb hand over hand up to the trapeze, she was transformed into a graceful princess of the air. It was the magic of the circus. Jenny loved it all, in spite of her dad.

After the season was over, they all went back to Florida, and Frank stayed with the circus that winter, which gave Jenny a chance to learn the wire act, as well as some other trapeze tricks. She went to school with some of the other circus kids, but none of them were her age, so she was still pretty much alone. The local youngsters were warned by their parents to stay away from the circus kids, as though they had some sort of contagious disease. Winter was fun in the warm Florida sun though, and Jenny grew like a flower.

Then one day it happened. At 13 years old, she was still sleeping on an army cot at the foot of her parents' bed, where Frank wanted her. She woke suddenly, aware of a strange wetness. She lifted her blankets and put one leg on the floor, then, horrified, she screamed."Mom!...Mom! Look, I'm bleeding!" She stood up and tried to stop the flow, her panic rising.

"It's OK, Honey," Mamie pulled her into the bathroom and helped her to wash herself off. Then she brought a soft cloth, folded thick, and pinned it to some of Jenny's old panties. I'll give you some more cloths, so change it when you need to, and wash it out carefully to use again. This happens to every woman, Jenny, it just means you're growing up. You'll go through this every month now for a few days."

Jenny was stricken. "You mean this is normal?" Her mom nodded. "You mean I have to go through this the rest of my life?" Mamie nodded again. "I can't do my act like this! I can't go out in public!" Jenny began to cry. Life had been hard enough for her before, and now this. It wasn't fair...it just wasn't fair! She refused to go outside for three days. She sent word to John that she was sick.

The worst thing of all was how her dad acted. He treated her with complete disdain, and said some terrible things to her. Things she didn't understand. Things like, "If I ever catch you letting a man touch you, I'll put you in juvenile hall!" and "You stay away from boys, you hear? If I see you hanging around any boys, you'll be in real trouble!" and "Anybody gets caught fooling around with you, I'll kill you both!" Jenny knew he meant it. He kept a revolver hidden in his suitcase, and she had no doubt he'd use it.

So somehow this had to do with boys, but she wasn't sure how. Nobody would tell her anything either. Even though she was in the circus and the carnivals, she was isolated and kept separate from other people. And she still was not allowed to associate with other kids outside of school. She was confused and upset. I wish I was at the Catholic school...I'd ask the Sisters about it. They'd tell me what's going on!

There was a church not far from the circus winter quarters, and with her mother's permission, Jenny started to attend the services. Sometimes, Mamie even went along with her. Jenny bowed her head and prayed, "Dear God, I need help. Please help me Lord!" But most of the time she prayed to the Virgin Mary. And sometimes she felt a little better when she came out from church.

The next summer's circus tour was a real success as far as Jenny was concerned. She had new tricks to expand her trapeze act and was a real star at last. And when she did the back-flip with the spotlight focused on her spinning little body and the drums rolling and the crowd chanting one, two,...one hundred fifty, one hundred fifty one,...until she stood dizzy and triumphant, arms uplifted, glowing with sweat and confidence, she was completely happy for a few moments.

The Angel was happy for her too.

CHAPTER SEVEN

1931

That winter they got their usual one room in Birmingham. "Why can't we ever once get a house or an apartment like we had in New Brunswick, where I can have my own room?" Jenny complained.

"You know your dad. Just between you and me, I'm afraid he's a sick man, Jenny." Mamie was unusually candid. She was lonely too, and Frank watched her as hard as he watched Jenny. She wasn't allowed any friends of her own either, only Frank's friends. She had developed a theory over the years while living with him. Now she shared it with her daughter. "He wants all his things around him right in one room where he can see them all the time, including you and me, Jenny." Her voice quavered, and she stopped and cleared her throat before going on. "I think he's afraid we might run away and leave him if he lets us out of his sight." She sighed, "And he's so restless...I don't think we'll ever have a house. He doesn't want to settle down anywhere." She looked around the room, "At least this room is bigger than most. And we have cross ventilation...and we only share the bathroom with one other couple!" She went into a fit of coughing. She coughed a lot lately.

The radio down the hall was playing sad songs like "All Alone" and "What'll I do?" And "Remember." Mamie and Jenny left their door open so they could hear. The mood of the music matched theirs perfectly.

Jenny started high school in Birmingham. At 14 she was still really innocent and childish in many ways. But finally she was allowed to associate with some of her schoolmates after hours this year, and Frank bought her a pair of skates that she begged for. "All the other kids have them Dad, and it's really good exercise. I'll be able to keep in shape for my act if I get outside and skate hard."

When she got the skates she spent all her after school hours on them, learning to do the most daredevil stunts, along with the boys. It was on a golden afternoon in late autumn when the trouble came. They had been skating down a steep hill and on across the street right into the traffic, without anyone being hurt. Now it was late and the other kids had gone in for supper, but Jenny was so eager to associate with them that she was standing on the corner, looking to see whether anybody was still out for one last trip down the hill.

She turned her head and swung her skate around just enough to trip over a tree root at her feet. She hit the ground hard, her arm coming down across the heavy root, and she heard a sickening snap as pain tore into her. She screamed and fainted, and the next thing she knew, she was in some doctor's office lying on a table, with her mom, dad and the doctor standing there.

The angel hovered overhead.

"Her bones are unusually brittle for someone so young. She doesn't seem to have enough calcium," the doctor commented, "you should make sure she drinks her milk...although its a little late now!"

Mamie glanced darkly at Frank, who hadn't let her buy milk for Jenny, saying coffee was good enough for her. Frank nodded, "Sure, Doc!" And he did let them have milk occasionally after that.

The accident marked the end of Jenny's school days. Frank wouldn't let her go back again, saying she didn't need high school anyway. "Well, then she'll study at home!" Mamie had declared, "She'll get an education somehow. I want her to have a chance for a decent life!" But Mamie herself had only gone through eighth grade, and couldn't help Jenny with the work, and it wasn't long before the schoolbooks got put aside in favor of novels.

Frank was restless again, wanting to leave Birmingham. He wrote to a theatrical agency in Baltimore and asked for work. They offered him a job running a 'museum' in downtown Baltimore. It was a place where sideshow people worked in the winter, earning money to live on. There were a variety of attractions: a fire-eater, a tattooed lady, a snake charmer, a knife thrower, a half man-half woman and his friend a ventriloquist, and lots of other games and acts.

The museum was in an old theater building. There was red velvet and plush everywhere downstairs, all very fancy. Upstairs had long ago been used for offices, but had long been abandoned. Frank was as tight-fisted as ever, and he determined to house his family there. "Now look Mamie, see, we can save a lot of money if we fix up a couple of rooms upstairs and live there for the winter. I know it's kinda dirty now, but we can clean it up and it'll do just fine!" Mamie wrinkled her nose in dismay, but she followed Frank, and Jenny followed her, and the three of them trooped up the narrow stairway and found their way through dark hallways to the front of the building.

The place smelled of dust and dry wood and a strange mustiness. It was obvious nobody had been up here for years. Plaster lay on the floor where it had fallen from the ceiling during the cold winters and hot summers when the flat roof leaked. There were torn stained shades at some of the windows, and one window was broken, where someone had thrown a rock, which still lay on the rough wide-board floor in the broken glass. A single light bulb dangled from the ceiling.

Mamie and Jenny stood in the middle of the room and looked around them in dismay. "You can't mean it, Frank! This place should be condemned!" Mamie finally gasped. "How can we possibly live here? We'll freeze to death, even if we manage to get the place clean enough somehow." She took his arm, pleading, "Let's find a place in a rooming house instead. It can't cost that much!"

"This'll be just fine, Mamie. Now don't make a fuss! I'll get a mop and broom, and we'll get the place cleaned up in no time. You watch, it'll be great when we get it finished!"

"But Frank, it's a firetrap up here! If anything ever happened we'd burn to death sure!" She coughed the deep raspy cough they were used to hearing now.

"That's enough, Mamie. I said it'll be fine, and it will be! Get started cleaning up, and I'll have our stuff brought up here. I'll find us some beds and chairs." He turned and strode back down the dark hallway, leaving Mamie standing there. She couldn't help herself. The tears started rolling down her cheeks. Jenny put her good arm around her mother as she stared at the mess around them.

Mamie wept for a few moments, standing there in the middle of the decrepit room, then shook herself and wiped her eyes. She dug in her purse for a cigarette, which she lit and took a deep puff. "Well, let's find the best room up here to start on," she said, resigned to their fate. Jenny followed her out into the hall. They turned left and opened the next door. That room was larger, with a sort of bay window overlooking the street below. The plaster was in even worse shape than the first room, but there was more light.

They went on from room to room, finally locating a bathroom of sorts. The stool was covered with filth, and rusty pipes ran from the floor to the back of a cracked sink. Small broken black and white tiles covered the floor, and the wall was painted a putrid green under layers of dirt. There was a skylight in the ceiling, but it was so covered with debris and dirt that hardly any light came through it. Mamie turned the faucet. Nothing happened.

"Mom, do we *hafta* stay here?" Jenny could hardly believe it. They'd stayed in some pretty bad places before, but this was the worst she'd ever seen. "I'll bet there's rats and bugs here too!" Her broken arm ached. It was still in a sling, so she couldn't do much to help. She felt hopelessness settle down around her like a tangible presence.

"We're going to make this into a home for the winter, since we have to, and it'll be a good one when we get through." Mamie raised her chin and started back down the hall. "Now let's pick the best room to start on." She opened the door on the room with the bay window. "I guess I prefer this one. It's the lightest one." Jenny nodded tiredly. Mamie coughed again, then bent and began gathering up the debris that littered the floor.

Frank arrived with broom, mop, pail, soap and rags. He worked on the plumbing until he succeeded in getting the water to flow. "We got water, but only cold," he told them. "I'll get us a stove to heat water on." Mamie turned her back on him and kept sweeping.

Jenny watched him tiredly. I wonder why he's so mean. He must really hate us...or at least me.

She tried to clean the windows with her left hand. It went slowly, but bit-by-bit the grime from years of vacancy was removed, and finally they had one room clean enough to sleep in. Some used beds arrived from somewhere. At last they dragged themselves down the dark hallway to the back of the building, down the rickety stairs, and back through the museum to the front door. They went on down the street to a small restaurant. "The Shamrock, Real Home Cooking," it said on a dilapidated sign out front. They opened the door to a homey-looking room with green oilcloth on the tables, and gladly went in and settled their weary bodies in a corner booth.

The Shamrock was run by a wrinkled Irish woman named O'Grady, whose motherly soul went out to the obviously exhausted and hungry mother and daughter. She eyed the dark man with them and sized him up immediately. Her own family had had its troubles, and she was quick to recognize the symptoms and to sympathize with Mamie and Jenny.

"New to the neighborhood, are ya?" she inquired in her rich brogue, as she brought them hot coffee. They nodded, grasping the cups gratefully, sipping the hot brew. "The special tonight is Irish stew and biscuits." She glanced at Jenny's sling. "It'll do ya good...give ya some strength to mend yer bones!"

They ordered the stew and ate it hungrily, and found that it did make them feel better. Then reluctantly they returned to the museum building and stumbled up the stairs to their new 'home'.

The angel sat on the stairs on guard.

Jenny's job at the Museum was to take tickets. Mamie sold the tickets and Jenny took them from the people. The museum was in a part of Baltimore where 'nice' people didn't go. Directly across the street was a burlesque theater featuring names like Gypsy Rose Lee, and Sally Rand. Even their music that one could hear quite clearly from the sidewalk sounded forbidden to Jenny's ears! Right next door to the museum was a lower-class girlie show, where strippers learned their trade before they graduated to the burlesque. There were bars and pawnshops between the museum and "The Shamrock." They weren't far from the docks so there were plenty of tough-looking stevedores and sailors, along with drifters and men just out for some adventure. There weren't nearly as many women customers. Many of the ones who did come were prostitutes who hung out along the streets. They came in with the sailors sometimes. It wasn't a place where most people brought their wives, except once in a while when Frank was able to book a really special act.

Jenny was far too young and innocent to be dropped into that environment, but Frank stood nearby all the time, and nobody dared to touch his daughter or make a pass at her. Frank would have killed them… or at least he said he would, and they believed it.

The Gibbs family made it through the winter somehow, and then spent the next summer going here and there from one fair to another, and to Carlin Park too. Jenny could hardly keep track. Frank was restless and jittery, smoking more than ever and drinking heavily too. He decided to take them back to the museum in Baltimore the next fall.

CHAPTER EIGHT

1932

Jenny stood in front of the mirror and regarded herself critically. She had turned 15, and was letting her hair grow out from the short bob of the flappers to a lovely shoulder length. It was the color of honey and she curled it at the ends to frame her face in a most flattering way. Her big clear blue-green eyes were wiser than her years in some ways, while completely innocent in others, with a hint of mischief in them. Long dark lashes dropped over them when the men made remarks about her. Her blue dress fell about 5 inches above her shoes, and it fit quite well. She felt satisfied with her appearance except for the shoes. She needed different ones!

Jenny had turned into a beauty, but Frank didn't seem to notice it particularly...until she asked for a pair of high heels. "Please, Dad, I really need new shoes...and I'd so love some heels like all the other girls have!" She turned to look directly at him, "I've been workin' really hard for you Dad, and I think I've earned them!"

Frank looked at his 'daughter'. She was almost grown-up! He was upset...he could hardly stand the thought of her being an adult. He swore and raged and threw things around the room, ranting that she was nothing but a 'whore' and calling her other even worse names she had never heard before. He accused her of terrible things, acting as though she were the lowest form of vermin. Jenny felt rejected, confused, and completely unloved. She rushed into the bathroom and slammed the door, while Mamie tried to reason with Frank.

"It's a wonder she doesn't turn into a prostitute, the way you keep accusing her of being one!" She put her hand on his arm and looked into his face. "Frank, why can't you treat her like a daughter?"

He shook her off and snarled, "Leave me alone, Woman! I'm just tryin ta keep her from going bad! She's gonna be just like all the trash that walks in those doors downstairs!" He lit a cigarette and stood looking out the window, unseeing. Jenny was his property. He'd invested a lot in her over the years, and maybe if any man were going to enjoy that sweet young body, it should be Frank!

Why does he treat me this way? Lord, why is he so cruel...I haven't done anything wrong! I just want to be like everybody else for once! Jenny sobbed and raged inside herself, staying in the bathroom for a long time. She was afraid to come out when she finally calmed down, for fear Frank would hurt her.

(Frank pushed the demonic idea aside, but it kept coming back and he treated her all the more roughly, while thinking his evil thoughts.)

At last, Mamie came to the door. "Come on out Jenny, he's gone. I think he'll be OK now."

Jenny unlocked the door and faced her mother. "Why does he hate me so much?" she demanded. "I didn't do anything wrong!"

Mamie nodded, miserably. "I know you didn't, Love, I know you didn't." She looked at her lovely daughter with a feeling akin to despair. Then she turned her back and said in a choked voice, "I think he just doesn't want you to grow up. He's afraid he'll lose you, I guess."

"I don't know why he should worry about that when he hates me so much!" A new thought struck her, "How in the world did you happen to marry him, anyway?"

Mamie turned and went down the hall to her room without answering. Jenny followed her, wondering even more. "Mom, tell me about when you were a kid," she coaxed. She perched on the arm of a broken-down easy chair and looked at Mamie curiously.

"Well, I had two sisters and we lived in a great big house." Mamie started slowly, remembering how it was. It hurt to think about it, but it was good too. "My Ma was strict like your Dad. It was nice sometimes, and not so nice others. But I had my sisters to talk to, and that helped." She looked up at Jenny, "I'm sorry you don't have any sisters or brothers, Honey. I guess God just didn't mean for it to be." She was silent then, thinking of the sacrifice she'd made so Jenny could have a 'home.' She wondered for the thousandth time what would have happened if she'd made a different choice.

From that time on, Jenny started planning to run away. She just <u>had</u> to get away from Frank Gibbs! Sometimes she pretended he wasn't her father, but that she really had a regular father who loved her and cared about her. Now she planned to go back to the circus, where she felt at home and appreciated. She could live with the Gandellas, she was sure. But how could she get away?

Slowly, she worked out the plan. There was a young sailor who kept stopping at the museum to talk to her. He wanted to date her, but of course, her dad wouldn't allow that. He kept hanging around, and even gave her his picture. Jenny decided to use him as her excuse. She wrote a long note to her parents, explaining that she was running away to get married to the sailor, and she tucked his picture in with the note. Then she packed her suitcase and hid it in the back hall under the stairs.

The next day she asked the fire-eater to call her folks, saying she was really sick. As soon as she saw her Dad coming toward the ticket booth, Jenny sneaked around behind it and started toward the back of the building, picking her way over and around the various obstacles behind the booths. She crossed the main hall quickly, so that nobody would see her. She had just reached the dark back hall and picked up her suitcase, when she looked up to see her mother standing at the bottom of the stairs in the dim light.

"Where do you think you're going?"

"I'm getting out! I'm getting away from here. I can't stand living this way any more! I can't stand the way Dad treats me! Get out of my way Mom, I'm going!"

Mamie grabbed the handle of the suitcase and tried to pull it away from her daughter. She pulled Jenny around until Mamie's back was against the door, both of them yanking the suitcase back and forth. "You can't go Jenny, you just can't! Your dad will kill us both!"

"I don't care any more, I just have to get away." Jenny let go of the case and pushed her mother hard, trying to get out the door.

Just as Mamie fell, Frank Gibbs loomed up in the hallway. "What's going on here?" he demanded. He held her letter in one hand, and the tone of his voice shrunk Jenny to pygmy size. His iron grip fastened on her arm as he shoved the letter at Mamie and pulled the pistol out from his belt. "I'll kill you, you bitch!" He kept his voice low because of the people just outside the hallway, but the menace was plain. Jenny braced herself, saying the Lord's Prayer under her breath. She really thought this was the end of her.

But Mamie grabbed Frank's arm and hung onto it. "No, Frank! No! Leave her alone...I'll take her back upstairs...it'll be all right...don't hurt her!" She pushed her own body between Frank and Jenny and moved toward the stairs, forcing Jenny along in front of her. They slowly fought their way up the steps, while somehow Mamie managed to loosen Frank's grip on Jenny, then shoved her on ahead, nearly causing her to go sprawling. In Jenny's room she made her daughter strip and get into bed, while she tried to calm Frank.

Jenny lay there shaking, her fists clenched tight. She prayed then, "Lord, please help me! I can't live this way...why can't I get away? Oh, God, please do something about this mess we're all in. Please, God!"

At last Mamie was able to get to Frank through his anger. Jenny watched him put the gun back in his belt and stomp out of the room, still swearing and calling her names. "If you ever try that again I will kill you...you can count on it!" he called back over his shoulder.

The angel, who had brandished a bright sword, slowly sheathed it once more.

This time Mamie was angry with her too. She was afraid of Frank, and Jenny didn't help to make things easier for them! But slowly life swung back to what for the Gibbs family was normal.

Jenny caught the flu that March and was in bed for a few days feeling miserable. When finally she was well enough to be up, but not well enough yet to go to work, she hung around the rooms trying to amuse herself. She did a puzzle, read a couple of books, then decided to clean out the cupboard. She took everything down from the top shelf and began to straighten and sort it all out. There was the green box that Mamie always kept special things in. Jenny had never been allowed to look in it by herself before, and now she opened it curiously. She looked at pictures that must have been her grandparents and aunts, and bits of nostalgia from Mamie's past, then she picked up a yellow envelope, an old telegram. She opened it and read, I'LL MAKE A HOME FOR YOU AND THE BABY. COME RIGHT AWAY. LOVE, FRANK. What? Lord, what does this mean?

Carefully, she folded the paper and put it back into the envelope. She picked up another envelope addressed to Mary Louise Shane. I wonder who that is?

She opened it. It was a government allotment check stub from a John Shane. Jenny sat on the floor with the paper in her hand for a long time, her thoughts spinning. He's not my father! Oh Lord, He's really not my father!

She could hardly contain herself. Carefully, she put everything back into the green box and returned it to the shelf, then replaced all the other things neatly.

The next day she screwed up her courage, and during a lull while she and Frank were running the ball game she asked him, "Are you my real father?"

"What?" He stared at her, "Why in the world would ya ask me that?"

"Because I found a paper in the green box. It was an allotment check from a soldier to Mary Louise Shane. I thought maybe he was my real father and he got killed in the war or something, and you decided to raise me instead?"

He roared with laughter. "You ask your mother about that tonight!"

When they got together for supper he said to Mamie, "Have Jenny tell ya what she asked me today."

Jenny repeated the question, telling about the allotment check, but her mother replied quickly, "Oh that belonged to Mary Louise Wilson! She was my best friend. You remember, I've talked about her before. She married John Shane and I guess I picked that up for her one time. Don't know why I've had it all these years though. Just one of those things, I guess."

Jenny, looking at her mother thought, she's lying to me! I wonder why? She didn't ask anything more though. But she *knew*. From then on, she knew that Frank Gibbs was not her real father, and she determined to find out one day who he really was.

That summer they went out to Carlin Park with the carnival again, and stayed until the place closed up in the fall. Jenny turned 16 that year, and was a real knockout. She'd managed to get some makeup, starting with the popular new Tangee lipstick that looked orange in the tube, but turned a lovely shade of pink when she put it on her lips. From that, she gradually worked up to brighter lipsticks and a dab of rouge.

Johnny Boyd, the young ventriloquist, began hanging around Jenny sometimes after his performance out front. He couldn't say much to her because Frank was always standing nearby, making it very clear that he'd better not. So he made eyes at Jenny from across the room, and Jenny was flattered. It made her heart beat faster. She'd never had a date, and she wanted very much to go out with a man. The juices were flowing and she was surrounded every day with temptations, learning a lot, mostly the wrong things, just by watching the people who came and went past her booth. Frank promoted her to running the ball game by herself, since she was an experienced shill and could bring in a lot of business, but Frank was still always nearby.

Johnny finally managed to ask for a date, and Jenny wanted to go so badly that one night she lied to her folks, telling them she was sick so she wouldn't have to work. Frank and Mamie had to run the ball game themselves, and it was open until late, leaving her time to go to dinner with Johnny. They had a lovely time, and Jenny was completely smitten by Johnny's smooth talk and manner.

"I think you're beautiful Jenny," he told her. "You're the most beautiful girl I've ever seen! Jenny, let's get out of here. Let's run away and get married!"

She caught her breath, "Get married!" She stared at him, her eyes wide."Johnny, do you mean it?"

He nodded, seriously. "We could get on the train and leave...just get away from here and make a new life for ourselves. What do you say, Jenny?"

She was dazzled by the possibility of getting away from her dad's tyranny, and here was someone who really wanted to marry her. *Why not?* she thought, looking at the handsome face across from her. "Why not?" she said. "When?"

"Let's do it Saturday. We may as well get going right away!" They planned and plotted their escape from the life of the museum. Jenny would tell her folks she was sick, so she could stay home and her folks would leave to run the ball game. Then she'd pack her suitcase and sneak out the back entrance to meet Johnny in the alley, and they'd get on the first train heading south. They sealed the bargain with a kiss, and Jenny sneaked back to her room with her head in the clouds. Finally, she would get away from Frank and his temper and his weird moods!

Saturday afternoon came and all was going as planned. Jenny packed her suitcase carefully, trying to take everything she valued, since she knew she'd never be able to come back. Dad would kill her. She was heading quickly down the back stairs, when Mamie started up those stairs. "What are you doing? Where do you think you're going Jenny? Answer me!" she demanded.

Jenny's chin came up and she answered defiantly, "I'm going to get married, Mom. Get out of my way."

"And just who are you planning to marry, young lady?"

"Johnny, the ventriloquist." She said it proudly.

Mamie screamed, "Johnny! He's a queer! Jenny, are you out of your mind?" She turned and yelled, "Frank...Frank!" The call was relayed down the building, and Frank came bounding down past the midway shows and slammed into the back hall. He took in the situation at a glance and grabbed Jenny by the arm.

"Hold on there my girl," he growled. His dark eyes, the folds of leathery skin on his forehead, and the straggly graying dark hair made him look even more sinister than usual in the light of the one dim bulb hanging over the stairs.

"Let me go!" Jenny pulled at her arm, trying to stamp on his foot, wanting nothing so much as her freedom.

"Where do you think you're going, anyway?" he demanded.

"She says she's running off to marry Johnny." Mamie was beside herself.

"Marry Johnny? Johnny Boyd?" he asked incredulously. Jenny nodded. "He's a @#* queer!" Frank looked at her, his lip curled, as he said, "You know what I caught him doing just the other day? He was in the alley down on his knees, and he was"...and he told Jenny in disgusting detail all about what homosexual activities her wonderful Johnny had been engaged in. It was the first time she had ever heard of a homosexual, and Jenny was completely overcome with revulsion. She could hardly stand to think about the things Frank was telling her. Finally, she pulled her arm free, turned and ran up the rickety stairs and down the hall to the bathroom, where she threw up until there was nothing left to vomit. She was empty in body and soul, and completely disillusioned and dispirited. There was nothing in the world to believe in any more. She walked woodenly back to her room, where she sat and endured the filthy talk from her dad without really hearing it.

Oh God, isn't there any help for me? What kind of a world is this, anyway? Isn't there any love or peace or happiness for me ever? Do I always have to stay here and listen to this stuff? If you're really there and you care anything about me, please help me!

Frank was still ranting about the half man-half woman and Johnny, his lover. Finally he stormed out, breathing hard, his hand on the gun under his belt.

The next day the half-man/half-woman and the ventriloquist had left town. Jenny knew Frank had threatened them. Their booths were empty the rest of the season and the museum lost money, but nobody mentioned anything to Frank about it. Jenny felt bad about that, since she didn't feel they had done anything to harm her. "He never touched me, Dad!" she kept repeating to Frank, but he didn't seem to hear.

The angel hovered overhead, holding out his hands to ward off the evil.

CHAPTER NINE

1933

Mamie's cough was even worse than usual, and Jenny was concerned about it. The rooms over the museum were cold and drafty, and there was never enough hot water for a good hot bath. Mamie and Jenny shivered in the cold, but Frank let his bottle keep him warm and didn't seem to notice. The rooms reeked of smoke, and ashtrays overflowed with cigarette butts. They were saving money though… the rent was very cheap!

The night it happened was cold and windy. They had made their way down to The Shamrock for some of Mrs. O'Grady's good Irish cooking, and by the time they got back it was late. They locked up the museum for the night and went to their rooms upstairs. Jenny was in her own room wrapped in a blanket, reading a novel she'd borrowed from the Fat Lady, and Frank and Mamie were in their room talking. Mamie went to bed to try to get warm, while Frank sat in his shabby old armchair reading the paper. He lit another cigarette and took a drag, then set it on the edge of the ashtray beside him. He turned the page of his paper, looking over the editorials, swearing under his breath at the 'idiots' in Washington. He didn't notice that the edge of the first section of the paper had dropped onto the cigarette...not until the paper suddenly flashed into flame. Instantly, the whole thing was burning in his hands. He dropped it on the floor and tried to stamp out the fire, but it was no use; the dry old wood and the loose cover of the old chair caught fire almost instantly. "Fire!...Fire!" Frank shouted, "Come on, get out of here! Fast!"

Mamie grabbed her blanket and her shoes. "Jenny!" she yelled.

"I'm here Mom!" Jenny called from the doorway. The fire was clearly out of control now. They ran for the stairway and almost fell down it. The fire crackled behind them, and thick smoke billowed through the air, choking them and making it hard to see. They stumbled their way down to the little hallway where Frank kicked the back door open and they spilled out into the dark alley. The wind grabbed them, pushing them back toward the building, chilling them to the bone as it rushed beyond them through the building's open door, making the fire burn even faster. The velvet draperies that decorated the booths on the first floor caught in another minute, and by the time the fire department arrived 5 minutes later the building was completely engulfed in flames.

The firemen battled bravely to save the surrounding neighborhood, but it was touch-and-go, what with the wind whipping the flames and carrying them on like great tongues hungrily licking up the old buildings. Mamie and Jenny struggled their way around to the front of the museum and across the street, where they huddled in their blankets and watched numbly, as the structures seemed to melt before their eyes. More fire trucks arrived, and firemen worked heroically pumping water into the inferno. Smoke and flames were everywhere, people ran to and fro, women screamed, children cried. Jenny pulled her blanket tighter around herself in a vain effort to get warm. "It's like a scene out of Hell!" Mamie said, and went into a spasm of coughing.

Suddenly Frank loomed up beside them. "Listen," he growled, "don't either of you say one thing about how this happened, you hear? Nobody needs to know anything about it!" Mamie nodded, shivering with cold. Jenny just stared at him.

When morning finally came the fire was out, but the museum was only a blackened hole in the ground, along with the burlesque house next to it and one of the pawnshops. As far as anyone knew though, nobody had been killed. Wrapped in her blanket over her flannel nightgown, Mamie stumbled along beside Jenny and Frank to The Shamrock. Mrs. O'Grady took one look and welcomed them into the back room, where she made them sit down while she went scrounging for some clothing. "You poor, poor things," she crooned over the women, as she helped them wash and dress. The clothes were warm if not stylish, and soon Mamie began to revive, the color coming back into her cheeks. She coughed a lot though, and Jenny wondered about finding a doctor for her.

Mrs. O'Grady brought hot coffee and then pancakes and eggs, which they ate gratefully. They were utterly exhausted and still in shock, so when Frank came back later to get them, they only wanted to find a place to sleep. He caught Mamie's arm, pulling her up."Come on, I rented us a room at the boarding house for now." They thanked Mrs. O'Grady over and over, as he led them out to the waiting cab. Then they rode in silence. Frank seemed really sorry for what had happened, and was much quieter than usual.

They spent a couple of weeks at the boarding house while Frank attended to some details for the insurance, conveniently forgetting to mention the fact that his family had lived upstairs. The various side-show acts went looking for other places to set up shop, and Mamie spent some time in bed, 'resting up a little,' as she said. She seemed feverish, and the cough didn't get any better. Jenny read to her and brought her cool drinks and hot soup.

On Tuesday, Frank came home and told them to pack up again. "We're going to an apartment. It's in a row house near the steel plant. I'm pretty sure I can get a job at the plant. I been talking to the guys, and Joe Pitts'll put in a good word for me." He threw a suitcase on the bed. "I picked this up. Guess it'll be enough for our stuff right now." He stopped talking long enough to take Mamie's hand and look at her closely. That caught Jenny's attention because it was so out of character for Frank.

Mamie started to get up, and had another coughing fit. "There'll be more room for ya, and we'll have our own kitchen. You'll like it better there." He patted her head awkwardly, another uncharacteristic gesture that Jenny took to mean he knew this was all his fault.

The apartment Frank had found was small, but furnished. It wasn't fancy, but it was warm, and a whole lot better than the rooms over the museum had been, except for the outhouse. A nickel and black stove dominated the living room, and in the kitchen a coal hod stood beside the range. In the basement of the building there was a bin to keep a reasonable supply of fuel. Frank had bought a bag of coal to start them out with, for which Jenny was grateful. Joe Pitts was there to help them settle in. When the women had looked around and were satisfied, Frank walked outside to talk with Joe. Jenny quickly laid a fire and helped Mamie get settled with a pillow and blanket on the rather lumpy brown couch. It wasn't like her mom to lie down at a time like this, and Jenny resolved to make Frank find a doctor for her, first thing.

To Jenny's surprise, he agreed and went out right away to look for someone who would be willing to come to the house. Sure enough, when he returned an hour later he brought a small neat man in a suit. The man carried a black case. "This is Doctor Melrose," Frank said to Mamie. "He'll check ya over and make sure yer OK." He stood by, frowning, as he watched the doctor take her temperature, look at her throat and ears and take her pulse.

When he listened with his stethoscope, Dr. Melrose looked serious. He listened again and again, and then left Mamie lying there coughing, as he beckoned Frank to the kitchen, where Jenny was anxiously waiting to hear what he'd say. "She has double pneumonia, and a pretty bad case!" he said brusquely, as he folded his stethoscope and zipped up the bag. "I'll arrange for her to get into the hospital right away...I'll send the ambulance for her. We've got to get this under control as fast as we can!" He reached for his hat and started for the door. "I just hope it isn't too late already," he muttered almost to himself as he closed the door behind him.

Jenny quickly put her mom's flannel nightgown along with her toothbrush and comb into a sack, and then sat beside Mamie holding her hand and talking, while they waited for the ambulance to arrive. "I just know it was that awful place we lived that did this to you! That, and being outside in the cold wind so long during the fire..."

She looked accusingly at Frank, who paced back and forth, frowning and feeling completely helpless. He could attack and punch out a person who would cause trouble for Mamie...but how could he fight this? "If you know how to pray, you'd best pray for your Ma," he growled at Jenny.

Jenny dropped to the floor beside the couch and began at once. She prayed the Hail Mary and asked for Mary's help, then she prayed the Lord's prayer and asked for God's help, and then she just said in her heart, Jesus, please take care of my Mom and don't let her die...please God, don't let her die!

The angel put his hand on her head.

It was a long, slow process...Mary Louise had not been in good health for a long time, and they almost lost her now. But finally she was able to come home. She was thin and pale and still with a cough, having to lie down often. They had a little family party to celebrate, and Jenny baked a 'welcome home' cake, which she served with strong tea, the way Mamie liked it.

****

It was 1934, Roosevelt was pushing his ideas to reform the government and take care of everyone and make sure every person who needed one had a job, but the depression still held the country in a merciless grip. Frank did manage to find work - not in the steel mill, but driving a truck hauling produce to the markets. Jenny also got a job selling curlers for a lady who made them. She had a little booth in an arcade in downtown Baltimore. Her booth was across from one that was run by a very handsome young man who sold wooden shoes and other Dutch items. She made eyes at the fellow across the wide hall when she wasn't busy. She demonstrated the curlers on her own hair and sold a lot of them. The lady, Pearl Jackson, was a skinny widow with dyed black hair. Pearl was happy with Jenny and treated her like a daughter.

But Mamie was not getting well. Doctor Melrose finally diagnosed tuberculosis. He said she'd have to go out to Arizona where the air was dry and clear, if she expected to recover. So one hot July day Jenny and Frank stood and watched the train take Mamie away from them. Jenny felt strange...she'd never been without her mother since she was born. Also, she wasn't sure how her dad would treat her now that Mamie wasn't there to take her side of their arguments.

Strangely enough, he eased up on her and began to let her associate with the neighborhood young people. She was in her glory now being able to actually make friends. Except for the worry about her mother, this would have been the best time of Jenny's life. And the best part of this best time was Bud Caldwell. Bud was a good-looking boy with brown curls, brown eyes, and a nose that was crooked from being broken once when he went back to catch a high fly ball and turned too late, just as he crashed into the wooden fence. He made Jenny feel strange when he came close to her, and when he smiled at her, she sort of melted. He smelled of Wildroot Creme Oil, which he used liberally to tame his unruly locks. She loved him.

They spent a lot of time together in the evenings sitting on the steps talking and flirting with each other. He held her hand, and she couldn't even speak for a few minutes. The new radio in the living room played "Let Me Call You Sweetheart" and Bud looked into her eyes meaningfully. It was almost unbearably sweet. Jenny lived in a dream and didn't want to wake up.

Once Frank even gave them money to go on a moonlight cruise on Chesapeake Bay. They stood at the rail watching the lights along the shore, the moon on the water, and the wake of the boat that made a trail behind them. Jenny felt his arm slip around her waist. "You cold?" he asked. It was a warm night, and the light breeze was refreshing but she made a fake shiver and nodded, to keep his arm there.

"Oh Bud," she sighed a long happy sigh, "this is so beautiful. It's like being in a fairy tale where I'm the princess and you're the handsome prince who came to rescue me."

He chuckled, "Yeah, some prince and princess we are! The poorest ones in history, I'll bet. And what have I rescued you from anyway?"

She turned toward him, looking up into his young facewith her lips slightly parted, her eyes half-closed. He did what any good red-blooded 17-year-old boy would do...what she wanted him to do...he kissed her. Then he kissed her again, pulling her tight against him. It was as though they were in their own little island of space and time and there were no other passengers along that rail in the moonlight. Jenny was completely happy. The rest of the evening passed in a beautiful romantic dream, and she lived it over and over in her mind and heart for days afterward.

Jenny worked hard every day selling curlers till she saw them in her sleep. But every evening she sat on the steps while Bud courted her and talked about what the future might hold for them. She was happy, feeling like a 'normal' person at last! The bubble had to burst of course, and it happened through Frank, as usual.

"You know Andy Ames?" he asked her casually one evening as she set the table for supper.

"Yeah, why?" She knew Andy by sight. He was a very handsome older man, married to a stylish woman named Harriet. They had a small boy. Jenny watched them walk past sometimes while she and Bud sat on the steps. They looked like the ideal young family. "They need a baby-sitter or somethin'?"

"Nah...it's not that...they broke up,and Andy wants to have a date with you. I told him it's OK."

"You *what?*" Jenny could hardly believe her ears.

"I told him he could come over tomorra night and take ya out. He thinks ye're pretty cute."

Jenny was totally confused. How could her dad let her date an older man...a *married* older man? She couldn't understand it. He'd always had a fit when anyone even looked at her. He'd called her terrible names for wanting to talk to any man or boy, saying he'd put her in Juvenile Hall...and now he'd made her a date with Andy Ames! Well, Andy was handsome and Jenny was curious, so she agreed. She really didn't have any other choice anyway, and she knew it.

She made an excuse to Bud, and dressed up the next night and waited for Andy to show up. Eight o'clock passed, then nine o'clock. Frank was getting really put out, and Jenny decided she'd been stood up. At nine forty five she was about to put her book away and start washing out some stockings for the next day, when the fellow finally showed up at the door looking flushed and talking strange. She knew he'd been drinking...that was how Frank got after a few beers. It was too late to go anywhere else so they sat on the steps and talked for a while. Andy mostly talked about Harriet and little Henry. He told Jenny how pretty she was and tried to put his arm around her, but she pulled away, giggling nervously. And just then she looked up to see Bud Caldwell staring at them from across the street. She wanted to die right there on the steps. She felt sick at her stomach as she closed her eyes for a moment, then she smiled weakly and went to wave at him, but he was gone!

Andy Ames left shortly after that, saying something about needing to go see his wife, and Jenny was left alone with her life...her whole world...in shreds and tatters. She lay on her bed unable to sleep, going over and over the scene in her mind. Bitter tears ran down the sides of her face and made her hair wet. Finally giving in to self-pity, she turned over and buried her face in her pillow to muffle the sound of her sobbing.

The angel sat on the end of her bed and waited.

Jenny's first real love was over. She grieved its death for a long time. But Bud never came around again. He couldn't forgive her for what he had seen. She had desecrated their love by sitting on the steps with a married man. He would never believe her again!

CHAPTER TEN

1934

Jenny turned 18, and in October Mamie came home! They met her at the station. Jenny was surprised to see Frank's reaction when Mamie appeared at the steps. He was at her side before she could set foot on the ground and swept her into his arms, carrying her to the waiting cab. She was thin and frail, but so happy to be back with them. She kept hugging them both and they asked questions back and forth, laughing and crying and talking all at once until they reached the apartment. Frank lifted Mamie again and carried her up the steps into the house, where he laid her on the living room sofa.

"I really can walk now, you know," she laughed at him.

"Ye're so thin...ya look like you'll break! Are ya really all over the TB?"

"That's what they told me. And I feel pretty good again. No cough! I'm sort of weak yet, but I'll build up strength just being here with you two again. Boy, how I missed you!" She looked at Jenny, "You've grown up while I was gone. You seem different, Honey." The blue eyes, now with wrinkles around them, looked deep into the clear young blue-green eyes of her daughter. "Are you all right?"

"Yeah, Mom! I'm OK...'specially now that you're home again."

They spent a happy Christmas together. Jenny and Mamie went to church together on Christmas Eve, where they sang the old carols, prayed, and took communion. Christmas day they exchanged gifts and had a wonderful dinner together with Joe Pitts and his family. Jenny opened a large box to find a lovely white satin blouse and a bright green skirt from Frank and Mamie. She held them up, her eyes shining. "Oh, thank you! Thank you so very much!" She put them on right away and wore them the rest of the day. She felt special and glamorous, and wished Bud would come by to see her looking so good. It was the nicest Christmas Jenny could ever remember. Frank didn't even get drunk as usual, though he did consume several bottles of beer. (For a while after Mamie came home, he even tried not to smoke in the house. That lasted until just after New Years sometime, and not long after that Mamie began smoking again too.)

The neighborhood football team planned a big party on New Years Eve to celebrate a successful season. The party was to be held at Pearl Jackson's house. Her nephew Irving Kragt, who lived with Pearl, was on the team, and he invited the whole gang to their house. Jenny really wanted to go to the party, but Bud was taking Betty Morrison. Freddy Farell's former girlfriend was going to the party with Izzy Olds, leaving Freddy as unhappy and as unattached as Jenny.

"We could go to the party together if you want," Jenny offered, "since we're both in the same boat. We don't have to spend a lot of time with each other when we get there." Freddy agreed and he took her to the party, even though they really didn't like each other very much. Jenny felt that Freddy was 'fast' and she wasn't about to let any guy get fresh with her!

They arrived at the party a little late, to find things going full swing. Irving had a neat phonograph and a lot of cardboard "Hit Of The Week" records with the latest songs, so music flooded the house. There were two groups of young people, the older kids on the main floor and a younger group in the basement. Bud was there, making eyes at Betty and holding her hand. This was the first time Jenny'd had a chance to celebrate her 'adulthood' and she decided now was the time. She was 18 now, so she could drink. And she did. She drank everything they put in front of her. She was feeling much better as she went upstairs to the bathroom. The phonograph played "You Made Me Love You." "I didn't wanna do it," she sang.

"Say, here's a cutie!" she heard someone say, as she made her way through the kitchen, dressed in her Christmas outfit, with a green bow in her long honey-blonde hair. She turned to see Irving grinning at her.

She looked up at him sideways through her long lashes, "You ain't so bad yourself," she smiled in her best imitation of Mae West. On her way back from the bathroom he made another remark, which she parried. A couple of drinks later, she needed to visit the bathroom again. She was feeling really strange by now, sort of tingly, but with numb feet. Her words came out sounding different than she meant to sound, and she laughed a lot over nothing. She flirted shamelessly with Irving, ignoring his date, a frizzy blonde in a bright blue dress. On the way back from the bathroom for the third time, she suddenly sat down on the top step, holding on to the railing, her head spinning...or was it the room that was moving? She didn't know. She didn't much care either. She laughed giddily, watching her shoe tumble down the stairs. She heard someone say, "It's only 9 o'clock and this one's out already!"

Someone took her hand and she looked up to see who it was. "Oh hi, Pearl!" she giggled. "You have a really nice house if it would just stand still."

"Come on Jenny, you better lie down on my bed a few minutes." Pearl was surprised and upset to see her this way. Jenny had always been capable and efficient and reliable. Now look at her!

Jenny lay down on the bed with her head whirling, and watched the room go up and down crazily. Suddenly she rolled off the bed and just made it to the bathroom, where she was sicker than she'd ever been before in her whole life. Finally, after there was nothing left to throw up, she staggered back to the bedroom, where she lay on the bed laughing and doing some of her old clown routines for a fascinated audience including Irving and his friends. Jenny was a skilled and experienced performer, and she gave a real show, flirting with Irving the whole time to try to make Bud jealous. Bud didn't notice, as he was busy with Betty Morrison, but Irving noticed...he fell in love with Jenny that night.

"What'll we do about her? We can't let her go home like this...her old man'll kill us!" Freddy, her date, was really concerned. He hadn't paid any attention to her and now look at the mess they were in!

"We better get her some spirits of ammonia or something!" one of the girls suggested.

"Yeah, maybe that'll bring her out of it!" They held the bottle under her nose briefly till she shoved it away and headed for the bathroom again. She was so sick she thought she'd die, but finally she crawled back to the bedroom.

"We'd better take her out for some fresh air!" Irving suggested. "Let's go for a drive."

They trooped out holding her arms to keep her from falling down, and piled into the car, Irving sitting between his date and Jenny. They rolled the windows down and rode around the city until they got so cold they couldn't stand it any more and went back to Irving's house. Jenny was feeling a little better until someone offered her a drink, then she was sick all over again.

Midnight came and she kissed all the guys, including Irving. By this time Irving was pretty much ignoring his date, and concentrating on Jenny. "I better walk you home," he told her. She agreed. She didn't know what had happened to Freddy, and she didn't much care. She carried on an animated conversation all the way home, and then, keeping on with the Mae West routine, arched her brow and said coquettishly "Why don't you come up and see me sometime?"

"Yeah," he answered. "How about going out Friday night?"

"Sure," she blew him a kiss. "See you Friday." Somehow she managed to make it to bed without Frank finding out about her getting drunk. She woke the next morning with a head that didn't belong to her body.

Things were a bit strained between Jenny and Pearl for a while after the party, but Pearl really liked Jenny, so she chalked the whole episode up to her "trying to grow up" and didn't mention it to Frank.

After Friday, Jenny and Irving dated as often as possible, in spite of the objections of his mother and Pearl, and Frank and Mamie. Irving was the sole support for his mother and younger sister, and stayed at his Aunt Pearl's house to be closer to his job at the garage. Jenny found excuses to go past the garage as often as possible, smiling provocatively at Irving and causing him to neglect his work daydreaming.

"What's the matter with you" his boss demanded? "You're making stupid mistakes, and that's not like you!" He handed Irving a wrench, "See if you can put that carburetor back on properly now!" He shook his head as he went back to the engine he was tuning up.

They sat in the back row of the balcony holding hands and kissing as they watched tender love stories unfold on the screen. Jenny didn't allow any more than kissing, remembering Frank's threats. They walked home slowly, holding hands, and kissed at her door. Then they each lay in their beds dreaming about each other, aching to be together. It came to a head one night on their way home from the Bijou. The stars were out and a warm spring breeze blew in off the water. Irving stopped walking and turned to look down at Jenny. "I can't stand this any more," he told her, "I love you. What do ya say we get married?"

"Oh, Irving," Jenny's eyes shone with love as she looked up at him. Then she stopped. "But how can we? They'll never let us, you know. We're too young to get married without their permission."

"I was talking to George Whiting, and he said when he and Ida got married, what they did was go down to the courthouse and get a license, and they lied about her age. Then they waited the three days for the blood test. They got the judge to marry them, and by the time her folks found out they'd already been together two weeks. They've got a nice little apartment now, and they're doing fine. I bet it would work for us too!"

"Oh, Irving, do you think so?" She was hopeful and doubtful at the same time. "My father will be furious! He told me he'd kill me if I ever let any guy touch me."

"He meant when you're not married," he assured her. "Anyway, once we're married I won't let *him* touch you!"

She looked up at him. She wasn't so sure he could really protect her from Frank. Then the hormones took over, and she took a deep breath and said, "OK, let's do it!" They talked and planned for two weeks, and Jenny only had serious misgivings once when she saw Bud walk by. She didn't feel exactly the same about Irving, but Bud wouldn't even speak to her any more. Her heart still hurt over that. She really loved him.

But according to the plan, on a fatal, rainy Tuesday Jenny slogged down to City Hall and applied for a marriage license. She told the clerk she was 18 and Irving was 21, and held her breath until he wrote it down and the document was safely in her hand.

"You gotta get a blood test, ya know." he said as she started for the door.

"Yes I know, thanks." She flew out of there before anybody could change their minds. Down a few doors, a Dr. Meyer had his office right on the street level. She walked in dripping, and smiled shyly at the nurse. Showing her the license, she explained, "I need a blood test to get married."

"Well, roll up your sleeve then. You won't need to see the doctor for that." The nurse took out a needle and tied a band tight around Jenny's arm. Jenny closed her eyes and turned her head as the nurse jabbed the needle into her vein. When it was over, she rolled her sleeve down, holding a small piece of cotton over the spot, and pushing hard.

"It'll be ready for you in a couple of days." The nurse said pleasantly, "When is your wedding?"

"Ah, it's next week." Jenny was flustered, but since that was natural for a new bride, the nurse didn't think anything of it.

"Got a pretty dress, I guess?"

"Oh, yes. Really beautiful," she lied. "Well thanks a lot, I'll see you Wednesday." She walked out and started down the street, dodging puddles.

The angel kept pace.

Jenny began to wonder. Is this really going to be OK? What'll my life be like now? And what about my feelings for Bud? Gee, I hope Dad won't kill me! ...

At the thought of getting away from Frank, she straightened her shoulders and walked more purposefully for a minute. Then the sky opened up and dumped its whole load of water. She sprinted for cover.

Rev. Morgan at the Methodist church married them the next Saturday, with George and Ida standing up for them. After the wedding the four of them went to a small restaurant for supper and ordered cake for dessert. Then Jenny went home to her folks' house, hiding her ring in her purse. For a week or so she lived in a dream world of suspense and fear, waiting to get free from her folks and start her marriage, but afraid to tell them. Then someone read an item in the newspaper citing the marriage licenses filed for the previous week and congratulated Frank on his daughter's marriage. Mamie didn't believe it, and sent a friend down to the courthouse to see if it was true.

Jenny worked hard all day selling curlers and arrived home tired and hungry. The secret gnawed at her insides, and she longed to be going home to Irving and her own house. She trudged slowly up the stairs. The door opened before she could touch it, and Frank's face greeted her. He smiled an evil greeting. "Whatcha doin' here, Missy? Why don't ya go to your husband?"

Jenny's heart nearly stopped beating. She felt faint, and shook her head to clear it.

"Well, why don't ya say something?" he sneered. You know I can report ya, and you'll go to jail for lying about his age! I may just do that, too! Gimmie one good reason why I shouldn't?"

"Frank, please!" Mamie's hand pulled at his arm and he turned on her.

"Your whore daughter has finally done it, Mamie! She's got herself into a whole kettle of rotten fish now! I guess we'll just let her stew in it!" He turned back to Jenny. "Get your stuff and get on out of here. Go live with your husband!"

Jenny's heart beat like a trip-hammer as she ducked past Frank and ran up the stairs to get her suitcase. She packed quickly, expert over the years of constant moving. Mamie stood in the doorway watching her with a strange expression.

"Mom, I had to...Irving loves me, Mom." She stopped, suitcase in one hand, a hatbox in the other, and waited for Mamie to move from the door. "I had to get away," she said softly so only Mamie could hear. "He's not my father. I know my real father wouldn't be so mean to me! I know my real father would love me!" She ran quickly down the stairs and out of her folks' house.

He was just walking up the steps as she got there. "Irving! Honey, I've come to be with you...my parents know about us!" She called to him as she ran up the walk. He turned, and his face registered surprise, joy, and fear in quick succession. She dropped her things and hugged him, and he hugged her back, looking over her head toward Pearl's house.

"I suppose that means Aunt Pearl will know too if she doesn't already." He let go of her. "I don't know what my mother'll say!" She was surprised to see he was shaking.

"Let's go talk to Pearl," she said. "It's better we tell her ourselves than let my dad do it. At least that way we can give her our side of it!"

Pearl was less than happy for them. "I don't know what your Ma will do without your support, Irving! You know she and your sister live on your income. How will you manage to support a wife too?" She frowned. "I hope you don't plan to stay here! I don't have room for anybody else."

Jenny raised her chin proudly. "That's all right Pearl. Irving and I will get our own place. I'm sure we can find a little apartment we can afford." Then she realized her situation and asked somewhat more humbly, "but can I stay for tonight at least? My dad won't let me stay there any more."

Grudgingly, Pearl let her come in and fixed a place on the couch for her to sleep. She joined Pearl and Irving for supper, and after the dishes were finished they talked about what to do next, until she was too tired to think any more. She slept on the couch, while Irving slept in his own bed. They both thought about how it would be when they could be together...and now there wouldn't be anything to keep them apart.

They found a place to rent the next day, and Jenny scrubbed and cleaned it until it shone. She made the bed up with clean sheets and took a bath as well as she could without a bathtub. When Irving came home, the smell of spaghetti cooking filled the little apartment, making it seem homey and pleasant. He didn't say much as he used the soap and water Jenny had prepared for him, and dried on the soft towel, but after his bath he turned to find her watching him. He reached out for her and she flew into his arms, and the kiss this time was different. It wasn't until much later that they thought about eating...and now they really were man and wife!

She took pleasure in cooking for Irving and trying to make things nice for him. They got along together fairly well after the first passion wore off. But once Irving could have his way with Jenny, it seemed he no longer wanted to - at least not very often. His friends came over night after night and hung around smoking and drinking and playing cards, making a lot more work for Jenny. She came home tired at night and had to cook for his friends and put up with their off-color jokes. To make matters worse, Frank wouldn't leave them alone either.

He spent far too much time at their small apartment, drinking himself into a mean mood. Then he'd rant and rave and say all manner of vicious things. It was just like before Jenny left home, except now she had Irving and his friends and a lot more work!

In spite of all the problems, Jenny really tried to be a good wife and to make the marriage work. She wanted everything to be perfect, and did all she could to make sure it was. She made Irving move to different apartments over and over, trying to find just the right place for them. She was never quite happy. But she was sure if they just found the perfect home, things would be much better. And then, after they'd been married just eleven months she discovered she was pregnant.

Irving was upset. He didn't want children. But Jenny loved children and looked forward to having her own child to love and care for. Things were not happy at their house, and Jenny couldn't seem to do anything about it. Irving had lost interest in her. There was no romance in their lives and Jenny craved romance and affection. She needed the closeness of sex, but he never came near her any more. She desperately waited for the baby, hoping that would make things better with them. Surely Irving would love her more when they had a child to love together!

In a few months the summer heat was upon them and Jenny was big and uncomfortable. Irving's grandfather had a cottage at a lake some miles North of the city, and Irving would take his mother and Aunt Pearl and his sister there on weekends to swim and cool off. They'd come home talking about how wonderful it was. But they wouldn't take Jenny along. "There's no room for you...especially in your condition!" Mother Kraght said, looking at her belly with obvious disapproval. "Anyway you shouldn't be riding now...it isn't good for the baby. You better just stay here and do your housework." She eyed the kitchen floor pointedly. "Well, come on Irving, let's get started!" He nodded and took his mother's arm and walked out to the car without even saying good-bye, though he did wave his hand as they drove away.

Jenny felt absolutely alone and abandoned, unloved and unwanted. She sat in the hot little flat and laid her head on the kitchen table amid the breakfast dishes and wept.

She finally put her foot down about his friends, and that made Irving even more remote. He went out with them almost every evening, leaving her alone at home. That was almost worse than putting up with them at her home. To make matters worse, his mother and sister picked on her constantly, criticizing everything she did. Jenny prayed, asking God to help her and to bless her child.

Frank and Mamie's attitude about the baby was entirely different. They insisted they be there at the birth, and hovered around her nagging her to eat right and take care of herself. Finally she gave in to their pushing, and agreed to move into a small house behind Aunt Pearl's place with them. They divided the house into two areas, even dividing the tiny kitchen! It was very difficult though, as any noise Jenny and Irving made bothered her folks and made for constant arguments. So they all moved again, into a larger place where they made one of the bedrooms into a kitchen. They still had no bathroom, only an outhouse! And the situation between Jenny and Irving didn't get any better. Frank and Mamie picked on him constantly.

The day she delivered started out like any other, only somehow Jenny's senses seemed sharper. The bacon she fried for breakfast smelled so strong it threatened to overcome her, so after she had washed the dishes and left her kitchen shining once more, she went for a walk. The warm late-summer sun felt like a blessing on her face and arms. She lifted her head and breathed deeply of the fragrance of the red roses that climbed and crowded along a fence in the next block. A bird sang in the tall tree overhead, and Jenny stopped and tried to see him hiding in the leaves. A child with a dirty face rode his tricycle right toward her, ringing its bell furiously. The sound seemed magnified somehow. She stepped aside for him and turned again for home. Her belly felt as though it must pop if it grew any more. She needed to sit down to rest it. And there was that nagging little pain in her back. It was getting worse as the day went on.

As she stepped through the back door into the kitchen, she suddenly felt a flood of warm water running down her legs. She stopped in surprise and watched a large puddle form on the floor. It was happening! "Mom!" she called, and the sound of her voice brought Mamie running. Then things became a blur. Irving drove her to the hospital and kissed her cheek as the nurse wheeled her away. He sat in the waiting room while she went through her ordeal. Frank and Mamie arrived soon after, and Frank joined Irving to wait, while Mamie went to Jenny.

Jenny was only vaguely aware of Mamie, the nurse and the doctor. She was busy with her own private world. The pain wracked through her back, taking her breath away. It grew worse and worse and came more and more often. She bore it as long as she could before she began to scream. Screaming felt good. It was a release from all the pent-up frustration of her life, as well as a protest against the pain. She worked and sweated and screamed for hours, and was at last rewarded with a tiny, ugly, wrinkled boy. Mamie brushed Jenny's damp hair back off her brow and whispered. "He's beautiful, honey. He's just perfect!" Jenny made sure he was all there and watched the nurse take him away to be washed and dressed. She dealt with the afterbirth and when she was at long last tucked into a warm bed, fell into an exhausted sleep.

She named the baby James Irving Kragt. His looks improved quickly, and by the third day he was very cute. She cuddled and loved him, holding him close to her breast and crooning little songs softly. "Sweetest little feller, everybody knows. Don' know what to call him but he's mighty lak a rose...."

The day she was to go home, her folks came to get her and little Jimmy. "Where's Irving" she asked?

"Oh, he had to work. Has to make all the money he can now that he has another mouth to feed! He's sure been livin' it up with you gone, though. Out carousin' every night, dancin' with the floozies and carryin' on something fierce. He an' that gang he hangs out with. You sure picked a fine one to get hitched up to!" Ashes fell from the end of Frank's cigarette as it bobbed up and down. He removed it from his mouth, blowing a great cloud of smoke that made Mamie cough.

Jenny's heart sank. This was supposed to be a joyous occasion, bringing home her first child. They were supposed to celebrate it together. Now it was all spoiled. What kind of life would Jimmy have? She almost regretted bearing him. She cuddled him close, watched him sleeping so peacefully, and her heart hurt for him. She'd do the very best she could to make his life better than hers had been.

The angel touched Jimmy's cheek.

CHAPTER ELEVEN

1936

Jimmy was a real joy to Jenny. She loved him with all her heart, and kept him clean, fed and happy. It was like having a real live dolly to play with. He smelled so good after his bath, and he smiled and cooed at her. "He's so sweet...why won't Irving hold him and love him" Jenny asked Mamie? Mamie settled him onto her lap and smiled at him, then raised her face to Jenny and shook her head just slightly. "I don't know, Honey, but he seems to have a lot on his mind. Jenny, is everything all right with you two?"

Jenny wasn't ready to admit there was a problem. She'd been so anxious to get out from her folks' care. "We're fine, Ma." She poured some coffee for the two of them. "It'd be easier if his family would like me." The plaintive words cut to Mamie's heart. She was used to burying her feelings though, over 20 years of pretending.

"You took their source of income away. They probably won't forgive you for that." She reached her hand across the table to touch Jenny's cheek. "Don't take it personal Honey, it'd probably be the same for anybody who married Irving."

For a few precious moments, Jenny felt comforted. Then the world came back.

Things went from bad to worse with Irving. He began going to the bar almost every night. It got to the point where he was hardly ever home. Finally, Jenny decided if she were going to save the marriage, she'd have to share his interests. (She read that in a Saturday Evening Post article) So one night she got her folks to stay with Jimmy and joined Irving at the bar. He was surprised to see her, but she was dressed up nicely and looked very pretty, and he soon realized that other men were eyeing his wife. That made him feel proud at first. Then after a few drinks, he discovered a way to capitalize on the situation.

"Say," he said loudly to one of the oglers, "you wanna dance with my wife?" The guy nodded, surprised. "OK, if you buy me a drink, then she'll dance with ya!"

"Right," the fellow agreed and ordered drinks for the table.

Jenny was horrified, but she didn't know what else to do so she danced with the man. She was a good dancer and he was pleasant enough to her, so it went fairly well. But having found a good use for Jenny, Irving wasn't about to give it up. So every time she joined him at the bar from then on, he sold her to other men to dance with. They bought Irving drinks and Jenny danced with them.

On weekends his family would take Irving to the cottage, leaving Jenny and little Jimmy at home. "The lake is no place for a baby!" Mrs. Kragt told her.

And while they were at the lake, Mrs. Kragt did her best to drive the wedge even further between Jenny and Irving. It got to the place where Jenny almost hated to see him come home after a weekend at the lake. Life was always even harder for her after Irving had spent time with his mother. She prayed about it, "Lord, why don't they like me? Why won't they love the baby, when he's so sweet and innocent? What should I do, Lord? How can I make Irving love me again? Oh Lord, help me!" she wept.

The angel spread his wings over her.

She slept, and dreamed of a beautiful place where there were clean marble halls, fragrant flowers in tall vases, and friendly people smiling and talking pleasantly around a sun-splashed lake. It was a place where she felt loved and protected. Then she woke up in the same cramped little house with the outhouse and a crying baby, only to find Irving hadn't come home at all last night. It was the last straw.

At the bar, the one friend Jenny had was a beautiful girl about her own age. Her name was Fern, and she always seemed so happy and full of fun that she made the place bearable for Jenny too. Fern danced with all the men too, and seemed to sympathize with Jenny. In her innocence it didn't occur to Jenny that Fern was a prostitute like so many she'd seen at the museum. Fern was a friend, and that was good enough for Jenny.

She began going to the bar to talk to Fern even while Irving was gone on weekends. She told Fern the whole sordid story of her miserable marriage, using her as a sounding board to talk about possibly leaving Irving. "I don't know what else to do...I've tried everything I can think of to make him happy, and nothing's worked. We haven't any personal life any more...haven't had sex in months...not even any hugs or kisses." She looked down at the table, playing with her napkin, creasing and re-smoothing it as she talked. "He's never happy to see me, and even picks on me about my cooking. He always used to love my cooking!" Fern nodded sympathetically, so Jenny kept on talking. "He doesn't seem to care anything about Jimmy, either. I'm seriously thinking of leaving him and going somewhere else to start over again. Except I know my folks would really give me a hard time." She frowned as she turned her glass of cola round and round on the table, not really seeing it.

"I know whatcha mean, Honey. It can get pretty hard when there's no love." Jenny was too preoccupied to catch the meaning behind Fern's words. Fern knew a lot about what Jenny was going through. She was an understanding friend, and after their talk Jenny felt stronger and able to cope with things while she tried to decide what to do.

One night soon after that, Jenny and Fern were sitting at a table at the bar, both looking beautiful...Fern in a revealing beaded gown, her red hair swept elegantly back from one side of her head to the other, and a jeweled earring dangling almost to her shoulder. Jenny felt dowdy beside her in a skirt and sweater, with her honey blonde hair curled gently at her shoulders. She looked young and innocent beside her friend.

As they talked, Fern's eyes constantly swept the room for prospects, while Jenny was hardly aware of the people around them. She looked up as someone said, "Hi there, gorgeous! Mind if we join you?"

The voice belonged to the handsomest guy she'd ever seen. He was with another fellow who was eyeing Fern with interest. They were both slim, dressed in white sailor uniforms, the bell-bottom pants snug against their tight rears. Jenny's heart jumped to her throat and she couldn't speak, only smiled shyly. But Fern answered, "Sure, sailor! and moved her chair over to accommodate another beside her. Jenny obligingly moved her chair closer to Fern's, and the men grabbed chairs from nearby tables and sat down with them.

"Name's Al Brownell," the handsome one said, "and this is Herb Grady."

"Hi, I'm sure" Fern responded. "I'm Fern, that's Jenny."

"Jenny," Al repeated, smiling at her. "You like to dance, Jenny?"

"Sure." She gave him a sideways glance.

He rose and reached for her hand. She colored as she extended it, and he pulled her into his arms on the dance floor. The band played romantic music and they floated, they glided, they sailed. It was as though they were meant for this. Jenny felt his strong arms around her, leading her in steps she'd never done before, but with him they came naturally to her. She felt his strong body as he held her close during a slow dance, and it seemed as though all the past years had been leading up to this night...this wonderful night with this handsome, romantic stranger.

Her heart beat faster, she could hardly breathe, she was trembling. She was swept by passions she'd never felt before, not even when her love with Irving was new. Jenny knew she was on dangerous ground, but for now she didn't care. It was like the story of Cinderella and Prince Charming. It was hard to remember she had a husband...and a baby waiting for her at home.

"How about taking in a movie tomorrow night?" Al asked, as Jenny slipped into her coat to leave. Fern and Herb had disappeared after only a few dances and a drink, leaving the two of them alone together.

"Oh, I couldn't! But thanks anyway, Al." She smiled at him sadly. "I guess I should have told you before, but I'm married." Jenny's heart hurt as she saw the surprised look on his face. It was over now, but it had been such a wonderful evening. She would always remember it, and feeling the way she had, she knew now without a doubt what she had to do. "I'm going to leave him soon, but I'm still married...and I have a baby, my son Jimmy. He's a real sweetie." She started toward the door, making her way along the dance floor, dodging a waiter, and edging around a couple of tables. Al followed her.

"I really want to see you again, Jenny. I'd like to meet your kid, too."

"You would? Really?"

Al nodded, "Listen Jenny, give me your address, will you? I don't want to lose track of you. You're a special lady, you know? We could have a lot of fun together, you and me!"

She looked up into his eyes and agreed. It would certainly be wonderful to have fun again with someone. She'd been a drudge for so long now, with no love, no appreciation...she couldn't refuse him. She gave him her address. He wrote it on the back of a matchbook cover and stuck it into his shirt pocket, patting it as he grinned at her. "You'll be hearing from me!" He pulled her to him and kissed her.

She kissed him back, then pushed away and left quickly, hardly knowing what to feel, only knowing it was good to have someone make a fuss over her. It was so long since she'd felt any self-esteem, and he was so handsome and funloving and wonderful! But she knew she'd seen the last of him. Now that he knew she was married and had a baby he'd go on to someone else and forget about her!

She lived on the memory of that night for four days, and then the letter came. His ship was docked in New York City and would probably be there for quite awhile. "If you're really going to leave your husband, why don't you come to the City and get a job? That way we could get together on weekends. I'd really like to get to know you better. You're so beautiful, and so much fun. I can't forget you, Jenny."

Irving came home that evening and Jenny tried to talk to him, to get him to hold her in his arms and say he loved her and they could put the marriage back together. But he pushed her away roughly, "Why do you keep hangin' on me? Just let me alone, will you?" He looked over his shoulder as he headed for the door. "I'll get something to eat at the grill. I'm gonna play pool with the gang tonight."

"Wait a minute, Irving." Something about Jenny's voice made him stop and turn. "I've had enough of this miserable so-called marriage. God knows I've tried to make you happy, but it's pretty obvious you don't love me any more." He started to retort, but she held her hand up in the stop signal position. "We'll get a divorce. I want to go to New York City and try to find a job, and I'll go as soon as possible. Do you think Aunt Pearl will take care of Jimmy until I get settled? I'll come back and get him as soon as I can, and then we'll be out of your way."

She watched a strange expression come into his eyes as she talked. First it looked like anger, but then she read relief there! It was a blow to realize she was right, then it was a relief to her too. The travesty they called a marriage had been over for a long time. It was time to bury it and get on with their lives. The only thing they had to show for their time together was Jimmy.

Irving simply nodded in agreement and left, closing the door softly behind him. Closing the door on Jenny and on their marriage.

The angel shook his head in sorrow.

CHAPTER TWELVE

1937

It was hard to approach Aunt Pearl, but Jenny swallowed her pride and knocked on the door. Pearl was surprised to see her, and less than happy to hear what Jenny wanted, but she reluctantly agreed to take care of Jimmy while Jenny went to New York to look for a job. "You never should have married in the first place! Look at the mess you've gotten yourselves into... I guess I can't stop you from leaving Irving, and I can't say I don't think he'll be better off without you!" She shook her finger at Jenny, "You make sure you're back in two weeks...or sooner if you find something!"

"I will, Aunt Pearl. I'll miss Jimmy a lot I know, but I just can't go job hunting with a baby on my hip. I'll leave you all the clean diapers, and enough food, and his formula and bottles and his crib and all....and he's such a good baby. I know you'll both be fine till I get back." She hugged Jimmy close to her breast as she said it, and turned to look at the calendar hanging on the back of the door. "I'll leave tomorrow. It's Sunday, so that should give me a travel day and time to find a place to stay, and I'll still have the rest of the week to look for work."

"I can't believe how irresponsible you young people are today. Why, in my day we would no more consider leaving our husbands and children than..." Pearl shook her head and pursed her lips.

"Thanks, Aunt Pearl...I really appreciate it. And there's one more favor I need to ask too." She felt desperate and wicked and excited and hopeful all at one time as she made her request to the older woman. "Could you please not tell my folks anything about this? I know it'll be hard to explain, but they just won't understand, and I can't take any more hassle right now. Things are hard enough already without that."

She gave Aunt Pearl a little kiss on her pale skinny cheek. "I'll have Jimmy here in the morning." She gathered her things and left hurriedly. There was a lot to do before morning. Pearl stood at the window watching her go and muttering to herself.

The trip to New York was mostly uneventful. Jenny carried her lunch so she wouldn't have to spend any more than necessary. She'd have to scrimp to make ends meet, but if she found a good enough job, and soon enough, they'd be OK. She knew Irving wouldn't send her anything. He'd be right back with his mother as soon as she was gone for good, and Jenny could just picture the satisfied smirk on Mrs. Kragt's face.

She worried about what Mamie and Frank would say. They were so attached to little Jimmy. Too much so, she thought. It made her uncomfortable sometimes, remembering how Frank had treated her as a child. If they knew she was going they'd insist on keeping Jimmy for her, and Jenny simply didn't want that. It was probably a good thing she and Jimmy'd be leaving. She sighed and closed her eyes.

But Jenny had a secret that made her smile in spite of her stress. Al would meet her at the bus station and help her find a place to live. When she'd called him and told him her plan, he said he looked forward to being with her. She certainly looked forward to seeing him again, too. Her heart beat fast at the thought of his handsome face, his trim figure, the way they'd danced together, and the kiss...she closed her eyes and almost felt again how his lips touched hers.

After a rest stop at Trenton, the bus rocked along the road, the engine droning endlessly, and Jenny fell asleep, her purse tucked securely under her hip, her head resting on her folded jacket.

She woke with a start when they pulled into the station at Woodbridge. It wouldn't be long now until they reached New York City. She hurried into the bus station rest room to clean up, comb her hair, and apply fresh lipstick. The rest of the trip she shared a seat with a silver-haired Baptist preacher who was going into the city to speak at a large church that evening. He smelled like Bay Rum aftershave, and that made her like him. "Do you know the Lord as your Savior?" he asked her kindly but nosily, she thought.

"I don't know what you mean. I pray the rosary, and I go to church when I can. I guess I'm as good as most people!"

"Well, young lady, I hope you'll take the time to come to Calvary church tonight and hear the gospel preached. Jesus loves you, you know. He died in your place. He took all of your sins on Himself on the cross, and paid the death penalty for you. So now if you receive His gift to you, you can live forever with Him!" The preacher's eyes shone with sincerity as he told her about her Savior and his sacrifice in her place.

They reached the station in New York City faster than seemed possible, and Jenny thanked the man. "I'll think about what you said," she promised as she gathered her things. Then she glimpsed a white sailor suit out the window and her heart beat fast with hope, and she promptly forgot all about the preacher's words.

"Hey, Jenny!" Al picked her up and swung her around, laughing with her. "Where's your suitcase?" She pointed it out and he grabbed it and headed for the taxi stand. "You hungry?"

She shook her head. "I need to get a room first."

"No problem. There's a hotel down near the docks...rents rooms by the week. Not very expensive, and you can have a hot-plate so you can even do some cooking if you want."

"That sounds good. Is the area safe?" She remembered the waterfront neighborhood around the museum in Baltimore, and how seedy and run-down those places were.

"Would I take you someplace you wouldn't be safe?" he teased. "Wait till you see it and decide for yourself. If you don't like that, we can find something else. Lots of the girls stay there though."

"The girls?"

"You know, the girl-friends of the guys on the ships." He grinned at her knowingly.

She had a momentary sinking feeling in the pit of her stomach. Oh Lord, I hope I'm doing the right thing!

Then the feeling passed and she smiled back at him. "I need to be somewhere close to where I can get a job."

"Subway's only a block away, and that'll get you anywhere you want to go."

"OK then, sounds good." She took his arm and he signaled for a taxi.

She rented a room at the run-down hotel and paid for a week in advance, then they went down the street to a little cafe' and had dinner together. Once more she felt like a Cinderella, rescued from the drudgery of her former life and being treated like a princess by someone who obviously admired her. "It was a wonderful evening...thank you so very much," she told Al as he unlocked her door for her.

"Too bad I hafta be back on the ship. I'd sure rather spend the night here with you!"

"Don't be so forward," she teased him. "We hardly know each other yet, and I'm still a married woman!"

He bent and kissed her, and made her head spin again.

"You'd better leave now, and thanks again, Sailor...see you...when?"

"Gotta stay on the ship till Friday now. Pick you up here Friday evening?"

"Right. I hope we can celebrate my new job by then!"

He kissed her again and she nearly lost her resolve, but pushed him away, smiling. She closed the door and leaned against it, feeling lost. She almost called him back, but took a deep breath and decided against it. Instead she got a towel, went down the hall to the bathroom she would share with three other rooms, and took a hasty bath. For the first time since she'd left Baltimore, she missed Jimmy.

She slept fitfully, and in the morning waited until the other guests had left before she took her turn in the bathroom to fix her face and hair carefully. Then she dressed in her good navy skirt and jacket, with a soft yellow sweater. "I look OK, she thought. She took a deep breath and stepped out into the hall, locked the door behind her, and made her way out of the hotel and down the street to a small diner. She picked up a newspaper there, and scanned the help wanted ads as she ate toast and coffee.

There were several jobs that might do, and she circled them with a pen. With a map and a phone book, she figured out where they were, and then crossed two of them off her list as being too far away. That left three possibilities: sales clerk at a large department store, cosmetics sales, and file clerk for a sewing machine manufacturer. The best pay was for the file clerk job, so she decided to try that one first.

She braved the subway system, and only got lost briefly. Got off at the wrong stop and had to walk a few blocks. The building was a big old brick place with small windows and a large smokestack, belching acrid black smoke. She found the proper door and went down the depressing ocher-colored hall, where a sign pointed to the employment office. Five women were there already, seated in a row, holding their application forms. They surveyed Jenny curiously as she crossed the room to the desk, sizing up the competition.

"I'd like to apply for the file-clerk job." Her voice sounded amazingly confident. The training from the ballyhoo days served her well.

"You'll have to wait your turn, miss. Just find a seat and fill out this form."

She did, and looked in dismay at the questions. They wanted to know what experience she had, where she'd gone to school, whether she had a college education. She glanced around at the other women again. They were a diverse group, but probably all of them were more qualified than she was for the job. She finished the form anyway, and sat back to wait. They went in one by one. Then the third one, an attractive dark-haired girl came out smiling, and waved at them. The woman at the desk announced the job had been taken. Jenny and the other two applicants left together.

It was after noon already, and she was hungry, so she grabbed a hotdog at a stand near the subway station and decided to try the department store next. She found it without trouble this time, and filled out the application with a lot more assurance. She'd had experience in sales, and knew she could do the job well. Her confidence apparently came across to the personnel director, and she was asked to check back with him Wednesday.

Back on the sidewalk, she checked her list again. OK, so what do I do now? Shall I go ahead and check out the cosmetics job, or would I rather wait on this one? I wonder what my chances are for this...pretty good, I think! Anyway, it's kind of late in the afternoon for getting to the next location...and then all the paperwork and interview...I guess I'll wait till tomorrow.

She decided to walk partway back to the hotel. It was good to be outside and getting some exercise. It helped her feel less anxious for the future somehow. She passed interesting shops of all kinds, admiring the variety of goods in the windows. A bakery had some wonderful sweet-rolls and éclairs in the window, and just as she passed the door opened for a shopper, and the aroma that came out took hold of Jenny and carried her in. She sat at a little table and savored every bite of the cinnamon roll, with a cup of coffee.

Then back on the street, she began to worry again. I'll have to find someone to take care of Jimmy while I work. And I can't live at the hotel with a baby. I need an apartment close to where my job will be. Oh boy, I just have to find a job fast, so I can look for a place to live.

She looked up to see a church across the street. It had a tall steeple and stained glass windows. Even as she watched, a man came out the big wooden doors, so she knew it was open. She crossed the street and pushed the big door hesitantly. Catching her breath, she slipped inside. As the door closed, the noise of the city died away and everything was hushed. Sinking down on a cushioned pew, she bent her head on her folded hands and prayed. The peace of the place slowly overcame her troubled mind and spirit.

The angel prayed beside her.

She spent Tuesday applying for a couple of other jobs. Not very interesting, she thought. She checked the paper for apartments. There were a few listed that she might be able to afford, but she couldn't look at them until she knew where she'd be working. On Wednesday she made her way back to the department store.

"Glad you came back, Mrs. Kragt. The personnel director waved her application form. You impress me as someone who can sell, and you look honest. When can you start?"

"I can start right now, sir, but I'll need time off after next week to go and settle my affairs in Baltimore."

"Done. Now here is the employment agreement and the store policy manual. Read these and sign them, and then I'll take you to meet Mr. Mulgrew in the linens department." They shook hands, and Jenny was officially an employee of Hamilton James stores.

Jenny turned on her charm for Mr. Mulgrew and demonstrated to him that she did know something about selling. She began work immediately, starting to learn about the merchandise. Mr. Mulgrew smoothed his thinning hair back and tried to hold his stomach in. Jenny watched him out of the corner of her eye, and knew she had him in the palm of her hand. She was right at home in a work environment. After all, that's where she was brought up. It came much more naturally to her than being a wife and mother did.

She worked Thursday and Friday too, doing such a good job that Mr. Mulgrew's department had the best sales week in a long time. He was happy, she was happy, and now it was the weekend and she'd see Al again! She was beginning to really miss Jimmy though. She looked at the phone. I'll call tomorrow and tell them I'll be back to get him next week.

Al was on time, and Jenny was ready. "Do we celebrate?" he asked.

"You betcha!" she answered, and told him all about her week, on the way downtown in a taxi. They had dinner at a nice little place with good food and a band. They danced the evening away, Al holding her close and making her dizzy with love and desire. She had a hard time getting him to leave when he took her home. Truth be told, if she hadn't had all the stuff Frank told her over the years going through her head, she'd have let him stay. But her resistance made her all the more desirable to Al. He could hardly stand it. Women always found him irresistible, and he was usually able to get his way. There was just something different and special about Jenny!

The phone rang several times before Aunt Pearl answered. "Jenny! About time you called!"

"Is everything all right? Is Jimmy OK? How are you getting along?" The questions came in quick succession, not giving Pearl time for an answer. Then the phone was grabbed out of Pearl's hand and Frank shouted in her ear. "How could you do such a thing? You lousy whore! You little bitch! You miserable excuse for a mother! Your baby is pining away because he misses you so much. What kind of a wretch are you anyhow? How could you do such a rotten, stinking thing as walk out on your own husband and baby?"

Jenny didn't have a chance to say anything before Mamie took the phone from Frank. "Jenny, you'd better come on home! Jimmy misses you so much, and he needs you. Your place is here with him and with Irving. You're a wife and mother now, you have no call to be running around the country causing such a ruckus!"

"Mom, I'll be coming back for Jimmy next week." Jenny answered, her heart in her throat. She'd known it would be bad when her folks found out, but it was even worse than she feared. "Is Aunt Pearl OK with Jimmy?" she asked.

"Aunt Pearl can't handle a baby any more. You ought to know that! We have Jimmy with us. We're doing fine, but you'd better get yourself home where you belong!"

"I'll come on Tuesday, Mom. I have to let my boss know first. I have a job here."

"A job? How can you have a job there, when your family is here?"

"I'll talk to you about it when I get there, Mom." Jenny felt as though the booth was about to close in on her. She hung up and stepped outside, taking deep gulping breaths of air, trying to stop the panic that began to rise in her breast. She was still afraid of Frank, and now she remembered his threats over the years, and the gun and his temper. She trembled. Lord, please help me! What can I do?

Deep down, she knew she should stay with Irving and be loyal to him, just like Mamie said. But it was either stay there and do what was expected of her while she died slowly from hate and boredom, or stay here and find a new life with hope and love and excitement. She knew she would stay. The die was cast.

The trip back to Baltimore went by in a blur as Jenny tried to plan her life and Jimmy's. She'd have to find a good place to leave him during the day while she worked. But they'd have evenings and weekends together, and she was sure she could work things out so they'd have a good life. She hoped it might include Al too, but whether it did or not, she had charted a whole new course for herself.

Dusk was falling as Jenny stepped off the bus, carrying her overnight case. She looked fearfully around, hoping Frank wasn't at the station waiting for her. She hadn't told them exactly when she'd arrive. She sighed in relief when she didn't see him. She had a few more minutes before the big scene. She knew there'd be one...she'd lived with Frank and Mamie long enough that she could almost predict what would happen. But she still wasn't prepared for what did.

When the door opened, Mamie stood there holding Jimmy in her arms. "Hi, Mom," Jenny reached for the baby and hugged him close, breathing in his clean baby-smell. "Oh, Mommy missed you, Jimmy! Are you OK? Did you have a nice time with Grandma and Grandpa?" She hugged him again, looking past him into the room.

"Come in here, Jenny and sit down," Mamie ordered. "We want to know what in the world you think you're doing? Just what do you mean running off to New York City...and taking a job there!" She had her hands on her hips, and although she didn't realize it, at that moment Mamie looked a lot like her own mother had looked all those years ago.

"It just got too much, Mom." Jenny looked at her mother, hoping for understanding, but seeing nothing but judgment. She hurried on, "Irving doesn't love me or want me any more, and his family all hate me! I just couldn't stand it any more, Mom! There has to be somewhere I can be happy! So I decided to start over again. Irving's filing for a divorce, and that's fine with me. I've got a job, and Jimmy and I will get along just fine by ourselves now." She fought against tears, swallowing hard. "I'll just stay the night and pack his things, and we'll go back to New York tomorrow."

"And just what makes you think we'd let a whore stay at our house?" The words tore through her, and she turned quickly to face Frank standing in the bedroom door. His face was contorted with rage, and his words were almost visible, as he snarled, "You're not fit to be a mother! Well, that's just fine! If you won't stay here and be a proper wife and mother, then go! But don't expect to take Jimmy with you!"

"What?" She sprang to her feet, clutching the baby to her, and backed toward the door.

"You heard me!" His arm came up slowly, aiming the gun straight at her head. His eyes bored into hers.

Mamie screamed, "Frank! You'll hit the baby!" She rushed forward and grabbed Jimmy out of Jenny's arms. He began to cry, and she said accusingly, "Now look what you've done! You've scared the poor little thing to death."

Frank waved the gun at Jenny. "Go!" She hesitated, and took a step toward Mamie. "Go on! Get out of here! You go to New York City and live like a whore, and go straight on to hell, but ye're not takin' this child with ya! The only way you'll get him is over my dead body, and most likely his dead body too!" And Frank turned the gun toward Jimmy. A pot boiled over on the stove, but nobody seemed to notice.

Jenny didn't know what to do. She hesitated, debating whether she could safely grab the baby and run, but then Frank turned the gun on her once more. "You still here? Ya don't value your life much, do ya?" Her eardrums nearly burst, and wood splinters flew as a bullet hit the doorframe beside her. Jenny let out a soul-rending scream, that blended with the terrified cries of her baby. Then she turned and ran. She knew he would do it...he really would kill her.

She stopped when she was sure he hadn't followed her. She fell to her knees, huddled beside some bushes. She shook uncontrollably, and gasped and sobbed. She looked back toward the house they had shared, not knowing what to do."Oh Jimmy! What have I done to you?" she wailed into the darkness.

The angel hovered over her, his sword drawn.

CHAPTER THIRTEEN

1938

Back in New York, Jenny was like a robot. She had two personalities for some time. The one she used at work was capable, efficient, smiling, though she seemed suddenly more mature somehow. She automatically got up each morning and went to the store where she sold sheets and towels and did her paperwork. Then she went back to the hotel, where the other Jenny took over. The other Jenny was a basket case. She wept and lamented for her lost baby. She cursed herself for what she'd done. She tried to pray, but felt God was judging her for her sins.

Al spent time with her, but he began to be impatient over her change in personality. "Hey, I know you're feeling bad about the kid," he told her, as they took a long walk. Yellow leaves were beginning to fall from the few trees they passed, and the breeze off the ocean had an edge to it. He patted her shoulder. "But you still gotta live! It's not like he died, or something, you know. Your folks'll probably take real good care of the little tike. And hey, maybe it's better for him to have a regular home instead of a big city apartment." He liked that idea, and elaborated on it. "Yeah, he'll probably be a lot better off growing up there in Baltimore with his grandparents than he would be here in New York City with baby-sitters and all."

"You don't understand, Al. The man is crazy! He nearly killed me, and I think he did kill a man at least one other time! I know what kind of a life Jimmy will have with him!" Jenny pulled her sweater closer around her, feeling a chill.

"Well, you made it, didn't you?"

"It wasn't easy, Al!" She thought back over her childhood, "It sure wasn't easy!"

Gradually, as the weeks passed, her grief dulled. She signed the divorce papers when they came, and sent them back. That chapter in her life was over. She buried it, along with her family. It was survival, pure and simple. She could let the past eat her alive, or she could put it behind her and go forward. Jenny was a survivor. She chose to live. Only sometimes in the night she woke weeping for her lost baby.

As the old Jenny began to emerge Al was more and more intrigued by her. She was funny and smart and entertaining. She could do a lot of things no other girl he'd ever known could do. And she'd been around...she knew how to talk to people. She constantly surprised him.

Jenny was the only one who realized she was always performing for an audience. She was still shy and unsure of herself, but she put that aside when she was 'on stage.' She dressed in whatever 'costume' her current role required, and played her part as well as any seasoned actress.

They saw each other most weekends all winter, except when Al pulled duty. It made life bearable for Jenny. In fact, that was the shortest winter she could remember. In March, he proposed. She didn't know what to say at first.

"Ya wanna marry a sailor?" was how he put it.

"Why?" she asked, then it hit her what he was asking, and her heart began to pound. "Al, are you asking me to marry you?"

"Yeah, I guess I am. Never thought I was the marrying kind...you know? But I can't getcha out of my mind. You're beginning to get in the way of my work! I guess that means I love ya." He reached for her hand across the table of the little Greek restaurant that was their favorite. Soft music played in the background. "Whadaya say?"

"I guess I say yes!" Jenny's heart was singing. *He loves me! He loves me!* Her blue-green eyes sparkled at him.

He nodded, "Well, OK then!" Then he added, "You know what happens when you marry a sailor, don't you? Sometimes we get shipped out, and you have to be alone for a long time. Think you can handle that?"

"As long as I know you love me, and you're being true to me, I can handle that." She remembered Irving, and added slowly, "What I can't handle is being ignored, treated like a fixture. I can't take that, Al. That's why I'm here, not in Baltimore."

"Honey, you're no fixture...not to me!" He got up and came around to her side of the booth, sliding in beside her. He put his arms around her, dipping his elbow in her plate, and kissed her thoroughly.

She leaned back against his shoulder happily. "When?" she asked.

"Now's good for me!"

"Oh, be serious, she laughed. There's the license and the blood tests and getting a preacher and all. It takes some time, you know. But maybe we could do it by next weekend. Can you get a pass?"

They spent the rest of the evening talking and planning, and for the first time in a long while, Jenny felt happy. She found a wonderful dress at the store. It was a sleek rose-colored silk that hugged her body in the right places, and swirled gently just above her ankles. She bought a little feathery hat with a veil in the same color, and spent more than she should have on some beautiful suede shoes with rhinestone clips.

When Friday night came again, she met Al, dressed in her new finery, feeling elegant and pampered. He was in his dress uniform, looking so handsome her heart swelled with pride. This wonderful, handsome man loved her! She was on cloud nine.

Al in turn was bowled over by how gorgeous she was. He could hardly believe this was happening, that he would soon actually be married! But this woman was so different from the others he'd known. He couldn't wait until he could take her to bed, all legal and formal, and she would no longer refuse him.

Al had invited a buddy of his, Buz Jamison and his girlfriend to stand up with them. They all met at the church where Jenny had prayed when she first arrived in New York. Soon they stood in a small chapel In the back of the building. "Do you take this woman to be your lawful wedded wife," the young assistant pastor asked? "Will you love her and honor her, and forsaking all others, cleave only unto her until death do you part?"

Al squeezed her hand gently when he answered, "I will."

Jenny felt somehow remote from the scene, as though she were watching it in a movie. It was a lovely wedding, she thought. Then she heard herself answer, "I will."

There were some more words from the pastor, and then she heard him say, "Kiss the bride" and All bent and kissed her...or was it a movie hero kissing a lovely starlet? The orchid Al had brought her smelled sweet, the music played by a young girl in a flowered dress might have been a fine symphony orchestra, rather than just a small piano. She looked down at her hand, where a shining new gold band decorated her finger. She looked up at Al, her husband, and smiled. He kissed her again. They paused for a few moments to sign some papers. Al paid the man, and the four of them were on their way to have dinner at a more elegant place than usual to celebrate.

Jenny hardly paid any attention to the other girl, whose name was Sarah. She was quiet and sweet, while Jenny was the center of attention, as usual. She entertained them with stories about the store and Mr. Mulgrew. She had learned to mimic him perfectly, and they all laughed a lot. Al watched her with pride. She was his now! He could hardly wait! He had rented a room at the Hilton for their 'honeymoon,' to surprise her. They had barely finished dinner, with cake for dessert, of course, when he began to thank Buz and Sarah for coming to be witnesses for them.

"But now, I'm taking my wife and leaving. Hope you two won't mind spending the rest of the evening by yourselves!" He winked at Buz, and took Jenny's arm.

"Thanks so much, Buz and Sarah," Jenny said. "I hope we can get together often now. It'd be fun to go to a movie or bowling or something?" They agreed, laughing together, and Al and Jenny stepped out the restaurant door into a magical night full of lights and people and noise. They turned right and started walking.

"Where are you taking me, husband?" Jenny asked, her eyes full of love for the handsome man at her side.

"I fully intend to ravish you, wife," he warned, playfully. He pointed down the street toward the hotel. "There's where it'll happen, so you better brace yourself, woman!"

She laughed happily. They registered, and Jenny saw her name for the first time as Mrs. Al Brownell. It sounded wonderful. They rode up to the 5th floor in silence, with the elevator operator grinning at them knowingly. As soon as the door closed and locked behind them, Al grabbed her and kissed her as she had never been kissed before. He was insistent now, and she had trouble making him wait until she took the dress off and hung it carefully in the closet. Then she stripped off her underclothes and gave herself to him.

Afterward, Jenny lay smiling, realizing she had never known what real married love could be like. She felt complete, fulfilled, and loved. It was all she had ever wanted, and she hoped it would last forever. Al pulled her close to him again, cradling her head against his chest. "Honey, you're the greatest!" he told her. This is gonna be just fine."

They had until Sunday night together, and they spent all of Saturday in the room. It wasn't until Sunday morning that they finally put their wedding clothes on again and went back to Jenny's room in the other run-down hotel. The contrast between that room with the shared bath, and the comfortable room they'd started their marriage in, was eye opening. "I'll find us a place to live this week if I can." Jenny promised. "Even if you only come on weekends, we'll need something better than this. It wasn't so bad for just me, but..." her voice trailed off.

"Yeah, let's find something a little more private, OK?" He grinned at her. "In here you can't even talk without the neighbors knowing all about it. And try to get a place with our own bathroom, will ya? Guess I'm spoiled after the weekend, but that sure was nice!"

She went to work Monday in a euphoric state, and Mr. Mulgrew stared at her often, she was so beautiful. She had a sort of glow about her. After work, she went looking for an apartment. There were several in the paper. After touring the first three, reality set in. She sat in a little diner, eating meatloaf and reading the ads again. They sounded so great until you saw them in person! She gave it up for the night and went back to the hotel room.

On the second try the next evening, she found it - the perfect apartment for two, with its own bathroom, and a little kitchen, living-dining area combined, and a small bedroom with a comfortable bed. The closet was small, but she figured Al wouldn't keep much of his stuff there anyway. She signed the lease and arranged to move in on Saturday.

When Al showed up Friday night, she was so excited about the apartment she didn't notice at first how quiet he was. When she did, a cold feeling came over her, "Al, what's wrong? I know there's something...don't you like the place I rented? Maybe we can get out of the lease."

"No...no Honey, it's not that. I'm sure it's a great place. It's this! I guess you didn't hear... Germany invaded Poland!" He pulled a folded paper from his pocket and waved it at her. She grabbed it and read it, then read it again to make sure. Tears welled in her eyes, "Oh, no! How could they do this to us! You've been here so long now, and they haven't even hinted about sending you anywhere else. Why now?!" She threw herself into his arms. "It isn't fair! We aren't even fighting this war!" Her words were muffled in his chest."How long will you be gone?"

"Whoa...one question at a time! We have a week before we ship out, so I'll try to get things straightened out for you before then." He lifted her chin and kissed her, "Meantime, let's not waste the time we have together!"

He helped her move into the new apartment, and stayed with her two nights before he had to be back on the ship. The following Saturday, she stood on the dock with a crowd of other wives and girlfriends, waving good-bye. He waved back briefly before he had to get to his post, and the ship began to move away from the dock. She watched as long as she could see it, before she turned, feeling abandoned, and started back home. "Jenny," someone called her name...she turned and saw Sarah waving at her.

"Hi, Sarah," she called back. She headed that direction, pushing her way through the crowd of unhappy women and parents. It seemed like a good time to be with someone else. They started back into the city, surrounded by other women. "Isn't this a rotten situation?" Jenny said. "Can you believe it? I just get married, and they ship him out! I guess the world situation is really getting serious though. Wish those crazy Germans would stay home and leave other people in peace!"

"Yeah, it's really crummy!" Sarah agreed. "Buz asked me to marry him, too, after we saw the two of you so happy together. We were going to set the date, and then the orders came out, and now he's gone, and who knows when I'll see him again. And, Jenny, I hear they're sinking some of our ships now if they happen to be in the wrong place!"

She sounded so forlorn Jenny put her own unhappiness aside to help her friend. She put her arm around the other girl's shoulders. "It'll all work out somehow, Sarah. It just has to! Al told me this could happen the night he proposed, but I sure didn't think it would be so soon! I guess we just have to be strong and find something to do to keep us busy while they're gone."

Sarah looked doubtful, so Jenny suggested, "Let's go somewhere and have lunch. Want to?" They got through the day together, encouraging each other to hang onto their good memories.

Later, at home, Jenny turned on her little radio for company and the strains of Irving Berlin's music filled the apartment, "What'll I do when you are far away and I am blue, what'll I do?" she sang with the music, her voice quavery with unshed tears, "What'll I do with just a photograph to tell my troubles to? When I'm alone with only dreams of you that won't come true, what'll I do?" Then she cleaned out all the cupboards and drawers to keep from feeling so sorry for herself.

Days passed as they waited anxiously for the mail. Finally the first letters came, and Jenny settled down on the couch in her little apartment to read, weep, and re-read until she could almost recite the contents. Then she called Sarah and shared some of the news with her new friend. She and Sarah were as different as could be, but somehow they complemented each other. They each needed a friend, and they met often for a bite to eat after work. The small diner near the store had good home-style cooking, and they felt at home there.

Buz wrote and asked Sarah to marry him the next time he had shore leave. Jenny celebrated with her and helped make plans for a quick wedding so they wouldn't have to waste time when Buz got back.

Jenny and Sarah became strong friends over the months and years, as their husbands came home for short leaves, and then left again for long months. They joined a bowling team to keep busy on weekends. They went to the library together, and they even learned to knit.

The war in Europe grew more serious all the time. Jenny and Sarah worried over it more and more. They survived 1940, seeing their men just often enough to stay acquainted. It wasn't easy for either of them, and at their age, temptation was everywhere. They were both young and beautiful, and they met a lot of young men. It wasn't easy to stay true to men who sometimes seemed like a fantasy. Jenny had an uneasy feeling sometimes about Al. It did seem to her that he drank a lot more than was normal.

The fellows had shore leave over Christmas in 1940. Jenny and Al made the most of their time together. They went dancing, and they took long walks, and Jenny cooked wonderful dinners for him. They snuggled together in their bed and had passionate sex, after which they lay there and talked ... or mostly, Jenny talked. Too soon, though, the leave was over, and she stood on the dock once more in the snow, watching the huge ship move slowly away from its slip and maneuver carefully through the traffic and out to sea.

Sarah stood beside her, tears streaming down her face. "I hate that war! Why do men always have to fight?"

They both knew how dangerous the sea had become. Germany had submarines out there that didn't seem to care whose ships they sank. And the RAF had just attacked Italy's fleet. It was becoming more scary every day.

"It'll be OK, Sarah... they'll come back safely. I know they will!" Jenny spoke with more conviction than she felt.

Jenny slid into the booth at the diner one evening a few weeks later and ordered her usual cup of coffee. "Hi, Sarah," she waved as her friend came in. Sarah sat down opposite her just as the waitress brought the steaming brew and set it down in front of them. Jenny was in mid sentence telling Sarah about Mr. Mulgrew's latest commands, when she got a strong whiff of the wonderful coffee fragrance. Suddenly her stomach rebelled, pushing up against her throat in a demanding way. She put a hand over her mouth and ran for the restroom, leaving Sarah staring wide-eyed.

"What's wrong?" she asked as Jenny came back to the table looking green and miserable.

"I dunno. I suppose I've got a touch of the flu or something. For sure I don't want any coffee! She pushed the cup as far to the edge of the table as it would go. Maybe I'll try some chicken soup. That usually calms my stomach." They finished eating without incident, and Jenny felt somewhat better after the soup. The next morning though, just the thought of coffee made her feel ill again. She ate some dry toast, and did some mental calculating. Oh no! Not that...not now! What a nuisance! But she was pretty sure she knew the problem. And every day that passed made it more certain. She was pregnant!

CHAPTER FOURTEEN

1941

Al was gone 8 months, while Jenny worked and grew bigger and more miserable every day. She felt awkward and ugly as her belly expanded, and when she surveyed herself in the mirror, she wondered whether Al would still love her in that condition. When his ship finally made port again, she met him at the wharf. She stood amid the crowd of women waiting. Sarah was there too, of course, looking beautiful in a new dress of copen blue. Jenny had dressed in her best maternity top and skirt, to try to be attractive.

He passed right by her... he didn't even look her way. Her heart was in her shoes, and she could hardly speak, but finally found her voice.

"Al," she called to him. He turned and looked closely toward her, then came pushing through the crowd and took her in his arms. He smelled of fresh air and the sea, and she held onto him like a life preserver.

"Baby," he breathed in her ear as he hugged her. Then he pushed her off and held her at arm's length while he surveyed her big belly. "Wow! You sure it isn't twins?"

She could see disapproval in his eyes behind the forced smile on his face. "I'm sorry, Al. I know I look a lot different than when you left...but I didn't do this by myself, you know!"

He took her arm and walked her toward the row of taxis. "I know, Baby, I guess I just didn't think of you as looking really pregnant, you know? You were such a pretty little thing when I left... "

"And now I'm just a big old cow, with swollen feet and wearing a tent!" She turned her face away to hide the tears.

"Aw, now, come on, it's not that bad, and anyway, it'll be over with soon now, won't it?" He was trying to convince himself as much as her, and she knew it. They went to the apartment and closed themselves in for a reunion, but it wasn't at all how she'd imagined it would be. Al was distant somehow. They made love, but in an awkward way, almost as though they were strangers....and they really were by then. A lot of living had gone on for both of them in the months apart.

The baby was born right on schedule, and Al took Jenny to the hospital, and then went down the street to a bar to wait. He spent a lot of time in bars these days she noticed... her first instinct had been right. After Irving, she was especially sensitive to that.

So Jenny went through the travail of birth alone, with the exception of a nurse who came and went, to keep track of her labor. When the baby was finally put into her arms some hours later, Jenny went through a whole range of emotions...love for the new little son God had given her, but sorrow and loss all over again for the first son she'd lost. She hugged the baby and alternately smiled and wept until Al arrived.

He surveyed the two of them through a haze of alcohol. "A boy, eh?...Tha's great! What'll we name him?"

"We decided on David after your father, remember?"

"Oh yeah, that's right. David. He looked down at the small red face and touched the tiny hand with his finger. "He sure is little, isn't he?"

"Yes, but he's plenty big enough!" She looked at David, then up at Al, and smiled wryly.

"I guess yer right, honey," he grinned. Then he took her free hand."Are you OK?"

Her heart melted. "Yeah, Al. We're both OK. And now we're all a real family!"

******

Davey took up most of Jenny's time, and most of the space in the little apartment. There was baby stuff everywhere, and a smelly diaper pail to contend with too. Al was proud of his son, and happy that Jenny was beginning to get a figure back, but he was more comfortable at the bar than at home. He had friends there, and when he wasn't on the ship, he was often at Tony's, playing cards and drinking.

Jenny was preoccupied with little Davey at first, and didn't pay attention to the situation; but suddenly one day it was as though she woke up out of a long dream. She looked around her with eyes newly awakened, and saw the mess in the apartment. In the mirror she saw a slob dragging around in a bathrobe and slippers, with stringy hair and no makeup. And the place even smelled bad! How had she come to a situation like this? She must have been in a coma or something! She hadn't even bothered to do much cooking since the baby came.

She shook her head. No wonder Al didn't want to come home! Who could blame him? She took a shower and selected an outfit she could fit her still flabby stomach into, then wrapped the baby carefully and went to the grocery store. When Al came home later, the wonderful smell of spaghetti sauce met him at the door, along with a pretty wife. She kissed him and let him into a clean apartment.

"I can't cook much of anything without a real kitchen, but I did manage spaghetti. And there's salad from the deli and French bread. How was your day?"

He could hardly believe it was the same woman and the same place he had left in the morning. He looked down at his wife and felt the love he'd been missing. That evening together made up to both of them for the miserable homecoming. They were together again, and they were happy. And now they were three. Davey nestled in his father's arms and hiccupped contentedly.

The drinking didn't stop though. Al still spent much of his time at Tony's bar, and when he was home, he brought a bottle with him. Jenny didn't like it. It reminded her of her dad and his buddies.

A month or two later, she brought the situation to a head. "I wish you wouldn't drink so much, Al." She put the baby down and faced her husband. His face was flushed and his eyes bleary. She could tell he'd already had too much to drink, and he was pouring himself another shot of whiskey.

"An' I wish you'd stay out of my business!" He settled down on the couch and turned on the radio. The ball game was on, and he turned the volume up too loud. She turned it down a little. He turned it up even louder and swore at her.

"Don't you talk to me that way! I won't listen to that kind of talk any more. I had enough of that when I was a child!"

"Listen to me, woman, I'll talk to you any *#* way I want to. You're my *#@* wife, understand? You better just get used to it, 'cuz that's the way it's gonna be!" He glared at her as he swung his shoes up onto the couch and leaned back on the pillows. Soon he was asleep and snoring, the radio blaring. Jenny took the baby and went out for a long walk to cool her temper. The crisp November evening grew dark early, as they covered several blocks.

"I don't have to put up with that kind of guff," she told Davey. "I don't want you to grow up afraid of your old man like I did!" She held him close and walked fast, and when the anger faded, she decided it had just been the liquor talking. If only she could get him to stop drinking so much things would be OK. She held Davey close to herself to keep him warm while she made her way back to the apartment.

Al was still asleep on the couch. She put the baby to bed, and snapped the radio off. Later she felt Al crawl into bed beside her, but he didn't say anything, and she pretended to be asleep.

The next day, she found all the liquor in the apartment and poured it down the drain, throwing the bottles into the trash-bin outside the building. Al came home after a stop at Tony's as usual and they ate dinner in silence after some trivial greetings. Davey lay in his drawer quietly, looking around and playing with his hands. After dinner, Al went to the cupboard for his whiskey, and found it missing. He looked suspiciously at Jenny, who turned away from him and busily washed the dishes. He frowned and looked in the cupboard again, then tried to find his gin and other liquors. She held her breath while he dug through the cupboards and drawers.

"All right, what've you done with it?"

The tone of his voice sent a chill down her back.

"Al, I did it for you, honey...for us! We used to be so happy before you started drinking so much. I think if you can just stop, things will be so much better...." she stopped in mid-sentence, as he grabbed her arm hard and pushed her against the counter.

"You *#@* bitch!" He hit the side of her face so hard she fell, screaming. His polished black shoe smashed against her hip, "Shut up, or I'll really give ya something to yell about!" His handsome face contorted with rage as he yanked her off the floor, threw her hard on the couch, and stood over her. "Don't you ever touch my stuff again, you hear?" He struck her twice more, then swearing again, he turned away and went to the bathroom, where she could hear him relieving himself. He stomped out of the apartment, slamming the door behind him, leaving his wailing baby and battered wife to deal with his anger.

As soon as he left, Jenny dragged herself into the bathroom and looked in the mirror. Her eye was swollen and turning black and blue. She spit blood into the sink. Her hip was bruised badly, and her arm had finger marks on it from his grip. She hurt all over physically, and she was terribly wounded in spirit. She picked the baby up and held him to her chest, rocking him back and forth as they both wept bitterly.

The angel covered them with his wings.

When Jenny was sure Al had gone to the ship the next day, she began to pack. He'd be on board ship for at least three days now, so she had time to get away. No way would she stay and put up with that kind of abuse! She cried as she folded her clothes into the suitcases. She loved Al, and she had thought he loved her too. Her dreams of a home with love and security were dead once more. And now she had Davey to care for too!

She stopped at Sarah's to say good-bye. "But where will you go? What will you do?" Sarah admired Jenny's strength and backbone, but she couldn't imagine being in her shoes. "How will you get along all by yourself with a baby to worry about?" Jenny looked terrible with her eye almost swollen shut. "Your poor face!" she moaned. "That beast!"

"It'll work out OK. I've got some money I saved...though not as much as I'd like! I've always wanted to see California, and this is as good a time as any." She rubbed her aching hip. "I want to get as far away from Al as I can. I'll file for divorce, but I don't want him to find me!"

Sarah nodded understanding and sympathy. She helped Jenny carry her things to the train station, and waved as she and Davey rode away to an uncertain future. (Sarah told her it had to be a better future than one spent with an abusive husband could be.)

Jenny stopped crying over Al, and resolved to look forward, not back. "If we look backward, we'll never do anything but grieve," she told Davey. "We'll make us a new life out in California, and it'll be good, you'll see!" She felt better herself as she said it. Hour after hour she gazed out at the endless prairies, then the desert, then mountains. Her eye was beginning to heal, though still tender and rather puffy. "Boy, I never realized just how big this country is!" she said to the baby.

"Yes, isn't it!" the lady across from them agreed, smiling. "Imagine crossing all this in a covered wagon or on foot! The pioneers certainly had grit and stamina, didn't they?"

"You bet." Jenny grinned. "Are you going west for the first time too?"

"No, actually, I live in California. I've just been back East to visit my sister and her family." She laid her book down and prepared for a visit with Jenny. "Where are you headed? Do you have family out West?"

"No....no, Davey and I are planning to start a new life in California. You see..." and Jenny poured her soul out to this total stranger, while the miles passed beneath the train wheels and Mrs. English listened sympathetically.

"I can hardly believe you've been through so much trouble...you're so young and beautiful. But now let me tell you about California. You'll love it there it's so warm and lovely, at least in the Southern part. You're planning to go to the Los Angeles area?"

Jenny nodded.

"Well, you'll do OK there, I'm sure. There are plenty of jobs right now, with so many young men going into the service. And there are sure to be women who will take care of your little one along with their own, to make a few dollars." She patted Jenny's knee. "If you're willing to work hard, you'll do OK!"

They chatted about the war, the jobs, their lives, as the train carried them farther and farther away from Al Brownell, Mamie and Frank Gibbs and little Jimmy, and all her past life. Mrs. English was encouraging, and Jenny found herself looking forward to whatever the future held for her and Davey.

The angel smiled at Mrs. English, approvingly.

Al arrived at the apartment on Friday night after his usual stop at Tony's Bar. He frowned as he noticed it was dark. Now where had Jenny gone? She'd better be getting herself home to cook his dinner. And anyway, the baby should be home, not out in the dark somewhere...anything could happen to him in the city at night. He swore to himself as he turned the key.

It took a minute for him to realize Jenny had left him. The apartment was neat and in order, no baby things lying here and there. He looked in the refrigerator...no food to be cooked for dinner. He swore again, as he crossed the little bedroom and opened the closet door. "Oh, no!" He sat down hard on the bed. Where could she have gone? He was angrier by the minute. How could she do this to him? That ingrate! Hadn't he *married* her, for heaven's sake? There were plenty of other women he could have married, but no, he passed them all by but her! And now see how she treated him. Oh, sure, he'd been mad about the liquor, but that was certainly understandable. Anyone would have felt the same! Damn women anyhow...nothing but trouble. Now he'd have to go try to find her and make up with her and all that stupid stuff women made guys go through. Well, she could just wait until morning. He'd let her stew in her own juice awhile. Maybe he'd just ignore her until she got tired of the game and came home on her own!

When he finally realized Jenny wasn't coming home, he went looking for Sarah. He stood at her door, his hat in his hand, looking contrite. "I guess I really blew it with Jenny, but you know I love 'er, and I wanna make it up to her now."

"I'd say you blew it, OK!" Sarah remembered how Jenny looked when they said good-bye. "Look, Al, you know Jenny isn't the kind of person to stay around and let you beat her up! You can't expect her to come back to you again, even if she still loves you."

"That's for her to tell me! You just tell me where she is, and I'll ask her myself."

"You won't find her, Al. She's gone." Sarah started to close the door, but Al stuck his polished shoe in the opening.

"Whadadya mean she's gone? Where did she go?" He glared at her, eyes narrowed. "Listen, Sarah, you'd better tell me, you hear?"

"Or what, you'll beat me up too?" Sarah's back stiffened, as she tried unsuccessfully to shut the door.

Al grabbed her wrist. "Enough of that! Now where is she?" He tightened his grip.

"She went to California!"

"Whaat? You're lying to me, aren't you? She's probably hiding right here somewhere, isn't she?" He pushed his way into the apartment and searched through the tiny space.

Sarah stood, holding her aching wrist. "If you don't leave, I'll call the police. And, as you can see, I'm not lying. Jenny and Davey are gone to California. Don't bother to ask me where, because I don't know. Jenny didn't know either, she just wanted to get away from you."

Al believed her. There was something about the way Sarah said it that convinced him it was the truth. Jenny was gone! He went to Tony's Bar and drank until he passed out.

The next day was Sunday, December 7, and in the early hours Japan attacked Pearl Harbor. Al reported to his ship and they left port within hours.

CHAPTER FIFTEEN

1943

It happened pretty much as Mrs. English had predicted. California was a whole different world to Jenny. The trees were different, and the hills were brown, not green. She was surprised to see huge geranium plants growing beside houses. The only ones she'd ever seen before were in little flowerpots. The warm air was nice, and it never seemed to rain…

Jenny rented a little house in the suburbs, and found a job in a factory that supplied parts for tanks. She worked long, hard hours, but made a pretty good income. The work kept her so busy she didn't have time to brood about Al, except in the night sometimes, when she was up with Davey. But now that he was almost two years old, he slept through the night most of the time, and usually Jenny was so tired from the hard work that she slept soundly too.

Their house was on the bus line and not far from her job. There were lots of other women working at the factory too. After Japan bombed Pearl Harbor, many of their husbands had joined the service, and now they all worked proudly at jobs usually reserved for men. They felt they were helping win the war, and they knew they were supplying vital parts for the war effort. Several other mothers had opened a childcare center for pre-schoolers. Davey seemed to like it there, and learned very fast from the other kids.

Jenny had consulted a lawyer, who drew up the papers for her divorce. He took care of everything, and she didn't ask Al for any support, deciding she'd rather cut all ties from him. The day her lawyer called to say the divorce was final, Jenny took herself and Davey out to dinner to celebrate. She was glad and sad at the same time. She was free, and able to do whatever she liked, without anyone's approval.

But as the months passed, she missed Al more and more. She still loved him, in spite of everything, and as time passed she tended to forget the bad times and remember the good. She caught her breath sometimes when she glimpsed a slim sailor, remembering how it was with Al at first.

Even so, the time had passed quickly, and now Davey was in his terrible twos stage and getting into everything. She missed having someone to share the good moments with. There were a couple of guys Jenny flirted with, but that was just for fun, there was no real interest. So she was lonely, even with Davey's company. There were lots of women friends, but no one special friend. She missed Sarah. She missed Al.

One hot day, she came home from work tired and dirty, to find a strange car parked in front of the house. She eyed it curiously as she walked up the front steps, carrying Davey. A moment later a man came up the walk and rang the bell. She put the baby down and opened the door. It took her a second to recognize him. "Al!"

"Hi, Baby!" He grinned at her, the old familiar grin she'd fallen in love with. He was as handsome as ever, and her heart still leaped at the sight of him.

"What are you doing here?" She pushed her hair back and glanced down at her dirty slacks. "And why aren't you in uniform?"

"Long story, Jenny. I'd like to see my son!"

She stood aside and let him enter. He picked Davey up and swung him into the air. "Hi, son! How ya doin'?" Davey laughed delightedly. "Gettin' ta be a big fellow, ain'tcha?" He looked over his shoulder at Jenny. "He's quite a guy. Looks like you're doin' a good job raising him, OK." She nodded, silently. He sat down in the easy chair, with Davey in his lap. "How about I take you to dinner?"

"I guess so," she faltered. She could hardly stand to have him so near. It was hard to remember the bad times any more. "Watch him while I get cleaned up, OK?"

They went to a small restaurant near by, where they could take Davey without a problem, and ordered their meal. Jenny watched him over her menu, as he looked over the choices. "How did you find us?"

"Went by the address for your lawyer. Then when I got here I went to the post office and told 'em I was FBI and needed your address. No problem."

"Oh great! So now I suppose they think I'm a criminal or a spy or something!"

"Nah, I don't think so." He grinned at her again. "Anyway, that just makes ya seem more interesting. You always liked to be mysterious, didn'tcha?"

She smiled slowly. "Yeah, I guess you're right, Al. So anyway, tell me why you're not in uniform?"

"Because I'm not in the Navy. They didn't like my drinking any more than you did, I guess. Anyhow, when my hitch was up they didn't take me back. Don't exactly know what I'll do now...maybe get a job here." He caught the expression in her eyes. "Hey, I've quit drinkin' now. I'm a changed, reformed man!" He nodded, "Yup, you just give me a chance, you'll see! I'm dry as a bone."

Jenny didn't know whether to believe him or not. She sighed. "I hope so, Al. For your sake as well as Davey's, I do hope so."

The next weeks were like when they first met. Al treated her like a princess. He swept her into his arms and danced they way they used to. He brought her little gifts...a flower, a locket...Jenny didn't know how to fight against her better judgment. She was in love again with the old Al - but an Al who didn't drink any more. And Davey seemed to flourish with his father around. She lay awake at night and reasoned with herself, but finally reason lost out to love.

They were remarried in a chapel in Anaheim and Al moved into the little house with Jenny and Davey. Everything was fine at first, except Al couldn't seem to find a job he liked. He finally took a sales job at an insurance office. That went fairly well, and he was settling into a routine there. Then one day a Japanese Sub managed to get close enough to the United States to take a shot at a ship anchored in the harbor at San Diego.

When Jenny got home the next afternoon, Al came out of the bedroom in an Army uniform. "You joined the Army?" She was incredulous. "How could you do that without even talking it over with me?"

"I had to, Jenny." He reached out for her hand. "I can't stand not being able to help fight those bastards! They'll be trying to come in and take over our country next if we don't fight 'em! Hey, they lobbed one right into the harbor already!" He pulled her to him. "I'm sorry, honey, but I just hadda do it. The army took me as a Sergeant because of my Navy experience too, so the pay'll be better!"

Jenny's heart was in her shoes. She began to cry. "Where'll you be stationed, Al? I wish you'd talked to me first! I was going to surprise you on your birthday next week… I'm pregnant again!" She began to weep in earnest. "Now you'll be gone again, and I'll have to go through it all alone again...it isn't fair! It just isn't fair!" She tore away from him and ran to the bedroom, slamming the door behind her. She threw herself down on the bed and sobbed with self-pity. When she was through, she washed her face and went out to the kitchen, where Al was feeding Davey some leftovers he'd found in the refrigerator.

"I'm sorry, Al. Now I guess we'd better talk about what we're gonna do next." She got out a pan and began to peel some potatoes.

Johnny was born while Al was fighting in France somewhere. Jenny got through it and wept over her beautiful little boy. Her third son. She wondered again how Jimmy was. Her heart hurt for him, even as she nursed her new son. The Red Cross got word to Al about the birth, and Jenny got a nice long letter from him. He was doing OK. Some of the guys in his outfit were killed taking out a bridge. There was death all around him. He was very glad to hear of the birth! He couldn't wait to be with his family again.

The war ended and the winners began to cut up the losers. Al was assigned to a post in West Germany. He was able to take his family along this time, so the household moved. In Germany, people drank beer instead of water, and Al was no exception. He began to drink more and more, and soon the terrible abuse began again. This time Jenny had to stay. She had two little boys to care for, and she was pregnant again!

The new baby was a girl! Jenny was thrilled, and she named her new daughter Karen. She looked like a little rosebud, so perfect and sweet. Jenny cuddled the soft little form to her breast, watching the baby suck earnestly.

She thought of her mother for the first time in a long while. "I wish you could see her, Ma. She's beautiful!" Then she remembered the last time she saw Mamie, and bitterness filled her heart once more. Why, Ma? Why did you do that to me? I know Frank isn't my father, so I understand how he could treat me so bad, but you...you're really my mother, aren't you? How could you treat me that way? How could you take my child away from me? She felt again the pain of that last time she saw her folks. "I'll never do anything like that to you!" she promised Karen as she touched her tenderly. "I'll take care of you and love you and keep you safe."

The angel sat on the end of the bed and nodded.

They spent a four year hitch in Germany, then returned to the States for a year. Al continued to drink, and regularly took out his anger and frustration on Jenny. He could be so loving and wonderful to her sometimes, and their physical relationship could be so great, and then he'd come home and hit her for no particular reason that she could see. He was good at bruising her where it usually didn't show, and she tried her best to keep him from becoming angry. She was ashamed to let anyone know what was happening, so kept to herself a lot. She lived for the kids, trying to be a super-mom and keep them from any harmful experiences. But Davey, at 8 years old, was beginning to notice things more. She was afraid he'd grow up thinking his father's behavior was normal for a man.

Jenny went to confession regularly, but the priest didn't have any help for her. He simply told her she must try to be the best wife she could be, and ask for God's help with her troubles, and pray the rosary daily. She tried that, but it didn't ease her heart. Privately, sometimes she dared to wonder how a priest could help with marital relationships when he'd never been married, but she tried to shove that thought out of her mind and just obey him they way she'd been taught. There didn't seem to be any way out of her trap, but she knew she'd gotten herself into it. Now it seemed she'd just have to live with her mistakes.

It was almost a relief when Al came home with orders taking them to Japan. At least it would be a new experience to look forward to, and maybe things would be different there...she hoped so!

CHAPTER SIXTEEN

1950

Japan was a whole new revelation to Jenny. The people were small and intense, and serious. And everything else there was small. It seemed as though the whole country was child-sized. It was hard for her to relate to the people, but she realized that if she were the one who'd lost family members and friends in the bombings, she'd likely be the same way. She felt big and ungainly next to the dainty little Japanese women. After her first few forays outside, she decided to stay close to the base. They had everything the family needed, and she felt safer there, although she chafed at the restraint.

The kids found friends right away at the camp school, and were busy with sports and games, birthday parties and lessons. There were movies on the weekends, good ones, starring John Wayne or Cary Grant, Bette Davis or Joan Crawford, or some of the other big names. So the Brownell family usually attended every Friday night. Jenny looked forward to that, but she needed more...she was hungry for something, but couldn't say what it was.

Al found plenty of friends, and drank even more than before. She dreaded having him come home after going out with them. He could be so mean...it reminded Jenny of Frank. She rubbed her bruised arm. What is it with men? Why do they have to think they own us? I wonder why they get that way? I've always tried to be good to him. Maybe that's the problem...maybe I should start being mean to him too! She tried out that theory the next time he came home drunk.

"You can just sleep on the couch! I'm not letting a drunk into my bed any more." She threw a blanket at him and slammed the bedroom door behind her. He was at the door in an instant. He flung it open and grabbed her arm roughly.

"Don't you *ever* try anything like that again, you hear me?" He snarled with rage as he twisted the arm, forcing her down on the bed.

"You're hurting me!"

"That's not all you're gonna get, either!" He held her down, while he forced himself on her. She struggled to get away, but he was so strong it was a futile effort. He tore her clothes off with one hand, holding both her hands down with the other. Then he took her. He was rough and aggressive, hurting her purposely. There was no love involved in this act, he simply used her to satisfy himself and show her who was boss. He finished and shoved her aside, stumbling into the bathroom.

She lay huddled on the side of the bed, not crying, but bruised and hurt, and angry to the core of her being. Now she knew what it was to be raped. That was it. There was no hope any more. Life stunk, and Jenny no longer cared what happened to her.

The angel wept for her.

She went about her routine woodenly after that. Something inside her was dead, but there were still things that must be done. The kids had to be fed and cared for, and there was laundry and shopping. Al tried to act as though nothing had happened, but Jenny didn't speak to him. She put all her attention toward the kids.

Davey sensed something was wrong and kept watching her curiously. Finally he followed her into the kitchen and gave her a hug. "Are you OK, Mom" he asked?

She hugged him back hard as she managed a weak smile. "Fine, Davey. I'm fine. Thanks for asking, though. You're a good kid."

Johnny and Karen were too young to be anything but self-centered. She was grateful for that now. One Thursday they went on a shopping trip through the PX. They had just turned the corner into the camera department to pick up some film when someone called her name. "Jenny...Jenny Brownell, is that you?" She turned to see Sarah coming toward them.

Her heart lifted out of its depression."Sarah! Oh, Sarah, I'm so glad to see you! When did you get here? Where are you staying? Are you stationed here now?" She hugged her friend. "Thank God you're here! If I ever needed a friend, it's now."

Sarah was nodding and smiling, and hugging Jenny and the kids. "Boy it's good to see you. I was hoping there'd be somebody here I knew...but you of all people! You're the answer to my prayers!"

"Come on home with us, and let's have a cup of coffee and catch up on each other. I'm all through shopping. OK?"

Sarah laughed. "I just have to pick up a couple of things. Only take a minute if you can wait?"

They dropped Davey off at the ball diamond on their way home, and Jenny sent Johnny and Karen out to play while she made coffee and set out a plate of cookies. "Now tell me about yourself." She settled down at the table.

"Seems a lifetime ago since you left, doesn't it? Well, it wasn't more than a couple of weeks until Buz got a promotion. We've been through a lot since then, but it's been good. I just got here a week ago." Sarah stirred her coffee, while she looked closely at her friend. "Something's wrong, isn't it?"

"Yes." Jenny stared down into her cup, then took a deep breath and looked into her friend's face. She let the breath out slowly and began to tell Sarah about the situation with Al. "And now I don't know what to do. I need somebody to tell me...I don't want to make another horrible mistake. I've made enough of them already."

Sarah had been listening and watching Jenny with compassion. " I think I know what you need, Jenny. And I believe it's the only thing that will help you...or, rather, He's the only one who can help you. The main thing that's happened to me since we left New York, is that I met Jesus." Jenny raised her eyebrows and opened her mouth to speak, but Sarah went on, "He's the answer to all of life's problems, Jenny. He's love and joy and peace and comfort...the friend you've always looked for. He's God's Son, Jenny, and he loves you so much he died for you, so that you can be together with him."

Suddenly, Jenny remembered the bus ride so long ago, and the silver-haired preacher. "I heard that a long time ago, from a nice old preacher. I told him I'd think about it, but I haven't. I'd forgotten all about it, until now. Now you're telling me the same things he said." She frowned, and added, "but I need somebody real to talk to. Somebody like you, who can talk back again, and relate to my problems."

"Believe me, Jenny, Jesus can relate better than anyone else to your problems. He was tempted in every way that you are, and he understands exactly how you feel. Only He never sinned. We always do, so we need a Savior. That's why He came and lived on earth, and died...for us! To save us...you and me. He loves us so much, Jenny. And he's a better friend than you'll ever find anywhere else. He knows your heart."

"I do pray, and ask for help sometimes, but I never get any answers."

"God can't hear your prayers except through Jesus. He's the only way to God for us." Sarah drew a square on the tablecloth with her knife handle. "See, it's like this. Here's a wonderful Christmas gift. God sent it to you. It's sitting right here on the middle of the table. You can have it any time. You can admire the shining gold and silver wrapping, and the beautiful ribbon. You can thank God for giving it to you, and you can just leave it there and look at it. Or, you can open it up and take out the wonderful priceless robe of salvation and put it on, and wear and enjoy it." She saw the doubt in Jenny's eyes. "It's right there. The gift is yours. The question is, will you just leave it there and admire the package, or will you open it up and use it?"

"How do I do that, Sarah?" Jenny asked quietly. She sensed now that this was her answer after all, and God had sent it to her twice now.

"You just tell God you're sorry for all your sins, and ask Jesus to be your Savior too, and then you thank him and praise him for doing it."

Jenny bowed her head and asked, humbly confessing her sins, as she pictured herself opening the gift and putting on the gorgeous blood-red robe. The Angel praised God for joy, along with a whole angelic host. They worshipped God, singing and praising, while she prayed. They saw the robe too, only from their side it was gleaming white! When Jenny looked up, the tears began to flow down her cheeks. She was surprised to see that Sarah was crying too.

"You're right, Sarah. I feel as though a terrible heavy weight is gone from me. I feel so light and free! Why didn't I listen to that nice old man and do this years ago? So what do I do now?"

"First thing to do is get a Bible and start to read and study it. That and prayer will give you all the direction you need, and a lot of strength, too." Sarah reached for her hand and squeezed it. "Then we need to find a church service where we can go to worship the Lord along with other believers. We'll need one with a Sunday school where your kids can learn too, and you can get some of your questions answered and find other friends." She stood up and wandered around the room, looking here and there. "Do you have a newspaper? We could look in there for a list of churches."

Jenny sprang up and headed for the carport. "Just a sec. I already threw yesterday's paper in the trash." She came back with it a moment later, and laid it on the table, smoothing out some wrinkles. They pored over the sections, searching. Then Sarah exclaimed, "Aha! Here it is! She started reading the list. It was a short list, and most of the services were held on the base. They selected a Baptist service and agreed to attend it together on Sunday.

"If we don't care for this one, we can try one of the others the next week." Sarah stayed as long as she could, talking and sharing and rejoicing with Jenny. "Now you're really my sister. We're both in God's family," she said as she picked up her things to leave. "I'm so excited and so happy I can hardly stand it!"

Jenny felt exactly the same way. She looked forward to Sunday, and in between she tried to prepare the kids for church. And she was kind to Al, since she forgave him for how he'd treated her. She felt him watching her suspiciously several times in the next couple of days. Finally he couldn't stand it any longer, and asked her point blank, "Say Jenny, what are you tryin' to pull on me anyhow? You planning to cut out and leave me again? Because if that's what ya've got in mind, you just better give that another thought, woman! We're in Japan, you know, and it's not as though ya can just run home to Mama now!" He tried to get her angry with that last remark, but she simply set the steaming mug of coffee in front of him and went back to stir the beef stew she was preparing.

"Of course not, Al. You're my husband." she replied quietly.

"Yeah, an' don't you forget it!" He eyed her closely. She was prettier than ever somehow. There was something different about her. It made him cross to think she had a secret. Maybe she had a lover. That was it! He knew he'd figured it out right. She looked like she'd looked when they were first married and she was in love with him! "Who is it, Jenny? Who are you havin' an affair with?" He walked over to the stove and grabbed her arm. "Don't you ever think I don't see right through ya! Now you just better tell me who he is, lady!" His grip on her arm tightened.

"Al, please don't do that. It hurts," she felt the fear rise up inside her, but she managed to keep her voice calm. *Please help me, Jesus.* He let go of her, and she turned to face him. Her eyes fastened on his, as she answered, "Yes, you're right. I do love someone...but that Someone is Jesus. I received Him as my Savior, Al. He's the answer to everything I ever wanted and needed. And He will be the same for you, too! He died for you, Al. He can change your life and make you happy if you'll just ask Him to."

She backed away as his eyes narrowed. "Are you out of your mind?" His voice was almost a shriek as he stared at her. "That's it...you're crazy! You've gone over the edge and now you want me to join you!" He grabbed the back of her hair and pulled her face close to his. "Well, you just listen and get this straight, woman. I don't ever want to hear anything more about that. You hear me?" He shook her head with each of the last words, pulling her hair and twisting her neck. He let go, waiting for her to break into tears.

She smoothed her hair and stirred the stew again. *Help me, Lord. Please help me!* Somehow she maintained her composure as she carried the stew pot over to the table and ladled some of the fragrant mixture into each of the bowls. "Dinner's ready!" she called, and waited while the kids came from their various locations. "Let me see your hands," she said to Johnny. "Go and wash" she directed. "Davey are your hands clean?" She set the bread on the table and pulled out her own chair. All the while she could feel Al's gaze on her.

He pulled out his chair and sat down heavily. He loved her stew. Always had. It was flavored with herbs and wine and tasted wonderful. She always served it with warm crusty bread. It was one of his favorite meals. If it hadn't been stew for dinner, he would have stamped out of there and shown her she couldn't yank him around. He ate in silence, and by the time his stomach was full of the warm, nourishing food, his anger had passed.

The angel nodded approval.

On Sunday Jenny was up early, getting the children and herself ready for their first visit to a church since she gave the Lord her heart. She could hardly wait to be with other Christians and hear what the minister would say to them.

Al lay in bed sleeping off the excesses of the night before. He'd come in very late, smelling of liquor and swearing as he stumbled around getting undressed. Jenny was quiet as she fed the children breakfast and wrote a note to Al, telling him which church service they were going to and inviting him to join them if he woke up in time. They met Sarah, who was coming to meet them, as they walked down the street toward the bus stop. The children were excited about their first visit to a non-Catholic church. "What will it be like?" Davey asked.

"I'm not sure, Honey. I've never been to a Baptist church either, but I'm sure it'll be really nice. They love Jesus there, I know, and that's all that matters. There'll probably be other kids there too.

"Then I'll like it," pronounced 6 year old Johnny. Karen, who was only 3 and a half, wasn't too sure. "Maybe I won't stay," she told Sarah, who was holding her hand.

"Oh, Honey, I bet you'll love it." Sarah assured her. "If you don't like the church service, I'll bet they have a nursery where you can play with other kids and color pictures or something."

"Well, OK," Karen agreed.

The big blue bus let them out at the building being used for services and they walked shyly in to join the group of people gathered in the foyer. A man gave Jenny and Sarah bulletins and guided the group to seats. They settled down and looked around at the others. It was a diverse group, mostly young service people and their families, but with some older Americans too, and a few Japanese. They sat on folding chairs arranged in two groups with an aisle between them. In front of the chairs was a sort of lectern with a table in front of it that held two candles and a couple of flat bowls. To the right side of the front was a piano.

In contrast to the reverence people showed in the Catholic churches, this crowd seemed almost sacrilegious to Jenny. They chatted with each other and the room was almost noisy. But they seemed cheerful and friendly, smiling at the new little group in their midst. A few stopped to shake hands and welcome them. Soon a young man took his seat at the piano and began to play some lovely music, and the crowd quieted down.

The preacher was a large balding man, in his 40's Jenny guessed, with a paunch he tried unsuccessfully to hide beneath his suit jacket. They sang some songs she didn't know, somebody gave some announcements about future events, they took up a collection and prayed, and then Reverend Pittfield started his sermon. At first Jenny was distracted by the children and the other people in the room, but soon her attention was completely captured by the message. It was all about how Jesus called his disciples, and how they simply dropped everything and left everyone and followed him. "Oh, they probably got a lot of flack from their friends and family. I'll bet they were called all kinds of names, including crazy and irresponsible, but they put Jesus first in their lives and obeyed His call."

Then he related that to each of his flock, asking whether they were willing to give up their own plans for making a living, for school, for their families, and simply follow the Lord's leading in their lives.

Jenny gazed at her hymnal. That's what I want to do. I just don't know how to do it. They stood up and sang the closing hymn,

"All to Jesus I surrender, All to Him I freely give,
I will ever love and trust Him, In His presence daily live.
I surrender all, I surrender all,
All to Thee, my blessed Savior, I surrender all."

She'd never heard the song before, but Jenny agreed with it with all her heart. By the end of the last verse, she was singing it as a prayer to her Lord. They shook hands with a lot of smiling people and with the Pastor, who stood at the door. "We hope you'll come back again!" He invited.

"Oh, I'm sure we will!" Jenny answered. Sarah just nodded and smiled shyly. Then they were out the door and walking toward the bus stop again.

"They have Sunday school before church, Mom," Davey told her. "I saw the room they meet in."

"Think you'd like to go next week?"

"Yeah...kinda."

"Me too then," Johnny agreed.

"Me too, huh Mom? Me too?" Karen jumped up and down to get her attention.

"What do you think, Sarah?"

"I was pretty interested, weren't you?"

"Yeah. Yes, I was. OK, let's plan to go again next week, and get there for Sunday school."

When they got home, Al was just getting out of bed. "Where've you been?" he growled, looking at how they were dressed.

"We went to church, Daddy!" Karen told him,

"Yeah, It was neat, Dad." Johnny agreed.

"Did ya bring home the Sunday paper," he asked?

Oh-oh, Jenny thought. "I'm really sorry, Al, but I forgot. We were so interested in the church service and all...I'll go back and get one for you though." She turned and started for the door.

"Don't bother yerself!" he drawled sarcastically, "I'm only your husband, and I guess that doesn't count with you any more! Hey? You're only interested in whoever it is ye're seein' behind my back! Don't give me any of that church business! Now ya got the kids lying for ya too! Don'tcha have any shame?"

"Al, you know that isn't true," Jenny said flatly. "You just want to torment me. Well, OK, if that's how you want our relationship to be, but just leave the kids out of it, please." She made shooing motions with her hands to them. "Go on and change your clothes now...Quick!" They went, but the joy was gone from their adventure now.

"Maybe you'd like to go along with us next Sunday, Al? Then you could check up for yourself on where we've been and what we've been doing"

"Don't start with me, woman! Just get me my paper, and get me some coffee! He stomped into the bathroom and she heard the shower turn on.

"Thank you, Jesus!" she breathed as she grabbed her purse and ran to get the paper.

They went to church every week from then on, and learned more and more about the word of God. Pastor Pittfield was a good teacher, and so was the lady who led the Sunday school class. Jenny was like a sponge soaking up the word. When she was home alone in the afternoons, she studied the Bible by herself, writing down questions she couldn't figure out, or just needed verified. Sometimes Sarah joined her for study and prayer over a cup of coffee. Sarah was growing in the Lord too. She was doubly blessed though, because after only a few more weeks Buz joined the little group at church, and not long after that he became a Christian too.

Jenny was jealous of their relationship and love, but tried not to be. "Lord, I'm glad for Sarah. It must be so wonderful to have a Christian husband. Please, Lord, let Al get saved too! Please let him turn to You, and set him free from the drink. He used to be such a nice guy, Lord!" Deep down inside though, she felt God was punishing her for leaving Irving and Jimmy and running away to New York to be with Al. Sometimes she wondered what Irving was doing now, and what kind of life she'd have if she'd stayed with him.

"That's not it, Jenny." Sarah told her. "You remember, all our past sins are covered with the blood of Christ, and God doesn't see them any more at all, so how can He be punishing you for something he doesn't even remember?"

"I guess so," Jenny said doubtfully, "but then why is Al so hard and mean to me? What did I do to deserve that? It must be to punish me for being so bad in the past."

"I don't think that's it at all." Sarah turned to a passage in her Bible. See, here in Hebrews 12:6 it says "Whom the Lord loves, he chastens, and scourges every son he receives." I think that means if he really loves you and you're a child of his, you have to be purified, even sometimes by fire, like being married to Al." She turned the pages again, and showed Jenny a passage in Revelation 3:21."To him that overcomes will I grant to sit with me in my throne, even as I also overcame and am set down with my Father in his throne." So that looks to me like we have to have problems so we can be overcomers. And Jesus will help us through the hard times if we just keep holding on to him and trusting him."

Jenny nodded, "I do trust him, Sarah. I want more than anything to be what he wants me to be, and do what he wants me to do. It's just that life would be so much easier and sweeter if Al knew him too!"

The children gave their hearts to the Lord too, and had their own trials and testings to endure, but they all kept growing in the faith. Then the next year a traveling evangelist visited Japan. Everyone in the church was excited about hearing the famous speaker, but there was some controversy too. "You have to be careful about hearing people like him. Satan can use people too, you know, and can cause confusion. I've heard there are a lot of strange things happening in his services," the pastor warned his people.

"Yes, but I hear people are being healed of all kinds of diseases and the blind are seeing and everything! That sounds exciting to me!" Jenny told Sarah. "Let's go find out for ourselves." She grinned at her friend, "Sounds like Pastor Pittfield feels about this guy the way I felt about his service the first time I went there. The Sisters used to warn us not to go into a Protestant church because the Devil was in there. That sure wasn't true! Well, and that's the same sort of reasoning this sounds like to me! Want to go and see?"

"OK, but can you get Al to let you go?"

"Sure, I'll bet if I tell him Pastor Pittfield doesn't want us to, he'll be all for it."

On the appointed day, they rode the bus into the city together, feeling like real adventurers. The service was being held in a huge auditorium in the center of town, and traffic was backed up for blocks around the building. They finally got out and walked the last few blocks, pushing their way through the crowded sidewalks. "I can't believe there's this much interest in an evangelistic meeting!" Jenny stretched her neck to try to see over the crowds to the signs ahead. "Are you sure we're in the right place?"

"I guess so. Wouldn't the bus driver have told us if we weren't?"

"Yes, but this is Japan for goodness sake. Most of these people must be Buddhists or something. Why are they all coming to a Christian meeting?"

"Probably for the same reason we are. Curiosity! They've probably heard all the stories about healings and miracles too. Everybody's always curious about that stuff. Remember when Jesus fed the multitude with loaves and fishes? That was a miracle. Then the crowds followed him all over, looking for more food. They just wanted to have their basic physical needs met. But when they realized there was a cost to following him, they went home."

They finally reached the doors of the auditorium and squeezed inside. The hall was nearly full already, and it was still an hour or so until the meeting was scheduled to start. Jenny and Sarah amused themselves by watching the crowd, trying to guess something about the various individuals and families.

At last the service began. There was wonderful music and much fanfare, but when the famous man began to speak, a hush came over the crowd. The word was coming forth with a power they'd never experienced. People were weeping and praying all around them. At the close of the sermon the speaker gave an invitation for those who needed healing, and the aisles filled immediately with people trying to get down to the altar. As they reached the front, the evangelist and his aides prayed for each one, and many started praising God for healing, running and screaming and praying and singing. A woman with a huge growth on her face was healed instantly. The growth just fell off! That was the most spectacular healing Jenny saw. But there were hundreds of people claiming to be healed.

Next, there was an invitation for those who wanted to be saved and filled with the Holy Spirit. "What is that?" Jenny asked.

"Don't know" Sarah answered. "Let's watch and see!"

"Remember when Jesus told his disciples to tarry in Jerusalem until they received power from on high? Remember when Paul and his followers asked the people at Ephesus, "Have you received the Holy Sprit since you believed?" Remember when Simon the Sorcerer tried to buy the power to baptize in the Holy Ghost?" The speaker leaned forward as though he was talking directly to

Jenny. "Well, if you're a Christian and have not been baptized into the Holy Spirit, you're missing the power you need to speak forth the word, to stand against the enemy, to do God's work in the world. You need the "tools of your trade" to do the job with. If this is you tonight, come forward and let us lay hands on you to receive the Holy Spirit." He said a lot of other things, but Jenny was on the way down the aisle and didn't hear the rest. She reached the front and stood with a crowd of others waiting to see what would happen next.

She closed her eyes and prayed, "Lord, if this is you, and if this is what I need to do your work and be closer to you, then please give it to me. But Lord if it isn't you, please protect me." She opened her eyes and watched as two men laid hands on the man next to her and prayed for him. The man sank to his knees and raised his hands. Then they were beside Jenny. Do you know the Lord?" one asked. She nodded. OK then Sister, receive the Holy Spirit now. Just breathe him into yourself," he instructed. Then they laid hands on her head and shoulders and prayed. She breathed in as they said, and suddenly she felt "electricity" coursing through her body. She fell to her knees, the feeling rising through her, now up from her waist, now through her breast, now coursing through her arms to the ends of her fingers, while her hands went up involuntarily. The electricity went on up through her head, and as it passed her mouth, new words began to bubble forth. She felt overwhelming love, such as she'd never felt before. It was a kind of love she'd never known was possible. She was loved with an everlasting, unquestioning love, and she loved the same way. It was unbelievable, unspeakable except in the new holy language that was streaming from her lips. There was such joy, such peace, such wonder...she realized she was singing in the strange language. It was amazing and she never wanted to stop. She was singing her love for the Lord in a language he gave her for that purpose. Her life would never be the same again.

The angel rejoiced and sang with her.

CHAPTER SEVENTEEN

1960

Jenny sat near the back of the sanctuary of the Community Church in Lompoc, California, watching and listening, praying and worshipping along with 150 or so other people. It had been a hard 10 years since she'd been so blessed of God. She understood now why he had poured out such an amazing gift of love on her. She'd needed it! She'd gone through her own private hell living with Al through those years. He beat her regularly, sometimes injuring her badly, in spite of anything she could do. She tried to be good to him and do what he wanted, as long as it didn't keep her from the Lord. But nothing seemed to matter. He just hit her whenever he felt like it.

Jenny's face and body weren't so beautiful any more. She bit her nails until they bled, and chewed her lips nervously. But her eyes showed the love of Jesus, and people seemed drawn to her for help and advice. She'd needed help and advice herself many times, and what the good people of the church had told her was that she must stay with Al and try to win him to the Lord. As long as he would stay with her, she must try to be a good wife to him they told her, and quoted the Bible to prove it. It didn't seem to make sense to her sometimes, but she stayed with him and tried her best to be a witness. He made her go with him to the bar sometimes, but not often any more.

Al was still very handsome, and looked much younger than his years. Other women thought he was wonderful, and often made a play for him. Jenny was surprised sometimes, that he hadn't left her for one of the pretty young things. She knew he wasn't faithful to her, but he wouldn't let her go either. She was thin and gaunt, and her once lovely honey-blonde hair was beginning to turn gray. She cut it and started to color it, hoping to look young and attractive again. Only sometimes when she looked in the mirror she saw her mother!

Jenny spent much of her spare time studying the Bible. She'd used a concordance so much it was falling apart, and she had several different translations of the Bible itself to compare. She didn't use perfect English, and her speech was peppered with rather salty expressions she'd picked up through her rough background. But she could teach the word better than most preachers. In fact, her dream ever since she'd met the Lord, was to be a minister for him.

Jenny came out of her reverie. The preacher was ending his sermon, and a few moments later they stood to sing the closing hymn. She walked out, looking around for Karen, who sat with some young people in the balcony. This was a difficult time for Karen. Al had just mustered out of the service. He took a job at Vandenberg Air Force Base, so they'd moved one more time. Karen was 13, awkward and loud and trying to grow up. You could see she would be a real beauty when she got through the transition, but in the meantime...well, Jenny prayed for patience and wisdom.

She needed both for Johnny too, who was 16, and having a hard time deciding how to be a man, with the role model he'd had. David was 18 and in the Air Force now. He'd fallen away from the Lord, and was Jenny's heartache. She missed him, and prayed for him. It was hard to teach her boys how they should grow and live, when they watched their father's example. He was tough and macho, handsome and popular with other men. It was natural for them to want to follow in his footsteps.

She felt proud now though, watching Karen mingle with the other teens. Karen was a natural leader, which was a good thing with all the moving they'd done over the years. She made friends easily once she got over the first shyness. Jenny watched her wave at the other girls and come toward her. "Hi, how'd it go?"

"Oh, OK, I guess. They're friendly enough...kinda square though."

"Oh?"

"Yeah. That one with the dark hair, see her?"

"The chunky one?"

"Yeah. All she talks about is horses! She's got one of her own. Her dad owns some business in town, so I guess they have money."

"She looks nice. Think you can be friends?"

"Yeah, I guess so. How about you?" She eyed Jenny sideways as they reached the car.

"I think it'll be OK too. Let's give it a try, yes or no?"

"Yeah, sure. If we don't like this one, there's a Baptist church in town, and I saw a full gospel church too.

"Well, I think maybe the Lord wants us here for now, but I don't know why. We'll see...I hope the guys didn't let the roast burn while we were gone!"

They drove back into Lompoc, through endless fields of flowers that covered the valley floor like a gorgeous quilt. Most of the flower seed companies grew their crops here. On three sides of the valley mountains rose darkly against the sky. The west side led to the ocean. The day was clear and windy, now that the morning fog had rolled out. The air was just cool enough for a sweater to feel comfortable, and it was perfumed with flowers. It was a beautiful place the Lord had led them to this time.

They eased into life in the community and in the church, and joined the various activities offered. Jenny volunteered to teach Sunday school, and became involved in the women's circle. There were many young wives of servicemen from Vandenberg Air Force Base, as well as a lot of women whose husbands worked at Lockheed there, trying to perfect and launch a space satellite. The group also included a sprinkling of older women who tried to keep the younger ones grounded in the word as they had learned it. Jenny stuck to their doctrine and bit her tongue often when she could have witnessed to the greater power of God. Those good, loving and earnest Christian women limited their own prayers by their unbelief.

Jenny was fascinated by the nearby Lompoc Correctional Facility, which housed many "white-collar" criminals along with the others. She volunteered with some of the church ladies who did visitation work there, and was in and out of the place many times over the years, helping prisoners see their need of a Savior. She liked that ministry a lot, and felt fulfilled doing it.

Inevitably though, one day she witnessed to a young woman at church. The Spirit that urged her was unmistakable... she knew the Lord was telling her to help this woman. She waited until Sandy was standing alone at the side of the room, and then approached her. "I've heard you pray every meeting lately to be filled with the Spirit," she observed.

"Yeah, you know the pastor has been preaching that we should be full of the Holy Spirit, and now they've made me the Spiritual Life chairman, and I'm really convicted that I'm not spiritual enough!" Sandy smiled at Jenny, sort of a sideways smile. "So I'm asking the Lord to make me what He wants me to be, so I can reach others for Him."

"Well, then what do you think about the gifts of the Spirit? You know, like prophesying, and speaking in tongues and teaching and all?"

Sandy looked surprised, "I don't know...I guess they're not for us today. At least, that's what I've been told, and I guess that's true because I've never seen anyone use them."

Jenny pushed the question further. "What do you do about First Corinthians, chapter 13 then?"

"Gosh, I don't know...but I'll read it and let you know, OK?"

"Sure. It's pretty interesting. And I haven't found anything in the word that says it's not for us today. If you like, I have a book on the subject you can read.

"Thanks," Sandy nodded to her as she moved away to speak to the church pianist, Jane Brody.

Jenny grinned ruefully to herself. I guess I've put my foot in it now, Lord. Oh well, this was a nice church while they let me be here, anyhow.

She was surprised when the following week Sandy made a point of waiting for her between Sunday school and church service. "I read Corinthians, and I see what you mean," she told Jenny. "I guess I'd like to read your book if you don't mind loaning it to me."

Little did either of them know what that simple action would lead to, but events happened fast after that, as both Sandy and Jane Brody received the Baptism in the Spirit, along with two or three other women in the church. Each of them witnessed to the pastor, and things were in turmoil.

At the same time, the elders and deacons of the church met to decide what they should do about all the disruption in their midst. "This can't be of the Lord, He wouldn't bring such discord and chaos! Why can't our men keep their women in control, and at home where they should be? If these people don't repent and turn away from this evil, we have no recourse but to ask them to leave our fellowship!"

They scheduled a meeting with the "sinners" where they called on them to renounce the evil spirits and turn back to the Lord. The newly Spirit-filled believers refused to turn their back on their newfound faith, and begged their friends to open their own hearts to this wonderful experience.

Soon the dissenters were invited out of the church. Jenny opened her home to the outcasts for Sunday services, and there in her spacious living room a new work was begun to glorify God. The little group found that trouble and persecution only made their faith grow stronger. They prayed for their friends back at Community church, but the Lord was leading them on into other pastures.

The angel praised God along with the "little flock."

It wasn't long before the group outgrew the living room. "It's been great meeting here, Jenny. We certainly do appreciate your hospitality, but there simply isn't enough room any more. We can't grow when there's no room for a new person to sit!" Sandy put down her coffee cup and looked around the family room. "Anyway, Al isn't happy with us, is he?"

Jenny looked down and sighed. "You're right, of course. It's been so good to have my house be the church... but Al won't stand for it much longer. He's making threats now.... and you're right about the room... so I guess we need to look for another location. Let's start the search after prayer meeting Tuesday, OK?"

"They found a small stucco house in the city that they could afford, and moved in immediately. They had work bees to remove the dining room and kitchen walls and make it into a suitable sanctuary. They used the bedrooms for Sunday school rooms. And the work kept growing.

In the midst of all the activity on the new church building, Jenny heard from her mother! The letter ignored the fact that they hadn't seen each other for all those years, and just said "Your Dad is very sick, and I don't have enough money to care for him any more. Can you help?" And it ended with a small acknowledgment that Jimmy was working in sales at a store in Baltimore. He was doing just fine.

Jenny's heart pounded as she read and re-read the letter. She'd tried to put her folks out of her mind because it made her feel so bad to think of them, but now all the old feelings came flooding back. And her son, her baby, Jimmy...she wept over him as if it were all happening again today. Then she prayed, "Dear Lord, please let me know what to do now. Please open a way for my mother and for Frank." (She couldn't call him her father any more.)

The only thing she could think of was to invite them to come to California and stay with her and Al and the kids. Al grumbled a whole lot when she told him the situation, but surprisingly enough he agreed to let them come... as long as they didn't get in his way. So she wrote and told them "pack your bags, and I'll be there in about a week to get you. You'll like it here in California, It doesn't snow here, and the sun shines almost every day."

The interminable miles went by, with Jenny praying, praising, singing, and listening to the radio. She stopped only when she was completely worn out, so covered the distance to Chicago in a little over three days. She saw the Chicago sign overhead. I wonder if they've changed at all...

Finally she located the address and a parking space. She combed her hair and checked her lipstick in the rearview mirror. As she swung out of the car and stood up, kicking dead leaves and a tin can aside, the trip caught up with her, and made her body feel heavy, her steps slow. But she shook herself and forced a smile as she climbed three flights of dimly lit stairs. Someone was cooking bacon somewhere down the hall, and the smell filled the hall and stairwell. The bacon must have been mixed with something else, because it didn't smell good... it was almost nauseating. The place brought back memories from her childhood.

Her knock resounded down the hallway. She heard voices, then slow footsteps, then the door opened, and a frail woman looked out at her. She was wrinkled and white-haired, with teeth stained by an endless chain of cigarettes, but it was Mamie, feisty as ever. "Hope you had a good trip," she offered. And ignored the years past, and the years passed, as she turned toward the window of the small apartment, where a bent and shrunken old man sat in a broken-down easy chair, wrapped in a large blanket. Jenny could hardly believe this feeble, bald old person was the man she'd feared so much for so long. But he was.

"So ya came," he stated. He coughed harshly.

Jenny nodded. "Of course I came. Mom said you needed me." She looked around the drab room. "Are you all packed?"

"What, you want to leave right now?"

"No, but I thought we'd get an early start tomorrow if that's OK?" She looked into the bedroom, where a few boxes were stacked in the corner. "I'll get some of your stuff loaded into the car now, and then we can see what needs to be done." She picked up two boxes and started back down the stairs. All went well until she reached the entry, opened the door, and tripped on the raised sill. She hit the porch rail, screamed with pain, and blacked out. The next thing she knew, she was in a hospital emergency room and someone was holding her arm. She couldn't feel it, and she couldn't see it because the person holding it had his back between her and her arm. "What happened," she asked? "Why am I here? And where is here?"

The doctor turned to face her. "You're at the hospital. You fell and broke your arm pretty badly." He frowned and looked back at the arm. "It's going to take some surgery to try to fix this. We'll get you into the operating room as soon as the Orthopedic Surgeon arrives." She groaned, and he looked at her more kindly. "We've given you a local anesthetic now, to ease the pain."

She couldn't hold back the tears, hard as she tried. "I'm s-s-sorry I'm such a baby. It's just I can't do this right now!" she wailed. I came here to get my folks because they can't take care of themselves any more. I have to drive them back to California, and now what am I gonna do?"

"Well, right now it'll have to wait, because you're not in any condition to drive!" He gave her a little white pill and a drink of water, and soon she slept.

She spent two weeks in the hospital, and had two operations on the same right arm she had broken so badly as a child. But finally, her arm still in the bandages and sling, she managed to get herself and Mamie and Frank into the car and headed back West. The trip went slowly this time, as they had to stop to rest often, both for Frank's sake and for hers. The long drive, confined in the car so closely, took a toll on all of them. It was hard to find topics to talk about that didn't cause arguments, so Jenny played the radio a lot. That caused almost as much trouble, as they had such different tastes in music. She gave in, mostly and listened to country-western with her folks.

When they finally crested the mountains overlooking the Lompoc valley, Jenny stopped at a scenic pull-off to let them see the view. The flower fields below them were in full bloom just before harvest began for the seed companies. It looked like the whole valley was covered with a gorgeous quilt. They admired the beauty for a few minutes while they rested, then began the winding trip down. It took all the skill Jenny could muster to maneuver with one hand through all the hairpin turns, but eventually they reached the valley floor, and straight roads.

.

Jenny took her folks home and got them settled into their room. She had tried to arrange a comfortable place for them. She remembered all the drab little rooms they'd stayed in over the years, and tried to compensate with a beautiful new bedspread and curtains, a comfortable armchair and a good lamp on a side table. The room smelled fresh and looked lovely. Her heart sank as she watched them light up cigarettes, but she said nothing, just brought ashtrays for them.

Frank was really sick. He had a very bad heart condition. Jenny had her own doctor examine him, and was told, "Just make him comfortable if you can. He doesn't have long to live." So that's what she did, as well as she could with her arm in a cast. She cooked good food for him, and kept him clean and tried to witness to him. He and Mamie seemed to take her care for granted and began to treat her the same way they had years ago. But Karen was their darling. She could do no wrong in their eyes. Johnny hardly ever came around them, so they didn't really get to know each other.

The church prayed for Frank, for his salvation. Some of them knew the story of what happened so long ago, but seeing the shriveled old body, it was hard for them to believe he could have been such a tyrant. (Anyway, everyone knew Jenny had a good imagination.) They avoided going to Jenny's house, but eased their good Christian consciences by bringing food now and then. And Jenny watched her lovely new white draperies gradually covered with scummy yellow film from an unending chain of cigarettes.

To add to the problems, Jenny's arm wasn't healing properly, so she had to endure another operation. There was an abundance of misery in her house, even though Jenny tried to praise the Lord and live a good example for Mamie and Frank.

Al stayed at the bar more than ever, after work. Karen started being a problem too, getting in with a rowdy crowd at school, and becoming sassy. But when Jenny tried to correct her, Mamie would stand up for Karen, and say things like, "she's just fine, Jenny! I remember you used to be a lot worse than that! Let her be!"

Time was suspended, just waiting for the inevitable. It came early one morning. Jenny was lying in bed, praying for strength for the day, when Mamie shrieked.

"What is it, Ma?" Jenny sprang out of bed and grabbed her robe, tying it over her sling, one-handedly, as she hurried across the hall. She took one look at Frank and called the ambulance.

They sat in the sterile waiting room, Mamie with tears running down her cheeks. And finally a green-gowned person appeared, "There's nothing more we can do beyond the Nitroglycerin tablets. His heart is too far gone...just shot! We'll try to make him comfortable, but..." He gave a lop-sided half smile, gestured apologetically and went back down the hall, his bootied feet making no sound.

Jenny sent for Pastor Bates, who came immediately, and sat a long time with Frank, quoting scripture, and telling him about his need for the Savior. And finally, at the very end of his life, after some questions and answers back and forth, Frank, with tears in his eyes, agreed that he needed the Lord. He repented of his sins, asked Jesus into his heart, and wept with the joy of salvation. That night, he died in his sleep.

Mamie traveled back to Baltimore to visit Jimmy for a few weeks, and Jenny tried one-handed to clean the yellowish crud from her house. Al ranted at her as usual, saying horrible things and, despite her broken arm, he landed one blow that made a terribly sore black and blue spot on her side under her breast. 15-year-old Karen came home late from a date, her clothes mussed up and her lipstick all over her face. They had a big fight over that, and Karen slammed her bedroom door after assuring Jenny, "I'll just do whatever I please, and you can't stop me!"

Jenny sat in the armchair in Mamie's room, trying to deal with her life. Gradually a cold heaviness came over her like a suffocating blanket, and slowly she lost her will to live. The Lord seemed far away, and a different voice wooed her. It was a subtle, soft, persuasive voice, and she listened, exhausted and discouraged. "There's no reason for you to keep putting up with this miserable life. It's so easy to end it all. You'll be out of all your pain, and in a far better place, where you'll be loved and cared for. And they'll be better off without you. Nobody needs you any more. Nobody loves you anyhow. Come on, just swallow these pills...." She held a bottle of medication Frank had left behind. She took the cap off and poured the pills into her hand. She looked at them as though she were hypnotized, and felt their hard edges when she squeezed her fist shut. Almost in a trance, she got up and went into the bathroom, poured a glass of water, and downed all the pills in a couple of big gulps. Then she sat down again to wait. To wait for whoever would come for her.

The angel fought a desperate battle with the dark enemy.

Slowly, she came to her senses. She shook her head to try to clear the dizziness, prayed, "Lord help me, Oh, please, Lord, forgive me!" and reached for the telephone. The ambulance reached her in record time, and she felt them lift her to the stretcher before she lost consciousness. They rushed her to the hospital, where the emergency crew worked on her a long time, before they were able to bring her out of the shadow of death. They kept her in the hospital to treat her for complete exhaustion. She slept for days, but finally began to regain her strength and recover the will to live.

The angel thanked God too.

By the time Mamie returned, Jenny was nearly back to normal, only thinner. And now she was able to talk with Mamie and ask the questions she'd always wanted to ask. Like who her father really was, and how Mamie had ended up with Frank, and about Mamie's family, and Jimmy...most importantly, Jimmy. "Does he know anything about me?" she asked.

"Well, he does now.

"What have you told him about me?" Jenny demanded.

"That you were married to another man, not his father, and had another family to worry about, so you couldn't be bothered with him." Her mother stated it matter-of-factly, but she looked just a trace sheepish.

"Mother, how could you do that to me? How could you let Jimmy think I didn't love him? I missed him so bad...but you know very well there was nothing I could do about it!" Jenny's feelings were in turmoil and she was having a hard time maintaining her Christian love for her mother. The scene from long ago came flooding back to her memory as clearly as if it had just happened. Apparently Mamie remembered too, as she turned her back and changed the subject.

"Your father lived on the place next to ours when I was a child," she said, as though she were continuing a conversation instead of starting another one. Jenny was shaken even more now. She wanted to talk about Jimmy, but she wanted to know about her real father too. She decided to go along with Mamie for the moment.

"Tell me about him."

"He was smart and young and handsome...and I really loved him." She looked off into space and remembered, her brow wrinkling from the hurt, even after all the years that had passed. "He was Scotch and Irish descent. His father came over from India. He'd worked there for the British government in some kind of job. Came into America at New Orleans, and moved on up into Georgia. He had a lot of sisters, so you probably have a bunch of cousins in Georgia."

This was a whole new revelation to Jenny. She began to ask question after question, as for the first time, Mamie talked about her childhood and her family. This was the first time in years she'd allowed herself to think about her childhood home and how she'd had to leave it a long, long time ago. She remembered her mother and the terrible rejection she'd felt from her. And she began to tell Jenny about some of the things that had happened to her. Jenny was fascinated, trying to picture her mother young and vulnerable with such hard choices to make.

"You mean if it hadn't been for me, you never would have married Frank?" Jenny became defensive. "I don't want to be responsible for that mistake! You didn't have to do that for me. We'd have been better off without him!" Scenes from her childhood flashed before her, and she remembered again how lonely and unhappy she'd been...and she knew Mamie had been too.

"I never did marry him," her mother admitted. "Never divorced your father either." She almost let herself break down and cry, but then hardened her heart again, as she'd done for all the years with Frank. "I wanted to leave him many times, and tried to a few. He would have shot me. And by the time you left, I was used to the life and had nowhere else to go. Frank did love me in his own warped way, you know."

"Yeah, Mom, I guess I know that. But tell me more about your family." Jenny was anxious to learn about her grandparents and their lives, and Mamie allowed herself to remember and talk about them and her sisters, and the way she had been brought up. Jenny was wide-eyed over the description of their home. She couldn't believe her mother could leave such a place to exist the way they'd lived with Frank all those years. But she understood more about her mother now.

Before they realized it, the afternoon was gone and it was time to make dinner for her own demanding husband. But now Jenny had names and locations jotted down, and resolved to make a trip to Georgia as soon as she could, to find the family she'd always wanted and never had.

Mamie's cough was worse than ever, but she still smoked endlessly. Along with that, she seemed to lose interest in life since Frank was gone and she had no more responsibilities. Within a matter of weeks, she was bedridden, becoming more frail by the day, and soon after that, when Jenny went to her room with breakfast, she found only Mamie's empty body. Her soul had gone to Jesus.

Jenny grieved for her mother, even as she scrubbed every inch of her house, ridding it of the filthy tobacco stains and trying to get the clinging odor out of her once-beautiful white draperies, and putting things back in order. She had written a long letter to Jimmy, telling him her side of what had happened, and how much she loved and missed him. He came west for the funeral, and Jenny went to meet him at the airport. She arrived an hour early and paced the big waiting room, wanting him to be there, and afraid at the same time. What if he rejected her?

Finally, the flight arrived, and as the plane emptied, suddenly, there he was. She recognized him at once, as he was the image of Irving, his father. She waved her hand, "Jimmy!" she called.

He turned and came toward her. She hugged him, and he responded stiffly. He was small and thin and looked like his father, and he was quiet and reserved, like Irving, not at all like Jenny. They talked about Mamie and the funeral arrangements, and anything else but what was so important to both of them. His voice was soft and flat, but with an undercurrent of feeling.

She understood that feeling. She knew he was an emotional cripple, afraid to feel, and she realized living with Frank had made him that way. She could relate! And she decided it was a lot better than turning out to be like Frank!

The chance came on the third morning of his visit. The funeral was behind them, and Jimmy and Jenny were finishing breakfast. She found the right opening during their conversation and asked, "Did you ever get the straight story of why I left you?"

"Grandpa said you were a whore, and you left me because you had another family and didn't want me."

Her heart ached for him, as she pictured a small boy being told his mother didn't want him. She steadied her voice and asked, "And you didn't ever wonder whether that was really true?"

"Well, yeah, at first... but then, you never came back... "

"Will you listen to what really happened, Jimmy? Can I tell you about it from my side of the story?"

He nodded, and she began, "Well, it will take some background, I guess. Maybe you'll understand some of this, if they lived the same way we did when I was with them..." and she began to tell her son the story of how and why he was born, and how and why he was left with Mamie and Frank to be his parents. "I just want you to know how much I missed you, and how much I wept over you and wanted you... there just wasn't any way to do anything about it back in those days. And finally, it was just too late."

She struggled to keep her voice from breaking, as she told her poor little boy that he really wasn't thrown aside, and that his mother really did love him. "Did your father help you at all?" she asked. She had wondered about that through the years.

"He didn't want me to live with him either." Jimmy spoke flatly, remembering how he'd wanted to be with his father, and had been rejected there too. "We moved around a lot, so he didn't know where I was sometimes anyway."

Jenny nodded. And he didn't care, either, did he? And that's why I had to leave him. She understood so well, she could hardly trust herself to speak.

Jimmy stayed for a week, while Jenny tried to pour 22 years of love and longing into his lonely heart. She talked to him of her life, and of his life with Mamie and Frank. She tried to get him to stay in Lompoc, but he said he needed to go back east. So she took him back to the airport and hugged him goodbye. When he was gone, she wept for him again.

CHAPTER EIGHTEEN

1970

As the months and years passed, most of the close friends Jenny had at the little church moved on to other jobs in other cities, and new people took their places. She no longer had anyone to pray with her who understood and loved her. She did hear from Sarah on a regular basis. Sarah was still her dearest friend, but she and Buz were living in Texas now, and Jenny needed someone close.

She and Al studied for licenses, and then sold real estate for a local company, which pleased Jenny. She was always good at selling, and could hold her own and- then-some in the business world. Gradually, she got caught up in the glamour and excitement of earning big commissions and living in a more lavish style.

The angel watched and shook his head.

Karen, who was a gorgeous, headstrong young woman, left home for Los Angeles, planning to marry a young businessman. He had money and a lovely house, and influential friends, and Karen was in danger of forgetting the Lord.

Johnny had joined the Air Force like his brother, so now Jenny and Al were "empty-nesters."

They both decided to study for their Broker's licenses, so they could open their own real estate office; therefore they signed up for the required courses at the Community College. Jenny put her whole self into selling, and into keeping her home clean and attractive, into cooking good dishes for Al, and now into studying too.

Things went along pretty well until one day in January of 1970 when Jenny came home after a particularly stressful day with a buyer, and started to get dinner ready for herself and Al, who was due home shortly. She opened the refrigerator to get out the meat, and suddenly gasped in surprise and pain, as a giant hand grasped her heart and squeezed. "Oh Lord, help!" she pleaded as she crawled to the phone and dialed the emergency number.

This time she was in the hospital for a few days, then out a few days, then back again...Doctor Blake sat down on her bedside and rapped his knuckles on her serving table. "You aren't going to like this, I suppose," he began, then seeing her expression, he hurried on, "I'm afraid if you don't get out of Lompoc, and away from the wind and fog...and the stress...well...I give you maybe 18 months to live!"

"You're kidding!" Jenny's eyes were wide. She'd known she was sick, but..."Where should I go?"

"I don't know that, but get out of this valley, while you still can, OK? That's the best advice I can give you now. And try to avoid stress!"

Jenny prayed about the new problem, and the day after she was released from the hospital she went to church. It always felt good to be with the body of Christ, and maybe there'd be an answer for her somehow. As usual, she asked Al, "Want to go along?" This time to her surprise, he agreed.

They listened to a gripping sermon, and some powerful singing, and when the service was over, Al went forward to take Jesus as his Savior!

Jenny was thrilled, of course, after all those years of prayer for him, but she was in and out of the hospital several more times, and didn't have a chance to meditate on the situation. Al didn't seem to change very fast, except that it was easier to talk to him about things he wouldn't even discuss before. She finally had to tell him what Dr. Blake had said.

"You know, we wanted to start our own company," she told him, "and now that you have your Broker's license, why couldn't we move up to the Napa Valley area? I've always liked that area when we've driven through there, haven't you? The redwoods nearby are so majestic and the air is clear, and maybe it isn't so foggy there...do you think?"

Al was still in shock over what she'd just told him. "18 months! Well, I guess we'd better get serious about this, huh? I'll think about it...ya know, though, I'd been thinking maybe the boys'd like to go into business with us. A family real estate business...whadda ya say?"

"Oh Al, that sounds great! We could call it Brownell Real Estate Company, and that would fit all of us! I wonder if David and Johnny would both get their licenses?"

"This is a great time to get inta real estate...things are booming all over the country right now, and especially here in California! You know how much more we can get for our house now than we paid for it?"

"Oh, that's right!" Jenny was excited now, "Al, why don't we pray about it, and then put our sign out, and if we sell fast, for a lot more than we paid, we'll know we should do it...go ahead with the move and the business and all!"

So it happened that the Brownells moved north. Within a month their house was sold and they had bought a mobile home in the Napa Valley. Soon afterward, they rented an office, and the Brownell Real Estate Company was in business. They joined New Life Center as their church, and Jenny started singing in the choir, something she'd always wanted to do, but never thought she really could. She loved the choir. She loved joining her clear soprano with the other voices in harmony. There were over 100 members, and they gave concerts all around the area. It was a meaningful ministry, and Jenny put her whole heart into it, as usual.

Al went to church too. He'd go to the 8:00 a.m. service and Jenny would sing in the choir, then go sit with him during the sermon. After that service Al would go home and open the office. Jenny would sing for the next service, go home and cook dinner, and go back to church for choir practice at 4:00.

One Sunday the guest speaker was Brett Homer, from San Quentin. He gave an eloquent speech about the problems of reaching prisoners for Christ, and ended his talk with a plea for volunteers for the M-2 program Prison Ministries. Jenny was deeply moved, and longed to be able to be involved in that kind of work for the Lord, but she knew it was out of the question for her, so she contented herself with praying the Lord would send ministers to the prisons, and give them power and grace to reach those desperately needy hearts.

Jenny was living one of her dreams with the choir ministry, and now Al wanted to live one of his. He bought motorcycles for each of them! "Besides, we can save a lot on gasoline" he told her. Jenny called on some of her old talents from the circus, put on her new leather jacket and gamely rode with him all over California. She found she enjoyed it. She liked the incredulous looks she got when she took her helmet off and people saw she was a woman in her 50s.

They made a trip down state to visit Karen, and on the way back, tired and hungry, they pulled into a gas station to fill up. Jenny swung her leg off the bike and instead of stepping on solid cement, she hit the curb, fell, and landed in a sea of pain, the heavy bike on top of her. It was her right arm again. This time it was so mangled they didn't think they'd be able to save it. She went through 4 operations over a few months, and lost much of the use of her arm. It was all a terrible trial, a major problem, and it was too much for Al. He began to drink again.

He tried to hide it from Jenny at first, but after all the years she'd lived with his drunkenness, she knew the signs well. He hid liquor in his golf bag, in the toilet tank, at his office, everywhere. He quit going to church, and when Jenny got home after the second service on Sunday, he'd be drunk already, and mean. Then the beatings began again. It got worse and worse, and over the course of four years of living in hell with her arm, she also lived with a nagging fear that if he didn't change, she might end up killing him. The church still insisted she had to stay with Al as long as he would stay with her. But when he came at her with his fist or his foot, she hated him, and pray as she might, she could no longer work up any love or respect for her husband.

She prayed God to forgive her, "Please, Lord, I know he's your child, and I know it's wrong how I feel. Please let me be what you want me to be. Please give me love for him."

But then on top of the abuse, she discovered he was making love to another woman. Not just his usual philandering, but one special woman. It was Billie Jean, a voluptuous blonde who ran the clubhouse with her husband Bernie. Every night Al went to the clubhouse to play pool. He didn't invite Jenny, but she got tired and bored with staying home alone, so she began to go there too. They had a really nice big organ, and she'd always wanted to be able to play an instrument well, so she'd go there and play the organ. Or try as well as she could with her injured arm. Only when she turned around, Al would be gone again, and she'd find him at home. But if she stayed at home, he didn't come in until time to fall into bed. He simply didn't want to be around Jenny, and it was increasingly obvious to her. And it hurt. Then Bernie died, and Al hovered around Billie like a father.

Jenny knew Al wanted the job of running the park with Billie Jean, but the park policy was to hire only a married couple. She figured probably Al's main motive was to save the rent money. But she could always find him there at the clubhouse with Billie Jean whenever he wasn't at the office working. And Billie Jean often looked at Jenny knowingly and smiled a wicked little smile.

Jenny took her troubles to her pastor. He seemed to care about what she told him. "I know she planned for me to see him coming out of her mobile home! They're having an affair, and she wants me to know it so she can have him! I've stood by him all these years, like the church said I should, but now he's making it impossible to stay there!"

The pastor put his hand on her shoulder and prayed for strength and love for her. She felt he didn't understand at all, and when later that month the trouble broke at church, she was outraged at him. It turned out the pastor had been playing around with some girls in the ministerial school. So he was the same kind of cheating skunk Al was! There was a big scandal, and ultimately the church and the choir fell apart, giving Satan a temporary victory, but by that time Jenny was gone.

Jenny felt the same rejection and humiliation she'd felt as a child and for most of her life. She prayed and wept before the Lord daily, until one day she seemed to receive an answer from Him. It was a strong impression to "Put your feet into the water...give him an ultimatum and see what happens."

That scared her even more! "What will I do if he takes me up on it, Lord? How will I live?" She had $90 a month from Social Security, and half of Al's pension was only $500 a month. "How can I go from several thousand dollars a month to only $600 and live?" Rent was very high in California...how could she do it?

But peace of mind was worth more than money, and she knew she could trust the Lord. So the next day on her way home from the hospital she decided, "OK, Lord, please be with me, because tonight is the night I'll do it."

She quietly served Al his dinner as usual, and then as he was getting ready to leave, she spoke up. "Al, do you think we could talk awhile? I need to talk to you."

He rolled his eyes, but sat down again beside the table and waited.

"Al, I can't stand your drinking any more. I can't take it when you're drunk. And Al, I know how you feel about Billie Jean! I can't take your rejection mentally, and I can't stand any more physical abuse. Can we get some counseling or something?"

"Are you crazy? You must be! No! I ain't about to see any fricking counselor!"

Jenny took a deep breath. OK here it comes then. "Well, then I have to file for separation, Al. No divorce, I don't believe in divorce, but I can't live with you any longer. I know you don't love me, and I don't love you any more either. Let's go our separate ways awhile and see." He opened his mouth to make some sort of retort, but she hurried to add, " I'll want the mobile home and the furniture, one of the cars, and some money."

Al looked at her with complete disdain, got up out of his chair and left for the clubhouse without even answering.

Jenny sat at the table in a daze. So it would really happen. "Lord, please guide me and take care of me," she prayed. "Please give me your wisdom and love. I need you, Lord." She began to cry softly, and as she washed the dishes and picked up, she alternately wept and smiled.

The next day she filed for a separation. Three days later Al moved out. Jenny was a bundle of nerves the night he left. She cooked dinner for Al and Joe, a friend of his who helped him move, hardly aware of what she was doing. Panic grabbed at her and tried to shake her faith. It reminded her of all the questions...what would she do? How could she live? She was 60 years old, and had no job and only $600.00 a month to live on. And rent alone was $170! Her car was old, and would soon need replacing.

She shoved plates of fried meat and potatoes in front of the men, then watched them eat, crying in spite of herself, while Al sat laughing at her as he ate. Then he left, and she knew he went to be with Billie Jean. She knelt and prayed, while panic fled and calm crept into her heart. It was time to get on with her life. Anything had to be better than what she'd been going through! She prayed, "Lord please don't let me hate Al...please don't let me end up a bitter old woman because of him. Be with me, please Lord..."

Jenny gave Al a bedroom set, the maple dining room set, and some living room furniture, as well as pots and pans and all his own stuff. He took the Buick, and left her with the older Toyota, and he took the largest bank account, leaving her with only four thousand dollars cash. She resolved to make the best of the situation with God's help. "I'll pack the rest of your things, and you can pick them up on Saturday," she told him when he stopped to get some tools he'd left.

He nodded "I'll be here after dinner. Don't try to pull anything on me!"

Packing went slowly, with lots of reminiscences over the various items. Jenny pitched a lot of stuff, and carefully wrapped the things that carried value for their good memories. It took a while to clean out the desk and file cabinet. She read every paper, before deciding which stack it belonged in. Old bills, old letters, years worth of correspondence. She opened another envelope. Why did we keep all this stuff?

She was almost at the back of the next-to-the-bottom drawer. She stopped and made a cup of tea, which she sipped quietly for a few moments. Oh well, I'd better finish this mess today so I can get at the kitchen tomorrow. She reached for the next hanging file. It held a packet of envelopes. I wonder what this stuff is…

She opened the top one and read: "Dear Al, thought I'd better let you know the situation here. Dad is real bad now, and the doctor says he doesn't have long. No need to come home, he wouldn't know you anyway. I'll handle the cremation, and Bessie says we shouldn't have any ceremony. He never went to church or anything. I'll let you know when it happens though." And it was signed Herb.

Funny he never mentioned to me that his dad was dying! She picked up the next letter.

"Dear Al, Just thought you'd like to know Dad's going to leave each of us one of his bank accounts. They're almost equal size, about twenty thousand each. You might want to do something to keep your wife out of the picture if you're planning to dump her anyway, like you said. It'll happen real soon now, so maybe you better speed up the plan. I'll keep you posted. Herb."

She put the letter back into its envelope and jammed it back into the file. So that's it! Al was trying to figure out how he could hide the money so I wouldn't get any of it. He obviously would have left me, if I hadn't left him first!

She struggled with that knowledge, but being honest with herself, she knew that in the last few years money had become more important to Al than anything else… including either herself or Billie Jean! She read the other letter, then shoved the whole file into a box with her important papers, just in case she needed them for evidence later. "Thank you, Lord! Oh, thank you for letting me know it was time to get out! Praise your Holy name, Jesus!" She went on praising God, while she lost even more feeling for Al. It was as though the past years had been a vast wasteland.

The angel hovered over her, nudging her mind.

Jenny fidgeted as she worked. There was a thought nagging at her somewhere… deep in the back of her brain. She was uneasy, but not sure why. She cleaned out the kitchen cupboards, putting all of Al's stuff in boxes, separating their belongings, as she was separating their lives. She stumbled as she started to kneel in front of the sink, and almost fell, but caught herself by grabbing the edge of the door. Something dropped from a narrow board that braced the side of the cupboard. Suddenly, the thought surfaced, even as she picked up the little packet. He won't let me go like this… He's going to try to kill me! He'd have to pay me alimony if I divorce him, and he'll never do that without a fight! Oh, Lord! What should I do?

Panic rose up inside her in a wave. She stood grasping the edge of the sink so hard her knuckles were white. I can't stay here tonight! He'll be here to get his stuff, and that's when he'll try to do it!

She straightened her back, raised her chin and took a deep breath. The Lord was with her, He had warned her, and He would help her now. She talked to the Lord as she began to work again, tossing things into boxes quickly, and sealing the full ones. The panic subsided, replaced by a strange calm... it was almost as though she were an observer, watching someone else go through the motions of packing up a lifetime. Carefully, she put the little packet back on the board it had fallen from. Better not to tip him off that she knew. She piled his things on the back steps, then locked and bolted the door.

She went to the bedroom and swiftly packed her suitcase and some personal things and put them in the Toyota. Then she locked the front door behind her, got into her car and drove away. When safely out of sight of the coach, she circled around and came back down the alley. She pulled in behind a neighbor's storage shed, where nobody would notice her. Then she watched.

It seemed a very long time, but finally she saw him. He was on foot. That alone was odd, but the way he kept looking around was even stranger. He went straight to the back door, and glanced at all the boxes stacked there. He tried the door, and then knocked loudly. When he got no response he kicked the door angrily, then stomped around to the other side of the coach and tried the front door. Then he got out his key and went inside. She could see him looking around for her. Searching the place. His shadow moved to the kitchen, and disappeared as he bent under the sink.

She held her breath. I'm so glad I left it there! Maybe he won't think I know what he's up to... Suddenly she realized why he hadn't driven. He'd thought he'd take her car... probably with her in it! She trembled at the thought. He's gone absolutely crazy! He's really sold out to Satan! Oh, Thank you Lord for letting me know in time! She watched as he finally left the house, locking the door behind him. Shakily she started the car and drove toward town. And the pastor said I had to stay with Al! Lord, what would have happened if I'd listened to him!

The angel beside her nodded.

She had even more trust in the Lord, who was watching over her through something the church, and some well-meaning Christian friends felt was sin!

She went back home in the morning, and finished packing hurriedly.

The angel watched her work, and kept Al away.

CHAPTER NINETEEN

July, 1978

Jenny was devastated over Al's betrayal, and scared about the future, but as always, she "hitched up her petticoats" and did what had to be done. She'd always been a survivor, and she'd live through this too. She still received the Lompoc newspaper, and one evening while she was sitting at the table in her small rented room reading it, she noticed a letter to the editor. "I'm all alone, from back east, and there's nobody to visit or call me," the writer said. "If anybody out there would like to write to a lonely man who needs a friend, I'll be real happy to write back. I'm a good person, not dangerous. I made a mistake, and I'm paying for it, but I need somebody to talk to." It was written by a prisoner at the Lompoc F.C.I.

She cut the item out and put in on her table. It lay there for a couple of weeks, while she was occupied with her own troubles. But she had wanted to be involved with prison ministries ever since she first heard about it, and writing to lonesome inmates was part of the job. So one evening she picked up her pen and started a letter. It was difficult to write with her injured arm, but she managed.

She wrote to the man, whose name was Terry Singer. "I'm no doubt old enough to be your mother, but I've been around a lot...traveled the world some, and maybe we'll have some things to talk about." She told him about being a Christian, and how she loved to sing in the choir, and she said she'd be glad to write to him if he wanted.

Only 5 days later, she received an answer. He was so excited to hear from her. He'd love to get to know her. He was terribly lonesome. His spelling was terrible, and she chuckled over his letter. But she answered it, and in the flurry of letters that followed between them, she began to get to know Terry. He asked if he could call her and talk. She said OK, and from then on they talked often. She enjoyed his soft voice, and his slightly southern accent. He sent her his picture. He was 29 years old, and nice looking. He also looked nice.

Jenny got caught up in an enticing and exciting game with him, never dreaming she'd ever see the man. But she stood before her mirror with a more critical eye than usual. Her figure was still trim except for a little tummy bulge. She'd better start to exercise! Her face had some wrinkles...no wonder, with what she'd been through! Her graying hair, though...she'd neglected herself lately. She could do something about that!

She walked out of Tina's Salon two days later, with a soft blonde coif, looking and feeling ten years younger. "I should've done this years ago! (Well, I did, as a matter of fact, but gave it up a few years back.) Makes me feel so much better!" she told her son Johnny.

"Yeah, Mom, you look great!" he agreed. "Wait'll Dad sees you now!"

"Oh well, Johnny, that's over with, and he's on to greener pastures. I did this for myself...wanted to look younger. I'm not so old, you know...at least not inside." She grinned at the expression on his face. "Well, what do you know? You're still just a kid!"

She sobered, looking over at her handsome son. "John, I've decided to move away from here. I don't like being where I have to see Al and Billie Jean all the time. It's time I found a new life in a new place."

He was surprised. The mother he knew had stayed and suffered loyally for as long as he could remember. Surely she couldn't just go off somewhere on her own now, at this age! "Where'll you go, Mom? What'll you do? You can't just take off on your own! Who'll take care of you?"

"I can still take care of myself, Johnny, thank you very much." She realized he was simply concerned because he loved her, and softened her tone. "I've been looking at ads for this new Mobile home park they're building down near San Diego. It looks really nice, and I think I'd like it there." She shook her head and grinned at him. "Well, actually, it's in San Marcos. The climate down there is great, and I can find another church to get involved in. I only need to sell this home, and I need to get as much for it as I possibly can. I've been praying about it, and this feels right."

"But, you haven't even seen that place, have you?"

"No, but I guess that's not too hard to change, is it?" She reached for the ad and handed it to him. "I want to get away from here anyway, so I'll go look at it, and if I still feel this way, I know God will help me sell this home for enough to buy one there and have a little left over." They sat and visited and planned, and Jenny felt closer to her son than she had in a long time.

She left the next week, driving the old Toyota at a leisurely pace down the coast on highway 1. The ocean sparkled under a bright sun, and around every curve was a scene more beautiful than the last, and Jenny praised the Lord often for his wonderful creation. She felt peaceful inside for the first time in a long while... a little lonely, but she knew Jesus was there with her. She liked to pretend he was sitting in the passenger seat beside her, and she sometimes talked to him as she drove. It helped pass the time and also helped her sort out her feelings,

Jenny liked the park when she saw it. It wasn't finished yet, but the location was great, and the plans were excellent. She signed on for a space and went home to sell her place back up north. The new park was scheduled to open on September 15th, and Jenny's separation would be final on August 31st.

She put her home on the market and sold it for $31,500. Johnny told her Al nearly fainted when he found out what she'd gotten for it, as they had only paid

$12,500. Jenny got a perverse satisfaction out of that, as she knew Al had thought he really got the best of her, and kept her from sharing his inheritance too. Now God had given her almost as much herself and Al couldn't share in that.

"I guess this is what the Lord wants me to do, John. He's certainly blessed me in this deal, hasn't he?"

"Sure seems like it...you sure you really want to move so far away from us?"

"Well, I expect you to come visit me sometimes! It's warm there, and close to the beach...a great place to vacation, you know." They both laughed, and Johnny agreed to move her things when she was ready.

A few days before she was scheduled to leave for her new home, she received a notice from the Prison Ministries. There would be a seminar in San Marcos at Father Bredesan's church. "Oh Lord, this is great!" she said, "that's just down the road from where I'm moving! You certainly work in wonderful ways, Father!" she rejoiced.

The mobile home she bought in her new area was bigger and nicer than the one she had just sold. She had it set up on her lot in the new park, and waited for the opening of the park so she could move in. Johnny drove her things down to San Marcos in a rented van on October 4th, but when they arrived, they discovered the park still had not been cleared for occupancy. She could move her furniture in, but she couldn't stay there yet herself.

They stood beside the new coach in the bright California sunshine. Workers were busy landscaping nearby. A gentle breeze blew in from the ocean. She breathed deeply of the warm, fragrant air, and told Johnny, "It's OK, honey, I'll be fine. I'll just have to stay in a motel for a couple of weeks, I guess." She sent him on his way back north, then stopped in at a small restaurant for a sandwich and coffee, while she took time to think and pray and take stock of her situation. She had only a few thousand dollars. She would need to landscape, and that would be costly. What to do?"

Then she thought of Terry. Might as well go back up to Lompoc and visit him a few days. Gosh, I never thought I'd ever meet him. Wonder how he'll take it when he sees I'm so old! Guess it's as good a time as any to find out!

She hadn't told him exactly how old she was, only that he'd be sad and upset when he met her. "But I'll still be your friend if you want me to." The whole thing was silly anyhow. Terry was going to be 30 in October, and Jenny had just turned 63! "I'll teach you about Jesus, Terry. He'll be the best friend you'll ever have," she had told him on the phone.

The day she arrived at the prison was a holiday weekend, so there were more visitors than usual. She wore a navy skirt, white blouse, and a soft pale blue sweater, which brought out the color in her eyes. Her short blond hair was brushed back on the sides, with a soft bang on her forehead. She thought she looked nice, but even so, her stomach tightened as her footsteps resounded on the hard tile. The familiar corridor seemed endless, then she waited forever in a crowded visiting room, her palms sweating. She looked up as the guard appeared, and then, there he was! She liked him on sight. He was slim and medium height, with short red-brown hair, and his smile lit up his whole face.

She threw out her hands, "Well, here I am, just like I promised. All 63 old-lady years of me!"

"And you're just beautiful!" He spoke in his soft southern accent that Jenny found so attractive, and he sounded like he really meant it. "I'm just so glad to see you after all these months of letters and phone calls." He looked deep into her eyes. "You'll never know how much it's meant to me to have you for a friend. And you know I love you, don't you?"

Jenny was flustered. He not only wasn't put off by her age, he even seemed attracted by it! They sat together and had a good talk, and she promised to come back the next visiting day.

But the second time she went through the doors of Lompoc Federal Correctional Institution was a whole different ball game. She discovered that the phone calls between her and Terry had been monitored and reported. The Lieutenant over Terry was a big, rough man who had once worked under Al, when Al had been in charge of the civil engineers at Vandenberg Air Force Base. After he retired from engineering, he got a job as a guard. Don Harper hated Al; therefore he hated Jenny too. He had just been waiting for her to visit Terry. Somehow he had missed her the time before. He would make up for that today.

"Hold on there, MRS Brownell!" he ordered in a loud, harsh tone. Everyone looked at her. He motioned to the female guard standing by the door, "Strip search!" She started toward Jenny.

"What?" she yelled. "You don't touch me, sister!" she warned, as the woman reached for her arm.

"No strip search, no visiting the prison!" Lt. Harper insisted. Several other visitors passed on through the room and into the long institutional-green hallway. "How come they didn't have to be searched," she asked?

"Never mind them. It's you we're dealing with here, and I just told you how it'll have to be! We know all about you and your precious Terry. Can't take a chance you'll try to break him out so you can run off with him and be his 'little love rose' " he sneered.

Jenny turned red with anger and embarrassment. She took a deep breath and turned on her heel. Obviously he knew all about her conversations with Terry, and intended to humiliate her completely. She left the prison, fuming. "Lord, how can they treat people that way? How can anyone let them do that? No wonder nobody visits these men!"

The more she thought about the situation, the more she realized she was the only one picked out for harassment. And she realized why, as she recalled how Al had treated the men under his command. She phoned the prison and asked for

Lt. Harper, and when she reached him, she cut loose at him. "I've visited that prison many times over the years, and I know when I'm being harassed!" she ranted."I know what you're trying to do, and you can't take it out on me just because you hate Al. I'll go straight to the warden and tell him all about it if you don't let me in to see Terry!"

Harper backed down reluctantly, and Jenny visited Terry the next day, and every day after that for two weeks, without further harassment. She got to know him better as he told her his whole life story. She couldn't believe what she heard! Oh, he deserved to be in prison, all right, but he had already been in for 4 years. His wife divorced him, so he'd lost her and his kids. He was from Appalachia...a Kentucky "hillbilly" as he put it.

"Daddy was a coal miner, and we had a bunch of kids in the family. I was the 6th kid, the 4th boy, and Daddy said I wasn't his, 'cause I had red hair." He gave her an embarrassed grin, then continued."After me there was another girl, Freida, and then Billy, and he had red hair too! But none of the other kids would play with me or talk to me because Daddy didn't like me. He beat me up all the time. It was really hard when I had to go to school, because I didn't know how to talk yet."

He went on telling about his childhood, as she wept a few quiet tears over him, she felt so bad for the poor lonely boy he had been.

"Then Daddy died, and Mama went out to Montana to stay with my brothers out there. And I met Lucy. She was from a big family in Ohio...ten kids. They all stuck together, but I didn't realize how much until I was married into the family. Then I found out they were a bank robbery gang! Well, I stayed out of that mess for a long time, while I had a job. I moved Lucy and the kids...two little redheaded girls. They're sweethearts." Terry paused and wiped his eyes.

"We moved to Montana where Mama and my brothers are. She didn't like it there. Missed her family. You know, they'd hung out in each other's houses every weekend, partyin' and drinkin' and such. Well, one day I came home from work and she was gone with the kids...just picked up and went back to Ohio. I went to Dayton and brought 'em home, but after a few weeks she did it again!" He looked at Jenny to see if she was sympathizing. She was, so he went on.

"Well, I got time off from my job one more time, and went back to Ohio to get my family again. But when I got there, little Joanie was sick. Doctor said it was rheumatic fever and she couldn't be moved. So I stayed there - and got fired from my job, of course. Didn't have enough money left to go back to Montana, so we had to stay in Ohio. Well, Lucy's sister Joan was married to a guy in Ohio state prison. He was a real gangster, and when he got out of prison he got all of Lucy's family organized into the bank robbery gang. Over time, they robbed about 40 banks in Indiana and Ohio."

He rubbed his hand over his chin. "I took a job at my brother-in-law's gas station. Turned out, he was washing all the money from the robberies through his business. He never did go to prison...came out of the mess in great shape. He's a rich man today! Apartment buildings and stuff like that." Terry grinned ruefully at Jenny, his eyes asking her for understanding.

"So what happened with you then?"

"Guess I'm awful stupid, but they finally convinced me to join the gang. By that time, though, they were really hot, and the FBI had infiltrated the gang. So my first time out we got caught. We were set up and handed right over to the FBI. Their agent was driving our get-away truck! Well, in the confusion of that robbery, somebody shot a bank guard! That made this one really serious." He looked her straight in the eyes. "I didn't do it," he said quietly. "But I saw who did. I was just sick about the whole mess. The guy had little kids and a pretty wife."

She believed him, and nodded. "What happened to the guy who did shoot?"

"He's in prison in Ohio. But the feds convinced me I owed it to the dead man's family to testify so he'd go to prison. They said if I'd turn state's evidence, they'd give me clemency and put me in the witness protection program for my safety. So I witnessed against Roy, and a couple of the others, but some of the gang lied, and said I was more involved. It was a rotten thing to do! But I guess I should've kept quiet."

He sighed and looked at the floor. "Didn't get no clemency. Got a 75 year sentence! But they sent me out here to California instead of putting me in with them in Ohio, and I guess this is as close to a witness protection program as I'll get."

"75 years! I can't believe it! They let horrible rapists and murderers out in 7 and 10 years these days!"

Jenny was shaken over Terry's story. Later on she did some checking through the library, and discovered what he'd told her was true. All the old newspaper clippings she could dig up verified what he said.

When she left Terry, she went over to see her friend Lilly Horner. Lilly was going to Oak to see her parents for a couple of weeks, and asked Jenny to house-sit while she was gone. That would save 2 weeks of motel bills so Jenny agreed. But first she went to San Marcos to get some more clothes and see how things were going there. She found she still couldn't move in, so settled into Lilly's house and visited Terry every day, while she pondered over his situation. She prayed, and she went to the library to read and study the law. She couldn't believe they could treat a man so unjustly. Lilly came back, and Jenny stayed on for a week or so, then finally knew it was time to leave, and reluctantly spent the money to rent a tiny apartment in Lompoc.

She drove down to San Marcos and got her clothes and TV set, letting the scenery soothe her mind and heart, and listening to the radio. "Some day he'll come along, the man I love... and he'll be big and strong, the man I love"... she sang along with Jo Stafford. All too soon she was back in Lompoc, where she settled in and prepared to go on with a "normal" life again.

Jenny attended the seminar at San Marcos, and learned a lot of useful information about prison ministry. She was full of zeal and new purpose when the meeting ended. And shortly after that she began to look into getting her ordination papers. They said she needed them so she would be allowed into the prison system without a lot of hassle.

She still wasn't able to move into her mobile home, as the park had a serious drainage problem and the health department wouldn't let them open. So Jenny's beautiful new home just stood empty, and Jenny was spending a lot more money than she could afford. She put up with the situation until December. She didn't hear from any of her family up north. Karen had gone overseas following a divorce she didn't want, and was occupied in her own problems.

When she went down to the mobile home park one day in December, Jenny discovered someone had stolen the new refrigerator and her sewing machine. They had completely ripped off some of the other homes, so Jenny knew she was lucky to get off that easy. But now she was faced with another decision. A new refrigerator would cost a lot, and she no longer had enough money to do the landscaping. Reluctantly, she gave up on the idea of living in her beautiful new home. She put it on the market, and left for Lompoc again.

She was driving along the coast, enjoying an occasional glimpse of surf pounding in, and sun shining on the white foam of breaking waves, when the transmission fell out of her car. "Oh no, Lord! Now what do I do?" She stood on the side of the busy freeway, looking sadly at the beat-up Toyota, and when a passing trucker stopped to help, she hitched a ride back to Lompoc. She had to have a car, so she was forced to borrow money against the home to pay for one.

By then, she had concluded that the Lord had only used the mobile home purchase as a way to save her investment money. The park's drainage wasn't approved until the following May. Jenny's rent didn't start until the park opened, and she had a month's rent paid on the space, but by June she was paying rent in 2 places. "Lord, If you don't do something pretty soon, I'll be out on the streets," she told him. Her prayers were always the direct to the point kind. She never had been the kind to indulge in a lot of religious palaver, but was always honest before him.

Stress was building up again, and she knew it was bad for her heart, along with the climate in the Lompoc Valley. There was nothing she could do but keep trusting the Lord, and praying. The home finally sold in November, for $2000 more than she'd paid for it! She stashed the money in the bank and settled in at Lompoc once more, only in a nicer apartment. Somehow, she couldn't bring herself to go back to the little chapel she'd helped to establish there. She 'knew' her friends there wouldn't understand all the things that had happened in her life. She judged herself as she thought they would judge her. Strangely, she was happy in the Lord and her new freedom, while at the same time, she felt guilty for not staying with Al, even though she knew she couldn't have stayed. She knew he'd have left her for Billie Jean, and in some dark moments, she even let herself remember how he would have hastened her demise. Even so, the years of indoctrination in wifely guilt dogged her.

Back up north, Al and his love, Billie Jean, spent much of their time drinking heavily together. Shortly before Christmas, they went to a party where the liquor flowed freely. "Al, honey, maybe we shouldn't drive?" Billie Jean suggested, as they wove their unsteady way toward the car.

"I'm perfeckly able to drive, an I'll get us home jus fine," Al assured her. He eased his brand new Cadillac out of its space, the radio blaring "Jingle Bell Rock," and headed for the exit from the parking lot. Another car steered for the exit from the other row. "Why that S.O.B....thinks he can beat me out, eh? " Al snarled, and stepped on the gas. They beat the other car to the exit all right, and shot out across the highway and with a horrible clanging crash, stopped abruptly against a telephone pole. The innocent pole cracked in two and swung from its wires over the disaster below. Al hung halfway out the windshield, his face torn and bleeding. Billie sat in the car, her broken neck at an odd angle, unconscious. The radio kept on spilling loud 'Christmas' music into the air.

The rescue squad moved Billie carefully and she survived. She spent 5 months in a brace and in traction, with one foot crippled beyond use. Al couldn't stand his guilt when he looked at her nor his own disfigured face when he looked in a mirror. He'd been so handsome all his life, and now his face was a mess. He drank more and more to blot out his problems, until one night he collapsed at the door of the clubhouse, with blood trickling out his mouth.

"You'll have to stop drinking, Mr. Brownell, or you'll soon be dead!" the emergency doctor told him. "I second that all the way," his own doctor agreed, on his way into the room. "You have several holes in your stomach. This is pretty serious, you know. You'll have to change your diet completely, and stop drinking entirely, or you'll end up in the morgue. Now here's what I want you to do...." and he handed Al a diet sheet and strict instructions about avoiding alcohol and stress.

For a few days, Al obeyed the doctors, but then he got drunk again. This time he nearly died. At last, Billie Jean was released from the hospital, and the two of them tried together to stop drinking. It wasn't easy, since their whole relationship was based around the bottle.

Back in Lompoc, Jenny became educated about the prison system, received her ordination papers through the church there. She learned about prisoners and their families...and about Terry. She grew fonder of Terry every day. Her nerves were relaxing at last, and she enjoyed her freedom, after so many years of fear and trouble with Al. It was almost as if she'd gotten out of prison herself!

Jenny had found a place for herself at the Foundations Church in Lompoc. They accepted her and used her gifts as a teacher. In the four years she was there, the adult Sunday school class doubled in size. She was constantly busy between the church and the prison, and the Lord used her to lead souls to Him. She was as happy as she had ever been. The Lord provided for her needs, and she was getting over the loss of her family and home and her old circle of friends. But she was learning a lot about some very unsavory people.

The prison at Lompoc was fertile ground for sowing seeds, and Jenny became an accomplished sower and reaper. She was able to reach some of the hardest men for the Lord, because of her background from years in the circus and at the museum. She wasn't put off by rough talk, and could speak in terms the men understood. A few of them came to know Jesus as their Savior because of her ministry. Most of the others respected her, and at least listened when she talked to them.

She worked hard on Terry's case, and within a year after she met him, Jenny had managed to get one 12-year sentence dropped. He had two other sentences of 6 to 25 years, and she was able to get them changed from consecutive to concurrent so there was one 6 to 25 year sentence.

"You're a real wonder-worker, Jen! I can't believe the Lord really sent you here to help me! What an answer to my prayers!" Terry reached over and took her hand. "I love you, you know," he told her again, with a gleam in his eye.

"And I love you, too. You're like another son to me." She ignored his crushed look and reached for the Bible. "Did you study all of that last chapter of Romans?"

He nodded and opened his Bible, and together they studied God's word, Jenny pointing out the meanings and reasons for different verses, and helping him learn to read with more understanding at the same time. His education had been sadly lacking. He'd left school after the 6th grade to help support the family. But he was bright and interested, and he learned fast. He had an open, honest heart and loved Jesus with all his being, and before long his education was a real challenge to Jenny. He studied when she was away and saved up questions and kept her on her toes to answer them. It was very good for both student and teacher.

Jenny loved Terry's sweet spirit and quiet ways, in such contrast to most of the inmates. If ever there were anyone who didn't seem to belong in prison, it was Terry Singer. She taught him faithfully, and brought them both closer to the Lord.

The angel sat with them and smiled.

CHAPTER TWENTY

1982

Then trouble hit again. God had kept him safe so far, but on that particular dark morning, when Terry saw the new inmates filing in, he nearly panicked.

He froze momentarily, thinking, *Oh no, it can't be him! I don't believe this, Lord...what is he doing here?*

Terry turned his face away and moved half behind his cellmate to keep from being seen. As soon as he could, he got to the phone and called Jenny.

"I've got a big problem, Jen! Vern, my brother-in-law just came in with the new prisoners!"

"Oh no! What's he doing there? Oh Terry, this is terrible! Did he see you?"

"No, I don't think so, but it's only a matter of time before he does, and then I'm in for it. He'll tell everybody I'm a snitch, and my life won't be worth a nickel in here!"

"OK, Terry, let's pray, and then I'll get right to work and see what we can do about this." She dropped to her knees with the phone still at her ear. "Dear Lord, please keep Terry invisible from Vern. Please protect him and get him out of there and away from this danger. Thank you Father that we know You care and will help us."

Jenny got on the phone immediately, calling everyone she could think of to call, telling them of the danger Terry was in. She reached Governor Brown of California and told him the situation. Brown called the warden, and within an incredibly short time, Terry was on his way to a state prison in Montana.

He left Lompoc in the back of a state police cruiser, and they headed south for Los Angeles. It was a beautiful drive along the California coast and through the mountains, and Terry hadn't seen the Pacific Ocean before, so he relaxed and enjoyed the drive. It was a long time since he'd been able to relax or really enjoy anything. It felt good. It almost felt free! But then they arrived at the city and made their way through unbelievable traffic to the county jail, where he was shoved into a cage with a bunch of other men, mostly drunks or addicts.

"You'll spend the night here, and we'll catch a plane for Montana tomorrow." The cop gave him a mock salute and left.

"Yeah...thanks." Terry responded.

The turmoil around him was disrupting, and after his quiet ride through the beautiful countryside, he was more disturbed than usual by the rudeness and swearing, the shoving and blaming and filthy talk going on around him.

"OK, everybody line up!" A red-faced young cop yelled at them. They all shuffled into a line, and Terry was pushed into the line with the rest of the men.

"Quiet!" the cop yelled. Nobody listened, and if anything they got even louder. "I said quiet!" the cop called again.

"Yeah, guys, get quiet for pete's sake!" Terry repeated.

Kwop! The blow to the side of his face knocked him down. The cop yelled for backup as he grabbed Terry's hands and snapped handcuffs on him, then yanked him upright and dragged him to a cell.

"This'll teach ya not to make fun of a police officer!" He gave Terry a hard shove into the tiny room, knocking him off balance against the wall and bashing his head. He landed on the floor, where he lay in agony, curled into the fetal position with his head covered by his arms, while several officers kicked him in the ribs and hips and struck him with clubs and fists. It was his worst nightmare come true, as 60 derelicts watched the beating, yelling and cheering and cursing.

Suddenly the desk sergeant showed up. "Hey! What the hell are you doing? Cut it out!" He grabbed the nearest cop and pulled him away. "This guy's a federal transfer. He's just here overnight! Leave him alone for crying out loud! Oh geez...there's gonna be trouble over this!"

Swearing profusely, they picked Terry up and carried him into another room where they left him alone, while the cops involved in the beating suddenly disappeared. He lay alone on a cot, his face and body bloody and battered. He ached everywhere. When he eventually came to himself enough to realize there was a phone in the room, he called Jenny and told her what happened.

"They what? Oh, Terry!" she gasped. "I wish I were there right now to help you! Will you be OK? Listen, I'm gonna call Washington and get the Feds on this! You really didn't do anything wrong now, did you?"

He just groaned a terrible wounded groan, and put the phone down, and arranged his aching body carefully on the cot once more.

Jenny made several phone calls and threatened a few people, and in a very short time two FBI men showed up at the county jail and made life miserable for the cops on duty.

"You were really lucky the sergeant got there when he did," one agent told Terry. "You'd probably have been the latest statistic from here by morning. These goons have a bad habit of 'just happening' to beat people to death."

"Yeah," the other Fed agreed, "this is one of the worst places in the country for brutality. We're always having to investigate deaths here."

"Well, thanks a lot for showing up," Terry said carefully, out the side of his mouth that could move without too much pain.

They transferred him to the hospital to heal up before sending him on to Montana, so it was a couple of weeks later before he entered his new "home" at Deer Lodge.

The cell door closed behind him, the guard walked away, keys clanking, and Terry stood a moment to take in his situation.

"Get away from the door, you're in my light!" The voice came from the bottom bunk. Terry moved further into the small space. A muscular arm reached out toward him, then grabbed onto the edge of the bed above, and pulled his new cellmate out of the bunk. "OK," he snarled, "there's rules here! First, ya don't touch any of my stuff! Ya don't sing and ya don't snore! I hate it when guys snore!" The scraggly beard somehow didn't fit the delicate Latin features. He scratched it. "Name's Tony Manici." He glared at Terry.

"Terry Singer." Terry swung his stuff up on the top bunk and asked, "How long you in for?"

"Life. You?"

"Twenty five years." He almost said he'd already done some of it, but stopped in time.

Tony regarded him with beady dark eyes. "Whadja do?"

"Robbed a bank." He didn't elaborate. "You?"

"Killed my wife. She had it coming though. She always tried ta aggravate me! Knew I liked the house clean and my dinner on time. Just didn't care. I hit her a few times, just ta teach her ta shape up. She jus never learned! So the next time I hit 'er harder...she jus' never learned!" He glowered at Terry, rubbing his hand across his scruffy chin. When Terry didn't respond, he sank back into the bunk, muttering to himself.

Terry took a deep breath of the ill-smelling air, placed his foot on the metal end of the bed and heaved himself into the top bunk. There he turned his face to the wall and prayed God to deliver him from the evil of this place.

Jenny couldn't stand it. She decided to move to Montana to be near Terry. She felt like a mother needing to watch over her boy...or so she told herself. She contacted Terry's mother, who lived in the mountains at Lonely Lake about 80 miles from the prison, and told her what was happening in her son's life. "So now he'll be near enough so you can go to visit him," she told Mrs. Singer on the phone. The response was vague, but Jenny supposed that was because she didn't know her. Terry's mother did offer to rent her a house in Missoula though, which she gratefully accepted. It didn't really matter to Jenny what kind of a place she lived in. It was enough to have shelter and food and warmth, so she could visit and minister to Terry and the other men in the prison.

She hired a mover, saw her furniture loaded onto the truck, and left the valley again. She drove the winding road through the mountains alone, marveling at the beauty and majesty of the scenery around her, even as she prayed God to keep her safe.

In Montana, she followed Mrs. Singer's directions, and drove on through Missoula into a seedy neighborhood, decorated with garbage cans and junk cars. "Oh, Lord, is this where you want me to be?" she asked, even as she recognized the street name, and arrived almost immediately at the house number. She sat in her car looking at it for a few moments before taking a deep breath and opening the door. "Well, OK, Lord, just please keep me safe here!"

She went to the house to the south and rang the bell. "Mrs. Webber?" she said to the huge woman who answered. The woman just looked at her, waiting. "Mrs. Singer told me to pick up the key to her house from you. I'm Jenny Brownell. Did she tell you about me?"

"Oh, hi, Honey. The deep raspy voice was friendly. I thought you might be another one of those bill collectors. I've had it up to here with those pushy dames!" She moved out of the doorway. "Come on in, and I'll get the key for ya." Jenny stepped into the room and was almost overwhelmed with cat smell. She looked around, fighting nausea, her eyes adjusting to the gloom caused by all the shades being drawn, and realized the place was crawling with cats. There must have been 20 cats, all sizes, colors and breeds. She held her breath as much as she could, nearly gagging, while she watched Mrs. Webber dig around in a kitchen drawer. Soon she came up with a key, and dangled it from her fingers as she came back into the room.

"Don't mind my babies. They won't bother you none." She chuckled good-naturedly. "They just seem to adopt me. Guess I got the reputation of being a good place to dump off cats people don't want or something. I just love 'em, and I can't seem to say no to the poor little things!" Jenny smiled weakly and nodded, reaching for the key.

"I'll just go on over with ya to make sure the key fits and everything is OK, y'know. You been traveling far?" She closed the door quickly behind them to make sure the cats didn't escape, and started across the driveway that separated the small yards.

Jenny followed, gulping great breaths of air. "Came from California. It was quite a drive through the mountains. Beautiful though!"

"That's the truth!" she shoved the key into the lock and pushed the door open, standing in the doorway so Jenny couldn't see in around her bulk. "You'll like it here. It's a good city. Nice place to live. What brings you here? You planning to stay long?" She was friendly, but nosy, and Jenny didn't know what to say.

"I'm not sure yet. I'm a pastor, and I plan to do some ministry work at the prison at Deer Lodge. Have to see how it works out before I know whether I'll be staying or not." She moved up one more step, backing Mrs. Webber into the living room of Jenny's new home. It wasn't at all fancy, and it was small, but it was reasonably clean. Jenny smiled, "Thanks a lot, Mrs. Webber. It's nice of you to keep track of the place for your neighbor."

"Least I can do!" She turned and started out the door. "Ministry work at the prison! That's a strange job for a lady like you! Ain'tcha afraid to go into a place like that? And anyway, it's at least 80 miles from here!"

Jenny nodded. "Yeah, it is sort of far. I'll have to see how it works out, I guess." She gave in to the woman, and added, "I know Mrs. Singer's son. Have worked with Terry Singer in prison, and that's why I rented from her. I'll be staying here for a while anyway. She'll probably be wanting to visit him too, now that he's so close by."

"Minnie has a boy in prison?" Mrs. Webber shook her head, her many chins swaying. "She never said a thing about that! Goes to show, you never really know a person, do you?"

"I'm sure it's a heartache to her," Jenny said. She was sorry she'd said anything. Obviously, Mrs. Singer didn't want people to know about Terry. "Well, I'd better get busy, my furniture should get here tomorrow, and there's lots to do!"

"You need anything, I'm right nearby!"

"Thanks a lot."

She watched the woman waddle back across the yard, and then took a deep breath and turned to survey her new home. Well, it'll do. I probably won't spend much time here anyway. Let's see, the couch can go here, and my good table....

Her furniture arrived the next morning, and she spent the whole day getting settled in, with a short break once after lunch, to provide a cup of tea for Mrs. Webber, who suffered from chronic curiosity. She finished her own cup, and then worked cleaning the few kitchen cupboards and lining them with paper while her new neighbor sipped tea and gave her the lowdown on the neighborhood.

The very next day, Jenny checked her maps once more and set out for Deer Lodge. It was a beautiful drive along Clark Fork River through the mountains, and she had time to spend praising the Lord for the beauty of his creation, and for his care and love. She prayed for guidance and help in working with the prisoners and dealing with the guards. And she prayed for Terry's safety, and that he would soon be paroled and get out of that terrible environment to a place where he could grow in the Lord and serve Him.

The ugly prison walls, high fences and guard towers were a sore and a scab on the beautiful landscape. Jenny sat for a few moments, her heart beating fast, as always when she faced a new and unknown situation. Then she took a deep breath and opened the car door. "OK, Lord, let's go." She walked quickly to the gate, showing a confidence she didn't feel, and showed her clergy card.

The guard looked her up and down insolently, with the sort of stare that made her blush in spite of herself. "You sure don't look like no preacher!"

"Yes, well, I am, anyway." She held up her Bible. "You know, Jesus died for you, too. He loves you, and he'll forgive your sins and turn you around and give you real peace, if you'll just ask him and believe."

"OK, Lady, you're a preacher!" He opened the gate and showed her where to go for permission to see the prisoners. She felt him watching her as she walked away.

When Terry was finally shown into the little visiting room, they were both so glad to see each other that the big hug was spontaneous. "I'm so glad to see you...I was worried about you after the beating. Are you OK? Let me see your face!" She pulled his face from side to side, studying it.

"You're like an angel! I can't believe you actually came out here to Montana to be near me! Yeah, I'm all healed up now. Just some soreness yet here and there. You get used to it after awhile."

They settled down on the hard chairs and talked non-stop until the guard signaled time. Then Jenny gave his arm a little squeeze. "I'll be back as soon as I can," she promised. "I have to set things up to visit other prisoners and do some family ministry for their wives and kids. Don't know how that'll work out yet with living so far from here, but I'll figure it out somehow..."

He gave her a lopsided grin. "I'll be waiting for you! I'll study Romans, like you said, and I'll have questions, too!" The guard turned him toward the door, and he was gone in a moment.

Jenny gathered her purse and Bible and went to talk with the warden.

The angel went ahead of her and softened the warden's heart.

Jenny settled into a routine at the prison, driving from Missoula nearly every day. The scenery was so gorgeous along the way she almost didn't mind the long drive. On occasion, she invited a few prisoners' wives to stay overnight, at her little house, knowing they had no money to be able to visit their husbands otherwise. She taught them the Bible in the evenings, as well as feeding them nutritious meals. It was a severe strain on her budget, but she felt led to do it, as she knew their bodies had to be fed before their souls could be reached with the gospel. Over the months, she led several women to the Lord. Those who were able, then began to help her with the work, and invited more women to the Bible study group.

Mrs. Webber watched the comings and goings from her kitchen window and wondered what in the world was going on over there. Finally she couldn't stand it, and in the middle of an evening Bible study one Saturday, she knocked on the door. "Oh, Hi, Mrs. Webber, I'm glad to see you...are you OK?" Jenny asked.

The woman craned her neck to see around Jenny and nodded, and Jenny caught on immediately. "Why not come on in and join our study?" She indicated the big easy chair as she closed the door, then got another chair from the kitchen and introduced her neighbor to the other women. "Judy, will you share your Bible with Mrs. Webber?"

The large woman settled uncomfortably toward the edge of the chair, and looked around at the odd little group. Judy wore tattered jeans and a flowered shirt, Beth had on a cheap but neat blue suit, and Mary Lou wore a tight sweater and mini-skirt, with 4 inch heels, while she chewed gum as though her life depended on it.

"We're studying the gospel of John," Jenny told her. Judy pulled her chair closer to Mrs. Webber and held the book out for her to see.

"Now where were we...oh yes...the third chapter. Mary Lou, what do you think it means when it says, "For God so loved the world that He gave His only begotten Son, that whoever believes in Him might not perish, but have everlasting life? Who do you think that refers to?"

"I know," Mary Lou said quietly. "It means God loves me so much that he sent his son Jesus to die for me."

"It means he doesn't see my sin any more," Judy added. "So I can live my life now as though I hadn't done all that stuff before. It's all clean now, and I can start over!"

Jenny nodded, her heart overflowing with joy, "That's right, He took all our sins on Himself, so we can live as though we had never sinned. And what do we have to do to earn that?"

They were quiet for a moment, and then Mary Lou said, "I think all we have to do is believe it."

"That's right. And ask him to forgive our sins, and include us in his sacrifice, and make us clean. If we just really believe Jesus is the Son of God, and that he came to die for us, then we can claim his death to cover our sins. Then we can live in his righteousness instead of our own miserable condition. Turn the page a minute to chapter five, verse 24. See, there Jesus is talking, and he says, *Truly, truly I say unto you, he that hears my word, and believes in Him that sent me, has everlasting life, and shall not come into condemnation, but is passed from death unto life!* That means that when you take Jesus as your own Savior, you have new life...everything is changed, and it's as if you're starting all over again, clean as a baby!"

"It's hard to believe that." Mary sounded hopeful though.

"Yeah, I know," Jenny nodded. "I remember how I felt when I first heard this too. But then I figured I might as well try it and see. So I prayed and asked forgiveness for my sins and asked Jesus to come into my heart, and He did, and my life changed...it was a miracle!" She smiled at Mary, "That's why I want you to know the same experience." She hesitated, then asked, "Any questions? Anybody want to ask Jesus to be your Savior?"

"I guess I do, Mary said in a small voice. Things sure can't get any worse than they are now...and if this is true, it's sure what I need!"

Jenny's heart was full of joy and gratitude to the Lord. She took Mary's hand and knelt by her chair, and Mary knelt beside her. "OK, just pray with me, and mean it. Dear Jesus, I know I'm a sinner, but you say you came to take my sins and die for me, so I can be made new." Mary obediently repeated the words after her. "Please forgive my sins and make me clean and new, and I'll live for you from now on. Thank you for hearing me, and thank you for being my Savior!"

Mary finished the prayer and dissolved in tears, weeping with joy and relief. Mrs. Webber watched everything, with one eyebrow cocked skeptically. Jenny and Judy, who already knew the Lord, hugged their new sister, and Mary Lou resolved privately to try praying that way sometime and see if it really worked.

The angel sang praises to God, and rejoiced with the heavenly choir.

Existing in the prison was hard enough for Terry, but living in the small cell with Tony Manici was almost more than he could endure. The man was a true maniac, with extreme mood swings that ranged from euphoria to depression to rage and back. It kept Terry on his toes to react appropriately to the current state of Tony's mind. And Terry had enough problems of his own trying to be a Christian in that ungodly place. He lived for the hours of exercise in the pen, and for the visits from Jenny. She was his lifeline, his hope for another life sometime, outside the prison walls. She made his existence bearable, and gave him things to study and think about during the endless hours in his cell. And even though she was older than his mother, he knew his feelings for Jenny were much more than friendship. His heart lightened when he saw her waiting for him in the visiting room, and he suffered as a plant suffers from lack of sunlight when she missed a day.

Terry witnessed to his fellow prisoners as well as he could, and several of them wanted to meet and talk to Jenny, so she was kept busy teaching from the Bible all day at the prison, then most evenings at home too. She was pressed for time to do the cooking and cleaning necessary to care for her prisoner families, but she loved the work and knew she was in the Lord's will doing his ministry. There were only a couple of other ministers visiting the prison regularly, and they were both men.

Sometimes Mrs. Webber joined the evening Bible classes, seeming to feel free to come any time she wanted to. Jenny always welcomed her, and prayed for her salvation privately. "Call me Marge," Mrs. Webber told the group one evening. "I want to be part of the gang here, and you all go by your first names."

"Great, Marge." Jenny grinned at her. "And you are part of the gang anyway, you know. We all miss you when you don't come."

The big woman smiled and eased back into her chair, holding the Bible she had recently bought. They opened the pages to the 19th chapter of John, and Jenny read to them, and elaborated on Jesus death on the cross. She painted a word picture so real that they could almost see Jesus standing before Pilate, while Pilate washed his hands and sent him to his death. They watched him carry his heavy cross up to Golgotha, and they heard the nails pounded into his hands and feet and the thud of the cross falling into the deep hole dug for it. They pictured the thieves on either side of him as the prisoners they knew, and were thrilled when Jesus told the repentant one he would be with him in Paradise.

"Why did God allow that? Jesus didn't do anything wrong!" Marge spoke up after they finished reading about Jesus death.

"Well, Marge, I'm so glad he did allow it, because if he hadn't, there wouldn't be any way for you and me to be saved! God sent Jesus here for that very purpose, because he loves you so much, and the only way for you to be spared from death and Hell is through Jesus' death and resurrection. Because that's the really good news, you know...he rose again from the dead! Death couldn't hold him! And because of that fact, we know we can believe him when he says we have eternal life in him. God sees us now through Jesus' shed blood, and we are clean in his sight that way...clothed with Jesus righteousness!"

"How can that be? I know he can't possibly love me after all the stuff I've done!" Janidy Prentis, who spoke, was clearly touched by the story. She had a drug problem, and had done all the things necessary to maintain her habit. She wound a tight black braid around her finger nervously, her dark eyes darting from one woman to the other.

"Because like it says here in Romans chapter 5, verse 8, *God commends his love toward us in that while we were still sinners, Christ died for us.*" He took our sins in his own body on the cross and God looked away from him because God cannot look on sin. That caused Jesus unbearable pain, terrible grief, and the load of our sins was too much for his body and soul to bear, and his heart broke with the horror of it all. He actually became sin for us! So it doesn't matter how bad the sin is...he took it all!" Jenny looked around at the little group. "Then he took it into Hell for us, but Hell couldn't hold him, and the third day he rose up from the dead, and that's why we know it's real! And he'll come and live in you if you let him, and he'll help you overcome all that stuff you've been into, and live clean and be happy!"

Janidy looked doubtful, but hopeful at the same time.

Marge Webber, though, made a strange gasping noise, and everyone turned to look at her. She was shaking and crying silently, her large body quivering all over.

Jenny went to her side and knelt down. "Marge? What is it? What's the matter?"

"I want that...that's what I need!" She pulled a tissue out of her pocket and blew her nose, then gasped again. "Can he do that for me, too?"

"Of course! He loves you so much, Marge! Come on, let's ask him, OK?"

Marge nodded, and together they went through the prayer of repentance, and once more the angels rejoiced at the salvation of another sinner.

Marge Webber turned out to be an enthusiastic Christian, dedicated to telling everyone about Jesus and how wonderful he is. "I just want to do what I can to help!" she said as she delivered hot casseroles or gathered clothing from the neighborhood to give to the women and children who met at Jenny's little house for food and help. She even noticed how dark and dirty her house was, and began to clean it up. She didn't get rid of any of her cats, though. "They need me, poor babies," she told Jenny. Then on Jenny's birthday, she brought a covered basket and handed it to her, beaming.

"What's this?" Jenny set the basket on the table and took the towel off the top. There sat the cutest little kitten...soft and gray, with white feet and face, and big eyes. Jenny didn't know how to feel. She loved the little creature, but it would be a lot of trouble owning a pet with her schedule. She hugged Marge. "Thank you so much! It's adorable...is it a boy or a girl?"

"Girl. Ain't she cute? And you need some company here. Cats are good for ya. They give ya something to hug, and they never pick on ya."

"Well, maybe you'll look after her for me sometimes if I can't be here for her?"

"Sure, Marge agreed.

Jenny held the soft, furry ball of life gently in her hands and looked at its little white face. "Let's see, I think I'll call you...Pansy. That's what your little face looks like!"

Marge chuckled and nodded. "I broughtcha some litter and a box. She already knows how to use it."

Pansy settled into Jenny's life, and soon it seemed she'd always been there. Jenny found herself talking to Pansy as though she were a person, and Pansy would sit and look at Jenny as though she understood, meowing now and then as though making a comment.

Life was comparatively peaceful, with no foreshadowing of the disaster soon to strike.

CHAPTER TWENTY-ONE

The months rolled by, as Terry resigned himself to his situation, and made the best of it, trying to fit into the prison routine without causing anyone to notice him especially. But Tony kept mentioning the bank robbery, looking at Terry sidelong to see his reaction. Terry usually just changed the subject, asking a question, to hear Tony's fractured philosophies.

"Yer a strange man." Tony told him on several occasions. "Always gotcher nose in that Bible. Whadaya get outa that anyhow? Never made no sense ta me!"

"You mean you've read it?" Terry looked at his roommate with interest. Maybe there was more to him than it appeared.

"Yeah, I picked it up a time or two. Looked like a bunch of begats and verilys and talked about the Israelites and Jews a lot. Don't even apply ta me!"

"I'd be glad to show you how it does apply," Terry offered. "You'd be surprised how important it is to you! Jesus died for the sins of the whole world, not just for those people. He just used them to tell the rest of the world about him."

"Nah...my ma took me ta church when I was a kid. Lotta guys prancing around in dresses, sprinklin' holy water or sumthin and talkin' an chantin' in Latin so's nobody could understand. I don' need that kinda business. Anyhow, they tried ta look so all-fired holy, then got Buddy Finelli...he was my pal, and they conned him inta bein' a altar boy." He glared at Terry as though he were the priest in question. "Got 'im in the vestry room an got inta his pants...really hurt im...he was bleedin' and cryin' and Father Baker told him if he ever told anybody he'd go straight to Hell. Told 'im that's what altar boys were for! Told 'im everybody knew that's what altar boys are for." So Buddy thought his ma knew about that stuff when she made him be one! He thought she approved of it! I got the whole story outa him one night.

Tony punched his pillow as though punching the priest. "Buddy was a good kid before that. He o.d.'d on heroin a couple years later. I ain't had no use fer religion. Only looked at that book when I was bored outta my skull an it was the only thing around!" His expression was so menacing that Terry let the subject drop and resolved to bring it up again some other time.

As the summer weather grew warm and dry, Jenny was able to visit with Terry outside in the courtyard. She brought Pansy along once, hidden in her large purse. Terry was delighted with the little creature, and cooed and petted her. But then he said it wasn't safe for the kitten there. Other men who saw Pansy might decide to use her for sport. So that was the last time Jenny brought her.

It was pleasant enough there in the courtyard, although sometimes she wished some of the married couples had more privacy. They did some pretty obvious sex right there in front of everybody else, the women sitting on their men's laps. She tried to ignore them, and she and Terry would sit on a bench with their backs to the others and talk. They were really close friends now, and Jenny could talk to him about things she couldn't even discuss with her family. They had deep discussions about the scriptures too, since she had taught him to read better, so he could understand more of what he read.

Jenny had noticed camping spots along the river here and there between Missoula and Deer Lodge, and one day she decided to invest in a tent and camp out at the one nearest Deer Lodge. She loved the mountain air and enjoyed the sights and sounds of the river. It saved her hours of driving time, which she could spend ministering to prisoners and their families at Deer Lodge. She went home every week to hold a Bible study at her house, but she told the women not to expect her to be there every night any more. "I just feel it's a good idea to save time and money and be closer to the men we're trying to reach for the Lord," she explained to the group.

"Ms. Jenny," Judy said after the meeting, "that's a really great idea! It's such a long drive back here to spend the night. I'd be able to go more often to see Buck if I could stay closer. Can I maybe rent some tent space from you?"

Jenny was taken back, but after a moment's reflection answered "Sure, Judy, why not? It'll be sort of like going to summer camp!" She didn't know how Judy would cope with camping out, but Jenny had done a lot of it when traveling with the circus years ago. She quite enjoyed sleeping out now, without Frank around to watch everything she did. And Judy was good company. Jenny left Pansy with Marge, while she and Judy spent most of the summer camping, except in bad weather. Fall came all too soon, with the colder weather that forced Jenny to move back to Missoula full time.

There was one particular cross Jenny had to bear along with Terry, and that was his family. Terry's whole family lived in Montana now. His mother at Seely Lake, only 80 miles away to the East, never came to visit her son. Terry's heart hurt every day when visiting time came and went without the announcement he waited for. Jenny ached for him, and she wondered how any mother could treat her son so coldly. She'd never had sisters and brothers, so she could no more than imagine how they should act and interact, but it wasn't like that ... just ignoring their brother!

One crisp golden morning in autumn, Jenny drove to Seely Lake to visit Minnie Singer, praying for wisdom as she drove. The drive through the mountains was beautiful, but tiring, as the road was narrow and winding. Just as Jenny began to think she'd never get there, a sign announced Seely Lake. It was a tiny town situated on a clear blue lake, surrounded by lofty peaks. The scenery everywhere was absolutely gorgeous. As her car pulled up a dirt driveway to the small ranch-style house where Terry's mother lived, two big shaggy mongrels came barking around the corner. She stepped out of the car and stood still, waiting for them. When they got close, standing and barking at her, she began to talk to them quietly.

"Here boy, what's the matter, eh? Come on, now. I'm not here to cause any trouble." Her voice was soothing and calm, and the dogs stopped barking after a minute, to hear her. They stood panting, watching her. "That's a good boy. That's a nice dog. Come on, now, let's be friends...what do you say?" She tentatively held her hand out to pat the closest dog. It jumped away, baring its teeth. "Oh come on now, I won't hurt you! I just want to talk to your people, OK?"

The door of the house opened and someone called. "Major! Trixie! Come on, now. The woman whistled and the dogs retreated to her side.

Jenny walked slowly up the slope of a small hill and then up the steps, where a gray-haired woman in jeans, shirt and an old ripped cardigan stood patting the dogs.

"Hi, are you Mrs. Singer?" she asked. No response. She held out her hand and said, "I'm Jenny Brownell. I rent your house in Missoula, and I visit your son Terry in prison."

The woman ignored her hand and turned back to the house, "Well, come in, I suppose. What can I do for ya?" She walked into the small, cluttered kitchen, where dirty dishes covered most of the work surfaces, as well as the kitchen table. "You want coffee?"

Jenny nodded, "Sure, that would be great." She didn't relish the thought of drinking coffee in that dirty place, but knew that talking over a cup is much easier than without one. And anyway, she figured you have to boil water to make coffee. She tried not to think about the cup.

Mrs. Singer rummaged around and found two cracked mugs, then poured coffee from an old thermos bottle, and set one mug in front of Jenny. "You take cream and sugar?"

Jenny shook her head. "This is fine, thanks."

"Well, whadda ya want?" the woman asked bluntly. She wasn't as old as Jenny, but she looked ancient, especially because of the deep lines around her mouth and eyes. And where Jenny was slim and walked straight and tall, with quick firm steps, this woman was heavy and bent over, and shuffled her feet as though walking was painful to her. She panted gently as she sat now, waiting for Jenny's answer.

"I just wanted to talk about Terry, and tell you that he'd really love to see you! He misses you and the rest of his family terribly."

"Hmph! He shoulda thought of that before he got hisself into so much trouble!"

"I'm sure you know the story behind his problems...don't you?" Jenny looked at Terry's mother, and could see she didn't know the story at all, so she began at the point where Terry met his wife, and related to his mother all the things he had told her, ending with his coming to Deer Lodge prison. "So you see, it was his fault, of course, but you can probably understand how it all happened, can't you?"

"Terry always did have trouble...seemed to make it for hisself somehow!" Mrs. Singer sighed a deep, resigned sigh. "I just had too many young'uns to look after. Didn't need Terry! Don' know why God gave me so many boys...and redheads too! My Henry never thought they was his...they was, though! I never looked at any other man! Not that I didn't have my chances, you know!" She looked at Jenny as though expecting her to argue that point.

Jenny nodded, "You must've been a looker when you were young."

"Wasn't no slouch!" She chuckled bitterly. "Well, you makes yer choices and then you lives with 'em."

"I'd be glad to take you to see Terry, if you'll come. He'd be so happy and surprised. He loves you very much...he told me! We can drive over to Deer Lodge and visit, and you can stay with me at your house in Missoula overnight. Then I can get you home by late afternoon tomorrow. Would that be OK?"

"Well...I suppose so...I oughta clean up this stuff first though."

"How about if I start on the dishes while you get ready to go?"

Mrs. Singer agreed to that with alacrity, and disappeared into the bedroom while Jenny started running water into the sink and looked for the soap.

The drive to Deer Lodge was a strain on Jenny. It was hard to talk to Terry's Mother. She was one of those people who respond yes or no to every question or observation, and seldom expand on an idea or offer one of their own. It took all Jenny's considerable talent for making friends with people, and by the time they stopped to eat at a neat little restaurant, she was almost sorry she'd volunteered to bring Terry's mother to visit.

They sat at a table near the window and Mrs. Singer ordered a hot beef sandwich and apple pie, which she consumed with evident pleasure. Jenny watched her mop up the last of the gravy, thinking, *no wonder she's in that condition!*

They arrived at the prison barely in time for visiting, and Mrs. Singer dropped her purse getting out of the car. "Oh dear," she cried as she got down to pick up the scattered contents. "I hope I ain't lost anything!"

Jenny stooped to help gather Mrs. Singer's belongings. "I think we got it all, OK." She took the other woman's elbow and started for the gate.

Mrs. Singer stopped. "I hate ta be a bother, y'know, but I really gotta go to the john!"

Jenny guided her to the rest room, and watched as Terry's mother tried everything to delay going into the prison. By the time they were shown into the visiting room, the woman was almost gasping with nervousness. Her eyes darted here and there, as though she expected to be jumped on at any moment. When the guard locked them into the room, she looked ready to faint.

"It's OK, Jenny reassured her. I do this all the time. They'll let us out again. Listen, when Terry comes, I'll leave you two alone, OK?"

Mrs. Singer looked at her vacantly. Just then the door on the other side of the room opened, and there was Terry. His mouth fell open, and he stood staring for a second or two, then he held out his arms, "Mama!" His voice broke.

"Hullo, Son." She hugged him briefly, and then sat down heavily, while he stood near her chair and held onto her hand, struggling to control his emotion.

Jenny signaled the guard, who let her out of the room, and she waited in the outer hall while Terry tried to make peace with his mother. She realized the meeting hadn't gone as well as she'd hoped, when Mrs. Singer hardly spoke to her all the way back to her house at Missoula. They had nothing in common, not even Terry, it seemed. They both welcomed bedtime when it finally came, as an escape.

The trip to Lonely Lake the next day was a strain on both women, and Jenny was glad to drive back through the beauty of the mountains alone, even though it was getting dark by the time she reached home once more.

The rest of Terry's brother's and sisters came all together one day to see him. That was the only time they visited while he was in Montana. From Jenny's viewpoint, he might as well not even have a family. She couldn't understand it...she'd always wanted a big family, and thought it would be great to have lots of sisters and brothers. But Terry's family didn't seem to care at all for him. She remembered what he'd told her about his childhood. She hadn't really been able to believe it at the time, but now she could see it was true. They didn't care for Terry at all. It wasn't natural. It made Jenny feel almost as though he'd been abandoned at her doorstep. Her heart went out to him even more than before.

Tony Manici worked on an escape plan. He kept hinting at it to Terry, but Terry tried to ignore him, to get the point across that he wasn't at all interested. Still, Tony studied and watched and plotted. Terry could almost see his mind working as he turned over the data he received and processed it. Eventually he worked out the details of his plan to suit himself. He knew it would work if the right men went with him. So he spent the next few days watching the others, and finally selected five, including Terry.

The prison laundry was a busy place, but there was one quiet spot behind the dryers, where prisoners could manage to talk privately sometimes. Manici met there with his friends, one at a time, "You figure you rather rot in this stinking place, or make a break for it?" He watched the eyes, to catch a reaction. When he saw what he thought was interest, he proceeded. "I figure we can get out of here if some of us work together on it. I got it all worked out. Now, here's the plan....agreed?" And one at a time, they signed on.

"Hey, I don't want to chance it, Tony!" Terry told him. "I'm no good at that kind of stuff, and they'd catch me sure! Look, it only took one job and they got me in here!" Never mind that he'd be eligible for parole from his Federal sentence in 6 months! Of course he couldn't let them know that, or he'd have been found dead some morning.

"Shut up! Tony snarled, his dark eyes glaring. Ya don't think I'm gonna leave ya behind ta rat on me, do ya? Not a chance! Ye're goin, and that's that, so quit whinin' and pay attention to what I'm tellin' ya. If ya don't, one way or the other, ye're gonna get shot...understand?" The evil in his eyes made Terry's stomach turn.

"We'll use him ta rob banks for us, so we have enough money ta get a new start," Tony told the rest of the group. He made it clear there was no choice in the matter for Terry..."ya'll go with us or they'll findja dead the next morning. We don't need nobody ta rat on us!" His eyes were dark drills, boring into Terry's head.

"When?"

"Ya don't have ta worry about that...when it's time, I'll letcha know! You just be ready ta go!"

"How many of us are there, anyway?"

"Six, and any one of 'em'll be glad ta shoot a traitor!"

Terry was beside himself! He managed to tell Jenny about the plan, and she went to the prison officials immediately. "Something's going down, and soon," she told Warden Biggers. "You've got to get Terry out of there. Tony's gonna make him go with them whether he wants to or not!" The man sat there like a rock, his lip slightly curled.

"Yeah, and what else is new?"

Suddenly Jenny had the urge to push his face in. She curled her hands into fists at her side and took a deep breath. Lord, help me remember I'm a Christian!

"Listen to me!" she pleaded. "They'll kill Terry if he doesn't go along. Please, please move him out of there before it's too late!"

"OK lady, just what is it you think's going to happen?"

"I don't just think it...I know it! It's a prison break! I'll give you the details as soon as Terry is safely out of there! You know very well I can't tell you now, or he'll be in even worse danger if they find out he's told! Listen...Terry's a Federal prisoner, remember? Come on, you've just gotta help him!"

"How do I know you aren't just saying this to get him moved to a better cell?" His tone made it clear that was what he believed.

She was infuriated by his arrogance and lack of concern. With difficulty she kept herself under control and continued to plead with him."OK, if it doesn't happen, you can put him back! Just, please don't let those men know that Terry's told us anything."

But the man was impossible to talk to, and she left Biggers' office completely frustrated.

Next she tried talking with the head guard, a huge black man who hated all whites, with some justification. He'd obtained his post by being mean as a Doberman guard dog, and wasn't about to jeopardize his position. He looked at her as though she were a crazy woman. "I'll think about it," he said, in a flat, even tone, "but it'd be a whole lot more convincing if you tell me when and how you think it's going down."

She glared at him in frustration. "I already told you that when you assure me he'll be put somewhere safe, I'll tell you all about it!" The guard shook his head, clearly unconvinced, and walked out of his office, leaving her standing there. Jenny was so angry she was shaking. Oh Lord, please help me. Please help Terry! Make these guys listen to me!

She knew she couldn't leave the matter there, so she called the warden at his home. "I'm a minister...I counsel with the men on a regular basis. Terry Singer is one of my converts, and I'm terribly concerned for him. He knows something big is going down soon, and he's going to be forced to be part of it if you won't help him. He's been told they'll leave his dead body behind if he doesn't participate! Please, please...he's a Federal prisoner with only a few months left on his sentence. Move him to safety, and I'll tell you all about the plans!"

"I'll look into it, Mrs. Brownell, Biggers snapped. But I can't guarantee anything. We can't go running crazy over every report we hear about things like this. I think this con's just trying to use you to get a better cell. Why don't you just go home and pray for him and leave the situation to us? Anyway, without more details, what can I do about it?"

"Listen, I have details, and I'll give them to you as soon as Terry is out of danger, OK? Then I'll tell you the whole thing! Please, he's going to be forced to be part of this, and nobody will help him!"

"You know what I think, ma'am? I think you're over-reacting, and being used by a fast-talking con! I'll think about it though." He hung up while she was still talking.

Jenny was indignant and scared. I know it's just because I'm a woman they won't listen to me... well maybe I'll call Pastor Gardner. Maybe he'll listen. She called and got an appointment to meet with Pastor Gardner the next day. She wasn't on the best of terms with him, as he didn't approve of a woman being a minister at all, and especially not in the prison. It was no place for women. It was stupid of her to think she could lead those tough men to the Lord. They only thought of one thing, even with an older woman like her! Everybody knew that!

They shook hands in greeting, and she sat across the desk from him and told him the whole story. He listened impassively, privately thinking what a crazy woman she was, and obviously enamored of a young prisoner. Probably had no idea he was just using her to get a better situation in the prison. Things like that happened all the time. He hardly heard what she told him.

"So will you take what I tell you and go to the Warden with it? Will you please help me to save this young man?" She looked at the younger pastor and her heart sank. He was shaking his head almost imperceptibly.

"Well, if he wants to meet with me and tell me this story himself, I'll listen to it and then decide what to do. You know these men, they lie to us all the time to get what they want."

Jenny became very quiet before she spoke, then she looked him in the eyes and said, slowly and clearly, "I pity you if they find this man's dead body in his cell some morning. I've told you the truth, and I don't know why you won't listen to me. I am not hysterical, and I am not being led around by a conniving prisoner. This is planned to happen, and it will happen if nobody does anything to stop it, and a young man who is innocent of this crime, and has told us about it ahead of time, will be forced to be part of it!" She picked up her jacket and purse and turned to leave, "And it'll be very hard for you to rationalize your behavior then."

Jenny didn't know what to do next, but finally decided to call the Governor in the morning. She didn't quite dare disturb him so late at night. But by the next morning everything had changed.

CHAPTER TWENTY-TWO

She stirred in her sleep, something was wrong ... Someone was banging on something...She snuggled into her pillow, but the noise came again. Her eyes snapped open. It was the door. Someone was pounding on the door! She looked at the clock. 6:00 A.M.! More banging. Someone was pretty anxious to get her attention. She shrugged into her warm robe as she staggered toward the back door. I hope it's not something wrong with Marge!

She fumbled with the lock. When she opened the door a crack she could hardly believe her eyes. There stood Terry, soaked to the skin in the cold October rain! She flung the door open and he stepped quickly into the warm kitchen. So all her efforts had been in vain. She felt so frustrated she was angry momentarily, but on the other hand, he was here in her kitchen and safe, not dead. She hugged him, wet as he was, and felt the cold water soak into her robe as he hugged her too, lifting her off the floor. Something inside her felt sort of like some singing... She quickly freed herself, smoothing her morning hair. "So they did it?"

"Yeah."

"How'd you get here? Where are the others?" "How many are there?" She looked anxiously out the window, hoping they weren't out in her yard, ready to force their way in.

"They scattered. Supposed to meet in a couple of weeks, after our trail's cooled some." Terry was shaking from cold, and dripping a pool on her floor.

She felt a great tenderness rise from somewhere deep inside herself. She pulled him to a kitchen chair. "Here, sit down, you poor boy! I'll find you some dry clothes, and then you'd better get out of those wet things and into a hot shower while I fix you some breakfast. Then we'll decide what to do next."

He followed her instructions mechanically, in too much shock after the events of the night to think any more. For now, it was good to have somebody who cared for him care for him. Fortunately, no prison wives had stayed with Jenny last night, so after he was clean and warm and fed she tucked him into the guest bed, with soft blankets and a good pillow. "I feel like I've died and gone to heaven!" he murmured, eyes closed. I haven't slept in a real comfortable bed for so long..." and he was asleep.

Jenny stood in the bedroom doorway watching him, feeling a mixture of relief and anxiety...and something else she didn't acknowledge. She closed the door quickly. She had to plan what to do next.

She picked up the damp newspaper from her porch and carried it into the kitchen where she spread it out on the table, and found the prison break story was already front-page news. She wondered briefly how they could do news so fast, and then read the article. It told in lurid detail about each of the men who'd escaped, warning everyone how dangerous they were. She scanned quickly looking for Terry's name, and sure enough, there it was, including the fact that he was a Federal prisoner being held in the state prison for protection!

Well, so much for the protection part of it! Now we HAVE to keep him from going back there! Lord, please help me know what to do now to help Terry.

By the time Terry awoke from his exhausted sleep, she was ready with a list of things to do. "We have to call the prison and tell them what happened," she told him. "I know, I know," she said, catching his expression. "It's great to be out and free, but you'll never be really free as long as they're all looking for you. The only thing to do is tell them the truth about what's happened and try to get you into a safer place."

Her heart ached for him, as she watched him wrestle with all the options she knew he had. It would be terribly hard for him to go back into that Hell voluntarily, now that he tasted sweet freedom. She reached out for his hand. "I'll stay with you wherever they end up sending you, Terry. You know that, don't you?"

He squeezed her hand and gave her a look that sent the blood flooding into her face unbidden. She turned away from him quickly.

"Jenny, I don't know why you're so good to me. I don't know what you see in this little ol' country boy with no education and no class. You're such a fine lady, with so much to offer...so many blessings…" His voice broke. "OK, go ahead and call them. Let's get it over with!"

She lifted the phone and dialed the prison office from memory. "This is Pastor Jenny Brownell." She told the warden. "If you remember, please, I've called you several times in the past few days to tell you there was something about to happen. You wouldn't talk to me about it, and now it's too late." She took a deep breath, sending up a prayer as she did. "Well I told you Terry Singer was being forced to be involved in the break-out against his will. You remember that?"

On the other end of the line, Warden Biggers motioned to his aide, who quietly picked up the extension. Biggers cleared his throat, ran his fingers through his thin blond hair, and tried to keep the anger out of his voice, not succeeding. "I remember you wouldn't tell me any details about it! You didn't have any proof!" His face was red now, his eyes beginning to bug out with the effort to constrain his rage. If it had been anyone else he'd have been yelling!

"Well, you've got your proof now, don't you?" Jenny also tried to be civil, but she had a hard time of it. She didn't like the warden. He was a cold, arrogant ass, in her opinion. "Listen, Warden, I know where Terry Singer is right now. He's unarmed and he wants to turn himself in, if you'll promise to put him somewhere else. He can't possibly go back to Deer Lodge prison now that the newspapers have told all about him. It'd be a death sentence for sure!"

"Listen, lady, if you know where he is, you'll be held as an accessory if you don't tell us and turn him in!" Biggers would have liked to get hold of that scrawny woman and shake some sense into her. Why couldn't she stay home and bake cookies or something like a woman should? "You have him turn himself in, and we'll go easier on him."

"OK, as soon as I have your word in writing that you'll send him somewhere else, not put him back into Deer Lodge. Then you can come get him!"

She hung up the phone and sighed deeply. "I think we'd better just pray, Terry. This is in God's hands now!"

They prayed, and then they waited. They waited all day, and nothing happened. The suspense was hard on them, but Jenny kept busy fussing over Terry, making up for some of the misery he'd been through in prison. She cooked way too much wonderful food, even baked him an apple pie. The fragrance of apples, cinnamon and spices filled the small house and he told her that must be what heaven smelled like. He ate as though he'd been starving for years. He had, but not only for food. It was the first time he could remember anyone caring enough about him to spend a day fussing over him and cooking and making him comfortable. He loved her. He thought about it a lot, and asked himself if he didn't really just love her like a mother or a sister. No, he answered himself, he'd never felt like that about his mother nor any of his sisters. He'd better not! But she was more than 30 years older than he. This was ridiculous, wasn't it? But no, there it was...he loved her. He gave himself up to the feeling, and wallowed in her care for him.

She felt his eyes on her as she moved about in her kitchen and smiled at him. It was good to be cooking for someone special again.

The angel watched both of them.

CHAPTER TWENTY-THREE

When they awoke in the morning and the police still hadn't arrived to pick up Terry, they weren't sure what to think. Jenny got the newspaper off the porch and read that three of the prisoners had been captured!

"I guess they've just been too busy up to now to bother with me!" Terry observed. "Wonder where Tony is now?" He shuddered involuntarily. "I sure wouldn't want to go back into a cell with that one again! Wouldn't last long, I know. You have to sleep sometime." He gave her a lopsided grin to cover his seriousness.

"You're right, Terry! And I don't know why I didn't think of that yesterday. I wasn't thinking they might catch all the guys again!" Jenny began thinking a mile a minute now. "Get ready, and I'll get some stuff packed. We have to get out of here as fast as possible! We can't take the chance they'll put you back in that place again, and they haven't given us any reason to think they won't!"

She pulled her suitcase out of the closet and began throwing clothes into it.

He watched her helplessly, not knowing what to do.

"Get some food packed, will you? We might need something to snack on...no, we might need to hide somewhere and do some cooking! Who knows where we'll end up tonight?"

Catching her urgency, he ran to the kitchen and began throwing things into grocery bags, which he then organized neatly in the trunk of her car, while she ran next door with Pansy, to ask Marge to take over the Bible study classes for her because she'd have to be gone for a while. And no, she wasn't sure when she'd be back. "And Marge ... please pray for me!"

"I will, Honey, you just take care, you hear me?"

And within 20 minutes they were on their way somewhere. Anywhere else but where the cops thought they were! Their first stop was at the bank, where Jenny withdrew most of her cash.

"Thank you, Jesus, for warning me in time," she breathed a little later, as they cleared the city limits, heading north.

"Amen" he agreed.

They kept the car radio turned on, to catch any bits of news about the prison break. And they drove safely and carefully, so as not to attract attention. Just north of a small town named Eddy, they stopped to fill the gas tank, before turning off the main road onto a narrower road winding through the mountains.

They drove for another hour before Terry asked, "Don't you ever get hungry?"

"Now that you mention it, yes. I guess I was just too hopped up with adrenaline to realize it!" She looked with new eyes at their surroundings. "It's a great day for a picnic, isn't it? Lets' find a good spot and have lunch out. What do you say?" She sobered and added, "There certainly isn't much traffic out here, and if we can find a place where we can tuck in behind some trees, I think it'll be OK. Keep your eye out."

She slowed down, so they could survey the roadsides more easily. Finally they located a beautiful remote spot where they hid the car behind a clump of trees and opened the trunk to examine what food Terry had brought. Jenny chuckled in spite of the situation, on looking into the bags. He'd brought most of her canned goods, and he'd remembered a can opener and a couple of pans. That wouldn't do much good out here in the open. She pulled another bag out and found it had stuff from the refrigerator. There was catsup and mustard and cheese and lunch meat, which he'd put into a plastic bag with the contents of the ice tray to keep them cold. He'd even brought some leftovers she'd stored in small plastic containers.

"Did you bring any bread?"

"Bread and crackers are in that bag, back there." He indicated which one, and then reached over to pull it out for her. "Here. You didn't have much bread left." He held up a partially used up bag of whole wheat. "But you had three different kinds of crackers, and some peanut butter!" He held up the jar, grinning at her.

"We might need those later on. Guess we'd better eat the most perishable stuff first. That means sandwiches!" He walked off into the woods as she spread mustard, meat and cheese on bread. When he came back they sat on the ground with their backs against a tree.

"Mmmm good," he said, with his mouth full.

It was almost like a real, planned picnic, as long as they didn't think about why they were there. Sunshine dappled through the trees, and lit up the gold of the few leaves still hanging on, but the breeze had an edge to it. "It'll be winter before we know it!" Jenny remarked.

"There's snow higher up, already, you know," he answered. The thought of it made him feel adventurous somehow...the danger of being out in the wilds in the snow.

"Let's go, we've been here long enough," Jenny felt an inner urging that suddenly made her want to get out of there. But they made sure they cleaned up every bit of evidence they'd been there, before they left. They were on their way again, feeling calmer after stopping in that peaceful place, and now with food in their stomachs.

The music on the radio was interrupted for a news bulletin, and they listened as the newsman told them once again about the escaped convicts, and to be very careful not to pick up hitchhikers.

"The police are still searching for three of the six men who escaped from Deer Lodge prison Thursday night. Please be on the lookout for these men, but do not attempt to confront them. They are probably armed, and are considered dangerous.

Anthony Manici, convicted of the brutal murder of his wife, is 5'10" tall, weighs 170 pounds and has straight black hair and dark brown eyes. He may have a beard, but probably has shaved it off.

Rafer Moliso, rapist and child molester, a black American, is 6'3" tall, weighs 250 pounds, has close-cropped black hair and black eyes. He has a scar on his left arm between his wrist and his elbow.

Terry Singer is a convicted bank robber, a federal prisoner who had been held in the state prison for protection. He is 5'9" tall, weighs 158 pounds, with short red-brown hair and brown eyes. If you see any of these men, please contact the nearest State Police Post immediately. I repeat, these men may be armed, and are considered dangerous!"

Terry sighed deeply. "Well, they haven't caught Tony or Rafer yet either. And I sure don't have a chance of any protection now, do I? They're blabbing it all over the country!"

"We can't let them take you back to Deer Lodge. We have to do something to stop that. You'd be as good as dead when you walked in that door! And you notice they didn't say anything about your wanting to turn yourself in again!" Jenny was hot with anger. Her expressive eyes flashed fire, and her foot pressed harder on the gas pedal, making the car careen around the curves. She didn't care...it felt good.

"Hey, don't kill us here instead!" he protested, putting his hand over hers on the wheel. "Come on now, ease up, and let's both calm down and think what to do."

She slowed the car and they drove in silence for a few minutes. The wind came up and the temperature dropped as they drove higher into the mountains. The road they were on ended at a town called Yakt. It was late afternoon when they turned right onto highway 2. A large sign said they were only a few miles from Kalispell. A little further on, they passed a small Ma and Pa motel.

"Maybe we should stop here for the night." Jenny asked.

"OK by me if you think it's safe," he agreed.

She did a turn at the next side road and they pulled up in front of the motel door. There were only 8 units, and most of them seemed to be vacant. Jenny went inside. The owner, who lived behind the office, hauled himself out of the comfort of his easy chair and hurried to the front desk, wondering about a lady her age traveling alone.

"I need a room for myself and my son," she told him.

"Oh, sure, Ma'am," he smiled. "I got one good one with two beds. You'll be just fine there!" He took her money and gave her the key, and she pulled the car up in front of the door to the unit. It was old and small, but it was also cheap and comfortable enough, so they arranged things to suit Jenny's sense of propriety, and then went across the road to Jimmy's Bar to find some dinner.

It was dark in the bar and smelled of stale beer, and there were enough people at the tables that nobody paid attention to them. Jenny was grateful for that, and settled down at a small corner table. She sat with her back to the wall, making Terry sit across from her, with his back to the room, just in case...They ordered hot coffee, and Jenny held the hot mug in her hands to warm them, breathing in the wonderful fragrance of fresh-brewed coffee. What a blessing small things like that could be sometimes. They were in luck, as there was a limited food menu, and they ate their fill of some surprisingly good fish and chips.

Outside, a state police cruiser drove by, but as it passed the motel, something caused the trooper to look away, and he never noticed either the motel or the bar.

After he passed, the angel drifted into the bar to wait.

When they'd finished dinner, they went back to the motel and turned on the TV. Reception was surprisingly good. "I suppose they don't have much else to do out here," Terry observed.

They watched a game show, and then the news came on. "Police have apprehended two of the remaining three convicts who escaped from Deer Lodge Prison two days ago," the blond woman reported. "There is only one convict still on the loose. Terry Singer." She went on to describe him, but Jenny and Terry didn't hear the rest, they were so surprised that Tony and Rafer had been caught.

"I wonder where Tony went wrong?" Terry said. "He had all the details worked out ahead...where he'd go, what disguise he'd use...he was sure he'd be able to hide from them forever!" He shook his head, "and Rafer...I think he even had a friend on the outside...Oh!"

"Yeah," Jenny agreed, "Maybe it wasn't such a great friend after all?"

"Hard to find a friend like you, Jenny," he told her, wanting to take her in his arms but knowing she wouldn't allow it, and not wanting to scare her away. He contented himself with her smile and her nearness, as they both consulted the map of Montana. They slept that night in the same room, each very much aware of the other. Terry lay there longing to hold the woman he loved, while Jenny denied her feelings, but had a hard time going to sleep.

Snow covered the ground in the morning. They prayed for safety and guidance for the day, then loaded their things into the car and left early, heading east again. "I'm going to find a telephone, and I'm going to call Governor Brown and tell him the story," Jenny told him. "Then let's get off highway 2 and find someplace less traveled, OK?"

Terry was awed by the fact that she could "just like that" pick up the phone and call the Governor. He simply nodded, watching her face. Soon he pointed to a phone booth beside a small gas station. She pulled the car up nearby, got out with her hand full of change, and reached for the dangling phone book. It was damp and tattered and it smelled somewhat musty, but she quickly flipped the pages until she located the number and punched it in, dropping her cold coins into the slot.

"I'm not going to stay on the line very long, sir, so I want to tell you this fast," she told the Governor when she succeeded in reaching him. He started to respond, but she stopped him.

" No, please just listen. Terry Singer was promised protection by the FBI, and they owe it to him. He told about this prison break before it took place, and I pleaded with the warden to transfer him to a different area so he wouldn't have to go along. Nobody would listen to me, and now Terry is the only one still on the outside...and he's the only one who didn't want to go! He wants to turn himself in, but only with the written promise that they won't put him back in Deer Lodge. It would mean certain death, and they all know it! Sir, if you can please, please get a promise in writing for us that they will not put Terry Singer back in Deer Lodge, he'll turn himself in! I'll call you again in a couple of days, Sir, and thank you. I have to hang up now."

She hung up the phone and stood for a moment holding onto it, leaning against the cold wall of the dirty booth. Then she took a deep breath and ran for the car through wet, swirling snow that was falling faster and beginning to make drifts. They drove into Kalispell and turned south toward Flathead Lake. The weather grew worse all the time, and Jenny worried about driving much further.

"That last place said it rents by the week," Terry commented as they passed some summer tourist cabins.

Without reply, Jenny turned the car around and went back to take a look. She drove past slowly. The few cabins scattered along the edge of the lake looked deserted except for one pick-up truck at the end unit. "Maybe this is a good place," she agreed. "If we park our car behind some of those bushes, we shouldn't be noticed...for a while at least!"

She found the office located in a house by the road, and signed up for a week, telling the proprietor some story about her 'son' trying to find work in the area so they could get an apartment. This place had a tiny kitchen, so they unloaded some of their food. It was better if they didn't go out any more than they had to.

Someone had thoughtfully stocked some jigsaw puzzles and old magazines in the cabin, so the fugitives had something to occupy their time while the storm reached it's peak and raged outside. Their heat was from a small wall furnace. When it turned on, the small cabin soon got hot and stuffy, and the blower whined in a high pitch. Then when it turned off, the place rapidly turned cold and draft and quiet. They soon adapted by keeping blankets on the backs of their chairs, which they pulled on and off according to the state of the furnace. They bent over 500 puzzle pieces on a small table, heads close together, and worked to complete a picture of a big white farmhouse in a field of ripe wheat.

The wind howled around the corners of the cabin, making the curtains blow out from the windows. "Be great if we had a fireplace, wouldn't it?" Terry commented. "But I guess we're lucky to have this smelly furnace." He glanced out the window and shivered. "I'd sure hate to be out there somewhere trying to survive!"

"You know, this storm might be a blessing to us after all. They aren't so likely to be out in force looking for us in this mess. And they aren't so likely to spot us either, with the visibility so low." She smiled at him. "Let's try to find something good to chew on...you know...comfort food of some kind. And then I'll tell you about growing up in the circus."

"No kidding! You were in the circus?" He eyed her curiously, trying to see if she was serious. "Oh, you're putting me on!"

"No I'm not. Just wait, and I'll tell you about when I flew on the trapeze, and all that." She dug into one of the bags of food, and came up with a box of powdered milk and some chocolate chips. "Here, maybe we can make some hot chocolate with this stuff. And we can eat crackers and jam or peanut butter with it, OK?"

"You bet! You mean you can really make hot chocolate out of that?"

"Just watch me!" she dug around in the bags and came up with the small saucepan he'd brought, which she set on the gas burner, added water, poured in some milk powder and stirred. Then she added half a bag of chocolate chips and a bit of sugar and stirred while it heated. Soon, sure enough, they were sipping hot chocolate out of some chipped mugs.

"This is really great!" He took another sip. "OK, so now tell me about the circus."

She spread jam on a cracker and popped it into her mouth. Then she took a sip of the chocolate, and began to tell him about her strange childhood. The storm howled outside, while she told him the true story of her life. He could hardly believe it was real. She must have been making it up! But no, he could see the pain in her eyes as she told about the fire. She stopped there, and he wanted to hear more.

"So what did you do then? I know about your marriage to Al, and I know you have children....

She nodded.

"Tell me about the rest of it."

"Oh, let's leave that for another time, shall we?" She wasn't sure she wanted to tell him about Al and all the problems she'd had with him over the years. She turned the knob on the small TV set and they watched an old John Wayne movie through the snow on the screen.

Privately, Terry thought the story wasn't nearly as interesting as the one Jenny told him earlier.

The storm died down sometime during the night. In the morning, there was at least a foot or more of snow outside their door. Terry bundled up the best he could in the hand-me-down clothes Jenny had found him. He grabbed a snow shovel that leaned conveniently against the cabin wall, and cleared a path to the car. Then he made a path to the motel office. Then he shoveled the driveway. When he finished he put the shovel back, and stumbled into the cabin, his cheeks and hands red from the cold. He held his hands next to the furnace to try to warm them.

"We have to get you some proper clothes if we're going to be out here very long!"

"Yeah," he agreed. "I could sure use some gloves!" His eyes were bright as he grinned at her. "But it felt good to get that kind of exercise again! Of course, I'll probably be sorry tomorrow!"

"No doubt!" She picked up her own coat. "Now since you've shoveled us out, I'm going to do a little shopping, and find a phone to call the governor again. You'd better stay here out of sight while I'm gone." She saw the look on his face and added, "I'll be back as soon as possible. Hey, you know I have to make the call!"

Driving was tricky until she got to a place where the plow had been through. She managed to find a grocery store in Rollins, where she picked up some food and other supplies, a deck of cards, and a pair of men's gloves. The gas station was nearby, so she filled the tank, paid and got some change, and then stood shivering out in the snow and used the pay phone.

"Hello Sir," she told the governor, when she'd managed to reach him again. "This is Pastor Jenny Brownell again. Have you been able to get an agreement for Terry Singer? He is anxious to turn himself in. He doesn't want to be a fugitive, Sir, but he just can not take a chance of being put back into Deer Lodge."

"Where is he now?" the governor's voice boomed over the wire. "Tell us where he is, and we'll arrange to have him picked up. We'll take care of him OK!"

"As soon as I have your word, in writing and guaranteed, that he won't be put back in Deer Lodge!"

"Lady, do you know how much trouble you're in for harboring a criminal? And for aiding and abetting an escaped convict?"

"Yes, Sir, I do, but I also know what will happen to Terry if I let you put him back in there! It would be as good as a death sentence, and I can't let that happen. I'll check with you again soon."

She hung up the phone, angry to the core.

"They don't plan to help you at all! We have to think of something else," she told Terry when she got back. "There has to be some way to get them to agree to move you!" She unpacked the grocery bag and tossed the gloves at him.

"Thanks, Jenny, these are great!" He tried them on, flexing his hands and admiring the fit. He was overwhelmed with gratitude for her thoughtfulness, but didn't know how to tell her. "Boy, thanks!" he said again.

"You're welcome, Terry." She grinned, watching him, then turned serious again. "What we need is a good lawyer!" She arranged boxes and cans and bread as she thought aloud.

"I had a lawyer in Ohio. He's the one who got me into protective custody in the first place." Terry sat on the chair next to the small table, his foot propped on his bed, bouncing absently. "He seemed to feel bad when they sentenced me so long."

"Do you think he'd be willing to help us now?"

"Maybe...I guess so. At least it's worth a shot, isn't it? He already knows the whole story, and that would save a lot of time and trouble, wouldn't it?"

"Right. OK, what's his name, and where is he?" She got pen and paper out of her purse, ready to write down the information.

"He's in Dayton. Name is Bob Fenton. I can't remember his address or phone number, but his office was in downtown Dayton, I think. He'll be in the phone book."

"OK, I'm going out and call him. You keep your fingers crossed and pray. Better yet, let's pray together now before I call him!" They bowed their heads and asked earnestly again for God's protection, and for wisdom to know what to do next. And they prayed that Bob Fenton would be able and willing to help Terry."

She reached the attorney with a minimum of difficulty and laid out the problem for him. "So you see, we're in a pickle here. We can't take the chance of turning Terry in without the assurance that he won't be thrown into the lions' den, so to speak. And we probably can't stay hidden forever, either. Can you help us?"

"Where are you now?" the lawyer asked, not really expecting her to answer, but in the habit of asking.

"Hidden out safely for now, I hope," she answered. "You won't be able to call us, but I can call you if need be. Will you help us?"

"Yes...yes, I will. I'll make some calls today, and see what I can accomplish that way. If necessary, I'll fly out to talk to the officials personally and plead Terry's case." He was silent for a second or two then added, "and I sure hope it turns out better than last time!"

"What time should I call you tomorrow, then?"

"Better make it about 1:00 your time. That'll be 3:00 here, won't it? I should have something by then, with any luck."

She hung up feeling somewhat more hopeful. At least somebody was now willing to listen and try to help. She certainly hoped he'd be able to appeal to the sense of justice and fair play that she felt the governor, at least, must have. She wasn't so sure of the others. Especially Warden Biggers. She wondered whether his pay depended on the number of men under his care. There must be some reason why he didn't want to lose Terry.

She parked carefully behind the trees, and hurried to the cabin. Terry flung open the door before she could reach for the knob. "Well?" he asked. "Come on, tell me!" he begged, as she teased him by not answering, looking serious.

She broke into a huge grin. "He'll help us! He's gonna call the governor himself and see what he can do, and if need be, he'll come out here and meet with him in person."

He grabbed her hands and pulled her close and they danced around the room, knocking over a chair, as they laughed together. Then they sat down to talk over what to do next, and how they could appeal effectively to the authorities. And above all they prayed for wisdom, and for mercy from the powers who had control of his destiny. Then, to keep from going crazy while they waited, they played card games one after another until it was so late they had to sleep.

"I've been thinking, Terry," she said in the morning. "Maybe we'd better move on to another place. Sitting too long in the same location may be a mistake. They'll eventually find us...you know how they always say if you get lost to stay in one place and somebody will find you?...well..."

"Yeah, maybe you're right. Anyway, should we be using the same phone all the time? Can they track us that way eventually?"

"I don't know, but I guess we shouldn't take chances." She spread the map out on the little table. "Let's go back and take highway 2 over to Browning and then cut off south to Choteau...or there's a little road here going to a town called Agawam. Looks like a real small town though. Sometimes that's a mistake. Everybody's nosy in a little place like that. They don't have much else to do but poke into everybody's business. No...let's try Choteau, it's a little bit bigger...what do you think?"

"We can drive over that way and check it out, at least," he agreed. If that doesn't look promising, we can always head on over toward Great Falls. Or we can just drive until we come to a place that looks good, like we did here."

They packed their things, carefully making sure they didn't leave any trace of a clue behind, and left the key in the cabin rather than going to the office. They were more than 20 miles down the road before the state police cruiser stopped at the motel to inquire about Terry.

"Only tenants we have right now are a lady and her son in cabin 6 over there, the owner told the big trooper. Looks like they're out right now though. But they're paid for the week, so I guess they'll be back. Why, officer, what's wrong?"

"Looking for an escaped convict. What does the guy look like?"

"Don't know for sure, except he's sort of a small man. Only time I saw him was when he shoveled the driveway for us. Real good worker, he is. Like to have that kind of people all the time! I don't think he's your man."

"Well, I think I'll just have a look around anyway. Thanks." The trooper walked down the path to the cabin and checked around the outside. Nothing there that looked suspicious. He stood around for a while, and then tried the door, not expecting it to open. When it did, he ducked back instinctively, waiting for trouble. Then, when nothing happened, he stepped inside. He knew instantly there was nobody staying in that cabin. He picked the keys off the table and swore, then ran back to the office and threw them on the desk. "Looks like the birds have flown," he said, and going to his car, he called out the information, then went back to talk to the owner.

"What kind of car did they have?"

"A white one...Buick, I think...not too old. I took the license number, it's here somewhere." He flipped a page, and turned the book for the officer to see. "I can't believe that nice lady is some kind of crook. She seemed real pleasant and ordinary."

"Yeah, well, you can't always tell, can you?"

Down the road, Jenny and Terry stopped at a gas station for hot coffee in Styrofoam cups. She picked up a small package of cookies, hoping they weren't too stale, and a newspaper too. Back in the car, Terry drove while Jenny leafed through the paper. "We're on the second page now," she told him. "That's a good sign, at least."

She kept looking, but didn't find anything else interesting, so folded the paper and handed Terry a cookie."Here, have a snack with your coffee. You know, I've been thinking again...maybe we should go into the city this time. If they find out we've been staying in little places like the cabin, maybe they'll keep on looking in those places. Maybe we should find a big motel and hide in plain sight a little while?"

He marveled at how she thought. "You know, you'd have made a real good criminal, Lady! You have a devious mind...but you're probably dead right." He chuckled, surprising Jenny, since he'd been so serious most of the time. "I'd hate to be the guys following us. They must be having a time of it!"

"I hope so. Anyway, what I think is, we need to try to think differently than an ordinary criminal would. They know how to predict what a criminal will do. I know they have psychologists to help them on that stuff. So we have to try to be normal if we can. She glanced over at him, sizing him up physically. "What do you think of becoming a lady for a while?"

He groaned. "Oh no! I can't even imagine being caught in drag! I'd never live it down if that happened! Isn't there any other way?" He looked so unhappy she laughed.

"Oh well, if it's going to make you so miserable, we'll try something else. I think you need a disguise of some sort, though. Maybe I'll bleach your hair."

He groaned again.

"Come on, you have to cooperate if we're going to stay free long enough for Bob Fenton to arrange things!"

"Well, what if I get a hat of some kind, and some glasses? I could live with that stuff."

She nodded. "OK, we'll try that and see if it makes enough difference. Your picture's been spread around enough that we need to do something though. All we need is for somebody to recognize you!"

As they drove into Great Falls, a large shopping mall loomed ahead on the left. She slowed and turned in. "OK, you stay in the car and pretend to read the paper. Keep it in front of you if anybody comes past. I'll see what I can find for a disguise."

She was gone so long he began to worry that she'd been caught. But then he saw her coming, carrying several bags.

"Where have you been, anyhow...buying out the whole place?" he demanded impatiently, then immediately repented. "I'm sorry. It's just I was worried."

"Sorry it took so long. I got a bunch of stuff to try. We'll see what works, and maybe we can change from one thing to another on different days." She shoved the last bag into the back seat and settled into the car again. "Now, let's find a good busy motel, where they mind their own business and ignore other travelers!"

They drove around the city eyeing the various motels, until a big "Best Western" place caught their fancy. It was called "The Ponderosa," and it had its own restaurant. "Looks like just what we need for now," Jenny said. Terry nodded his agreement. She went in and signed up for a room as Mr. and Mrs. Henry Stearns, and this time they left their food in the trunk out of sight.

She put all the bags of stuff she'd bought on his bed and left him to sort through it. "I'm going to call Bob Fenton, and then I'm going to use this bubble bath they've provided and just soak in the tub for maybe an hour!"

He grinned at her. "Sounds good to me, he agreed. I might do the same. Been a long time since I've soaked in a tub!"

She went out again to find a pay phone far from the motel, and called Ohio. "No luck, so far," he told her, when she reached the attorney. I guess I'll have to come out to Montana and meet with the governor in person. Hate to have to do that, but sometimes it makes a big difference. I'll plan to be there in a couple of days. Are you OK?"

"Yes, so far. We've managed to keep out of their clutches up to now, and I don't plan to let them catch us until we're ready for Terry to turn himself in. Where will you be when you're out here?"

He told her, and she wrote down the information, telling him she'd contact him when he arrived. Then she went back to the motel and filled the tub with wonderful warm suds. She sighed as she eased her tired body down into the water's soothing embrace. She could feel the tension slipping away, and the soreness of her joints and muscles fading. She sat there until the water cooled too much, then reluctantly got out and dried herself, rubbing vigorously, making her skin tingle. She stepped out into the bedroom wrapped in a large towel, to look for some clean clothes to wear.

Terry's face, when he glanced up from the TV, was a give-away of his thoughts, and Jenny's face flushed, but then something inside her broke. She had been so starved for love for her whole life, that now she simply forgot everything but that this man loved her and wanted her ... and she loved and wanted him! She smiled at him coyly, and let the towel slide a bit. He rose slowly from the chair, then crossed to her in a couple of fast strides, and took her in his arms. This time she didn't resist his touch, yielding herself to him as he loosened the towel and dropped it to the floor.

A long time later, she turned to look at him. Joyfully she said, "I'm starved, how about you?" He propped himself up on one elbow and grinned.

"Yeah, I guess I am too, now that you mention it. Let's go down and eat. Of course, you realize that means we'll have to get dressed again?"

"Well, I should hope so!" She waited while he showered, and then took over the bathroom while he dressed. She arranged her hair differently than usual, wondering whether she should dye it black or something, and applied more makeup than she normally used. When she was dressed comfortably in clean slacks and shirt, she stepped back into the bedroom to check on Terry.

He turned to face her, and she stepped back involuntarily. "Oh!" Then she laughed. "I really didn't recognize you!"

Straight brown hair hung down over his ears, and round, wire-rimmed glasses framed his sad brown eyes. A brown sweater over a plaid shirt, with khaki slacks completed his makeover. He looked different, but he looked good. You had to look hard to tell it was a wig.

"Well, whadda ya think?" he asked anxiously.

"I like it! I think it'll work for a while, too!"

"Great! Then let's go eat...I'm starved!" He grabbed her arm and headed for the door. "By the way, what did Bob say?"

They enjoyed dinner at the restaurant downstairs...it was a good-sized one, where they could blend with the crowd. Soft music from the big-band era played in the background, and the plush seats were soft and comfortable. They lingered over several cups of tea and dessert, then walked slowly back to their room and watched television until bedtime.

As they snuggled together in bed, Jenny felt a combination of guilt and happiness. "Lord, is it a sin to be so happy and to love this man who needs me so badly?" she prayed silently.

The angel stood guard outside the door.

They moved on again the next day, heading east toward Lewistown, then south to Billings, where they again found a big motel for the night. It was off-season, so the rates were fairly reasonable, but still Jenny began to worry about her dwindling supply of cash. So the following night they found a little place in the Bighorn Mountains, just sort of tucked into a bend in the road. Not many people traveled that way in the snow, so they had the little motel pretty much to themselves.

"I'm afraid it's not as safe for us, but maybe with the new disguise it'll be OK," Jenny said, grinning at her new companion, who sat glumly, wearing a skirt and sweater under his long jacket. His shoulder-length dark hair made him look vaguely Indian, and the deep wrinkles around his mouth suggested he'd spent too much time in the sun without protecting his skin. She'd at least given him sneakers and socks instead of making him wear the pantyhose she'd rather have had him use. She signed in as Mrs. Parmalee and her daughter Brenda. That night they used their food bags again, in their room.

When they contacted Bob Fenton the following afternoon he still had nothing to report, but he did have a meeting scheduled for two days from then. They spent their days on the run, driving through the mountains on obscure roads that sometimes were barely passable in the snow. Once they had to turn back because a road was closed. Terry managed to find all the country and western stations on the radio, and they learned all the words to a lot of songs while driving. Sometimes they stayed in a city, when Jenny couldn't stand the little "cabin in the woods" places any longer. Time seemed to her to stand still, while they were endlessly driving, moving, hiding.

Bob Fenton's meetings with the governor dragged on, and Jenny worried about paying his bill, too, along with everything else.

At last the day came when the attorney could report, "Yes, they've promised not to put him back in Deer Lodge! They've promised to turn him over to the Feds instead of the locals! I have it in writing. You've won, Jenny. Now he can turn in!

Terry was happy and sad at the same time. He'd miss Jenny terribly. He loved her more every day, and he knew she returned his love. Holding her close and feeling her warm arms around him was such a joy to his love-starved heart. She was a really remarkable person, and the only one who'd ever taken any time for him or done anything special for him. He had to turn in, if only for her sake. His heart broke as he told her, "I want you to get out of the state now before I turn in though. They might try to pin something on you for helping me. I don't want to take that chance. Promise me you'll move right now...please, Jenny!"

She felt his strong arms around her, and breathed in his clean manly smell, and could hardly stand to think of being without him again, but she knew in her heart he was right. Reluctantly she answered, "Yeah, of course you're right, Terry. They may try to convict me of something. Yes, I'll move...as fast as I can arrange it." She closed her eyes. But how will I live now without you?

Later she called Karen and told her some of the story, and that she wanted to move back to California. "Sure, Mom. Come on back, and we'll get a house together," Karen promised. "Just go ahead and call the movers, Mom, and I'll take care of the bill for you."

So Jenny called Baker's Movers and arranged to have her furniture picked up. She called Marge to ask for her help, and the big lady agreed to take care of packing for her and see that things were done properly. "Thanks so very much, Marge. God will bless you, I know. You're a good friend! It wouldn't be easy to take Pansy either, at least not right now, so can you keep her? I really love her, Marge. Thanks for letting me have her for a while anyway."

At the last minute though, Jenny just couldn't stand it. She had to go and take care of things for herself. She made sure Terry was holed up safely, and then drove back to her house in Missoula. She was in the middle of the mess, directing movers here and there, stuffing things into boxes, when the Marshall drove up. He stomped up the steps and came in without knocking. "Just where do you think you're going?" He poked around at the boxes, as though he expected to find Terry in one of them.

She kept on packing. Oh no, Lord, it can't be they'll arrest me now, after all this! Not now, when I'm so close to being free!

"I'm moving back to California," she told him, putting on a cheerful face. "Now that it's safe for Terry to turn himself in, I can leave." She hoped that was true.

"Your precious Terry has not turned himself in yet, and we know you've been helping him! We're watching you, lady! If you have the guts to go where he is, we'll get you sure!"

"I can believe it, officer. Well, don't you worry... he's only waiting to make sure I'm safe. As soon as I'm gone, Terry will turn himself in. It's all arranged."

"You'd better be telling me the truth, Lady! It'll go hard on the two of you if you aren't!" He shook his finger close to her nose. She gave him a weak smile and nodded, as she reached for a stack of books to tuck into the box she was packing. The Marshall poked around some more, nosing into everything, but finally headed for the door. "You'd be well advised to get on out of Montana... and fast, Lady!"

"Yeah, yeah!" she muttered under her breath. She grinned at the movers, who were looking at her with obvious curiosity. Without any explanation to them she went over to Marge's for the cup of tea she'd been offered. When the movers had finished and her stuff was all gone, Jenny finished cleaning the house, while she debated what to do about picking Terry up again. Finally she decided she'd just have to take the chance, so she drove as cautiously as she could back to where she'd left him. The car seemed to her to stand out like a beacon now, but she prayed, "Lord, please don't let them stop us now ... please Lord, let this work out safely for both of us." And miraculously, she was able to get Terry to Butte, where he hid out alone again, and she went to a motel.

She ate some dinner without really tasting it, and then went back to her room, where she spent the evening watching the news and praying. She was just about to get ready for bed when loud banging on the door startled her ... "Police, open up!"

She started to turn the knob, but the door crashed open and several cops charged into the room, nearly knocking her over. "He's here somewhere, all right! He hasta be!" one of them yelled. But they didn't find him, of course. Jenny stood watching politely. Finally, one of them grabbed her arm in frustration. "We're taking you downtown!"

As he pushed her outside ahead of him, making her bad arm ache with his rough grip, Jenny glimpsed men with machine guns stationed on the roof opposite her room! That shook her up somewhat. She caught her breath. It's like something out of the movies!

They shoved her into the back seat of a squad car and drove away, lights flashing, but thankfully, no siren.

She prayed for wisdom and guidance, and once in the interrogation room downtown, Jenny began to tell her story. She told them how she had tried so hard to stop the escape. How she'd gone to everyone she could think of to ask for help for Terry, and nobody would do anything for him until it was too late, and he'd been forced to break out with the others. Then how she'd called everyone including the Governor to get help so he could turn in safely, and how nobody would help with that either.

"It just seems that once you're convicted of a crime, that's it! You can never overcome that, or really reform. Nobody will believe you again for anything, no matter how innocent you really are. You have no rights at all!"

They all stared at her, grim-faced. Then the sheriff shook his head. "Tough, but that's how it is! We'll have to keep you overnight," he growled.

"On what charges?" she asked.

He ignored the question.

"What charges do you have against me?" she asked again. Then seeing he wasn't going to answer, she became angry. "It's as bad as it was at Lompoc!"

"What happened at Lompoc?"

"One of the guards at the F.C.I. there bled me of over $3,000 to keep Terry alive!"

"You better be careful how you accuse people, Lady!" he warned.

"Oh, I'm careful all right! I happen to have proof of this one!"

"What kind of proof?"

"I have letters he wrote. They're all the proof I'll need!" She was indignant, but prayed silently that she could keep cool.

"Where do you have those letters?" He looked at her, a crafty smile crossing his face... "In your car?"

"Yes"

"Pretty stupid place to keep them, don't you think?"

"No, officer, not unless you try to steal them now to protect one of your own kind!"

He glared at her angrily.

"Officer, I'm on my way to California, and I'll be out of your hair entirely. As soon as I'm safely out of the state, Terry will turn himself in, now that he has the signed agreement that they'll put him somewhere else, not at Deer Lodge. That's all he was waiting for!"

"You'd better be right, Ms. Brownell. If he doesn't, there'll be hell to pay!" He frowned and banged his fist on the desk as though wishing it were Terry. Then he turned to her, his lip curled in a sort of snarl. "Get out of here, and get on out of the state!" He stalked out of the room, leaving her with a young recruit who ushered her out of the station.

The angel dusted his hands as he followed her to the squad car.

She didn't say anything during the drive back to her motel, and neither did the young cop. It was a strange, silent ride.

She fell into bed and slept fitfully for a few hours until dawn, when she rose, dressed hurriedly, and shivered in the cold car as she drove toward the state line. She stopped once at a small diner for a take-out cup of coffee on her way.

When she finally crossed into Idaho, she found a pay phone and called the number she'd memorized. He answered on the first ring, and she told him, "It's OK, I'm in Idaho and on my way!"

He gave a deep sigh, "I'm glad you're safe!" His voice broke as he added, "OK, then I'll give them the call. I love you, Jenny! And thank you for all you've done for me. I can't wait to be with you again, my dear Love ..."

"I know, Terry! I love you, too. It's breaking my heart ... I'll go now, and I'll be praying for you!" She hung up the phone and leaned her head against the receiver in her hand, as she prayed God to keep him safe from harm.

The angel stood by, waiting.

CHAPTER TWENTY-FOUR

They lied! As soon as Terry showed up at the station officers cuffed him, shoved him into a patrol car and drove him to directly to Deer Lodge. "God must have been watching over me," he told Jenny later. "It's the only reason I can think that I lasted even one night there, much less a month!"

"What did you do? How did you keep them from..."

"Told them a big story about hiding out in the mountains, and how I stayed one jump ahead of the law all the time... they were so hyped on thinking about my fooling the cops for so long, they kind of forgot about the Federal prisoner bit somehow!" His eyes told her more than his words. "And I prayed a lot!"

She was in Sacramento. Karen paid for the move, but she didn't buy the promised house. Instead, she took her mother to Napa and left her with Johnny and his wife. Johnny didn't know what to do with her, so he got her an apartment in Sacramento. "I'll be moving there soon too," he promised. But in the meantime, Jenny was left alone in a city where she didn't know a soul and had nothing to do. She got a job in a local real estate office, where she felt like a fish out of water.

She wept when she heard the news. They had put Terry in terrible danger, right back into the same cellblock he'd left! How could they do such a thing, when they had given her a signed agreement saying they wouldn't? She was furious. I'll sue somebody over this! But who? And how? He'll have to stay there in Deer Lodge now until the trial, and who knows when that will be?

She had no friends, no family near, no reason to stay there, and every reason to want to be with Terry. She prayed, "Lord, what am I doing here? What should I do?" She couldn't afford to move her furniture again, and her pride wouldn't let her ask Karen to pay again, so she prayed and put an ad in the paper. By some miracle of God, the heaviest of her furniture sold at her asking price to the first looker. With that clear answer she quit her job and went back to Montana! She did call Johnny and tell him goodbye, but gave him no time to protest.

"I have no life here, Johnny. I'm needed and wanted there, and I'm going." She didn't add, "and I hope they don't put me in prison," but she thought it. She packed the car and rented a large trailer, which she filled with the remainder of her possessions. Then with a quick fervent prayer, she took her place behind the wheel and drove off, not looking back.

The roads were slippery, but she drove carefully. She'd never pulled a trailer before, and was nervous about it. She was OK until she got into the mountains, then she prayed constantly as car and trailer wound around the sharp curves, sometimes with sheer drop-offs to the side. She had chains put on the tires at

Salt Lake City. Then she headed north toward Montana. The roads were pretty clear as she started, but the further she went into the mountains, the worse they got. She stopped overnight at Pocatello and had supper at the motel.

"Where ya heading," the friendly waitress wanted to know?

"Have to get to Butte," Jenny replied. "But I'm pulling a trailer, and it's a real adventure!"

"I'll bet!" She poured hot water over the 2 tea bags in Jenny's little metal pot. "I hear we're in for some weather, too! Maybe you better stay over another day!"

"Oh no!" Jenny groaned." "I'll have to get a real early start in the morning ... I just have to get to Butte tomorrow!" She finished the meal and went to her room, where she took a long hot shower, and then watched the weather report. Sure enough, they were predicting snow in the mountains for the next day, and advising people to use chains and to carry emergency equipment if they had to drive. She took an aspirin to help her sleep, and set the alarm for six.

Snowplows were out next morning, sanding the slopes. There were a few regular snow flurries but things went OK until about 3:00 in the afternoon. She handled the situation pretty well. Then, somewhere in the mountains, the sky lowered. Snow fell fast and continuously, and the wind picked up more and more force, until Jenny could barely see the road. It was hard to tell where she was, as the snow blew in sheets in front of the car, creating a complete whiteout, so she had to almost stop. She was afraid to do that, though, for fear someone would hit her from behind, not seeing her in the blizzard. That's what it was, all right, a real blizzard. She was scared and tired and alone ... but not alone, either."The Lord is here with me, I know." She told herself out loud. "He promised he'd always be with me. Help me now, Jesus! Please take me safely there."

A few minutes later she started around a curve, turned the wheel too sharply, and the trailer jackknifed! "Oh no! Lord, help!" she cried as she hit the brakes and felt the car slide. It came to a halt only a few feet from a drop-off. She wasn't good at backing the trailer, but she prayed and backed and jockeyed, and at last managed to get straight again and headed down the mountain once more. She was soaked with sweat in the cold, and her whole body shook as she realized the danger she had been in. It was a miracle nobody had crashed into her! "Thank you, Lord! Thank you!" she kept saying over and over, and "Oh Lord, help me!"

And the angel guided her white-knuckled hands and steered with her as the trailer swayed back and forth seeming ready to overturn at any moment.

At last, after what seemed forever, the wind eased and the snow let up to a normal fall again. Deep drifts had formed across the road, and she hadn't seen another vehicle for a while. "I wonder if they've closed the road. I'll bet they have. It's really terrible out here!" she told herself. "I can't believe I was able to get out of that jam ... it had to be an angel or something. I couldn't have done that by myself!" She began praising God as she drove, easing through the drifts, as evening came on and darkness fell rapidly.

She drove and prayed, and passed a plow and a pick-up coming the other way. There didn't seem to be any place to stop, and she needed to get to Butte, so she kept driving and somehow got off the mountain at last and drove into another blizzard! The windows iced up and the heater hardly made a difference, it was so cold outside. "Maybe I'm gonna die out here by myself," she said, "but maybe that angel hung around ... I sure hope so! I really want to get there and help Terry!"

The angel smiled as he held the wheel with her.

She was so tired now it was hard to keep her eyes open, and the snow seemed to hypnotize her. She was tempted to stop along the road somewhere and sleep, but she knew if she did that she'd probably die out here in the snow. So she kept inching along, trying to keep the trailer on the road. At first she thought she was hallucinating when she made out some dim lights, but then she realized it was really a city ... she was in Butte ... she had made it! She could hardly see the city lights through the blowing snow, but she'd made it! She felt as though she were an arctic explorer who'd just found the Promised Land or something.

Now to find a place to rest! It was 10 o'clock at night, and she realized the town was pretty well closed up. Nobody was out. Nothing was open. She turned in at the first motel sign she came to. A fleabag that looked like a palace to Jenny! She pulled the trailer as far out of the road as she could, and stepped out into the minus fifty degree cold and nearly fell. She pulled her coat close around her, burying her chin as far as possible in the turned-up collar, and stumbled into the office. They had a room and hot coffee and food ... not good, but edible, and she was grateful for safety and shelter as she huddled in bed, her coat on top of the blankets, and slipped into an exhausted sleep.

Next morning she found she was too late after all. They'd hurried Terry's trial. They convicted him of escaping and sentenced him to four additional years for that ... the others, including Manici, got three years! Jenny'd had no chance to get there in time to help defend him. She felt it was a "kangaroo court" and the whole thing was a farce.

Setting her jaw grimly, she determined the first thing to do was find a place to stay. She couldn't afford a motel every night, even if it was a fleabag! She bought a paper and scanned the ads. There was a mobile home for rent in a near-by park. She made an appointment and met the owner there, and before mid-afternoon she'd signed a rental agreement and was carrying her stuff in from the trailer in the bitterest cold she could ever remember. Once she had everything inside and could keep the door closed, the place began to get a little bit warm, but there was still frost on the inside of the windows and the door, and even on the front wall. She bundled herself into as many clothes as she could manage, and still shivered.

She had to go out one more time to turn the trailer in at a gas station that handled rental trailers. Then she picked up a few groceries and went back to the mobile home, wrapped herself in a blanket, and settled down at the table. She took out pencil and paper to plan what to do next. Her bad arm ached deep in the bones from the terrible cold.

She called Terry to tell him what she was doing, and when they wouldn't put her call through she insisted on talking to Warden Biggers. "Warden, I must talk with Terry! I have to know that he's safe for sure after you people went back on your word!" She was taking a breath, ready to really let the Warden know what she thought of him and the whole system, when he got a word in.

"Your precious Terry is on his way back to California. Should be getting there about now, in fact!"

"What?! Are you serious? Where in California?"

"We sent him to Soledad," Biggers told her. Then he added, "Hope that suits your fancy! I'm glad to be rid of him and of you, Lady! Don't come around here pestering me again, you hear?"

He hung up on her and she fell to her knees, still clutching the receiver, and wept from relief, grief and frustration, and cold and loneliness. She cried as though she'd never stop, releasing pent-up emotions and tension she'd stored up for months.

When finally the flood of tears slowed, she prayed. "Lord, what am I to do now? I thought you led me back here and opened the way ... but for what? Is there something I'm supposed to do here, or should I just turn around again and go back to California?" She was exhausted and weighed down with stress, frustration and cold. She crawled into bed fully clothed, thinking just to rest for a few minutes while she decided what to do next. It was only mid-afternoon, but she huddled in a little cocoon of warmth and soon slept a restful, restoring sleep. Like a hibernating animal, she slept clear on through the night. She finally woke at about 6:00 the next morning in the cold dark trailer. It took her a minute to remember where she was. It came in on her mind like a wave, and she woke completely then and found her way to the bathroom.

She brewed herself a pot of hot strong coffee and drank two big mugs of it. Slowly the fog cleared from her brain, and she began to think once more. She spent the day writing out an account of all that had happened to Terry in Montana. The next day she went to some local radio and TV stations with it, telling the various reporters about how crooked the system is. She told about the weeks of hiding out while she tried to get the prison officials to agree not to put Terry into danger again, and how they'd lied and gone back on their written word. And she told how they hadn't listened in the first place when she begged for help so he wouldn't have to break out, and how the others who planned the break got 3 years sentence and Terry got 4.

They wouldn't use any of her story! Some of them even believed it, but they covered up the truth to protect the prison officials ... and their own jobs. She couldn't understand it ... the whole world seemed against Terry. He was just one small, helpless man against the huge, evil system. After trying for a month without success to get someone to air his story, Jenny took stock of her situation once more. Her rental agreement had run out, and she had gotten nowhere with the media. There would be no justice there for Terry. She'd had enough of Montana. She packed up again and started back for California.

This time though, she was headed for the coast south of San Francisco. She didn't even stop to see Johnny ... she'd call him later. Instead, she steered south from Sacramento, driving almost on 'automatic pilot'. Now and then she looked around in surprise, hardly realizing how she'd gotten to wherever she was at the time. The angel kept his hand over hers on the wheel, and she made it safely over the treacherous mountain passes and through California's brown and green landscape.

She worried about Terry, but tried to leave him in God's hands. Then she worried again. She worried about what she'd do when she got to Soledad, then tried to leave that in God's hands. Then she worried about it again. She kept praying though, and the miles passed steadily under the wheels of her car until she was surprised to see the sign for San Jose'. She was almost there! It was nearly dark, and she decided it would be better to get to the Soledad area in the morning when she was fresh and could think better. She stopped at a motel, hardly even noticing which one it was. She was operating almost like a robot, mechanically doing the expected things.

She entered a small Italian restaurant and ordered something, which she ate without really tasting it, though she loved Italian food. Then suddenly, as she lingered over a cup of hot coffee, something changed inside her as though a switch had been thrown, and she seemed to wake up. It was as though she'd been asleep for a long time, like coming out of a dream. Her mind cleared and she began to function well once more.

Back at the motel room she sat down as she usually did, and began to plan. First she'd visit Terry and make sure he was OK. She needed to check his situation before she made any real plans for herself. She wouldn't make the mistake again of renting a place before she knew the situation! Then if it looked as though he'd be in Soledad for a long time, she'd rent a house and start a ministry for the prisoner's families again.

She looked forward to working with the women once more. It seemed forever since she'd had to quit teaching her classes back in Montana, and she remembered how hungry the prisoner's wives were to know about the Lord. And she was hungry again to lead them to her savior.

"Lord, you've been so faithful to me all through this mess. Thank you for keeping me safe, and please help me to learn whatever it is you want to teach me with all these trials. And please Lord, keep Terry safe, and let me be a blessing and a help to him and to others too."

The angel listened, and smiled a golden smile.

CHAPTER TWENTY-FIVE

Mid-morning brought clear blue skies and a stiff wind. Jenny pulled her light coat tighter around herself as she hurried up the long sidewalk that led from the parking lot to the prison entrance.

She entered the cold, forbidding structure, and went through all the now - familiar ritual one has to endure to visit a prisoner, her stomach churning with rebellion against the rules and questions and restrictions. But finally she was allowed to see him. This prison at Soledad was a protective housing unit and Terry was in phu2. She waited while he came down through endless echoing hallways and locked doors that clanged behind him, to the visiting unit. Then he eagerly entered the room through one door, while Jenny was allowed in through the opposite door. The only furniture in the room was a long table and some chairs. Terry opened his arms and she went into them and he held her close for a long moment, disregarding the guards watching through the window. They broke away before the guard could come in and protest, and sat down at the table.

He took her hands across the table and held them in his. "I thought you'd never get here! I've missed you so!" His voice was tight with emotion, and his eyes spoke more than words.

"I came as soon as I could, Love. I tried to do something about the rotten system in Montana first, but they wouldn't cooperate ... They're all just worried about their own skins. Nobody cares about justice any more." She said it bitterly, but then paused and shook her head. "No, I can't feel this way. God has some reason for all of this, and I will not let the enemy use me that way. Somehow, Terry, there's a reason for this."

"I only wish I knew what God's reason is." He sighed, "but I suppose that's what faith is all about, isn't it? He kept her hands in his as she asked about his surroundings, his cell, whether he had a cellmate.

He had two of them. It was even more crowded than Deer Lodge. "They're just kids! Bucky got in trouble for dealing drugs and Joe, the younger one, is in for forcible rape. Both of 'em were abused real bad as youngsters." He sighed again, "I can't believe people treat their kids as bad as they do ... and how the poor things survive is to get hard and mean. Kids are meant to be loved and cared for ... Anyway, I'm tryin' to be a witness to 'em."

Jenny nodded, tears in her eyes, thinking of Terry's own boyhood and how he'd been treated. "I'll pray for them, and for you to be able to lead them to Jesus. You're right, Terry ... it's hard to be a kid these days!"

She told him about her adventures driving over the mountains with the trailer in the storm and the cold. "I know there was an angel with me ... it's the only way I could have made that trip safely!" she declared. "God is so good, and he's with me in everything I do... but why doesn't he answer my prayers for you? I wonder why you can't get out of this place? It doesn't seem fair, when other men who have even committed murder are let out in only 4 or 5 years sometimes!"

He nodded, "I can't imagine what he has in mind ... I'm gonna trust him no matter what! But I'm sure gonna keep praying to get out of this hell-hole too!"

"Me too!" she promised. "In the meantime I guess I'll find some kind of house to rent, where I can work with the wives and families again. They need so much help, Terry! They need food and beds and somebody to care about them ... and most of all they need to know Jesus as their Savior. That's what I'll be doing here while we're waiting for you to get out of this place."

She started to say more, but the guard came in and took Terry away, not even letting him look back. She followed the other guard back out to the waiting room, where other women were going through the process of being searched before they were allowed to visit their loved ones. It was a cold, dehumanizing routine, and it made Jenny sad to watch them. She left the prison, and went to buy a newspaper.

The house she found to rent was in Salinas. It was an older two-story stucco place that needed work, but it was livable and could hold up to six people besides herself. She bought cleaning supplies and a new elastic arm brace, and spent a week scrubbing and fixing the place up. Then she laid in a supply of groceries and got out all the Bibles she'd gathered over the years. She was ready to start her work in this new place. She prayed for God's blessing and guidance, and went out to find the lost sheep.

Sally Jane Foley sat in her beat-up Ford in the parking lot at Soledad prison, waiting for visiting hours. She'd spent the night there in her sleeping bag, and had found a gas station with hot water and soap in the rest room. Sally was almost at the end of her rope. There was no money for anything more than the rent and heat and light, and some pretty lean rations for herself and Tommy. It was hard to scrape up enough gas money to come to see Andy even once a month. She checked her hair and lipstick in the rear-view mirror ... it was almost time. She watched as an attractive older lady walked toward the car.

Jenny waved at the girl in the Ford. "Can I talk to you a minute?" she called. "It's all right, I'm not selling anything and I'm visiting a prisoner myself," she assured the wary woman.

Sally Jane opened the window halfway. "What?"

"I was just wondering whether you spent the night in your car?"

"What if I did? I didn't bother anybody, did I?"

"Guess not. Hey, I'm Pastor Jenny Brownell, and I have a house in Salinas, a few miles down the road, where you can sleep tonight if you want. I'll feed you a good dinner too."

"What's the catch? I mean, why would you wanna invite a stranger to your house ... what are you, some kind of pervert?"

Jenny laughed."No, but I can see why you might think that. I'm a pastor, like I said, and the catch is, you'd have to sit through a Bible Study class."

"That's it?"

"Yep."

Sally Jane unlocked the door, opened it and got out. She stood looking down at Jenny, who was at least 5 inches shorter than she. "Ya don't look crazy or anything," she observed.

"No," Jenny agreed.

"Well, where's your house?"

"Tell you what, let's meet here after visiting hours and you can follow me there … it'll be easier that way, don't you think?"

"OK, I guess."

"And hey, if you know anybody else who needs a place to sleep, I can take a couple more women. Just tell them to meet us here." Jenny held out her hand. "I didn't get your name?"

"I'm Sally Jane Foley, and you must be crazy, but I'll go along with you, I guess. There are a couple of other wives in the same boat as me. If I see 'em, I'll let 'em know about your offer."

They walked into the prison together and went through the process, not looking at each other again. It was an embarrassing procedure, and neither of them wished to share it with anyone.

Jenny told Terry about the meeting with Sally Jane. "Hey, that's great … I told Bucky and Joe about you, and Bucky's gonna have his wife talk to you too. Looks like you have a start, Pastor Jenny!"

She grinned and then sighed. "It'll seem good to get back to the Lord's work… I only wish you could be involved in it with me… not shut up in here! Oh, but I know you're being used here, and maybe that's why you aren't out yet. Maybe there's somebody you have to talk to first."

"Guess I'll have to talk to everyone I meet then, so maybe I'll find the right one and then I can go free!" He made a wry face. "I'm already getting a reputation as 'The Preacher.'"

"Is that bad?"

"Depends … it can get me in hot water sometimes. But then, God knows about that too, doesn't he?" He changed the subject. "Tell me the lesson you're planning for tonight. Then I can study it too."

They spent some time looking at scriptures together, and it seemed they'd just begun when the guard came back for Terry. "I'll see you soon … keep your chin up!" Jenny called after his receding back.

She waited outside in the sunshine for Sally Jane and the two of them went home to Jenny's place.

"Just bring your bag right in here, Honey." Jenny opened the door to the biggest guest room. It was simply furnished, but clean and neat with a comfortable double bed. Sally stood looking at the bed and the picture of the ocean hanging over it.

"It's nice." She set her bag down.

"Here's the bathroom, and these are your towels. Just make yourself at home, Sally. I'll be in the kitchen." Jenny busied herself making a simple but tasty meal for the two of them. Sally was quiet most of the time, but ate with obvious enjoyment. When dinner was over and the dishes put away, Jenny got two Bibles and opened them to the book of Romans.

"This is a good place to begin our study," she remarked, and started reading out loud. To her surprise, Sally found it very interesting and soon began asking questions. Then Jenny was in her element, explaining scriptures with scriptures until Sally understood. They spent an hour studying, and then Jenny said, "Well, you've put in your time, Sally Jane. If you've had enough we'll quit for tonight."

"It's really interesting, Pastor Jenny ... funny, I always thought the Bible was a dull book." Then she gave a sheepish grin, "Of course I never really read it, but just thought I couldn't understand it anyway."

Jenny laughed. "I remember when I thought the same thing."

Sally pointed to a verse they'd just read and said, "But what does this mean, 'while we were yet sinners, Christ died for the ungodly'? Don't Christians have to be good?"

Jenny started to explain the plan of salvation again, and they went back into the Word for another hour. Then Jenny closed the book and prayed for Sally, and for her husband, and for Terry. When she looked up, Sally was staring at her thoughtfully, but she didn't say anything.

"Want a cup of tea?" Jenny asked

"No, thanks. I'm tired, aren't you? I just want to go try out that lovely bed!"

"Sure, Sally, go ahead. I'll see you in the morning."

That was the beginning of Jenny's ministry in the Soledad prison. Sally came back the next week and brought two other women. They brought a couple of others and two children with them. They always had a good home-cooked meal, then a feast of the word of God. And one by one they invited Jesus to come into their hearts. It didn't stop there, either. They took Jenny's lesson plans into the prison and taught their husbands and told them about how Pastor Jenny was taking care of them. She began to be known among the inmates too.

But Jenny realized that she needed some fellowship with the body of Christ herself, as well as someone to keep her accountable, so she joined a local church. She told them about her work in the prison and tried to share some of the details of her life with them. Some people found her too coarse for their liking, and turned away from her. (She had associated with a rough crowd for most of her life, and often her language was a bit crude.) Others saw through the colorful vocabulary and appreciated the honest heart underneath her tough shell. They brought things to donate to the women and children, and sometimes they helped her with food ... a casserole or a cake now and then. And they prayed for her work, and that gave Jenny a lift too.

Things went along well for a while, although she didn't get far with her attempts to have the four-year unjust sentence taken off Terry's time. Then one day the enemy struck a major blow. She went to the prison as usual, but was not allowed in to see Terry.

"It's a new rule, Pastor Brownell. Only relatives can get in to see the prisoners. You're not a relative, so you can't visit. Sorry!"

She argued with the guards but didn't get anywhere, so she demanded to see the warden. She made as good an argument as she could, citing the fact that she was a member of the clergy and should be allowed to help those who wanted religious training, etc. It was all to no avail. It was like talking to a wall. The man simply didn't hear her.

Jenny raged all the way home. Then she quieted down and took her troubles to the Lord. She wrote letters to Terry telling him what was happening, and why she wasn't able to visit. "I wish I were your mother or something," she wrote, and suddenly the thought hit her... why don't I adopt him?

She wrote and asked him if he'd go along with that plan. "Adopt me? he protested, "I want you to <u>marry</u> me! I don't want to be your son, I want to be your husband!"

"I know, Terry, but I can't divorce Al. If I do, I'll lose all my income, and I just can't live on nothing!"

Finally, reluctantly, he agreed to go along with the adoption. At least that way he'd get to see her again.

She went to the courthouse in Salinas and started the paperwork going, and within a month she was officially Terry Singer's mother! She brought some cupcakes to the prison to celebrate when the papers were signed. The warden put her through a lot of hassle, but finally had to let her see him.

"Hi son," she greeted him when he finally came through the visiting room door.

"Yeah, Mom," he choked, and hugged her close to himself. Neither of them was happy with the situation, but they managed to cope with it. Jenny spent time teaching Terry the same lessons she taught her home classes, and he studied hard and asked questions she sometimes was hard-put to answer. It kept Jenny on her toes too. And Terry passed the lessons on to his cellmates too. He led Bucky to the Lord, and Joe gave them both a very hard time for weeks, until finally one day he asked Terry to pray with him too! Terry was jubilant. "This must be why I'm here!" he told Jenny. "These men need Jesus so bad." Slowly during the years he spent in Soledad, more and more prisoners and their families came to know the Lord through Jenny's and Terry's witness.

Pastor Jenny, as the women called her, was becoming well known among the prisoners' families. As her church people gave clothes and food for the work, she passed them on to the needy ones. And always, in return, they attended a Bible class. The word went forth, and the harvest in souls grew.

The Angel attended and rejoiced over each new convert.

But of course, Satan couldn't let that situation go on without a challenge, so one bright, windy day when Jenny went to see Terry, she found they were transferring him again. He had finished one of his sentences, and was now due to be sent back to Ohio to do another sentence there.

"If they send me there I'll be dead within a week!" He looked so dejected she could hardly stand it.

"I'll fight it! I won't let them do that to you, Terry! I'm going right now and talk to the warden. I'll talk to whoever it takes. You pray and hang in there and have faith, Terry ... God can't be going to allow this! Anyway, he says if two of us agree on anything we ask in Jesus name, he'll do it! So let's ask, Love." She took his hands and they bowed before the Lord and poured out their petition to Him together.

Jenny found the warden entirely cold to her pleas. She left the prison and hurriedly called the governor's office, and when she was able to reach him, she explained what was happening and that Terry's life was in danger. "The government promised him protection, and now they're going back on their word again! Can't you do something for us?"

The governor was willing to help, and he at least arranged to have Terry housed in the Salinas County jail while Jenny tried to appeal his case. So she wrote and called everyone she could think of who might be able to help. Senator Rach of Delaware was looking into some questionable dealings of the FBI at the time, so she called him and spent hours on the phone explaining Terry's case and all that had happened over the years. Senator Rach studied the records and agreed to do what he could to help Terry. "This is certainly not fair, nor is it according to what the FBI promised Terry Singer when he cooperated with them. I'll put some pressure on this case in Washington!" he promised.

Both Governor Conner and Senator Rach worked on Terry's behalf, while he stayed in Salinas County jail for six months. But finally he was sent to Ohio State Penitentiary anyway, and Jenny almost had a stroke over that!

She spent hours on her knees before the Lord, pleading Terry's case at the very highest court, while Terry prayed too on the too long, too short flight.

The plane landed at Columbus and Terry's escort took him through the airport, out the revolving doors and into a state police cruiser. Then they drove to the prison, where he waited while a burly officer with a handlebar mustache booked him. But then instead of throwing him in a cell, the guard took him right back to the police cruiser, back to the airport, through the terminal and onto a plane for California again! Terry praised the Lord for his mercy half the way back to California, before he fell asleep, exhausted from the stress of the situation. This time, they took him to California Men's Colony in San Luis Obispo.

They let him call Jenny, and the two of them rejoiced together over the phone. "God was watching over me all the time!" he exclaimed. "I did trust him, but I sure didn't know how he was going to keep me safe at Ohio ... I almost lost it when they booked me there. And then, what a feeling, when I went right back on the plane!" She heard him chuckle hoarsely. "It seems strange to be thanking God for being in this prison, but I guess that's what I'm doing!"

"Praise God!" Jenny breathed, at the other end of the line. "At least you're safe, Terry! We won! Satan didn't get his chance at you after all! I'll come to see you as soon as I can get there!"

But the next testing came fast. The enemy doesn't like to be defeated, and he fights dirty.

CHAPTER TWENTY-SIX

The state was in the process of turning CMC into a 'psycho' unit. There were some really bad criminals there. Watson, a killer in the Manson case, for one. And there were a lot of others very much like him. "A" unit was the honor unit though, and Terry was put into "A" unit so he was a little bit removed from the worst of the prisoners.

Jenny arrived in San Luis Obispo the day after she heard from Terry. She entered the huge, cold building confident that she'd soon be with him again. That hope was soon dashed, as she answered the questions on the sheet the guard handed her. She filled in the information that she was Terry's adoptive mother, along with all the other pertinent data, then handed the form back and waited to go through the search she knew was coming.

"Mrs. Brownell?" She turned to see a tall, bald officer holding the paper.

"Yes."

"I'm sorry, but you will not be allowed to see the prisoner."

"What?! Why on earth not?" She was stunned by the refusal. What could be the trouble, she wondered?

"It says here that you adopted Terry Singer, and we do not recognize that relationship as legitimate. Only real relatives can visit prisoners here. I'm sorry Ma'am, but you'll have to leave."

"But I'm a minister, sir. I should be able to visit the men to help with their spiritual guidance anyway. That's always been allowed wherever I've gone before." It was a white lie, she thought.

"Not here, Lady. I've just explained it to you. The only visitors here are real relatives!" The guard motioned her toward the door. "Write him a letter," he said sarcastically, as he turned away.

She walked out in a daze. Now what should I do? Lord, I thought I did the right thing adopting Terry. Maybe I missed it somehow ... what should I do about it, Lord? Please help me figure out what I should do next!

She went home and wrote Terry a long letter, telling him what had happened and how much she missed him.

By return mail she got a letter back that said

My Dear Love,

You know I never wanted you to adopt me in the first place. I don't want to be your son, I want to be your husband! I love you Jenny Brownell, and I need you. If the only way we can see each other is to be relatives, then let's get married! I can't live without you, Love. You're as necessary to my life as breathing or eating. Can't you see it's the only way either of us will be happy?

And don't mention the age difference again, Jenny. It doesn't mean a thing to me. I love you no matter how old you are or how young you are. Really, I think I'm as old as you are by now with all I've been through anyway. And with your enthusiasm and drive, you're as young as I am!

Say yes, Jenny. Please say yes and be my wife!

I love you always.

She put the letter down and fell on her knees. "How can I deal with this, Lord? I'm married to a man who doesn't love me ... and you know I don't love him any more. But I need my share of his income, Lord. I earned that for all the years I gave him and all the grief he put me through. Dear Father, what can I do? Lord, Terry loves me ... doesn't he? You know his heart, Father. If he really loves me as he says, and you know I love him ... Lord, is it possible we could be happy together? Can I marry him somehow?" She stayed on her knees a long time trying to sort things out with God.

The angel prayed with her.

She pondered over the situation for a few days, reviewing her life. She thought about the difference between Al, who was mean and selfish and abusive, and free - and Terry, who was kind and loving and caring, and behind bars. It didn't seem fair. One mistake... well, two, maybe. Maybe Terry shouldn't have testified against the family after all. What a shame! But then, if he hadn't she never would have met him, and surely God must have provided Terry to meet her heart's desperate need.

Finally she resolved to leave it directly in the Lord's hands. She knelt and prayed, "Oh Dear Father, I don't know what to do, but you know all about it. If I'm supposed to divorce Al and marry Terry, please let the government make some sort of provision in the law that will let me still get half Al's pension. Lord, make it very clear so there won't be any mistake, because I can't act on just a hope or a feeling. I need it to be down in black and white. Thank you Father, because I know you hear and care about me, your child. Praise you, Lord... Thank you Lord ... "

She left it in his hands then and went back to the work of teaching and helping prisoners' families in Salinas. Every night after the women and children who were in her care for that night were bedded down, Jenny wrote to Terry. She told him about things that happened at the classes, and little stories about some of the funny things they said ... and how much she missed him. And every day she got a letter back from Terry. They were wonderful letters, even though his spelling still lacked a lot, and they gave her even more insight into his character, telling her how much he had grown in the Lord, despite the hard trials of his life. She prayed much for him that the continued injustice he faced wouldn't make him bitter. And she prayed for him to be set free.

Sally Jane had grown in the spirit, studying the Bible for hours, and asking questions that sometimes made Jenny go searching for the answers herself. It was good for both of them. Sally was a true friend, a real blessing to Jenny. It was always a joy to see her coming, and Tommy came with her more often now. He came to know Jesus as his Savior too, and even at 10 years old he was being used by the Lord to witness to his friends. So Jenny was glad when she saw them coming up the walk one late afternoon.

"Hi!" she called. "You're just in time to help me with dinner!"

"Great." Sally returned. "You sound just like my mother used to."

They went into the kitchen and got out the food for the evening meal. "Here, Tommy, you can set the table please," Jenny told him, handing him a stack of plates. "You know where the silverware is, don't you?"

He nodded and began setting the plates neatly in their places.

"Pastor Jenny," Sally began, then she hesitated.

"Yes?"

"I... well I'd like to talk to you... I mean seriously."

"OK" Jenny stopped chopping the onion and looked at her. What next?

"I think I'd like to do what you do ... I mean, you know, help other wives and kids and teach them like you do. Do you think I could?"

"Oh Sally!" Jenny hugged her, feeling joy rise up inside her as she stood back again and looked at her young friend. "Of course you could! If God's calling you to do this work, he'll give you everything you need to do it with! Do you want to start a place of your own, or do you want to work here?"

Tears stood in Sally's eyes as she answered, "I'd like to work with you at first, and then maybe start another place like this."

"You know, Sally... I mean you're aware that Terry has been moved to the California Men's Colony?" Sally nodded, watching her. Jenny went on, "I'd love to be closer to him there, even though they won't let me visit him ... at least not yet." Jenny was talking as she thought. The idea came almost full-blown into her mind. "Why don't you take over here, where you can be close to Andy? Then I can feel free to go to San Luis Obispo and start another work there!"

"Really? You really want to do that? You're not just feeling like you have to do it for me or anything, are you?" Sally looked into her face to see whether she really meant it.

"Really, Sally! It's an answer to prayer. Listen, I'll have to help you study harder for a while, so you can get ordination papers. Then you're less likely to have anyone give you static about what you're doing. But we can work at that if you can stay here with me for a while. Can you move here soon? You'll have to put Tommy in school here and all. You'll want to start going to my church so they can get to know you. You'll need their support to keep this place financed, you know."

Somehow dinner got prepared for the evening group. The smell of onion and green peppers browning filled the kitchen while Jenny cooked, and Sally put the crisp lettuce and other vegetables together for salad, even while they talked and planned and rejoiced over the new venture. Sally was quieter than usual during the evening lesson, but when Jenny looked at her she could see the peace radiating from her friend. Jenny's own heart felt good about the whole thing too. It was time to go on to another new beginning. It was right.

The Angel touched her head, and Sally's.

CHAPTER TWENTY-SEVEN

The place Jenny found near the Men's Colony was just a small ranch-style house in Morro Bay. It was located a little behind the main house owned by an older woman, Florence Bassett. The cottage was pleasant with trees out front, and only a couple of miles from the ocean; where Morro Rock jutted out of the bay, a dark sentinel guarding the shore.

The house had only two fairly small bedrooms besides Jenny's own. But prices were very steep in the area, and Jenny couldn't afford any higher rent. She drove down to the shore and walked the beach, breathing in the ocean breeze, gazing at the inscrutable rock, and watching the waves try over and over to reach beyond their boundary. It was soothing and peaceful and lonely. She watched a lone gull spiral on a thermal out over the surf, and thought she understood how he felt.

After visiting various services a few Sundays, she found a non-denominational church where she felt comfortable. She made an appointment and talked to the pastor about her work. "And you see, Pastor Carlson, I have helped a lot of women and children. I've kept them off the streets and given them a place to stay while they visit their husbands in prison. And a lot of them have come to know the Lord. But I need a church to sponsor my work. One that believes in what I'm doing, and can help with some finances and food and clothing and all the things these families need. It's so hard for some of them with the main provider for the family in prison ... and some of the kids will be on the streets selling drugs or their bodies if we don't help them!"

The pastor leaned back in his chair and eyed the thin-faced, earnest-eyed woman opposite his desk. She was obviously a dedicated Christian, although a bit crude in her speech sometimes.

"You say you're an ordained minister?"

She nodded ... yes, with the Holy Gospel church. I was ordained through the Foundations church. I went through their training process. You do have to be able to answer their questions about the Bible, and you do have to believe the fundamental Christian truths about Jesus' virgin birth and resurrection. That He is the Son of God, who died for our sins and rose again, so that we can be saved from sin and death. I'm not running some cult or anything like that! And I don't hold church services like you do ... only classes for the women and children, the prisoner's families, who won't go to a church. I teach them about Jesus' love for them. They need that so badly. It touches their hearts when I tell them how much Jesus gave for them."

She looked strong and vital, her eyes shining with the zeal of the Lord. "You can't imagine, Pastor, how great it is to see the Lord change a life like that! And then they take their new faith into the prison and share it with their husbands. I've seen a lot of men come to know Jesus as Lord through the faithfulness of their wives!"

Pastor Carlson reached across the desk for Jenny's hand. "I believe you're doing a work for God, sister Brownell. And I think our people here will support you in that work. Let's pray about it together, and then I'll take it to the church board to see what we can do."

"You're welcome at any of the classes, Pastor Carlson. Just drop in any time as soon as I get going. I'll let you know when I get some women started coming. And thank you so much for the help I get from your services on Sunday! I have to admit I'll carry some of your ideas right over to my classes too! I hope you don't mind too much?"

He laughed. "I guess not, as long as you keep to the scriptures. It's kind of flattering. In a way, it gives me a bigger outreach too!"

The church embraced her work and supported her with some cash, food and clothing drives, as well as occasional personal help from one or another. And prayer ... that was the most help of all!

She had almost given up on getting into the prison to visit Terry, when one day the mail brought a newspaper from the Army. Jenny looked through it with surprise, as usually 'The Afterburner' went to Al, not to her. But this one, the September/October 1982 issue, was addressed to her. She stopped cold as her eyes saw the heading on page 2 that read "Retired Pay to Ex-Spouses." What? Lord, what is this?

She read: **The third piece of key legislation affecting retirees was included as a compromise amendment to the DOD Authorization Act FY 83 permitting state courts to include disposable retired military pay along with other property for division in divorce settlements, regardless of the number of years the spouses were married.**

Termination of payments upon remarriage of either spouse was not approved.

She put the paper down in her lap, "Lord, does this say what I think it says? Oh Lord, please let it be what I think it says!"

She picked up the paper and read the whole thing through thoroughly, and found that not only did it say she could collect half of Al's income if she divorced him, but it said that she *had* to do it before a certain date to get the benefits. It applied only to people in the exact timeframe she fit into as far as when and how long she'd been married. It even gave her healthcare benefits as well as Base Exchange and commissary privileges, since she'd been married to Al for more than 20 years!

And they couldn't take those benefits away if she remarried! If she had divorced sooner, she'd have missed the timeframe. And if Al had divorced her she'd have missed out also. "Praise the Lord! Oh, thank you Jesus!"

She read it again, to make sure she wasn't hallucinating or something. Then she read it once more, to be absolutely certain. Then she fell on her knees and praised and thanked God again and again for answering her prayer so precisely. He had shown her exactly what He would have her to do.

Jenny danced around the house rejoicing in the Lord and his love and mercy for her. It was such a special and personal thing ... as though God had written her a letter by His own hand ... just to her!

The angel thanked God too.

Jenny started divorce proceedings the next day. When she wrote to Terry and told him what was happening, she enclosed a copy of the paper for him to read. He was ecstatic. "How can I tell you what I feel, my dear Love?" he wrote. "God is so good to do this for us! Now you can be my wife as you should be. I can hardly wait! What will you do about this cursed adoption, though?"

She went to Salinas and filed papers to annul the adoption. The judge was not gracious about it, to say the least, and she had to really work to convince him to grant her petition. Terry wrote a letter too requesting the annulment, and finally the Judge gave in and signed the paper dissolving the adoption. Now all they waited for was the final divorce papers.

When she went to Salinas to pick up the annulment papers, she stopped to see how Sally was doing with the work there. Sally ran to hug her, getting flour on her back from the pie crust she had been rolling out. Then she stood back and looked more closely at her mentor, as she washed her hands at the sink."You look so happy, Jenny! Like the sun is shining behind your eyes!" Sally Jane dried her hands, and hugged Jenny again."Come on, I'll pour you a cup of coffee and you can tell me about it. I know just looking at you that something's going on!"

"You're right, Sally!" Jenny laughed. "I just un-adopted Terry Singer!"

Sally's eyebrows lifted in surprise, "but I don't understand ... I thought you loved Terry?"

"I do, Sally ... " she paused and looked into her friend's face. "I don't know if you'll understand Sally, but I'll tell you anyhow and hope you will trust me enough to know this is God's will. I do love Terry, just not as a son! I have filed for divorce from Al. I know God told me to do that now. And I'll marry Terry as soon as the divorce is final."

She watched Sally's reaction, expecting to see the rejection she would get from most devout Christians. But Sally trusted Jenny. She knew her friend always followed the Lord's leading, so she waited to hear what Jenny would tell her. "How did God tell you that?" she asked.

Jenny told her the story, right down to the miracle that God did for her by having congress make a law covering the exact things Jenny had asked Him for. And in the exact timeframe to fit Jenny's circumstances. "Do you know the chances of that happening, Sally?"

"Yeah, Jenny ...slim and none!" She grinned at her mentor. "I guess God really did tell you to marry Terry Singer. I hope it's the best thing that ever happened to you!"

"Me too, Sally! Thanks for being a friend and understanding! I know most people will only see the difference in our ages and the fact that he's a prisoner. But Sally, he loves me and I love him, and age just doesn't seem to matter! Nobody has ever loved me like that before. It's such a blessing from God! He makes me so happy, and he treats me like a queen! I've never been treated like that by any man before. I didn't know love could be like this."

They talked for a couple of hours, as Sally finished her pie, and set it on the counter to cool. Too soon it was time to prepare the rest of the dinner for the class coming that evening. They worked together on that, and Jenny sat in on the class, watching and listening as Sally, who so short a time ago had been lost and uncertain, led the women in an unusually insightful Bible study.

Back at the mobile home park, Al received the divorce papers and sat for a long time looking at them, wondering what the catch was. He squinted his eyes and rubbed his hand over his chin and thought about it. He didn't trust Jenny to just suddenly set him free out of the goodness of her heart. He puzzled over the reason, but couldn't see anything obvious.

"Maybe she's found someone else." Billie Jean volunteered.

"Maybe, but she's such a religious stick in the mud that I don't think she'll be able to remarry. I can quote you a bunch of stuff the church told her over the years! Unless something drastic happened, she won't dare remarry or she'll go straight to Hell!" He shook his head, worried that he was missing something in this deal.

"This means we could get married now you know, Honey," Billie Jean reminded him, running her finger around his ear as she sat next to him.

"Yeah," he admitted grudgingly. Al liked the arrangement they already had. No ties. But he finally signed the documents and sealed them back up in the envelope provided. "I just hope I'm not making a mistake here," he muttered.

When Jenny got notice that the divorce was final, she danced a jig in her front hall. Then she stopped suddenly and sat down in a kitchen chair. "It's over," she said to nobody. "It's really over, after all these years." She thought back on the old life ... it seemed a long time ago now. A different person in a different lifetime had lived that old life. She thought of Terry and his love for her, and smiled. "Thank you, Lord."

She called the prison and asked for Terry, and when she got through to him, she said, "Terry Singer, will you marry me?"

He let out a whoop. "Will I? You just get here with a preacher and we'll see how fast we can say "I do!" His voice softened, "You got the papers?"

"All signed, sealed and delivered."

"When can we do it? Can you get permission from the warden? Who's gonna stand up with us? I know, I'll get Kenny James. He's a good friend. Who'll you get?" He rattled on like a child looking forward to a special treat.

They talked a few minutes longer, until the guard came and took the phone away. Then Jenny called Sally to ask her to stand up with her at the wedding.

"Of course I will, Jenny! I'd be honored," Sally told her.

"I'll let you know when I can get the wedding arranged. It'll just be the four of us, and maybe a couple of Terry's friends."

Jenny was on cloud 9, feeling like a schoolgirl as she picked out a lovely pale blue suit to wear for the ceremony. She arranged with the prison for a little reception with a cake for the six people who would be allowed to be there: Herself and Terry, Sally, Kenny James, the prison chaplain and the warden, whom she invited on the spot when he gave permission for the union.

"I assume you know what you're doing, Ms. Brownell... you're old enough to have been around the block a few times," he told her dryly.

She laughed, not even upset with his reference to her age. "I guess I do, Sir. And Terry and I'd be honored if you'd be a witness to our marriage."

He seemed a bit taken aback, but surprised both of them by agreeing. So on a bright morning in August, 1983, near her 67th birthday, Jenny found herself saying "I Will" in reply to the questions asked, and then being kissed passionately by her new husband. She was Mrs. Terry Singer!

They ate cake and celebrated for a couple of hours before Sally had to leave and Kenny was taken back to his cell. Terry had been given two nights at the mobile units the prisoners used for conjugal visits. He led his new bride into the one assigned to them, and closed the door. "It isn't what I'd like to have for our wedding night, Jenny, but it feels like a palace to me right now!"

She smiled at her handsome young bridegroom. "It's fine for now Dear, and some day we'll take a real honeymoon together."

He gathered her into his arms. "You're my wife at last! And now I can show you how much I really love you. Thank the Lord for answering my prayers ... I never want to leave you again. Now I really have to get out of here!"

"I know, Terry... I know, Love ... but for now, let's just make the most of this time we've been given."

The angel waited outside, along with the prison guard.

CHAPTER TWENTY-EIGHT

1987

Jenny opened her eyes in the half-light of early morning. She swung her legs out her side of the bed, muffling a groan, as it seemed every bone in her body made its separate protest. She looked over at Terry, still asleep, his head half buried in the pillow. He'll have to wake up soon, poor guy ... he's sleeping so hard, I know he needs another hour or two. Not going to get it today though ... entirely too much to do!

She padded into the bathroom barefoot, and turned the shower on. Maybe the hot water would ease her stiffness. With all the work lined up for today she didn't have time to be bothered with a rebellious aging body!

The shower worked its magic and she felt better as she toweled off and reached for her toothbrush. It always surprised her to look in the mirror. She still felt the same inside as she had as a beautiful young girl, but now the face that looked back at her was that of an old person. Some old person who'd been through a lot of hard living... though she was still attractive. The eyes were the same bright blue-green, except half covered now by drooping lids. It's a wonder I can see at all! Wish I had the money for a face-lift!

She sighed and brushed her permed blond hair. I wonder what Terry sees in me ... and why he doesn't leave me for someone his own age ... but thank God he still loves me! What would I do without him? Well, for one thing, I wouldn't have so much laundry! she answered her own question. Being 71 wasn't so bad most of the time, except when that tightness came around her heart.

The aroma of bacon and eggs and fresh coffee roused Terry, and she heard him getting dressed as she put breakfast on the table.

"Mornin', Love," he said in his usual cheerful soft voice as he entered the bright little kitchen. He sat down at the table and she slid into the chair opposite his with her coffee cup.

His trash-hauling route took in a large area around Morro Bay. She watched him eat. "Lots of stops today. I have the route all mapped out for you. Mrs. Reinch wants you to take away an old stove. I hope you can manage that OK?"

He nodded. "I'll put a couple of boards against the truck and slide it up on those. It'll work fine." He spread peanut butter on a piece of toast. "One of these days maybe we can afford to hire some help. We're doing pretty well lately, aren't we?"

"Better than I thought we'd do so soon. If we can manage to get the truck paid off and get out from under those payments, then we'll be in good shape."

"And when I get off the stupid probation we'll be able to move somewhere else ... maybe somewhere with a lower cost of living." He looked around the little house. "I'd like to get you a better place to live. You deserve more than this, Jenny."

"This is fine, Terry. You're working as hard as two men already. You can't do any more now. We just have to be really careful to keep from doing anything to provoke Quincy. He sure takes his job seriously!"

"You can say that again! I don't dare even look cross-eyed at him!" He pushed his chair back and drained the last of the coffee from his mug. "Well, where's the list? Guess I'd better get going."

She handed it to him, along with a bag lunch and thermos."Call me at noon and I'll let you know if there are any more stops to squeeze in, OK?"

He pulled her to himself and kissed her thoroughly. "That'll keep you till tonight... love ya!"

She watched him cross the yard to the big green stake truck and climb into the seat. She waved as it roared away. The landlady was standing outside her bigger house in front of theirs, observing them while pretending to pick up the paper. Jenny waved at her and retreated into the kitchen. She didn't want to talk to nosy Florence this morning! Some people just couldn't believe Terry was really married to her. She had to agree it was pretty unlikely. But it was true nonetheless... and none of their business anyhow!

Life had been a lot different before Terry finally got released from prison. She'd had to fight the authorities with all the strength, knowledge and money she owned to get him released, even when his term was finished. And now he was on probation for another year. It didn't seem fair when he was such a harmless, good person. But they couldn't forget about the fact that he'd been able to elude them for so long after the prison break. She supposed that was her fault somehow... and the system could forgive anyone for anything, including murderers, or even pedophiles ... but not for bank robbery, and not for being a snitch! So they had to put up with Quincy dropping in without announcement any time he felt like it and putting Terry through the third degree. This wasn't quite the way she'd envisioned life when he got out.

Truth be told, she'd really figured he'd leave her when he got free. He was young and good-looking and more than 30 years younger than she. She knew a lot of other people were surprised Terry was still with her also. But the love between them was real on both sides, and Terry didn't seem to notice the age difference. She loved him all the more for that. And God blessed them together.

Most people looked down their noses at the December/May marriage, but Karen and Johnny both made their peace with the situation, and even seemed to like Terry, once they actually met and talked with him.

Jenny missed her other life sometimes, though she didn't want to admit that, even to herself. But she'd felt so used of God when she helped the prisoners and their wives and taught the Bible classes. She'd led many of the men and their family members to the Lord over the years while she tried to get Terry released from prison.

I wonder how Sally's doing now... wish I could get over that way to visit. She pushed that thought aside and loaded several pairs of Terry's dirty jeans into the washer. He liked to look neat, and wore a clean pair every day. Later that day she ironed them lovingly, sweat running down her cheeks and the back of her neck. She wanted to do it, but knew it took a toll on her body.

As she ironed, she fancied there was a strange calm outside. It was nothing she could put a finger on, but she went to stand on the porch, feeling vaguely uneasy. Was the sky an unusual color? But it was time to start fixing dinner so she tried to ignore her premonition, and went into the kitchen, where she sliced a steak into thin strips to make stroganoff. Terry came home tired to the bone, and she forgot about the weather as she tended to his needs.

That night the rains started. The water came down in torrents, turning the roads and valleys into streams. It rained for two weeks straight, in an area where the hills were normally brown. The landscape that didn't dissolve into mudslides turned lovely shades of green. Reminded Jenny of Maryland in the spring.

"I can't go to work, " Terry said.

"I know."

"What'll we do? We can't pay the truck payment! We'll lose the truck and all our business if I can't get out of here!"

"I know.... I know"

"Well, what do you suggest we do?"

"Let's pray about it. God knows our situation. He won't let us starve."

"You're right, but it sure looks hopeless." He knelt, and she eased to her knees beside him. "Lord, you know our need," he began, and laid their troubles at the feet of Jesus.

They prayed alternately, and praised too, as the rain drummed on the roof above them. Finally, they said Amen and got up. "I feel better about it now, anyway." Jenny held the kettle under the faucet and set it on the stove. "Let's have a cup of tea."

"Sounds good. I could eat something."

She got out the bread and some cheese. "How about a grilled cheese sandwich?"

"Great!" Suddenly he was ravenous, and he got the grill out of the bottom cupboard and put it on the burner to heat while she sliced cheese and placed it on the bread. The kettle boiled and she poured the contents over tea bags in the pot, while Terry turned the sandwiches over. Later, while they lingered over a second or third cup and talking about various things, the rain slowed. And soon they realized with a bit of shock that it had stopped! The constant drumming on the roof was gone, and all they heard was dripping from the eaves.

"Thank You, Lord!" Terry said with feeling. "I'll be able to work tomorrow, Jenny!"

"Yes, I know! But you'll have to be really careful, Terry. Some of the roads may be washed out you know, there are so many slides. I'm glad we live up here so high. It must be awful for those poor folks whose houses have filled with mud and water, or have washed away completely!"

"I'll try to help some of them if I can. Maybe I can haul some of the ruined stuff away with my regular loads."

"I'm sure that would be a real blessing! I can't imagine having to try to clean up such a mess!" She glanced out the window. "Look, there's actually some sunshine peeking through the clouds!"

"There should be a rainbow up there somewhere... I'm going out and look for it! Wanna come?"

"You bet! Just wait'll I get my rain boots on!"

The next day dawned with a cloudless sky, and Terry rose early to get at his route. The trash was piled up, he knew, and he planned to spend extra hours at work. He kissed Jenny goodbye and pulled out of the driveway with high hopes for some extra income. The world smelled different after the unaccustomed floods. The usually dry air felt heavy and damp, and he could see steam rising in places where the sun was at work putting things right again. The side roads were muddy and slick, but his truck handled conditions well and he had half a load in no time. He drove carefully toward San Luis Obispo, noticing all the damage from water and mud, and then as he rounded a curve on a steep side-hill he saw too late that the road was gone.

Before he could react, the truck hit a huge lake of water. He thought maybe he could make it through and tried to accelerate, but that was the wrong move and in another second he realized it was all over. The truck was sinking fast. Terry pushed the door open and managed to climb up on the roof of the cab, just as the water rushed into it. He was just ready to dive into the water and swim for land, when he felt the wheels settle. There he stood on the roof of his truck, with the muddy water flowing rapidly around him carrying his hopes and dreams along with it. He couldn't help it... tears of frustration flowed down his cheeks. A man can take just so much before he gives up!

He took a deep shuddering breath, wiped his face with his bandana, and took stock of his situation. And then Quincy drove up from the other side. Terry's heart sank, but he waved anyway and managed a crooked smile.

"What in the blue blazes are you doing out there?" Quincy commented.

"Waiting for the bus. I understand it's due any time now. Thought I'd skip town."

"Oh, funny!

"Could ya help me out here, Quincy? I'm not in a very good position to call for help. I need a tow truck to pull me out of here."

Quincy's eyes narrowed as he evaluated the situation."You're gonna need a miracle to save your business now!" His head reflected the sun as he removed his hat and scratched gently. "Yeah Terry, I'll call the tow truck for ya. Guess we'd better try to get you off there somehow too."

"That'd be real nice, Quincy! Real nice."

He watched as Quincy eased his fat frame into the car and turned it around. The water continued to swirl around the truck. Was it coming higher? Hard to tell, but gradually other cars were arriving at the edge of the disaster. People milled around yelling suggestions and making comments. Terry stood on his roof and tried not to lose his cool.

It seemed like forever before Quincy pulled up again, this time towing a little boat on a tiny trailer. People helped him unload and launch it, and soon Terry was rowing him back to shore. Then they both stood with the others and watched as the tow truck arrived. After much discussion and a lot of struggle, the men were able to get a chain hooked to Terry's truck, and the tow truck slowly backed away. The green truck emerged from the water bit by bit, dripping with mud, and with some of the load still in the bed. Terry hated to think where the rest of it had gone. They hauled his truck to the garage, where they told him it would take weeks to fix all the damage.

He called Jenny. "Can you come get me? There's been an accident and the truck's at the garage outside of San Luis Obispo."

"An accident! Oh Terry, are you OK? What happened?"

"Yeah, I'm OK. The truck isn't. Come get me Jenny, and we'll talk about it then. I can't talk now… oh, and don't come the side road! Take the main road into town, hear?"

"I hear you, Terry. I'll be there as soon as I can." Jenny prayed as she hurried to the city. "Lord, how can this be? How can we go on without the truck? We can't make a living without it! We can't pay the bills. Lord, you know how much we still owe on that truck. Please Lord, help us! What can we do?"

She pulled up to the garage and saw Terry standing there looking like a whipped puppy, and her heart tightened. Sometimes these days it felt like it would come right out of her chest. She swallowed hard and took a deep breath, waiting for it to ease. Then she went to Terry and hugged him. I'm so glad you're all right, Love!

He gestured toward the side of the garage and she saw the truck. She hardly recognized it. The green was covered with brown mud. A window was broken, and mud oozed out the open door. Her heart sank. *Lord, what'll we do now?* "What in the world happened? Did you drive into the river?"

"Might as well have. Come on, let's go home. I'll tell you about it on the way."

She listened in stunned silence as he told her the story. "And I don't know what we'll do now, Jenny. I don't have enough money to fix the truck and make the payments on it both... I just don't know how we'll make it."

"Well God knows, and He owns everything." She swallowed. Her words sounded hollow even to herself. "And Karen owns a lot of it too! Maybe we can ask for her help. She has so much... surely she would help her own mother." But she was far from confident of that. Karen had her own life, involved with a lot of rich and famous people. Her life certainly didn't include a weird mother who had married a convicted felon. Still...."Well, she is still my daughter, even if she is so uppity now she won't admit she has any parents! I suppose if I were in her shoes I'd feel that way too, what with the way our lives have gone, but I'd still help if I could. Maybe she will." She looked over at Terry, who was staring out the side window obviously unconvinced. "I'll call her when we get home."

Karen was in Paris again. When they finally reached her she sent a check, along with a personal letter to Jenny saying some very unkind things about Terry. Jenny was so angry she nearly ripped the check in two instead of cashing it. She did rip the letter in pieces before Terry could read it and be hurt again. It was hard not to be bitter against her children. They had so much, and she had so little... they had no idea how hard life was for her, and they didn't seem to care. Her grandchildren were growing up and she hardly ever saw them. Not that she didn't want to, but there was always some sort of excuse why they couldn't come to visit. And they always had a reason why she couldn't go to them. She knew they were ashamed of her. They led "normal" humdrum lives centered on their own selfish interests, and they didn't need her weird preaching or want their friends to meet her "hillbilly" ex-con husband. So they stayed away. Jenny's heart ached for them sometimes, but she had learned from childhood not to count on her family for love or support.

"Say, this was really nice of Karen! She's O.K.!" Terry said when she gave him the check. "This'll at least pay for the repairs, and that's a load off us now." He folded it and put it in his wallet. "I've been lining up some more work. If they get the truck fixed soon, maybe we can make it yet!"

Jenny turned toward the kitchen. Lord, there's gotta be something you want us to be doing. What is it? Help us find it soon, please Lord!

The angel prayed with her, and watched.

CHAPTER TWENTY-NINE

The prayer was answered within the week. Terry was busy trimming the overgrown shrubbery when Quincy drove in, bringing someone in the car with him. Terry straightened up and brushed the dirt from his knees, and waited while Quincy hauled his bulk out from behind the driver's seat. His passenger opened the other door and stepped out. Terry's jaw dropped in surprise. She was gorgeous! About 36 years old he guessed, with long brown hair that curled engagingly around her face and down her back, and a figure with enough curves to make a man want to touch ... Terry shook his head to stop the unwelcome thoughts.

Quincy and the woman advanced toward him, and Terry finally remembered manners and met them half way. She met his gaze with eyes the color of jade he'd seen once in a gift shop."Singer, I want you to meet Phyllis Rymer. She's wantin' to start a Bible study of some kind at the Men's Colony. I told her you'd be the people to talk to about helpin'.... "

Terry took the slender, strong hand in his own. "I'm pleased to meetcha, Ma'am."

Then she spoke, and her voice was high pitched, but sweet as honey, with the same southern drawl as his own! "Mighty nice to meet you too, Mr. Singer. I'm hopin' we'll become good friends."

Terry was hoping that too, and fighting a lot of conflicting emotions. "Come on in and we'll talk over some coffee," he invited.

Jenny was just finishing changing the sheets, and her usually neat house had laundry stacked on some of the chairs. She wore a pair of old jeans and a baggy shirt and hadn't taken time to do her face, so she looked older than usual. She ran her hand through her short blond hair, trying to make it neater. Oh drat! I wish people would call before they just come over!

"Come right in, Quincy. I'll just move some of this stuff...." She hurriedly transferred the clothes to the bedroom and closed the door.

"I'd like you to meet Phyllis Rymer," Quincy said. "She'd like to talk to you about ..."

"About doin' some prison ministry, Ma'am."

At the sound of the soft drawl and the sight of the lovely woman, Jenny's radar went on instantly. Oh-oh!

She glanced at Terry, who was gazing at the newcomer with an inscrutable expression. He caught her eyes and gave her a little smile.

"I told 'em we'd talk over coffee, Jen."

"Oh, of course, where are my manners? Please, sit here by the table, won't you?" Jenny quickly put the coffee pot to work and fixed a plate of cookies, which she set on the middle of the table. The others made chitchat about the weather and how the rain had damaged everything, and about Terry's accident with the truck, until Jenny brought the coffee and poured it. Then she sat down with them.

"Prison Ministry?" Jenny looked inquiringly at Phyllis. "Where? At the Men's Colony?"

Phyllis nodded. "It's such a challenge, don't you think? Those men need to hear the gospel and I'd like to try to bring it to them, only I'm not quite sure how to begin... "

"They wouldn't let me into the complex when I wanted to do ministry there. I had to work with the women and children instead." She looked at Phyllis again. She seemed so young, and she was too beautiful. She made Jenny feel old and ugly in contrast. "They only let close relatives into the prison to see the men."

"Well, they do admit ministers now." Her soft drawl was almost lyrical. "But you have to meet some pretty tough requirements. They weren't too happy with my bein' a woman, you know, but with the Women's Liberation movement makin' such inroads lately, they're afraid to turn me down for fear I'll sue 'em or somethin' I guess. Anyway, they're gonna let me teach a class on Sunday afternoons, if anybody wants to come. I don't know how to advertise it so they'll be interested. That's the first problem... and there are lots more. Can you help me do you think? I mean, with your experience and with Mr. Singer's ... you two should be able to give me a lot of advice." Her long lashes dropped, then opened and the green eyes looked up into Jenny's. "It must've been very hard havin' your son in prison so long."

"Yes," Jenny agreed, "It was hard having my husband in prison such a very long time!"

"Oh! I'm sorry, I didn't mean ...

"It's all right," Terry answered. "We're used to that." He raised his cup in salute to Jenny. "My wife worked long and hard to get me released from prison. She brought the gospel to a lot of men, and reached even more of them through teaching their wives and helping them with food and clothes and all... There aren't many people who would do what Jenny did!"

Quincy harumphed, trying not to laugh.

"I think we'll help, Phyllis. It would be good to be used of the Lord again. It's been hard being away from that work. If the door is really open now, I'll be glad to do what I can to help reach those miserable, lost men. It always amazes me how God can change them when they reach out to him. They've had such rotten lives, some of them, you'd think it would be impossible to make anything different of them... but God can do anything, as we've seen over and over. I think Terry will want to work with you too?" She looked at him inquiringly.

He nodded, slowly, thinking several things at one time. "I sure relate to the work, since it changed my own life so much! But I do have to run the business, too. We have to have some income or we can't live! And how can I run it alone, Jen? I need your help too!"

"We'll just have to manage our time more efficiently, I suppose. I feel this is the answer to my prayers though, Terry. I know there's more important work to do than just hauling trash."

She caught his hurt expression and hurried to add, "Not that our trash business isn't important to the world... I'm sure it is... and necessary. But I mean important for the Lord and His kingdom. I am getting older, although I try to deny that fact, and I think of going to meet my Lord soon, and standing before Him to account for my life. Somehow, I don't want to end it just trying to earn survival money. He always said he'll provide for our needs, and he always has done so! Remember how he changed the law for me?"

Terry nodded."Yeah I do understand, Jenny. It's harder for me though. I'm the one who's supposed to provide for our livelihood. I think God expects me to make a living for us too, and I'm tryin' to do that."

He was very much aware of Phyllis, and of a strong attraction to her. *Please, Jenny, throw me a lifeline here! There's danger... can't you see?*

"Well Phyllis, we'll take some time to discuss this together, and we'll let you know very soon what we can do. And I'll try to make out a plan for you too. It's good to know someone will be reaching that terrible place for the Lord. It's a stronghold of Satan though, and there's real danger for a Christian there. You need to be clothed with the whole armor of God and standing strong in the word."

Phyllis rose and put her arms around Jenny. "Thank you, thank you! I'm so excited about the work! I know the Lord has everything planned! I'll call you in a couple of days to work on some details. Will you be ready that soon?"

Jenny nodded, "Yes, I think we'll be able to make our decisions by that time." She looked at Terry, who nodded.

Quincy, who hadn't said much during the visit, but had done away with most of the cookies, pushed his chair away from the table and got up. "Well, if you're working at the prison, at least I'll know where you are! Just take care who you talk to over there, Singer!"

After they left, Terry went back to his yard work and thought over all that had just happened. He couldn't get the woman out of his mind... her looks, the feel of her hand, her fragrance, her voice... and she was a Christian, too! For the first time, Terry had a small flash of regret about his marriage. Satan had his foot in the door just a crack....

Jenny knew though. So this is the test, Lord... And it's coming through one of your servants, and through a work I love. What will you have me do now, Lord? How should I handle this trial? Should I run from it... just get Terry and the truck and move somewhere else and try to protect my dear love, or should I embrace it and trust you to bring us safely through? And what will be the effect on Phyllis? Is she really your servant, Lord? Or is she willing to be used by the enemy? If we do this, will you help us win the souls of those hardened men for you?

The angel looked to heaven for an answer to his question too.

Of course they decided to go ahead and help with the work, and soon were up to their necks in plans and details and meetings, as well as planning how to run their hauling business more efficiently to give them more time. As Jenny put it, "How can we not do this, when it's obviously such an open door to a work for the Lord?" But they neglected to pray for the Lord's clear leading. They just took it for granted that because they had done this work before and it was a good work for the Lord, it was what they should do.

Jenny went with Phyllis to the prison to set up the schedule and arrange to get word about the meetings to the men. They began the work on a Sunday afternoon a few weeks after their first meeting. A strong breeze blew the morning fog away, and the sun came out as they arrived at the prison and set up their meeting room. Phyllis had found a young girl to play the accordion for the service, and they started playing and singing some choruses while waiting for the men to assemble. When 3:00 o'clock came, there were only 8 men in the room, but Phyllis began the meeting with a prayer. When they looked up, 4 more men had arrived. Guards stood at both doorways, watching.

The service went well, with Jenny giving the main message and Phyllis handling most of the rest of the service. Terry gave the men his testimony of how God had changed his own life when he was in prison. Phyllis sang "Amazing Grace" accompanied by the accordion. She had a clear, sweet soprano voice, and looked like an angel as she sang. The men made lewd comments about her to each other, which she tried to ignore. Terry glared at them and moved closer to her, protectively.

Jenny was in her glory talking about Jesus and his mercy again. She laid out the plan of salvation for those hardened hearts, and they ignored it. But she knew a seed had been planted somewhere... "The Bible says His word shall not return void!" she told the others when they were on their way out of the building again. "We've made an impression here somewhere... maybe even in the guards. We just don't know. Our job is to speak the word, and the Holy Spirit has to take it from there."

"Yes, I guess that's true," Phyllis agreed. "At least we've been faithful to do what God led us to do." She looked out across the parking lot pensively, "But still, it's discouraging... I was hoping somebody would get saved today."

"These are hard men, with past histories you wouldn't even want to hear about. It'll take us awhile to crack through their shells... and most of them wouldn't dare let the others know if they were interested! They'd really have to stand a lot of abuse then." Terry spoke from experience. "You can't let this service discourage you. Actually, it went pretty well!"

She smiled at him, "You're a real inspiration to me, Mr. Singer. It's because of you that I know this ministry will work."

He beamed at that. "I wish you'd cut that Mister stuff and call me Terry."

"Oh, all right Mr.... Terry." Her voice was musical. He felt important and handsome, and appreciated.

Jenny watched, and thought she understood what was happening. Lord, keep us in your hand, and don't let the enemy get a foothold here... please Father!"

The angel was already fighting with the enemy.

As the weeks passed, the little group became a well-adjusted team of evangelists. They gave the word out faithfully, with no visible results for a long time. Then finally there was a small break-through. One of the prisoners asked to talk with Terry after the service. Terry made a time to visit him, and went to the room where he and Jenny had often met.

It felt weird being on the other side of the table...being the one who could walk out free after the meeting, although it was a bit scary too. He talked with Mike Justin, a former drug dealer, and answered a lot of his questions and told him again how to receive Jesus into his heart and be forgiven and cleansed. "If he can do it for me who used to be a bank robber, he can do it for you too. He'll come into your heart and make it clean... and he'll take away the drug habit and make you into a worthwhile man. I don't know whether you'll get out of here any sooner, but it can't hurt any! And you'll have peace, and even some joy in your life while you are here. I know it doesn't seem possible, but I've been there and it's true!"

"I guess I'm ready to try it then, Terry. I'm having a hard time believing what you say, but I'll give anything a try! I've been really rotten though and Satan has his hooks deep in me! I want to be free!" There was a look of quiet desperation in his eyes.

"Then let's pray right now!" Terry bowed his head, and Mike did the same and prayed the words Terry told him to pray. And Mike meant it with all the faith he could muster at the time. He looked up afterward with moist eyes and began to thank Terry.

"Don't thank me, Mike! Thank God! And tell somebody else what's happened to you." And just then the guard arrived to take Mike back to his cell, and that was the end of the visit. Terry left feeling really good.

"It was so great, Jenny! He was such a tough nut, and he actually had tears in his eyes after we prayed. Oh man, I'd almost forgotten how great it feels to lead somebody to the Lord!"

"I know, Love. It's the best feeling in the world, isn't it?"

That was the breakthrough they'd been waiting for, and from then on, slowly they began to see results from their work. Phyllis was on cloud nine over the work. She had begun to give the messages herself, taking turns with Jenny, and feeling really blessed of the Lord when she got through a service without having anyone make rude comments. She looked up to Terry, who in his quiet way was able to be such an influence on the men. She couldn't quite imagine his ever being one of them. He was a bit rough around the edges sometimes, sure, but a real gentleman most of the time. Surely he had been a victim of circumstances, not a criminal like those she preached to.

For his part, Terry tried not to think about Phyllis at all, but that was almost impossible for him. She was constantly there with him and Jenny, either at the meetings or in planning sessions and for other reasons. They kept being thrown together somehow, try as he would to avoid her. He tried not to admit it even to himself, but sometimes when he made love to Jenny, he imagined it was Phyllis. Then he had to pray for forgiveness. It was a hard trial for a man who hadn't had much experience with women.

The business was growing too. They had to hire a part-time helper to keep up with the demand. That made more bookwork for Jenny. She was willing to do it, but as the months went on she had a harder time keeping up with everything. So much responsibility and so little time, and a body that sometimes wouldn't respond. She washed and ironed a pair of heavy jeans for every day of the week for Terry, who liked to look clean and neat. He came home every night hungry as a wolf after working hard all day with heavy trash. So she had to cook big dinners for him, which she loved to do ordinarily, but sometimes she almost wished she could just eat a bowl of soup and go to bed and sleep and sleep...

One day when she woke and tried to swing her legs out of bed to start the day, she couldn't do it. She just couldn't get out of bed. She was tired... so tired... Terry came to see where she was, when his breakfast wasn't ready, and found her with tears flowing down her cheeks. "I can't get up. I just can't do it, Love. I'm so tired.... "

He took her hands in his and kissed her cheek. "It's OK, Jen. You just take a day off then. You've been workin' so hard... I forget sometimes, you know... Hey, do you want me to call the doctor?"

"I don't think so, Terry. I think I'll just rest. I think that'll do it for me... " She turned on her side and closed her eyes, while hot tears squeezed out from under her lids and ran down into the pillow. He tiptoed out, and she slept. She slept for three days, and then feeling like Lazarus resurrected, she got up, showered and fixed her hair, and went out to her kitchen.

Phyllis jumped up from the table where she was sitting with Terry. "Oh Jenny, you're up! Are you feeling better?"

Terry rose and came to her. "Phyllis volunteered to cook for me while you were sick. Are you OK? Here, come sit down and I'll get you some coffee."

"You must be hungry, Jenny. I'll cook you some breakfast too." Phyllis started to get some eggs from the refrigerator.

Jenny looked from one to the other. It's a good thing I wasn't down much longer. These two look pretty cozy. Oh, maybe I'm just in the way now. An old lady with a young virile husband... I know it's not natural.

"As a matter of fact I'm starved, Phyllis. Make those over medium, please." She sat at the table and let them wait on her for a change. It was almost funny watching them. They so obviously felt guilty. And she was pretty sure they hadn't done anything in particular to feel guilty about. It was just that they were young and vital, and she was getting old. She ate the eggs and toast Phyllis served her and drank two cups of coffee while they brought her up to date on the events of the past three days.

"Well it looks like I have a lot of book-work to catch up on, Terry. I'll do that today." She looked at them again. I think I'll skip the prison service tomorrow. You two can handle it without me this time.

"Oh Jenny, are you sure that's a good idea?" Phyllis' voice sounded worried, but her eyes were alight as she looked at Terry.

"Yeah Jenny, are you sure you want to do that?" Terry echoed, eyeing her questioningly. "You love to do the prison service!"

"You'll do just fine without me this time." She looked at them, and then smiled at their expressions, "Well, it won't be forever. I'll be back with you before you know it! I guess I forget how old I am, sometimes. Just try to keep up with you youngsters, and I get exhausted." She took another sip of coffee. "Well shouldn't you be getting to work, Terry?"

He jumped up, "Oh Lord, yes! I forgot what I'm doing. Did you fix me a lunch, Phyllis?"

She handed him a sack, and he gave Jenny a quick kiss and ran to the truck. She heard it roar away. Phyllis was cleaning up the kitchen, and Jenny let her finish. That was entirely out of character for her, but she felt like a different person somehow. It was almost as though she were outside the room watching what went on inside. Strange!

"Phyllis, are you in love with Terry?" She heard herself ask the question she'd thought for so long.

Phyllis stopped wiping the counter and looked at her, startled. A bird sang outside the window. The day was bright and sunny, with a warm breeze blowing in off the ocean. Life went on all around them.

Slowly, Phyllis finished the counter and put the dishcloth away. "I don't let myself think about it Jenny, but maybe I am. Yes, I guess I am... I'm sorry!" She sat down across from Jenny. "I didn't mean to love him, but he's such a sweet person. It's hard to believe he was ever a convict! And those stories he tells sometimes about the prison and all... it's like pure fiction when you look at him. What am I going to do, Jenny?"

"I don't know. I think we all need to pray about this, because its' a big problem. We can't keep on working together as though nothing happened. I think Terry probably loves you too, although I'm not sure he realizes it. He loves me too, you know... only in a different way, I'm sure." She sighed a deep resigned sigh. "I always thought he'd probably leave me for someone younger some day. I've heard that your fears are usually realized if you dwell on them."

She looked at the lovely face opposite her, "I don't know whether God brought you here, or whether the enemy brought you. But we're all going to be thoroughly tested before we're through. Whether it's right or not, God knows, but Terry is my husband. We pledged to love and honor each other until death parts us. I love him very dearly, you know."

Phyllis nodded. "I know. And I understand. I'll have to leave... although it will kill our work at the prison if I do."

Jenny was thoughtful a moment, "No, I think maybe Terry should go and visit his mother in Montana for awhile. I don't know how we'll manage the business, but the Lord has always watched over us and I have to trust him now. I'll talk to Terry about it tonight and try to thrash it out. And we'll pray about it, Phyllis. You know, I don't think we prayed enough before we started the ministry with you. This time, we'll pray!"

The angel nodded with Phyllis.

CHAPTER THIRTY

Terry left for Montana on a dull Tuesday in the rainy season. "I sure hope this isn't a big mistake, Jenny! What if we have floods like last year? How will you be able to cope with everything?"

"Henry will help me if that happens, I'm sure. He seems pretty capable, and he's learned the business in the past few weeks. We'll handle it together. You go on and visit your family. You haven't seen them for a very long time now. And your mama is getting old!"

He grimaced. *She's younger than you.* He didn't say it, although they both thought it. "Why now? Can't it wait awhile, Jenny? We're so busy with the prison ministry, and there's a lot to do to keep the business growing, even if Henry keeps doing so well."

"Terry, I think you need to get away from here for awhile and go somewhere else where you can think clearly and sort things out for yourself. Think about our life and your goals and how you can best live your life now."

"It's our life Jenny, not just mine!"

She smiled at him and kissed his cheek. "Keep in prayer Love, and God will sort everything out for us. But it will be better if you put some distance between us. Anyway, you really have neglected your mama." She handed him his suitcase and a bag of sandwiches and homemade cookies. "You'll be going back through some of the territory where we hid out."

He grinned, "Yeah ... say, those were great times, you know? Exciting, even if I was on the lam! You're some gal, Jenny. I love you ... always have, ever since I got your first letter! " She followed him outside, where he kissed her goodbye and left, driving their old Falcon. She hoped it would hold up on such a trip for him.

"Will I ever see him again, Lord?" Only the wind answered.

It rained the next day... and the day after that, and the day after that. Henry did the truck route, slogging through the mud. Jenny was afraid he'd quit if it kept up, but finally the rain stopped and the sun shone for a couple of days, on hillsides turned green again. She worked on the books, and she worked on the message for Sunday, and she cleaned her house thoroughly, and she prayed. In the night sometimes she cried.

It seemed as though she was always alone... her whole life she'd been alone. "I wonder if everybody feels this way, Lord? Or do other people have friends and family that keep them from feeling so separate from everyone and everything? Lord, where are my children? Why don't they care about me? Is it because I've tried to serve you with my life? Is that why nobody wants to stay with me?

She remembered some Bible verses about leaving your earthly family to follow Jesus and responded, "OK, Lord. If the loneliness is because I love you, then so be it. I know you were lonely too. I'm sticking with you, whatever happens. Your will be done. Please keep Terry safe, and please keep Phyllis in your will for her too. And please help us each to do whatever it is you want us to do.

As she prayed, the angel was able to chase the enemy far from the area. He sheathed his sword and rested.

The days went by. The rain fell, and the wind blew, and the sun shone, and the grass was green, and as she worked and prayed, Jenny slowly came to a conclusion. She had always in the back of her mind expected Terry to leave her when he got out of prison. It really was an unnatural relationship they had, wasn't it? He was young yet... only 40. He had a long life ahead of him, and it wasn't fair of her to expect him to stay hitched to a 73 year old. She'd soon be a real drag on him, as her arthritis was getting worse, and her heart gave her a lot of trouble. It scared her sometimes, though she didn't let him know. Yes, it would be better if she set him free.

She began to plan her life without Terry. Maybe she'd go back to Lompoc first. That was the place she felt most attached to on this earth. God knew she'd lived in a lot of places. She remembered back to her childhood, traveling around the east coast cities. No, she didn't care to go back there. Anyone she'd known in the circus would be gone by now, and most of the rest were bad memories. Remembering her past reminded her of Al. She hadn't thought of him for a long time. Now she wondered how he was. Probably drinking himself to death, if he isn't already dead!

But no, she was still getting the same pension checks, and anyway, the kids would have talked about that. She thought of the kids. David hardly ever contacted her. He was busy with his career and his family. He kept in touch with Al, she was sure, but Jenny hadn't heard from him in a long time. Johnny told her sometimes what David was doing. Johnny... she couldn't count on him for anything. He was having a lot of trouble with his wife. Probably end up with a divorce. His kids were having trouble with their own marriages. Johnny had too many other things on his mind and heart to worry about his 'weird' mother.

Karen. I wonder if she's back from Paris? Did she marry the oil millionaire from Iraq? Maybe I'll call her and have a talk, to see how she's getting along. Maybe she'll help me out one more time.

She dialed the apartment in Beverly Hills and waited. The maid answered. "No, Madam is at her office now. She'll be home at 6:00 though. Shall I have her call you? Or would you like her office number?"

"Yes, please. Give me her office number. I really want to speak with her today." She'd started this, now she was going to pursue it.

She dialed the new number. "Keen Consultants," the young voice answered. "Yes, Ms. Keen is in, let me see if she's available. Whom did you say is calling?"

The girl seemed surprised to find that Karen had a mother.

"Mom! Are you OK?" Karen still sounded like her daughter. It was hard to believe she was the owner and director of such a big business. Jenny had been told that Keen Consultants did business with some very impressive clients, and even had close connections with the current Whitehouse!

"Hi, Karen. Yes, I'm OK. I just miss you, and wondered how you're doing. It seems a long time since we've talked."

A shade of irritation entered Karen's voice. "Well, I'm just fine, Mom. Very busy, as usual. We're in the middle of some really important negotiations here. I'll be leaving on Monday for meetings with some bankers in Switzerland. What are you up to? How is Terry? Did you get the truck paid off?"

"Terry's visiting his family in Montana right now. I'm thinking of taking a vacation while he's gone. Karen, can you send me some money so I can do that? If you can spare it, I mean." (She knew Karen had millions, but didn't want to push too hard and alienate her any worse.) "I may be out of touch for awhile, and just thought I'd let you know so you don't worry. Thanks to you, the business is going pretty well. Henry is running it while Terry's gone, and he's doing a fairly good job of it. He's pretty reliable and works hard. I think Terry can make a good living out of this company if he puts his mind and heart into it." She wondered if Karen would pick up on the implication, but her daughter was as wrapped up in herself as always, and didn't hear.

"Well, I hope you have a good time, Mom. I'll drop a check in the mail for you, sure. Take care of yourself, won't you? Is your heart OK?" Not even a where are you going?

"I have a little bout with it now and then, but I have my medication. You be careful in Switzerland! All those big-shots…do they really care what you think? It must be quite a feeling being so powerful." She meant it seriously, but Karen took her wrong, as usual.

"You don't have to mock me! I'm doing very well, thank you very much! … in spite of everything! I'm sorry, Mom, I'm busy, and I have to go. I'll call you sometime." And she was gone. The dial tone sounded loud in Jenny's ear, and she reluctantly hung up the phone. So much for her children caring about her.

Jenny packed carefully, trying to take everything she'd need for a long time, along with some small things that meant a lot to her… pictures, mementos from her past. She sat at her kitchen table and wrote a note to Terry. "I'm setting you free, Love. You're young, and you should be able to live a more interesting life than you can have with an old lady for your wife. You need someone like Phyllis to be a partner with, and to work for the Lord. I probably shouldn't have married you at all, Terry. But I'm glad I did, and I thank you for loving me and for giving me so much happiness. Now it's time for your life to go on to another phase that doesn't include me. Don't worry, I'll be fine and I'll contact you before too long and arrange for the divorce papers. You'll be able to make the business grow if you use good common sense. Get someone you trust to do the books. That's where you'll need to be careful not to get cheated. I hope you'll keep up the prison ministry as much as you can. It's important work, and God will bless you for it! Goodbye, Terry Singer. I'm leaving you because I love you."

Then, drying the tears that threatened to blot out her writing, she began a letter to Phyllis. "It's time I let Terry lead the life he deserves, without being tied to a sick old woman. I'm pretty sure he loves you. If you love him too, then please take care of him and make him happy. The two of you will make a fine team for the prison ministry too. I'll set Terry free legally and stand aside for what God has for you. I'm going away for a time, but I'll come back after awhile and then we can settle everything. After you've both had time to sort things out and make decisions. I love you both."

She set the letters on the counter where they could be found easily. *Why don't I go and find my dad's family... or my mother's? I've always wanted to know my cousins. What better time than now?*

The more she thought about it, the better the idea felt. *Lord, if I don't find them now, they'll probably be dead and gone!*

She had a long discussion with Henry about the business. He said he'd be OK with the work on his own for a while, at least. How long did she plan to be gone? "Oh, Terry will be coming back in another week or so," she told him. "He'll be ready to get back to work fast then. Probably getting all fired up with new ideas while he's gone."

Karen sent the check, true to her word, and surprisingly, it was very generous. Jenny thought of buying a plane ticket, but couldn't quite bring herself to spend so much. She ended up putting some of her things in storage and buying a bus ticket to Georgia. She bought herself some crackers and peanuts and apples to snack on so she wouldn't have to spend so much on food on the way. Then she decided she really couldn't carry all that stuff, so stashed most of it in the cupboards and took a few granola bars that she could get into her purse. *Oh well, I'll get more in bus stations on the way.*

She wore her good navy slacks with low-heeled shoes, and a jacket. It could be chilly even in some parts of the South in early spring. She stood in the bus station restroom and eyed herself in the long mirror. Facing her was an attractive older woman, who looked about 65. Her short blond hair was done in a soft perm, and framed a face beginning to show some wrinkles, though not nearly as many as most of her acquaintances who were in their 70s. Her 5'4" body was slim, bordering on thin, and she stood straight in spite of the arthritis that had begun to plague her. Her eyes were still bright, the part of them you could see with the lids now drooping down so much. She frowned. I hate that... maybe I should have my eyes done.

Still, she wasn't unhappy with her appearance, except when she had to compare herself with someone like Phyllis. Jenny raised her eyebrows, opening up her eyes somewhat. Hey let's face it, I looked a lot better when I was her age too!

She turned away, picking up her overnight case and purse. It was almost time for the bus to arrive. Looking at her, a casual observer would not have realized her heart was breaking.

The trip took 4 days and 3 nights. The scenery was interesting, though not as pretty as it would be a little later in the season. They went down to Los Angeles and took the southern route. As they moved further south and east, the temperature climbed gradually, and by the time they reached Mississippi she no longer needed the jacket at all. Blossoms decorated the trees all through the south, and the air was gentle when she walked outside at the frequent bus stops.

Life seemed surreal somehow. Had she really lived all that time in other places and done all those strange things? Or was it only a dream and she'd wake up in the circus, ready to go on the trapeze one more time? But no, the ache in her breast witnessed the reality of her journey.

As they reached the outskirts of Savannah, she tried to picture her mother living in that area as a child. Now and then they passed a pillared house on a rolling hill in the distance, and she wondered if it could be the one where her grandparents had lived.

Then they pulled into the bus station and it was time to disembark and gather her things and decide what to do next. She stepped down from the security of the bus, moving stiffly at first. It was 3 o'clock, so there was time to look around the area a bit. She got out the notes she had written down when her mother finally told her about the family. Her grandparents' name was Wilson, but her mother had only sisters... Millie and Lucy, so she didn't know what their names would be now. And her father's name was John Shane. She decided to start with that, and looked in the phone book, where she found a whole list of Shanes, including three Johns!

Then she realized that of course her father would be dead and gone by now. These must be cousins, or she hoped at least some were. She put the phone book back in its place, picked up her bags and started toward the exit. I should've left half this stuff home! It weighs a ton.

She struggled with it to the taxi area and was relieved when the driver helped her load things into the trunk. "I need a not-too-expensive motel," she told him. "And it would be nice if I could be somewhere near the library."

He nodded "There's a ma and pa type not too far from downtown. Most of the big chains are out on the highway though."

"The ma and pa will be fine, I think. I'll be staying for awhile, so I guess I should rent by the week."

He took her to the little motel, which had only 12 rooms and was surrounded by shops, restaurants and other businesses all laid out in a square, with a little park in the center. They had a room available and she checked in and dropped off her things, then went for a walk to see what was around her.

The whole area was quaint and pretty, with a feel of age and history about it... not at all like the atmosphere in California. People strolled along the streets and sat on the benches under shady trees. Flowers crowded their beds along the sidewalks, smelling sweet as she passed. Jenny fell in love with Savannah. It felt like home somehow. She discovered that there were a whole series of squares like little towns, all joined together. Each had its green space in the middle, with a park or a fountain or a special building in the center. There were trees everywhere, and flowers. It was all very lovely.

She found the library after asking directions a couple of times, and told the librarian what she wanted. He was young and studious looking, and eager to display his knowledge. He quickly helped her locate information from various sources about her mother's family. It helped that the Wilsons had been prominent in the area at one time.

It turned out that Millie and Lucy were both dead, (and Mary Louise had disappeared mysteriously) but she found the names of some of their children listed in the obituaries. She did an eenie-meenie-miney-mo type choice and called Mary Sherman.

Hello, she said, when a woman answered. Are you Mary Sherman? At the affirmative, she said, "Well, I think I'm your cousin. I'm Mary Louise Wilson's daughter."

Southern hospitality kicked right in, and very soon a taxi arrived and the friendly young driver took Jenny from the motel to a lovely home outside of town. The house sat well back from the road, with a sweep of green lawn in front. Several different species of trees offered shade here and there and flowerbeds lined the walks. It looked like something out of one of her old storybooks. Mary Sherman welcomed Jenny like a long-lost child, although she felt rather like a thorn in the midst of the rose bushes. Mary was a little younger than Jenny, and reminded her of Mamie.

"You look a lot like my mother," Jenny told her.

"And you remind me of cousin Joanna." Mary's voice was sweet and cultured. She was Lucy Ann's daughter, and she had obviously had the education Jenny was denied. The contrast was very clear. But they managed to ignore their cultural differences, and settled down with tea and little cookies, to talk like old friends. Jenny told Mary what had happened to Mamie, at least as much as she knew. Mary could hardly believe what she was hearing was the truth, but Jenny's speech and manner told her as much as her words.

Mary told Jenny about the rest of the family history. "I think I was named after your mama," Mary confided, "and Grandma never called me by my name. I was always "Missy" to her.

Jenny stayed for dinner, and was pleased when Mary arranged a family get-together on Saturday so she could meet the rest of the cousins. And she was overwhelmed when Mary insisted she move into the mansion for the remainder of her stay.

The guest room was elegant, and Jenny settled into the luxurious pillows that night thinking that the Queen of England surely didn't have any nicer place to lay her head! She imagined what it would have been like to be raised in these surroundings, and compared it with her own life. For a little while she was very angry with her mother. Then, going over in her mind the love story Mamie had told her, she knew she would have reacted exactly the same way herself. Well, God knew all about it and surely there was a reason why her life had unfolded as it had. But I wonder what it is? I wonder why I had to go through all that misery with Frank?

Before she could dwell on it any longer exhaustion took over and she sank into a deep, restoring sleep. When she woke in the soft perfumed bed, surrounded by beautiful furniture, rose colored carpeting, and flowered draperies with sun shining through the sheer curtains, it took a few moments to remember where she was. Then the events of the previous day came flooding back, and the joy of being with her newfound cousins fought in her with the sorrow of leaving her closer family.

She closed her eyes again and prayed earnestly for all of them, and for herself to be in the Lord's will. Then she lay for a few minutes enjoying the comfort of the luxurious bed and wondering what she should wear for the day's activities. Finally she took a deep breath, slipped out of the high bed and prepared to face the day.

And later that same day in California, Terry arrived home to find the note.

CHAPTER THIRTY-ONE

He came into the empty kitchen and knew immediately that something was wrong... "Jenny" he called. "Jenny, Honey, I'm home!" There was no answer of course, and he dropped his bag and walked through the little house quickly, half expecting to find her passed out or dead or something... he didn't know. He wandered back into the kitchen, and saw the notes on the counter. Now the feeling in the pit of his stomach threatened to cause real trouble... He picked up the note with his name on it and read it over and over, not able to take in the meaning at first. Then he shook his head, hoping the whole thing was a joke and Jenny would soon pop in and laugh at him. "Aw, now what have you gone and done, Jenny?" he asked the air in the very empty little kitchen.

There were several messages on the answering machine. Three were from customers with extra trash to be picked up. One was from Karen asking whether the money had arrived safely. What money? Two were from Phyllis wanting to set up a meeting to plan the next service. He punched her number, taking out his frustration on the phone. When she answered, he just said, "Phyllis, we've got a big problem here and I think you'd better come over as soon as you can."

"I'll be right there, Terry. What's wrong?" she asked.

"Jenny's gone."

"Gone? Where?"

"I don't know, Phyllis!" His voice was brittle. He took a deep shuddering breath.

She heard it and said, "I'm on my way. I'll be there in a few minutes. Take it easy, Terry... you hear?" And the phone went dead.

She arrived so quickly he knew she'd broken all the state speed laws. He pointed to the note with her name on it, and she snatched it up and read, then reread. "Oh no!" she breathed, "So that's why I couldn't reach her." Her legs went weak, and she fell into a chair by the table."Oh Terry, what are we going to do?" He sat down opposite her and handed her his note. She passed hers over to him. They were silent as they read, then put the notes down on the table between them and just looked at each other.

Guilt rose up in Terry's mind, and he frowned at the worried face across form his own. "It's all my fault, Phyllis! I was attracted to you and it looks like Jenny knew it. But I didn't mean anything by it! I love Jenny... she's my wife! And I don't know where she is!"

"Stop that Terry! It's as much my fault as yours! And I feel as badly about this as you! We have to find her, of course!" She had mixed feelings as she watched his face. Obviously he was terribly upset, and that made her feel even more drawn to him. Sure, sometimes he was crude, but she could certainly understand why, given his background. A man can't spend that much of his life with hardened criminals and not be affected by it! But underneath the rough exterior there was a tender caring soul. "Who can we call?" she asked.

"I don't know... oh, Karen, I guess! There's a message from her on the phone wanting to know if the money got here safely!"

"What money?"

"That's just it, I have no idea what she's talking about! And Jenny didn't have any extra money, and the checkbook is here." He searched for Karen's office number on the phone list taped to the inside of the cupboard door. He punched in the number quickly, and dealt with the secretary with impatience. "I'm her step-father! And I need to talk with her now... it's urgent!"

That got a reaction on the other end of the line, and soon Karen's voice was asking, "Is that you, Terry? What's wrong?"

"Do you know where Jenny is?" His voice was tight, almost accusing.

"I have no idea, Terry! Don't you know?"

He felt close to despair. He could tell by her tone she didn't know. "She's gone, Karen. She left me a note."

He told her part of the story, but left out the part about Phyllis. "There was this message on the phone about money, so I thought she might be with you."

"No. I've been in Europe until yesterday. She did call me Terry, and ask for some money so she could take a vacation, but I didn't think to ask where she was going... Well, we have to find her! I can't believe she'd pull a stunt like this! It's always something with her."

"No." Terry was starting to recover his reason. "No Karen, I don't want to do that to Jenny. She's an adult, after all, and she's been taking care of herself for a lot of years. I guess she's still able to do that. And the note says she'll come back so we can settle everything. Don't call the police or anything. We'll just wait awhile for her to contact me. I can't believe she'd leave me just hanging here wondering and worrying about her. She's not like that!"

"Well ... well, if you think so, we'll wait a few days. But you keep me posted, Terry. I have some good contacts who can pull strings to start looking for her. I'll check back with you next week. And Terry, if you hear anything for goodness sake call me! I have enough to think about without having to worry about Mom too!"

"Right, Karen, thanks! Oh, and thanks for sending her the money she needed. At least I don't have to worry about that!" He hung up the phone and sat back down in the chair dejectedly.

"Now why in the world would she think I'd want a divorce, Phyllis? I never gave her any reason to think I wasn't happy with our life together!"

"It's probably my fault, Terry." Phyllis' voice was tight with emotion. She looked toward the cupboards."You want a cup of coffee? I could sure use one!"

He nodded. "Might as well. Doesn't seem to be anything else we can do right now." Then he realized what she'd just said. "What do you mean, your fault? You didn't do anything."

"Well yes, I guess I did." She talked while her back was to him, pouring water into the pot. She put the coffee in and turned the switch on, then got out mugs and spoons. "There's no cream."

"What are you talking about, Phyllis? And what do I care about cream at a time like this! What in the world did you do, anyway?"

"Well, Jenny asked me one day flat out, was I in love with you?" She flushed and looked away from his eyes. "I said yes Terry, but that I wouldn't let it interfere in the work here. I said I'd leave but she said no, and that's when she decided you should go visit your mother." She faced him again as the tears began to flow. She mopped her eyes with a napkin, "I didn't mean to love you! I don't want this to happen, but it did and now I don't know what to do about it to make things right!"

He had conflicting emotions. He was upset and worried over Jenny. He was angry with Phyllis. And he was thrilled to hear her say she loved him. He sat as if in shock, not responding to her revelation. Phyllis could hardly stand the silence. Once you've told someone you love him, you want more than anything else to hear that the feeling is reciprocated. She poured the coffee as silent tears flowed down her cheeks.

"Sit down, Phyllis. We need to talk. And we need to pray. If I ever needed God's help, I need it now!" His voice was soft, but strong. She sat. "I vowed before God to love and honor Jenny through good times and bad, rich or poor, in sickness and health, and to be with her alone until death parts us. Now, I happen to believe God holds us to our vows. I can't believe Jenny would do this to me, to cause me to break my word to God. I surely can't even think of letting her divorce me! The only reason for divorce that I can find in the Bible is adultery, and we certainly don't have that one! It was a whole different thing when she divorced Al. He had run around on her for years... and he beat her too! She had every reason to be able to leave him. And God gave us a real miracle to show we should marry. So I can't see why she'd do this!"

He looked at her sitting there in the dim kitchen with tears in her eyes, and knew she loved him. "I feel real bad about this for you, Phyllis. I could love you... I know I could if I'd let myself. But I prayed about that and God gave me the strength to put those feelings away. I do love you as a sister in the Lord, and I can't pretend it wouldn't be a temptation to let myself feel more than that. But the Lord is stronger than the tempter, and he's faithful if we ask for his help you know, so ... "

He rose and paced back and forth from the kitchen to the living room doorway. "I really am angry with both of you women though. What makes you two think you can decide my life for me? What gives you the right to play God?

Don't you think you could at least have talked to me about this… taken me into the decision-making loop? You've treated me like a child here, and I darn well resent that! I'm the man of this family, and I'm the one who should lead it, not Jenny… even though she is so much older!"

He slammed his fist on the counter and stopped pacing to face Phyllis, his eyes flashing, his form seemingly growing larger before her eyes, and his voice hard - even dangerous sounding. She shrunk back, in surprise and fright. "Stop, Terry… please! You're scarin' me!" She edged closer to the door. "We need to pray about this, not lose control. I'm sorry about what we did… we shouldn't have talked about it behind your back, you're right, Terry. I apologize for both of us. I'm sure Jenny will feel the same when she thinks about it!"

He deflated slowly, took a deep breath, and turned his back from her for a few seconds. Then he poured himself another cup of coffee and sat again at the table. She edged into her chair again too, watching him.

"OK then Phyllis, you're right. We'll try prayer and see what happens." He bowed his head and began, "Lord, you know all about this whole mess. You know why it's happening, and you know where Jenny is, and you know how I feel about it. Now Lord, what do you want us to do?"

Phyllis continued, "Lord, please forgive me for hurting Jenny and Terry. I didn't mean to do that, you know I didn't. If Satan used me, please forgive me for that and help me to make it right. Jesus, please touch my heart and ease the pain, and help me to feel as I ought to about Terry… and please be with Jenny wherever she is and help her through this too! And please Lord, don't let all this mess up our ministry to those men in prison. I see now what's happening I think, Lord. Satan doesn't like what we're doing here, and this was his way to try to put a stop to it."

Terry chimed in, "Lord, that's right! Now, please show us what to do about it! Make all this trouble work for good to us and to your work here somehow. We can't see how, but you know all about it. Give me the right attitude here, and give me wisdom to know how to go forward with my life and your work, and whatever we're supposed to do here for you."

They finished praying after a few more minutes, then, in accord once more, they looked up and knew they had to deal with their immediate situation first. "I guess I'd better go home, and I'll stay away as much as possible Terry, with our work still going on." She picked up her purse where it had fallen under the table and asked, "We can still work together, can't we?"

"For now I guess, Phyllis, unless I get some word otherwise. It would be too bad to let the enemy undermine all our work now. We have some guys right on the edge of coming to know Jesus. How can we let them down?"

She nodded, pushing her hair back from her face tiredly. "I can't believe we got into such a mess, when we were just trying to do God's will here. I only meant to do good, and I almost really put my foot in it! Goes to show how much we need to keep in prayer, doesn't it?" She opened the door and looked back at him with a strained expression, "and it'll take me a lot more prayer to get myself straightened out. Pray for all of us, won't you?"

His look was enough. She left, and he watched her car go down the driveway and turn onto the road. What am I gonna do, Lord? And deep in his heart the answer came...*trust me, and wait. Do your work. My son, have I ever let you down?*

He couldn't deny that... and he knew it had been the Lord's voice inside him. He got out the books for the business, called the people who'd left messages for pick-up, and settled in to wait. It wouldn't be easy, but he'd sure had to do a lot of learning and waiting during the prison years. That experience would stand him in good stead now.

The prison services went on much as though nothing had happened, and they simply told the men who asked that Jenny had gone on a vacation. "She'll be back soon." They carried on their parts of the service, and then went their own ways after a brief meeting to decide what the next week should bring. The music wasn't the same without Jenny's soprano leading out, but they had Einer Jacobs, a big Swede with a strong tenor voice who joined with Phyllis' clear melody. Einer had grown up in church but had gotten into bad company when he left the small mid-western town of his childhood. He carried the music along when he knew the songs, so they made sure they sang the ones he knew. It all worked out OK.

Jenny had been in Georgia three weeks. It had been a wonderful time of meeting her family. She loved most of them dearly. She learned a lot from the stories her cousins told about their parents. Her father's family members were somewhat harder to warm up to. They weren't sure they wanted to know about her at all. It wasn't a pleasant thought to know their father and uncle had been such a rotten egg that he'd abandoned his young wife when she was with child. But Jenny did meet some of them and found out about her background. She discovered she was of German and English descent. That alone was interesting to her, and she resolved to delve into genealogy and history as soon as she got the chance.

When she reflected on the situation she thought, I guess I understand how they feel. If I were in their shoes I wouldn't want to admit it either. I wish my real father had been strong and wonderful and dependable. It's interesting how our character and decisions affect other people's lives. And we don't have a clue for the most part, do we?

Suddenly a new thought occurred to her. What have I done to Terry? And what have I done to Phyllis? Oh Lord... I'm wrong! I have to get back home and try to undo what I've done!

She almost panicked with the realization, and began to pack on the spot. "I have to get home now," she told Mary Sherman. "I've had such a lovely time with you and all the others that I almost forgot about my family in California."

The angel nodded his approval.

Privately, Mary thought it was about time, as Jenny wasn't an easy person for her to live with, given her rather course speech and sometimes pushy manner. But Mary was gracious as always, and helped Jenny get organized. She insisted that her cousin take the plane rather than the bus back to San Luis Obispo, and even paid for the ticket!

"You're such a love, Mary!" Jenny told her. "I can't tell you how much I appreciate all you've done for me. You're real true family, and I love you very much." Her eyes were misty as she hugged her cousins and said goodbye at the airport. Then she got on the plane and buckled into the seat, impatient to get home. Do I still have a home, Lord? Or have I really bolixed this up? What's next? She watched a not very good movie off and on, and thought and prayed and hoped and napped a little. She switched to a commuter plane at Los Angeles and finally arrived at San Luis Obispo.

When she had collected her baggage at the terminal, she looked around for a taxi. She was eager to get home to Morrow Bay and see Terry. She checked her face with the small mirror in her purse, and put on some fresh lipstick, powdered her nose, and hoped she didn't look as old and tired as she felt. Suddenly she felt almost shy, as she neared the place. The cab rounded the last corner and she saw the small rented cottage. It looked like home to her now. She got out of the cab, paid the driver and stood by the driveway with her baggage, wondering what sort of reception she'd get.

She bent to gather her things, and suddenly there he was! Neither of them knew what to say, so he just took her in his arms. "So you're finally home! It's about time!"

She dissolved in tears. It was so good to feel his arms around her again, to nestle against his chest and smell his special smell, and know she was loved. "Oh Terry... can you ever forgive me? I'm so sorry, Love! I wasn't thinking right I know..." then she drew back. "Oh... what about Phyllis? Did you..."

"No! No, I didn't, and I can't believe you'd even think such a thing! Come on, Jenny, we have a whole lot of talking to do!" He picked up her bags and started for the house and she followed, thanking God in her heart.

It took a long time to get everything sorted out. He told her all about his time in Montana, and she told him about her family in Georgia. "They're all such nice people, Terry... so refined and elegant. I really didn't fit with them, I guess. But it was great to finally meet them... sort of like a fairy tale come true, you know?"

He nodded. "Yeah, I can imagine, Jen. I should have known that's where you'd go." He frowned then, and his eyes clouded over. "I can't believe you'd let me worry like that for so long. It was like Hell here, not knowing where you were or how you were..."

"I must have been out of my mind, Love! I can't believe I did that either! I guess I let the enemy get in, and I thought you'd want to be with somebody young and beautiful, and not be stuck with me! I'm older than your mom, after all, and you're young and handsome...it's a shame to waste your life like this!"

"And that's another thing," he looked very stern. "No more deciding my life for me! Understand?"

She nodded, looking contrite."I'm sorry."

"You should be! I'm an adult, Jenny, able to make my own decisions. And I'm supposed to be the head of this family, not you!" Then he told her how he felt about their marriage vows and about his talk with Phyllis.

She felt the rebuke strongly, and knew it was justified. "I can't believe I didn't understand all that, Terry. You're right, and I was wrong, and I'm sorry. I'm really deeply sorry. Will you forgive me?"

He held out his arms and she went into them. He took her into their bedroom and made her know how much she was loved. It was very good to be home.

The angel sat in the yard under a tree and watched for the enemy.

CHAPTER THIRTY-TWO

1989

When the phone rang that windy Wednesday morning, Jenny heard it from out in the yard where she'd been working on the petunias growing in the border along the walk. She hurried in, wiping the damp earth from her clothes and shoes as she went, and caught it on the 4th ring. "Hello," she said, out of breath, ignoring the tightness around her heart.

"Mrs. Singer?"

"Yes"

"Please hold for the governor, Ma'am."

She sat down in surprise. What? The governor? What could he possibly want with her?

"Good morning, Mrs. Singer."

"Good morning, sir." She waited.

"Is everything going all right with you now? Are you in good health?"

"Fine thank you Governor, yes. Is there something I can do for you, sir?"

"We're having some hearings on conditions at the various prisons, and in the process of investigation we came across some letters you had written concerning your work there and your husband's troubles with the system."

"Oh? Yes, I did write to you at various times."

"I wonder if you'd be willing to come and discuss things with the committee studying prisons? If you're not up to it I understand, Mrs. Singer. I know from the files that you've had some trouble with your health, and I wouldn't want to jeopardize that."

"Oh no, sir! I'm just fine... and I'd jump at the chance to talk about what I know about the conditions at several of the state and federal prisons. When will you want me there?"

"Can you be ready by tomorrow morning? We'll have a seat reserved for you on the 10:00 o'clock flight if you can make it?"

When she put the phone down, she sat for a few moments. "Lord, you've finally given me a chance to tell those people what's going on! Help me know what to say and how to act to get the message across to them. Give me wisdom Lord, please!" She already had the incentive and enough confidence to go and talk with the elected officials.

Jenny hurried to her closet and surveyed her clothes. She wanted to look as credible and authoritative as possible. She did some quick laundry and began to cook some things to put in the freezer for Terry. She knew he could fend for himself, but wanted to let him know she cared about him enough to fuss over trivial things to make him happy.

By the time he got home a little late because of extra pick-ups that day, she was pretty well ready to leave. He eyed the suitcases on the bed as he went to get cleaned up for dinner. "What's going on, Jen? You leaving me again?"

"Not hardly! You'll have a hard time getting rid of me now!" She grinned at him. "But wait until you hear what's happened, Love... the State Prison Committee wants to talk to me about conditions in the various facilities. It's all because of the letters I wrote to the governor while we were trying to get you back into the prison, and then while we were trying to get you released!"

"No kidding?"

"For real, Terry! This is the chance I've waited for so long. Remember when I tried so hard to get the radio and TV stations in Montana to listen when they pulled all that stuff on you? And nobody would even give me half a chance to talk about the corrupt systems then. Now it's finally going to happen! And maybe God will give me a chance to help other guys like you, who are forced to do things against their will... I'm sure it happens all the time! And there were so many unfair things you went through... I can't wait to tell them about it!" She waved a notebook before tucking it into her large purse. "I'm gonna make some notes while I'm on the plane. Or maybe you can help me start tonight. It's a pretty short flight, but I've had so much to do today I haven't had time to sort out my thoughts yet."

"How soon do you have to leave? And how long will you be gone?" He sounded like he'd sounded when in prison and she'd had to leave him. "I wish I could go along," he added. "I'd like to tell them a few things myself!"

She nodded, "I know Love, but I'll try to do it for you. Give me the stuff you really want to say, and I'll try to work it in." They both knew he would never be allowed to say it himself. She sniffed, "Oh good grief, the potatoes are burning!" she exclaimed, and rushed to the stove.

They talked over dinner, lingering as long as possible over the pot of tea afterward. Between them, they recalled and jotted down dozens of events and suggestions and criticisms. Then they prayed over the list, that the Lord would work his will through their past suffering, and make it work for good to someone else.

"I wonder how Sally's doing with her work now? Haven't heard from her in a while. When I get back, let's take a little trip over there and visit her, OK?"

"Sounds good to me. Maybe we need a little vacation together. We get so busy with the everyday stuff we forget to pay enough attention to the important things."

She was surprised at his insight. "You're saying exactly what I was thinking! Isn't it interesting how we do that sometimes!"

He gave her a sidewise grin. "That's what happens with us old married people… we begin to think the same thoughts. I read somewhere that if you live with someone long enough you begin to look like 'em."

"Well, that'd be fine in my case, but I don't know whether you'd get such a good deal …" she pulled her cheek flesh up to her ears to tighten the jaw-line. "Lots of wrinkles and sags…"

He laughed and swatted her hands playfully. "I never even see them until you do something like that!"

The committee was made up of five men and one woman. They were seated at a long table in a conference room. A skinny secretary ushered her in and gave her a seat opposite them, then took her place nearby. Jenny noticed a tape recorder too. Looked as though they'd take down everything she said. It was sort of like something from a movie she'd seen. She remembered that in the movie they'd jimmied the tape to say what they wanted it to though. She certainly hoped that wouldn't happen to her testimony!

Jenny wore her navy blue suit with a white blouse and silver earrings. Her hair was nicely curled, and she'd applied make-up carefully. She looked as "credible" as she could manage. She sat with her back straight, her notes in front of her, and pen in hand. She was ready for whatever they threw at her.

The day fairly flew by for her, as they asked questions and she answered. They let her tell them stories about various things, instead of just making yes and no answers. She was relieved that it wasn't like testifying in a courtroom. She'd sort of thought it might be… too many movies! But these people did seem to listen, and they took notes and asked questions. It was very satisfying to Jenny after all the years of frustration and wanting someone to listen and do something about the corruption.

As she was leaving the room, she overheard a senator telling the governor "Well, I understand she's Karen Keen's mother…" she didn't hear any more than that. I wonder how Karen will take this? Oh, I hope this won't just embarrass her and make things worse between us! Well, God knows all about it, and I'm not going to do anything different anyway, so whatever happens, happens!

The angel walked out of the room beside her.

The hearings continued for a week, and then she was sent home. It was sort of anti-climactic, as she hadn't a clue what they'd decided, if anything, but she left it in the Lord's hands. "I really thank you for letting me have a chance to get that all out in the open anyway, Lord. Please use it for good somehow."

Terry met her at the plane and gave her the hugs she'd been missing all week. He surprised her with dinner at an Italian restaurant in town. They sat in a corner booth with a red cloth and soft lighting. A Strauss waltz played in the background. She tried to remember all the details of the meetings to tell him, and they talked excitedly over big plates of pasta and hot breadsticks and olive oil with herbs.

"Well, the Lord gave you the experiences and the chance to talk about them, and now I guess we'll just have to leave it up to him to work out whatever is supposed to happen there." Terry put his hand over hers across the table. "I think our work is done now. God must have wanted me in the prisons so you could meet me there, and together we could bring all these things to light. And I guess if that's what it took to accomplish his work, then it's OK with me... hard as it was to go through!"

"Yeah," she agreed, nodding, "We probably won't ever know what this was all about until we get to heaven and ask him. She savored a bite of the pasta. "Oh well, all the Lord really requires of us is that we're faithful to do what he tells us. It's sure hard sometimes though, just trying to make the right choice... just trying to stay in his will." She looked off across the room, seeing into the past somehow. Al, and his physical and verbal abuse of both herself and the kids flashed in pictures across her mind again.

She brought herself back to the present, with an effort. "It was so tough all those years for instance, when people kept telling me I had to stay with Al no matter what happened to me and the kids. I must have been crazy to listen to them." Then she shook her head. "No, I was just really trying to follow what God wanted me to do. He knew I was sincere and eventually he got me out of there. " Her gaze came back to him. "And look what he gave me for my reward!" She squeezed his hand and smiled into his eyes.

"I love you, Jenny." His voice was soft and the trace of southern accent made it sweet to her ears. "I can't believe my luck when I look back over my life. Without you, I'd probably have ended up dead on the floor of that cell. The best thing that ever happened to me was that first sweet letter from you!"

Jenny's heart overflowed with tenderness and joy. "Terry Singer... my sweet husband... you've made me so happy!" Her voice quavered, and threatened to break. She swallowed hard, "I lived so many years looking for love, and sometimes I thought I'd found a little... but I never really knew what love was until you came into my life. You are my miracle, Love. And I don't care what people think about us anymore. Anyway, I believe souls are ageless, aren't they? So what does it matter if I've had a few more earthly years than you have?"

He looked into her blue-green eyes and frowned, "I wish I were older, Jen... but I am older in my mind than in years, and in the broad scheme of things you're right. It doesn't matter a bit." He signaled the waiter for the check. "Let's go home, Jenny."

The earthquake hit San Francisco the next week, so Television crews swarmed to that area and concentrated all their airtime on that terrible event. That meant there wasn't a lot of news coverage on the prison hearings, which frustrated Jenny. She got a nice letter from the governor's office thanking her for her participation, and telling her that some substantive changes were in the works. She wondered what that meant.

They went to visit Sally to check on whether the work there had suffered from the quake. Things were fine in Salinas, which was a relief. They sat with Sally at her kitchen table while Jenny told her about the hearings and asked her to keep an eye on things to see if anything changed at the prison.

"I can't believe you had such a chance, Jenny. But if anyone could do that job, it's you. I always knew God had something big in mind for you!" Sally gave her friend a hug. "You guys will stay for my class this evening, and meet some of my new recruits for Jesus, won't you?"

They stayed and helped prepare the meal, and enjoyed her class with the women and children who came. It was good to get back to that work, Jenny thought. She'd missed it. She was only 73... if she just didn't have to take care of Terry ... and then there was her heart... She knew with certainty and still regretted, that the prison work was behind her now. At the Men's Colony, Phyllis was handling things very well. On occasion, Terry went to a service to help, but Jenny didn't go there any more. She blinked back a tear. But I think I did something important, didn't I, Lord?

It was a good trip, but it marked a turning point in Jenny's thinking. She knelt beside her bed to talk with Jesus, and the angel knelt beside her. "Is there some other work for me now, Lord?" she asked. "Surely there must be something else meaningful for your kingdom that an older lady can do? And Lord, what about my kids and my grandkids? Father, please remember my family ... Lord, you promised if I trained them up in the way they should go, that when they got old they wouldn't depart from it," she reminded him. "And Lord, Karen, my baby, is already 47 years old! I know I made mistakes... I know they think I'm weird, Lord, but I always tried to do what I thought was best... what you wanted me to do! Please don't let my kids have to pay for my mistakes!"

The very next week Karen came to visit. She arrived unannounced on Thursday afternoon, driving a new dark green Jaguar. When it rolled into the driveway Jenny looked up from her ledger at the kitchen table. She saw an elegant lady step out of the expensive car. It took a second, and then she let out a shriek and ran outside to greet her daughter.

"Hi, Mom!" Karen said, as though nothing had ever happened to make friction between them.

"Karen! It's so good to see you!" Jenny hugged her joyfully, then stepped back to look at her. She was casually dressed in pants and a sweater the color of a cloudy day, that must have cost more than a month's rent for Jenny. Her dark blonde hair was shoulder length with just a hint of curl at the ends, and was clipped with a large gold bar. She smelled heavenly. "Oh, Karen, I'm so glad you came!" Jenny said again.

She brought out the good cups and saucers and made coffee for the two of them. It always helped conversation to have a cup in front of one, Jenny thought. She was glad she'd made cookies the day before, for Terry's lunches. She got some out of the jar and arranged them on a plâte. Karen sat looking around at the plain little kitchen, like a queen visiting the commoners. She ate a cookie though, and sipped at the coffee.

They made small talk for a few minutes before Karen got down to the reason she was there. "Mom, I thought I ought to be the one to come and tell you before you heard it from someone else. And I don't quite know how you'll take the news... but Dad died on Tuesday. His funeral will be tomorrow, at the funeral home in Napa.

Jenny was silent a moment. She closed her eyes. I wonder how Karen wants me to react? Then she opened them to ask, "How did he die, Karen?"

"He was leaving the clubhouse after closing. He'd been drinking again, after the doctor warned him over and over that it was dangerous, you know... just dropped dead right in the street. Almost got run over by a car, too, but they missed him by a whisker."

"How's Billie Jean taking it?"

"She's in a wheel-chair, you know. Has been for a long time now. It'll probably be really hard on her."

Jenny took a deep breath. Lord, please give me wisdom. Help me to be a witness to my daughter for you.

She didn't feel anything. Strange... after all the years spent together with Al, and raising his children... she felt nothing for him but...yes, some pity.

She didn't want to go to Al's funeral. Far from it, she was even glad he was gone. But suddenly she realized it would be a chance to see her family again. Surely all the children and grandchildren would gather for this event.

"Thank you for coming to tell me, Karen. I think I'd like to go to the funeral. Can I go with you?"

Karen nodded. "Sure, Mom. I'll get a room at 'The Breakers' for the night, and we can leave early in the morning." She picked at a non-existent speck on her sweater. "Will Terry expect to go along?"

"I don't think so, Honey, but he'll be home a little after five and I'll ask him then. I can't believe he'd want to go though. Besides, he has a lot of work to do, and probably can't afford to leave right now."

Karen looked up then and grinned. "Fine then, we'll plan to stay overnight there, and we'll see how it goes... we could stay longer if we needed to for some reason." She stretched her long legs out and leaned back in her chair, the way she had done as a teen. "It'll be nice to see the boys again, anyway. Seems a long time since we've been together." She frowned, looking out the window. "When you come from such a dysfunctional family as ours, it doesn't encourage reunions much. I haven't seen David for ages now, and Johnny's been through so much hell the last few years it hasn't been a great idea to visit him either."

Jenny nodded. "I know, Karen. It's not easy to deal with all we had going on while you were growing up. I'm sorry about that. If I could have made it otherwise, I would have." But that's not true, she realized... If I hadn't listened to all those good but misguided Christians, I'd have left Al and gotten the kids to a better environment. It's my fault.

Then she shook her head. No... it's Al's fault! How could he have treated us that way... his own family? Well, I wonder where he is now? I hope his conversion was real all those years ago, and that eternal security is true, or else Al is in a very bad place right now! His will be a funeral where I should weep.

And she did. She sat in the folding chair behind her family in the chapel and wept silently for Al. The organ played softly, some of the hymns she'd sung with the choir back in another lifetime, and she wept for the wasted life he'd had. She wept for the lost chances with his children, and for herself and the kids and all he'd made them suffer over the years. You can't go back and undo things like that. What a waste of a precious life!

She felt sorry for Billie Jean, who sat in the wheel chair looking old and ugly and unloved. She was a bitter old woman who had nothing good to say about anyone, including Al. Jenny looked at the down-turned mouth and the deeply wrinkled forehead. He must have had a miserable life with her. I wonder why he stayed? She had some kind of hold on him, but I surely don't know what it was. Hmmm. Well, maybe it was just that they were drunk together so much he couldn't function well enough to make a serious decision any more!

Jenny's grandchildren were strangers to her. They were a varied lot of people, from smart and cultured, to a couple she suspected were druggies. David had two sons and a daughter, and Johnny had two daughters, by two different wives. They were all married and Jenny had four great-grandchildren. She had not been included in their lives... their parents' choice, not hers. They considered Jenny very weird and not a fit influence for their children. First it was her Christian testimony, and then going so far as to be a prison minister, then and worst of all, the divorce and marriage to someone younger than her son. One could hardly blame them, they reasoned, for not wanting their kids to get well acquainted with a Grandma like that! So their kids had grown up without her, and had only the benefit of her prayers.

She was shocked to see David. He looked at least as old as she did. "How are you, son?" she asked him, when she got a chance to be near him in the crowd. "I've missed you," she added. She looked into his dull eyes. He looks ill! I wonder what's wrong?

"I'm doing fine, Mother. I hear you've been as busy as usual too. All that business about the prisons..." David was privately surprised to see her looking so young and trim. Dad had been a whole different type of person, and had looked old for some time. He'd always been younger-looking than Mom before, but now here she was, looking pretty good for ... how old was she now anyway, 73 or 74? Well, he guessed she took better care of herself than Dad had. Too bad she hadn't stayed and taken care of him that way too... A wife shouldn't just leave her husband like that!

She read his mind. She put her hand on his arm gently and said, "I had to leave, David. You know I stayed as long as I could. He would have killed me if I hadn't left."

He removed her hand, shaking his head.

"If you want to know the story, I'll tell you about it sometime," she offered. "I hope you're still going to church, Son. Just because your parents disappoint you, don't give up on God. He never fails you."

"You're still just as nutty as ever, aren't you?" He remarked coldly. Then he turned away. "Nice to have seen you, Mom."

She had the strong feeling that David didn't have much time left on this earth. She resolved to write him a long letter soon. He's sick, and it's serious... Lord, help him make peace with you soon!

Then she was swept back into the busyness of the day. She actually talked with her grandchildren, and was able to leave them feeling somewhat cheated that they hadn't known this interesting Grandma. "She's cool, isn't she?" David's grandson said to his cousin.

"Yeah, it might be fun to ask her about the prison stuff sometime. She must be a lot younger than Grandpa, huh?" Then they turned to the buffet table the club had prepared for the family and friends, and proceeded to stuff themselves with sandwiches and sweets. Billie Jean presided over the gathering, and everyone, one at a time, went to give her a hug and tell her how sorry they were. Jenny didn't. She wouldn't be that much of a hypocrite!

Karen took her and Johnny to dinner at an elegant place later in the evening. There were linen cloths on the tables, and candles in lovely glass holders, pretty china and silver, and soft semi-classical music in the background. Karen ordered a wonderful wine, and they toasted to good days ahead. It was a peaceful atmosphere, and it gave them a chance to talk over old times. They chose to remember the good times, and laughed over things that had happened back in Japan, and growing up later in Lompoc. Jenny enjoyed her children. They were nice people when they wanted to be. She grew serious over coffee though, and when there was a break in the conversation she leaned over to Johnny. "What's wrong with David?" she asked.

His eyes widened in surprise. "What makes you think...?"

"Come on, Johnny. This is Mom! You know I can tell when something's wrong with one of you. And this one is serious, I know. He's very ill, isn't he?"

Johnny looked uncomfortable. "I'm not supposed to tell you," he said. "But since you already know... I don't know how you do that, Mom!" He and Karen both stared at her.

"Yeah, it's weird" Karen agreed.

"I'm sorry you think that. I still want to know what's wrong with David?"

"He's got some rare blood disease. It isn't leukemia, but something like that… they don't know what to do about it."

"How long do they give him?"

"I think he said a year or two if he's lucky. He'll be really mad at me for telling you!"

Jenny nodded and looked down at her plate, moving the food around with her fork and waiting for the now familiar tightness around her heart to subside. After a minute it eased, and she raised her head and pretended nothing had happened.

"I guess he's really bitter about my leaving Al, hmm?" She knew she was right, and saw it confirmed by their expressions.

Johnny nodded. "Well, he was gone at the end there, when things got so bad. He didn't see any of that stuff like I did. And he didn't believe me when I told him what you said about his planning to kill you. He thinks we all ganged up on Dad and it broke his heart, and that's why he began to drink so much more." He patted her arm. "I'll try to talk to him again after he's had some time to get over this. He's feeling really bad right now, you know."

She nodded, "Yeah, I know… and now that it's too late, I understand that I should have communicated with David more. I did so many things wrong. And I meant to do things for you so much different than my folks did for me! I see it didn't turn out any better for you kids though, and I'm really sorry. I did try… honest I did! Only I couldn't do it by myself and Al wouldn't help. I know now that we should have left him a long time before I did. I should have gotten you away somewhere and given you a more stable home life somehow. But hindsight is 20/20 isn't it?" She half-grinned, ruefully. "I hope you're doing better for your family than we did? This chain of dysfunctional families should end with you. You still have a chance to do something for your kids and grandkids. It's too late for me, I think. You're all getting older too, though, so don't wait too long."

She looked across the table at Johnny and saw him as he really was now, instead of as a young man, the way she usually filtered his image. This was a grandpa, for heaven's sake! He had a large bald-spot, which he tried to disguise, and a potbelly too. He really should take better care of himself! She realized with a shock that he was nearly 50. It made her feel suddenly old.

And there was Karen, her baby, who hung out with movie stars and senators, who had been married twice to multi-millionaires, back when she was young and gorgeous. She was still striking, but looked hard, for all her style. Her life was spent in the business world, when she wasn't dallying with some Sheik or Earl or something. Her newest idea was to open her own bank, and she talked about that constantly. It gave Jenny mixed feelings of pride and shame to consider Karen's life. Jenny was pretty sure she'd had an abortion some years ago when she divorced her first husband. And there hadn't been any children after that. She supposed Karen was too busy and important to bother with them.

"It's too bad it takes a funeral to bring families together," Jenny said. She reached a hand out to each of them. "But I'm so glad we had a chance to do this... I've missed you both so much! And I love you more than you can know."

There was an embarrassed silence from her children, then Karen laughed and reached for the check. "Yeah, it's been nice. But I guess it's time to get out of here now and let John go home to his wife."

"Yeah, if she's still there." He glanced at Jenny. "I wish she had come with us, but she's probably at the bar again. I guess bad taste runs in the family!" Then he turned and said quietly, "But I do love her, and I'll try to do better like you said." They left the restaurant, to go on with their 'real' lives.

The angel walked out with Jenny.

CHAPTER THIRTY-THREE

1991

"Singer Trucking," Jenny answered the phone. "Yes, I'll see that our driver reaches you today. Yes, I understand. Thank you."

She flipped the switch on the mike beside her. "Henry, are you there?"

"Roger," came the answer. "Making the Brewster stop next, in about one minute."

"Great, you're right on schedule! I need you to work in a stop at Mrs. Shiveley's place to pick up a couple of old easy chairs. I know it's a ways off your route, but she's having guests tomorrow and can't wait for the regular stop. OK?"

"Roger that, Jenny. I'll get her right after the Riley's. That'll be about 2:00 O'clock as I'm going now."

"Ten-four, Henry. Oh, if the chairs are any good you could drop them at the Salvation Army. You know the Shiveleys ...those might be nearly new!"

"Right. I'll check 'em over! Mobile 2 out."

Jenny flipped the mike off and took a sip of her iced tea. The weather had turned really hot for the past week. It made her uneasy, and she went to look out the window at the sky again. Not a cloud in sight! The National Weather Service had been talking about the possibility of earthquakes in the Los Angeles area for a few days now. That was quite a long way south of Morro Bay, but still... She closed the blinds a little to keep out some of the heat. I wish we'd get an answer to the ad! This is just getting to be too much! I really need to ease off a little instead of working harder all the time.

She pulled at the elastic brace on her arm. It was hot and uncomfortable despite the air conditioning, but she really needed it more than ever now that they had the business on computer.

There were three green trucks on the routes now, with "Singer Trucking" in proud letters on the doors. Terry drove #1, Henry was in #2, and a young parolee, Buster Jacob, had just taken on a route in #3. So far he was doing very well, but since his arrival Quincy was on the scene regularly again. Buster was one of the converts from Phyllis's services at the prison. Jenny and Terry were no longer involved in the prison work, but Phyllis was more dedicated to it than ever.

Terry had interviewed Buster carefully before hiring him, and he felt good to be helping another ex-con get a new start in life. The business was in debt to Karen, but at the rate it was growing, it shouldn't take long to pay off the loan. Except they really needed a different location. It hadn't been much problem when they had only one truck, without a name on the side. But now it was against the zoning to run a business from a residential address. The men each took a truck home at night, but that wasn't a good practice either.

Jenny sighed, and sat down at the computer once more. If we ever get time, we just *have* to locate a commercial place for the company! I wish somebody would answer my ad and take over this 'office' for a while so I could go find one!

She looked around the small kitchen, which was piled high with files and papers, organized as well as she could get them, given the cramped conditions. "Singer Trucking, may I help you?" she answered the phone automatically, with her pencil poised over the order pad.

"No, the position has not been filled. I'd be happy to interview you." she answered the inquiry. She quickly checked her schedule, and penciled in a name. "Please come at 4:00 if you can. We begin to wind down by then, and I have more time to talk." The voice on the other end of the line was friendly and courteous, but sounded very young to Jenny. But then, she reflected, everybody sounded and looked very young to her these days! It was amazing how the older she got, the younger everyone else got... probably a "Murphy's Law" in there somewhere.

She tried to straighten the place up as well as she could between phone calls. It was a losing battle. Jenny hated having her kitchen taken up with all the clutter. She'd always been a neat housekeeper, but now it was almost impossible to keep order. And they had to eat their meals in the little living room, since the kitchen table was converted into an office desk. It was a real pain!

She straightened a pile of invoices, and cleared the books off a kitchen chair so Christy Smith would have a place to sit when she arrived for the interview. Well, one good thing about all this is maybe we'll be able to buy a house some day if business stays this good! And I'll have a big kitchen and a bigger bedroom, and closets!

Then the phone rang again with more business to handle.

She was so engrossed in the books that she was startled when someone knocked at the door. When she glanced up it was 4:00 o'clock already! Strange how the hours fly sometimes! The woman waiting outside was a chubby redhead with a friendly smile. Jenny smiled back and opened the door for her. "Come on in," she invited. "I can't believe it's four already."

They sat at the table/desk and talked. Christy was a single mother, with a six-year-old daughter. She lived in an apartment on the north side of town, and she had experience running an office. Her present job was in San Luis Obispo, and she wanted to be closer to home for her daughter. And anyway, she hated to drive so far in traffic. She was a giggler, but it wasn't an irritating giggle. Her voice seemed to have music in it, low and liquid.

Jenny leaned back in her chair and watched her as she talked. So, Lord, is this the right person? Is this the one you've sent me? I think I like her.

Christy finished telling about her last job and sat still, waiting for Jenny to respond.

"You'd have to work here in the kitchen to start with, you know. We're hoping to get an office soon, but this is it right now." Jenny gestured at the stacks of papers. "But if you want to take a chance on a little company with a lot of potential for growth, we're it."

Christy nodded."It looks like the kind of challenge I'd love."

Jenny grinned at her. "Well then I'd like to check these references you've given me, and talk it over with Terry (that's my husband) but you'll most likely be hearing from us very soon. We need someone now!"

So Christy Smith became part of "Singer Trucking," and part of the family too, it seemed.

Once she'd taught Christy the ropes, having her there to answer the phone gave Jenny a chance to go looking for new quarters for the company. She scouted the area carefully, driving as far down highway 1 as San Luis Obispo, and as far north as Cyucos, and up highway 41 almost to Atascadero. She scouted Los Osos and Morro Bay particularly, as she really wanted to find a place close to where most of their business was, and that was mostly in the beautiful Estero Bay area and inland toward San Luis Obispo.

It was on her third hunting trip that she spied a small storage business tucked behind some larger buildings on Main Street. She pulled into the lot and stopped to look around. There was a small office near the front of the long row of storage units, and there was space behind the building. She figured there was room enough for parking at least 3 or 4 trucks. It was a great spot for their business, but it wasn't on the market… at least there was no sign.

"This would be so good, Lord." she said under her breath. Then, with nothing to lose, she stepped into the office. A wizened little man looked up from his newspaper. Then he put it down and stood up. "You looking for a storage space?"

"Well, yes, and no." She hesitated, then asked. "Are you the owner of the business?"

"I don't need any more insurance!"

"That's OK, I don't want to sell you any." She held out her hand. "I'm Jenny Singer, from Singer Trucking. I don't suppose you're interested in selling the business?"

That caught his interest. He shook her hand. "Aintcha a little old to be looking to buy a storage business?"

She grinned. "Yeah, I guess. But my partner is a lot younger, and he'd like a place like this. Is there a lot of profit in storage?"

He looked as shrewd as a fox eyeing a fat hen. "Well now, that depends on a lot of things… "

Jenny turned on the charm, and with her past experience in real estate she was able to cut through the chaff and get down to the heart of the matter in a pretty short time. The more they talked, the more sure she was that this would be the right location for Singer Trucking - and Storage! He named a price and she countered, and he countered, and she agreed. She sat down and scratched out a preliminary purchase agreement on a piece of his stationery, which they both signed. It was subject to his wife's approval, and subject to Terry's approval, but they were both pretty sure this was a done deal!

She drove home with her mind working overtime, planning all the things they could do with the new location. "Come on, you two, I want to show you what I've found!" she called to Terry and Christy as she burst into the kitchen.

"What?" Terry asked... "What have you found?" He was hungry and tired after a day on the route, and hardly in the mood to go look at anything, and Christy needed to get home to her daughter.

"Come on Love, and I'll buy you some dinner afterward, OK? And Christy can follow us to the place and go on home from there. It isn't very far."

"Well, I suppose if it's all that exciting..." he grumbled. "Give me a minute to clean up first though."

Christy looked after him sympathetically, "I think he's tired. He had a couple of extra stops today too."

"Well I bet this'll do wonders for him. And you too, I should think! Or do you really love working in these conditions?"

Christy giggled. "OK, OK, you're the boss." She put her sweater on and gathered her purse and keys. "I'll wait for you in the car."

When they drove into the parking lot Mr. Castelado was just locking up.

Jenny waved at him and pulled up by the door. "This is Mr. Singer. I brought him to see the place. I'm really glad you're still here! Can we look in the office a minute, please?" She caught his expression and added, "We'll hurry, and not keep you too much longer!" She pulled Terry into the office and beckoned Christy to join them.

Terry just grunted as he looked around, but she saw the gleam in his eyes. Then he went outside to walk around the grounds and try to picture how his business would fit in that location. Christy stood in the little office and mentally put everything into its place. "You'd have to run two businesses here though, you know," Jenny told her. "We'd be buying the storage business too of course, since you can't move buildings off the property. Anyway, a storage business would work perfectly with our trucking, wouldn't it?"

Christy nodded and turned to leave, as Jenny motioned her out. Mr. Castelado pulled the door shut once more, and turned the key in the lock. "I'll just let you walk around by yourselves if you don't mind. I'm late for dinner now!" He drove away as Terry came around from behind the buildings.

"Well, what do you think?" she asked, "I thought we could park the trucks behind, over there, and the storage business would be extra income with little work."

"It's a good location all right, Jenny. But probably cost us an arm and a leg to get it, though."

"What do you think, Christy?"

She nodded. "I think it'd be fine. I could handle things out of here with no trouble at all, and it's closer to Becky's school too!"

Jenny nodded. Good. We'll see you tomorrow, thanks for coming with us!" They waved to her as she drove away.

"Come on, and we'll talk over dinner." She took him to his favorite place, where they served good food, not too expensive, with man-sized servings. They sat in a corner booth and ordered wet burritos. She leaned back against the cushion. "What do you really think, Terry?"

He nodded at her gravely, "It would be a terrific location, Jen. And you're probably right, the storage business would add to the trucking, and give us more income. It's a good match. But it's gotta be really expensive, isn't it? And how could we make the payments on a thing like that?"

She pulled out the agreement. "OK, here's what we can do if you want. I figure we can do some good advertising to promote the storage business more. Mr. Castelado hasn't done anything to bring anybody new in lately. He really just wants to retire! So with some increased hauling business from this location along with the extra income from the storage, we can meet the payments easily and expand even more in a year or two."

The waitress brought their food and they ate hungrily in silence for a few minutes. Then Terry sat back and studied her. He was constantly surprised by Jenny's ability to talk with just anyone about anything, be it a warden or a governor, a senator or a storage owner! She always seemed to come out on top of a situation. He couldn't begin to imagine doing the things she did. It irritated him sometimes, though he tried not to let it.

She looked across at him over her cup and raised her eyebrow. He nodded. "Yeah, it's a good deal, Jen ... it's a really good deal. Thanks for finding it and going after it."

"In a few years you'll be doing really well, Terry... mark my words!"

She caught her breath then and waited while the hand gripped her heart. It eased, and she relaxed again. He was talking...

"and maybe add a couple more routes then." He signaled the waitress for more coffee. "This may be the beginning of a whole new phase of my life. Jenny, when we close the deal, we'll have to really celebrate!"

But the day the deal closed, they signed papers at the title company's office and then walked out into the oppressive heat. It struck Jenny like a blow after the chill of the air-conditioned building. She gasped, and felt the hand grip her heart again. Only this time it didn't ease up. She fell, clutching her chest as everything turned black.

The angel touched her gently.

When she woke, she was in the hospital with an IV in her arm, and a monitor beeping beside her. Terry sat beside her bed with his eyes closed. She didn't know whether he was sleeping or praying. Whichever one, it was good. She stirred and he opened his eyes. "What happened?" she asked.

He stood quickly and took her hand. "You're awake! Oh, thank God!" He rang for the nurse before he answered, "You had a heart attack, Jen. Scared me silly! I guess it's my fault for making you work so hard all the time. I forget about your heart sometimes. You seem so healthy I don't remember your age, either. I'm sorry, Love!"

"How long have I been here?" her voice was weak and unlike the Jenny he knew.

"Three days. It's been touch and go, but now you're gonna be fine!"

The nurse arrived then, and took over, with tests and charts and all manner of hospital-type things. "Best let her rest now," she said to Terry when she was finished. Then she left the room again.

Jenny asked, "Did you move into the new office?"

"Yeah, I guess so. Christy's been moving stuff out of the kitchen, I know, and I think she's had a new telephone line put in the place for our trucking customers. She must be near finished by now. The guys seem pretty excited over the change." He rubbed his eyes wearily. "I haven't had a chance to really keep track of what's going on. But the crew seems to be taking care of things."

"They're a good group."

"Yeah." He gave her a half-grin. "I notice Buster is hanging around the office as much as he can lately, helping carry stuff over there in his spare time too. Seems to find our Christy pretty attractive!"

"Oh? Say, that's interesting," she responded weakly. "I hope he's on the straight and narrow. Then that would be good for both of them... and Becky too. She needs a dad."

"Yeah." Terry was silent, and she knew he was thinking of his own daughters who'd grown up without him. She wished she could have taken back the words, but ... "Has Quincy been around?"

"Not yet, but I'm sure it won't be long now. He doesn't let much peace go by between his visits. I remember that well!"

Jenny barely heard the last part, as she drifted into sleep again. She was just so tired...

Terry went home to get some rest, now that Jenny was going to be OK. He drove past the new location on his way. It looked good. He'd have to order a new sign and get the truck doors re-painted to say "Singer Trucking and

Storage." That sounded really good. He said it aloud a couple of times, feeling a mixture of pride and trepidation over the big step he'd undertaken.

Christy had all the stuff moved out of the kitchen and was fast organizing the new office. She wore her jeans and a t-shirt and hauled boxes and files around, cleaning as she went. "I can't believe how much dirt there is in here!" she remarked to Buster, as she swept up a whole pile of it she'd gotten from the corners.

"I guess that's what happens when a guy runs the office!"

She giggled. "Well yeah, but sometimes guys are very neat too. My dad used to keep his kitchen shining! We'd have to spend hours after his restaurant closed just getting things clean again for the next day!" Her brown eyes clouded as she leaned on the broom a moment, thinking. "Seems like another life-time! Dad's been gone forever, it seems. He died before Becky was born."

Her radio was playing a plaintive country-western tune that had to do with love and loss. He watched her, his heart feeling a sort of tenderness that it hadn't felt for a very long time. And something else too... she was just so little and soft and sweet, and her eyes were the color of melted chocolate, and her red hair curled in little tendrils around her damp face. "I'll try to get that air conditioner working better tomorrow if I have time."

She nodded, pushing her hair back. "That would be just wonderful, Buster! And it would save some money for the company if you can do it, too!" Then she thought again and turned from her sweeping. "Oh... or did you want to be paid for doing that?"

"Not that I couldn't use the extra income you know, but no. I'll do it for Ms. Jenny... and for you, of course." He stared deep into her eyes for a moment until she blinked, turned away and giggled nervously. "Well, it'll sure be appreciated, Buster!"

"You want to go have some dinner with me?" he asked, looking out at the parking lot.

"You mean now?"

He nodded. "Yeah. in case you hadn't noticed, it's almost 5:30."

"Oh good grief! I'm late to pick up Becky!" She shoved the broom into the corner and grabbed her purse. "I can't go tonight, Buster... have to take Becky to her music lesson." She smiled back at him as she locked the door behind them. "But I'd love to another time, thanks!"

The heat didn't ease at all in the next week, and Jenny came home to find a new air conditioner in her bedroom window. "That's so good of you, Terry... thanks a lot!" She smiled, and gave him a hug. He had tried to make the room homier by putting some of her pictures and plants on the dressers and adding some extra pillows to the bed. She thought she detected Phyllis' hand in it, but kept that to herself and just said, "It looks so nice and comfortable now!" She spent some time there writing letters to people she hadn't seen or talked to in a long time. She wrote a long, rambling letter to Sarah and Buzz, and another to Marge Webber. She wrote to her cousins in Georgia, and even to her sons and Karen. When she went out to the kitchen the heat wrapped her all around like a heavy blanket and threatened to suffocate her. She did what needed to be done there, and retreated to her room again.

The TV news and weather talked again about the probability of an earthquake in the Los Angeles area. The program went on, telling about past quakes and the damage they'd done. She turned it off and prayed, "Lord, please keep us safe from disaster like that!" Then she added, "but Lord, help us to be ready when your judgment falls on us!"

The angel said Amen.

CHAPTER THIRTY-FOUR

1993

Karen woke in the early morning hours of November 2nd to the strong smell of smoke. She got up and looked out the window. To the south everything looked almost normal. Then she went out on the back deck. Across the canyon, flames leaped upon houses and trees and brush, feeding voraciously, and reaching out for more. The fire was coming fast!

She ran back to the bedroom and dressed quickly. Then she grabbed her purse, her jewelry box and a photo album and ran for the door. The fire had already spread across the canyon to her garage a few feet away from the main house, and was even then devouring her car. She sprinted down the driveway, mentally cursing the environmentalists who had blocked the planned burning of underbrush. The wind was carrying the fire in gusts, leap-frogging over some areas, and starting again beyond.

The narrow blacktop road was already blocked by fire in both directions, and Karen quickly decided the only chance she had was to go directly down the hill through all that brush to the road where it wound back again far below her. She plunged into the bushes, which scratched at her skin, grabbed her clothing and slowed her progress. On the way, she dropped her album and the jewelry case, but the purse was slung over her head and under her arm, and that stayed with her. Thick smoke swirled overhead and gusted down at her. Choking, she crouched as low as she could while still running.

When she looked back, she could see the fire was fast closing in on her. She prayed. For the first time in a long, long time she called on the Lord for help. "Please Jesus, help me!" she pleaded. Then she fell and blacked out. She knew she was in the midst of the blazing scrub, but when she woke a few moments later, she was at the edge of the road below, and there was a fire truck coming toward her. She stood and waved frantically, and the firemen hauled her aboard and drove her back to a safe spot.

As they left her and headed back to the fire, Karen fell to her knees in the dirt. "Oh thank you Lord! Oh praise your holy name Jesus! Lord, please forgive me ...Lord, please take me back. Oh Lord Jesus, I'm so sorry for all the years I've ignored you and gone my own way! I know it must have been your angel who got me out of the fire... that's the only way it could have happened! Father, forgive me for making fun of Mom when she talked about angels watching over us. Oh, thank you Lord!" She wept, the tears making tracks through the soot on her face.

A woman came up to her and asked "Are you hurt, Ma'am? Can I help you?" and gently helped her to her feet and guided her to a van that would take her out of the canyon.

"I'm not hurt, thank the Lord!" Karen wept and smiled at the same time. "I prayed, and God sent an angel and carried me out of the fire!" She saw the woman's expression and went on "I know it sounds crazy, and yesterday I would have felt the same, but I know I was in the middle of the fire. I blacked out, and when I came to I was down on the road!" She stopped and looked back, trying to see where her house was. The whole side of the hill was blazing. Her house was undoubtedly gone.

They reached the van and she stumbled into it and sank into the seat, weeping with sadness for the loss of her house and all her things, relief at her safety, and joy for her salvation. When the van left her at a school the authorities were using for a shelter, she went from one person to another, telling them of her miracle. Then a reporter saw her and stuck a microphone under her nose and she repeated the story again.

In Morro Bay, Jenny and Terry watched the news on CNN, and saw the raging fires in Laguna Hills. "That's Karen's street! I wonder if she's OK?"

"We'd better pray right now that God will keep her safe!" They bowed their heads and Terry led in prayer for Karen's safety and that God would open her eyes to her need for him. "Maybe she's in Europe or somewhere else... I hope!"

Then an update came on, and the reporter told them, "The owner of Keen Consulting Company, Karen Keen, was one of the homeowners who was burned out today. We found her at the shelter at the foot of Canyon road. Her story is inspiring, but controversial to say the least!" And then there was Karen telling all about her rescue by an angel, and how good God is. Before Jenny could even react to that, the phone rang and she snatched it up. "Mom! I'm OK, I got out of the fire... and Mom, praise God! It was an angel that rescued me ... I didn't see him, but that's the only way it could have happened!" Karen told her the story again, and Jenny relayed it to Terry, and they all rejoiced together.

When they finally hung up the phone, Jenny danced around the room thanking God for the answer to prayer for her daughter... both for saving her from the fire, and for bringing her back to himself. "Finally Terry, after all these years of praying, finally it's happened! And Karen witnessed to the whole country about the Lord! God is so faithful to me!" She raised her hands, "Oh thank you, Jesus!"

Then she sobered and added thoughtfully, "I know there are angels watching over us, Terry. In the first place the Bible says so, but also, several times over the years I've just known there must have been an angel with me, or I wouldn't be here now either! I even think I saw one once! God really is so faithful, and so good to us!"

Terry nodded, "Yeah, I know… I figure the only way I survived back in prison when they put me back in with Tony was that an angel helped me. I know he'd have killed me if God hadn't stopped him."

They praised God together and then had an impromptu Bible study, looking up places where the Word talks about angels helping God's people. It was a blessed time together for them.

Phyllis came by in the evening and they told her all about Karen's experience. They sat in the roomy eating area in Jenny's new kitchen and talked for a long time. Jenny watched Phyllis and Terry together, and felt again that they really belonged with each other. They had matured a lot in the few years since she'd left for Georgia, and she knew they'd never do anything to be unfaithful to her, but she just had a strong feeling that they were meant to be a team. Not just in ministry, but in life. She glanced back and forth at them. And what should I do about it, Lord? Show me the way, please.

"How's Singer Trucking and Storage doing these days?" Phyllis asked Terry.

"It's really prospering. We just added another truck, and that makes 8 now. We'll need to add another location soon. I figure we can let Buster and Christy run one location, and hire another office manager here. Jenny sure knew what she was doing when she bought that place!" He grinned at his wife.

"Well, I may be old, but I'm still able to function mentally!" Jenny nodded at Phyllis. "I turned 77 last month. It's gettin' hard for Terry to put up with me these days." She took a cookie from the plate and stared at it reflectively, "You know, I never thought I'd last this long, especially after that bad heart attack two years ago. I wonder why God didn't take me home then?" She put the cookie down on her saucer. "I'm ready to go, you know. I'm tired. I'm tired of fighting this body too, and now that I know Karen's gonna be OK… I'll just trust Jesus to bring Johnny back. Well, maybe Karen can get to him! My heart still aches for my other two boys, but I trust the Lord for them too."

Phyllis patted her arm. "God knows you've done everything you possibly could to bring the gospel to others. He wouldn't let your own children die without knowing him!"

"I just want to say this, while the two of you are here." Jenny put her hands over one each of theirs… When I die, please don't burn my body. I want to be buried, like the people in the Bible. But please don't put my body out for display either, OK? And I want a celebration at my funeral. I want a lot of music and singing and food for everybody and all… you know?"

Phyllis nodded. "I think I do, Jenny. It sounds like the same way I'd want to go." She reached over and patted Jenny's shoulder. "But I hope that isn't for a long time yet for either of us!"

Terry cleared his throat loudly. "Well now Phyllis, about the sermon for next Sunday. I thought maybe we could use the story about Daniel and the lion's den, and how God sent an angel to protect him." He opened his Bible and they talked over the possibilities, while Jenny watched and listened and put in a word or two.

Jenny felt very heavy... she was so tired. She went to bed right after Phyllis left.

At about two in the morning the angel stood in the doorway, as the big hand tightened one more time around Jenny's heart. This time it stopped beating for good, as Terry slept on, in his own bed. The angel wrapped his cloak around Jenny, and together they began to rise. They stopped just a moment while she looked back at her body, and at Terry's sleeping form. God bless you, Love. Thanks for loving me and for staying with me. Now be happy! With that, they were gone.

EPILOGUE

In the great throne room, Eelima/Jenny arrived to stand with the angel before Yahweh. Music such as she had never heard before filled the air, as a huge choir of angels sang praises to God and to the Lamb. In the hand of the High Serif was a paper containing a long list of names, which he read in a strong, clear voice before the throne. He finished and bowed with his face to the floor. "These are the souls that Jesus the Lamb, and Eelima your servant have brought to lay before you, Almighty God, Lord of Heaven and Earth."

"Well done, my good and faithful servant," came the voice like thunder. "Enter now into Paradise to wait for the rest of my servants to finish their courses."

Huge gates opened opposite the throne room. There was light and joy, and old friends waiting to welcome her. She stepped forward into the brightness... Jenny's long journey was over. Eelima was home at last.

END

ABOUT THE AUTHOR

C. S. Hanson, or Sue, as her friends know her, is recognized in her hometown of Northport, Michigan, as a playwright. She has written and produced several musical comedies (with a partner writing the musical scores and directing), as well as creating a musical docu-drama depicting the origins of Northport. That was produced with great success as part of Northport's 1999 Sesquicentennial Celebration.

The team of Hanson and Bloomquist has also completed a Musical History of Michigan for 4th Grade, which will soon be available on their website. Sue has also written other song lyrics, as well as poetry and stories for children.

She and her husband have lived in Alaska, Indiana, California, and Michigan. Sue spent over 20 years doing real estate sales and then business brokerage in the Grand Rapids area, before retiring to Northport, where she and her husband grew up. They live in a small house with a gorgeous view of Grand Traverse Bay.

SOMETIMES ANGELS WEEP is her second book. The first, TO HIM THAT OVERCOMES, is yet to be published.

9 780759 623866